CARESS OF A WITCH

DARKNESS RISING - THREE

S.G. SLADE

S.G. SLADE

Caress of a Witch
Darkness Rising - Three

Copyright © 2024 Samantha Grosser, writing as SG Slade
All rights reserved.

ISBN: 978-0-6489635-9-2

Cover design by Anastasia at GetCovers.com

ABOUT THE BOOK

This darkly spellbinding adult fantasy series is as compelling as it is unique. With suspense, dangerous magic, and romance, the swirling darkness of the witches' world will captivate you from the very first page. Lose yourself in a richly imagined world of desire, witchcraft, and shadowy threat.
This is the standalone third book in a series.

Please Note: This series contains explicit content and dark elements that may be triggering to some. It includes dark magic, explicit romance, seduction, and mature language.

THE HAGUE 1648

IN NATURE'S INFINITE BOOK OF
SECRECY, A LITTLE I CAN READ

The midwinter sun had barely crept above the rooftops when Kate Winter stepped out of the house and into the street. A pale light peeped between the chimney pots and lit the attic windows above her, but the cobbles at her feet were still in shadow, and puddles of dirty water filled the ruts that had worn between them. Kate picked up her skirts with her free hand and though she trod with care, the wet still caught at the hems – she could feel the weight of the fabric dragging at her legs as she walked. With her other hand she held the parcel closer to her chest. A little way down the road, a servant sweeping a front step nodded good morning and Kate flicked the old woman a brief smile before hurrying on: she had been caught in endless conversation that way before.

A sudden breeze lifted the edge of her cloak and she pulled it more tightly around her. The season had turned bitter these last few days and the air held a biting chill. Shivering, she quickened her step, but when the great Binnenhof Palace rose up before her at last the weather was utterly forgotten. It was an impressive sight: warm brick and myriad chimneys and dozens of windows that gazed out to the lake where ripples danced in the breeze. In spite of the frigid air and the urgency of her errand, she stopped to run her gaze across the building's face.

An unexpected memory of herself as a young child flickered through her thoughts. She had stood just here, she remembered, her hand held tightly in her father's as he pointed out to her all the different rooms he could name, counting off the windows. Then they had watched the swans gliding on the water of the lake. They mate for life, he had said, and laughed at her awe; afterwards she had always gone with him to the palace whenever he was called.

But that was long ago and now she had come here alone for the first time, her father dead and buried, his bloated body dragged from the tide with seaweed in his hair six months since. It was that last image of his lifeless face that haunted her – pale, waxy, cold. She could barely recall his living look any more; the changing blue-grey eyes that had always held a smile for her, his warmth and love, the safety of his protection. His death had been so sudden – he had simply failed to come home one day – and she had not been ready to give him up. The anger of her grief still burned so fiercely under her skin that at times she had to tense every muscle in her body to brace herself against the pain and to remain upright, dry-eyed.

Taking a long deep breath to steady herself, she gripped the parcel tightly with both hands, stepped around the edge of the lake, and headed for the side door that would take her through the servants' entrance and into the kitchens.

The door was opened by a flush-faced woman with sweat in beads above her lip and a look of irritation in her eyes, but she recognised Kate straight away and stood back without a word to let her enter. As the warmth of the kitchen billowed out to engulf her, Kate gave her a grateful smile, and in the wash of sudden heat the weariness of the sleepless night seemed to wrap itself across her shoulders so that she had to quell an almost overwhelming urge to find somewhere to lie down, close her eyes and sleep. She found herself searching the corners of the kitchen for a likely spot.

The woman took the parcel with red, chapped hands, then

turned away to talk to another, handsomely dressed woman in a low-cut gown of dark satin. Kate waited, watching as the two women exchanged words she could not quite catch above the clatter and roar. Then, giving up the effort to hear, she let her gaze wander beyond them across the vast kitchen that rang with activity in spite of the early hour. Great fires roared in the double hearth, young boys turning roasted venison and boar on their spits, and every surface seemed to be laden with food at all stages of preparation. Men chopping and rinsing, stirring and dressing. It was hard to imagine the vastness of a household that required so much food and so many people to prepare it. But the clatter of knives and pots and porcelain, the crackle of the fire as the meat fat spattered, and the sweet scent of roasting flesh was strangely comforting. It felt familiar, she realised, from all the hours she used to wait here for her father as he went beyond the kitchen's confines to the more secluded reaches of the palace to measure and pin and suggest new designs for the courtiers' clothes. Before he died, he had begun to tailor for the Prince of Wales himself, as the young English royal kicked his heels in Holland and waited for his chance to help his father keep his throne.

Now, in the parcel that the red-faced woman was holding so carelessly in her fingers was the first shirt Kate had stitched for the Prince herself, and though she knew she had a rare skill with a needle, still she was nervous. It was no small thing to embroider for a prince.

Her presence apparently forgotten, she stepped further inside, and when she took off her gloves and slid her cloak from her shoulders, she was abruptly conscious of the sweat at the nape of her neck. She cast another glance across the kitchen, searching for a place to wait that would be out of the way, and in the far corner in the shadows away from the firelight she noticed two women sitting together, apparently oblivious to all that was happening around them. Their heads were bent close together, and one of them was examining the other's palm. Kate watched, intrigued – telling fortunes was a dangerous pastime when the church's spies were everywhere. But perhaps they had no power here. Perhaps the English princeling was allowed to indulge such heresies.

Kate shifted closer, curious, skirting the vast table that held centre stage and side-stepping the cooks as they moved in their complex dance around it. She had heard of such palm readers and glimpsed them now and then in secret corners of the fair that came to the city sometimes. But her mother had always drawn her away, distracting her with some other thing, and till now she had never thought to question why. A shiver ran over her and in spite of the warmth in the kitchen her skin began to bubble with goose bumps. Sliding a glance to the servant with the parcel, she saw the woman was still absorbed in her conversation, one hand sketching details in the air as she talked.

When Kate returned her gaze to the shadow of the corner, the fortune teller was alone. Briefly, she searched for the woman who just a moment before had occupied the empty stool but she could see no sign of her. The palm reader caught her gaze. She was a handsome woman in her mid-forties, Kate guessed, with green eyes that were arresting against an ivory complexion and dark honey hair. Her own hair was just a little lighter: there was a likeness between them, she thought, and for some reason the notion pleased her. Then the woman smiled and beckoned with an almost imperceptible gesture of her head and Kate's breath quickened in anticipation. Wiping her palms on her skirts in an automatic movement, she took a step towards the proffered stool. And though at the edges of her thoughts a faint bell of warning tolled, she chose to ignore it.

The woman watched her approach and Kate dropped her eyes away from the scrutiny, self-conscious and suddenly confused. It was unlike her to care much about others' judgements of her, but this woman's gaze was intense and unnerving, and the alarm bell in her head struck more loudly. Dismissing it with an abrupt toss of her head, Kate slid onto the stool and waited. She could not have said what it was she feared – the woman was only a fortune teller after all – but her mouth was chalky and her heart knocked hard in her chest as a ripple of risk ran through her blood, a new sense of danger ahead. The feeling was intoxicating – she felt reckless, and the desire to know her future almost overwhelmed her.

The fortune teller said nothing, merely observing her new customer, patient and watchful, and the light of the other woman's attention pricked an unfamiliar thrill. Finally, the woman spoke.

'Would you like me to read your palm?' the fortune teller asked, in English. So she was an outsider too. Kate wondered what had brought her to the Hague, and if she was running away from something.

'I have no coins,' she answered. She remembered the old tales of fortunes told for a payment of silver.

'No matter,' the woman said. 'Some things cannot be bought and sold.'

Kate was silent, unsure if she agreed. In her life it had seemed to her that most things could be bought for the right price. Then she thought of her father, dredged from the tide, and reflected that all the money in the world would not have saved him.

'Then, yes,' she said, 'if you are willing, I would like you to read my palm.'

With the first touch of their fingers, a charge seemed to flicker between them, an unwelcome connection that made Kate want to snatch her hand away, to turn and run.

Don't be absurd, she scolded herself, forcing her body by strength of will to stillness. You're imagining things. Don't be so weak. She let her right hand drop to rest on her thigh, fingers curled and awaiting their turn. The woman's grip was unexpectedly firm, almost hurting as she stretched back the fingers and ran her fingertips across the lines on Kate's palm. She did not look up.

'Long fingers,' the fortune teller murmured, 'a water hand. We are alike.' Her mouth curved into a small smile, but she did not lift her eyes to meet Kate's. She said, 'I see an illness when you were a girl, perhaps seven or eight years old ...'

A terrible fever, Kate remembered, that her younger brother

had not survived: he had died in her arms just as her own fever broke. She had not allowed herself to think of it in years, but now the pain of the memory swelled inside her, a physical force that seemed to hollow her out. She planted her feet on the floor to stop herself from swaying. She hadn't thought there was any room left within her for more sorrow.

'… and in recent days the loss of someone you loved very much,' the fortune teller said.

Kate said nothing, feeling suddenly exposed before this stranger she instinctively did not trust. At her silence, the other woman raised her eyes at last, searching. Kate met the look for an instant of confusion then lowered her head, but she did not withdraw her hand. In spite of the doubts and the growing sense of unease, some unknown force compelled her to remain and discover more.

'You have a guardian angel. See?' The fortune teller pointed to the heel of Kate's palm. 'Here, this line. Someone is watching over you. Someone on the other side.'

My father, Kate thought. Who else could it be? But she had never once sensed his presence since he died, never even dreamt of him. Surely she would know if he was watching her. Surely she would feel it.

'What else do you see?' She wanted to distract herself from thoughts of her father. The grief was too raw, the lack of him still a physical wound.

The woman seemed not to hear. She had her eyes closed, running her thumb across Kate's palm as though feeling for a truth. Kate waited with quickened breath, aware again of the connection that ran between them, a link that bound them together in some indefinable way. The thought of it both intrigued and repelled her. Finally, the fortune teller opened her eyes and the look in them stopped the breath in Kate's throat.

'You have witchblood in your veins,' she whispered. 'I can feel it.'

Kate let out a startled laugh: it was absurd to imagine her parents as witches.

'Not me,' she managed to reply.

'Oh yes,' the woman insisted. 'From both sides, but from your father most of all.'

Kate was silent then, disturbed by the fortune teller's words and reluctant to believe them, even as a small part inside of her half recognised the beginnings of a truth.

'You don't believe me.' It was not a question.

'My father was no witch,' she said.

But as the words left her lips she realised that he could have been and she might not have known. For all their closeness, he had always carried a private sorrow, a hidden darkness. Then she remembered the six fingers on her mother's left hand and the other children's taunts when she was a girl that her mother belonged to the Devil.

''Tis the truth,' the fortune teller said. 'Ask them, if you do not trust me.'

'My father is dead,' Kate snapped, and flinched at the pain of the words.

'And your mother?'

Kate swallowed, and certainties she had trusted all her life seemed to slide away beneath her. In her blood she sensed the woman was speaking the truth – why would she lie? But how could she know such a thing from the mere reading of a palm? Gently, Kate slid her hand free from the fortune teller's grasp and let it rest on her lap where it tingled with the memory of the other woman's touch, the energy still lingering. She rubbed at it with the thumb of her other hand as though to wipe the taint away.

The fortune teller regarded her with eyes that held a softer light than before, one that was easier to meet.

'Ask your mother,' she said. 'And if you wish to know more, come back to me here. My name is Isabella Last. I will wait for you. Your future lies in discovering your past.'

Kate was silent. She felt weak, legs like sand, and with no energy to rise from the stool where she sat. She let her gaze drift away, forcing herself to focus on the mundane world of the kitchen around her – the cooks weaving their dance between the plumes of rising steam, plates of meat, fresh bread, fruits she had never seen before that had come from far-off places, the scent of herbs: rosemary and thyme, sage. One of the cooks was preparing a sauce for the meat – onions with vinegar and butter, sugar and cinnamon; it was fragrant and enticing. But all of it seemed to be at a distance, as though she were outside a window looking into a world she was barred from. Then the red-faced woman with the parcel of shirts stepped into view and the last vestiges of strangeness slipped away.

Kate gave a smile of thanks to the fortune teller, got to her feet, and waited to hear what the other woman had to say.

2

FULL FATHOM FIVE THY FATHER LIES.

An hour ago Kate would have been nervous and excited to meet the young prince, for what girl doesn't dream of being a princess? All the gossip in town painted him as tall and handsome and with an eye for the girls. But as the servant led her through the maze of corridors, shoes sinking into carpets thicker than she had ever walked on before, she paid her surroundings little mind, her thoughts turning instead on the fortune teller's words.

Witchblood.

From your father most of all.

Was it possible? On first consideration it seemed unlikely and she was tempted to dismiss the suggestion out of hand. But the woman had planted a seed, and for all her doubts Kate could not let it go. Searching her past for clues, she found nothing suspicious beyond her mother's herb garden and strange, six-fingered hand. But what exactly did she expect to see? The presence of an old crone with a black cat? Memories of curses uttered at midnight? If her father had been a witch he had kept his secret close to protect himself, she supposed, and to protect his family also.

Ahead of her the servant halted to let two women in fine silks and too much make-up sweep past them along the corridor. Kate lowered her head with instinctive deference. Though her father had often been welcomed here this was not her world and she was unsure how to behave in such a place. But they met no one else in the passages. The hour was still early and she guessed the royal Court slept late. She hoped the Prince would not keep her long; in spite of the honour he was showing her she was resentful of this summons when her head was filled with questions for her mother she was desperate to ask. But Prince Charles himself had requested her presence in recognition of the fineness of her stitching. He must be bored indeed, she decided, to want to meet his seamstress, but still, she dared not refuse him.

At last they came to a pair of great double doors with handles of gold, and she realised she had given no mind at all to the way they had come. A sense of disorientation slithered through her. She should have paid more attention – she would struggle to find her way back, and the knowledge disturbed her. She cast a brief glance around her, taking in the portraits on the walls, the precious ornaments set out on small tables, the bright-coloured carpet underfoot, but she could not say which way was north, and there were no windows to the sky to help her.

The servant rapped hard on the door and, as the knock echoed in the silent passage, Kate took a deep breath to force her mind back to the scene before her – a meeting with the English Prince. The door swung open. The servant who had accompanied her from the kitchen bowed and backed away, leaving her to face the opening alone. A man appeared, his face in shadow so that she could only form a half-impression, but she could see enough to make out that he was finely dressed in crimson silks, and even through the gloom, she saw his eyes were dark as he regarded her. She dropped a curtsey and waited.

'You must be the seamstress,' he said.

He was English, with no trace of an accent. Part of the Prince's retinue, she supposed, exiled along with his master. The war in England had gone badly for the royal family.

She raised her head slowly. 'I am,' she replied.

Opening the door wide, he stepped back and she followed him into some kind of anteroom that seemed unkempt, as though many people had decamped within its walls. Coats and cloaks and hats were spread across the backs of chairs and benches. Trunks, some half-open, were stacked against the walls and a scent of stale tobacco and brandy hung across the room. A dull morning light filtered through the single window, and she was relieved to see the sky again and reorientate herself beneath it. The gentleman crossed to the window and looked out briefly, then turned back to her with a smile. She saw him more clearly now – a high, wide forehead, regular features, and a smile that lit eyes that would otherwise seem sad.

'Wine?' He gestured to the jug on the side stand.

She shook her head. 'It's a little early for me.'

'For me also,' he agreed. Then, 'Prince Charles is dressing – he is most pleased with the shirts.'

'I am honoured my work is to his liking.'

'The Prince takes great delight in small pleasures – it's a gift to be able to do so when his young life has been so beset by misfortune.'

She smiled her agreement, aware of the man's open observation of her – it was a look she had grown used to. Conscious of her own beauty from a young age she wore it carelessly, but she enjoyed the attention it brought her.

'You are English also?' he asked.

'My parents came from there before I was born. I've never been.'

'What brought them here?'

She lifted one shoulder in a shrug. 'The desire for a new life.' It was not a question she had ever paused long to consider, though she wondered now at her lack of curiosity. What might have driven her parents to leave a whole life behind them and begin anew in a strange country?

Witchblood. The fortune teller's voice whispered in her mind.

'And you are here to serve the Prince?' She rested her fingers on the back of a chair and the carved wood was smooth and warm beneath them.

'Aye. As I served his father.'

'You fought for him in the wars?'

'I did.'

She regarded him then with more open interest, this courtier-soldier. It was hard to imagine him in the heat of battle, bloodied with a lust to kill in his eyes. He seemed so reserved now before her, so refined. But perhaps it explained the sadness she had glimpsed before.

He said, 'Forgive me, I did not introduce myself. Rafe Tyndall, at your service.' He smiled and dipped his head in a bow that delighted her. He was a great man in the service of the Prince, and he was bowing to her, a tailor's daughter.

'Kate Winter, sir,' she answered, sweeping low into a curtsey that she hoped would convey her pleasure and respect. 'I am truly honoured to be here.'

They shared a smile, and briefly the fortune teller was forgotten. The room began to feel warm and Kate was conscious of the pinkness of her cheeks.

'Perhaps I will have a little wine,' she said.

'Of course.' He poured for them both and she realised he had abstained only to keep her company. His courtesy impressed her.

'To the King,' he toasted, lifting his glass.

'The King,' she repeated, though she knew his cause was all but hopeless now. He had lost the battle to keep his throne, his power stripped away by Parliament as he awaited his fate in a prison cell. They said he was a tyrant, though it seemed to Kate they simply wanted his power for themselves, and in the fight for it they had divided the realm and killed tens of thousands. Now the talk was the King would be put to the sword, and so all the Royalist hopes for the future had come to rest on the young man beyond the door who was dressing himself in a shirt her hands had wrought.

The wine soothed the dryness of her mouth and throat, but it was neither the heat of the room nor nerves at meeting the Prince that disturbed her composure. She risked another smile at Rafe. He was watching her, interest clear in his eyes, and though many men in her life had looked at her that way before, this was the first time she had felt an answering heat inside. She took another mouthful of wine. It was full-bodied, blood-red, and she let the pleasure of it ooze through her thoughts as her gaze travelled the walls and floor of the room, unable now to meet Rafe's look. Kate was no stranger to the company of men, but not one of them had ever touched her with their eyes the way that this man was touching her. He seemed to have reached inside her and found a new chord to play, and although her body filled with the lightness of pleasure, her mind was less certain, sensing a new capacity for weakness, an unfamiliar vulnerability. Draining off her wine, she tightened her feelings against this new emotion. She would not allow her head to be turned by the first courtier to show an interest.

Rafe lifted the wine jug to offer her more but she shook her head, already beginning to feel its effects as the edges of the world started to soften. Then one of the inner doors opened with a slam and they both wheeled towards it. Kate dropped abruptly into her deepest curtsey, eyes fixed on the floor before her, tracing a swirl in the intricate pattern of the carpet.

'What do you think?' the Prince asked.

Hesitantly she raised her eyes and slid a questioning glance towards Rafe. She had no clue about the proper behaviour before a Prince. He nodded lightly and so she rose from her curtsey and faced the young man before her. He was about her own age, she guessed, with a glossy mane of dark curls and full, sensual lips. He was regarding her with interest and though she was flattered and aware of the possibilities such a liaison might offer, he awoke no flicker of answering desire as Rafe had done.

'The shirt,' Prince Charles said impatiently. 'How does it look?'

'It suits you very well, sir,' she replied, and it was true. It was rare to see her work being worn and the Prince was a commanding figure – tall and strong. The fine linen hung becomingly across his shoulders.

'I like her.' The Prince turned to Rafe. 'She will make all my shirts from now. See to it.'

Rafe nodded his acknowledgement, and in his glance towards Kate his eyes were bright with merriment. She dropped her head away to hide her own smile, and the Prince, having delivered his message and inspected her, turned and returned to his quarters, the door rattling on its hinges in his wake.

'I will see you out,' Rafe said.

In the passage he walked beside her along the narrow corridors, and once again she paid no mind to the way nor to the many treasures and paintings they passed that should have sparked her admiration. Her thoughts instead were filled with the awareness of Rafe's closeness, their arms brushing now and then as they walked together. She could feel the heat of his body, and sense the blood that pulsed through his muscles. Her own heartbeat quickened in response.

Too soon they reached a door that led to the outside and they stood for a moment before it.

'Thank you,' she said, with a light curtsey, though she wanted to say more.

'The pleasure was all mine,' he returned. Then, unexpectedly, he raised his head and met her look with a light in the pale grey eyes that she could not quite read. But the same warmth travelled through her in the heat of his attention, and she lowered her gaze away, self-conscious.

'If you should ever find yourself in London, Miss Winter, and I can be of service in any way, leave a message for me at the Bull's Head on Bankside. I will be returning there very soon, and I would be pleased to aid you in whatever way I can.'

She swallowed, surprised by the offer. Why would she ever find herself in London? Or in need of aid from Rafe Tyndall, for that matter? She was just a seamstress, after all – pretty, but of no account. Still, it was a generous offer, and she was flattered.

'Thank you,' she managed to murmur, 'I'm honoured.' She was aware once more of the colour in her cheeks, her heartbeat quick under his gaze, and she dared not meet his eyes again.

'Till next we meet,' he said, with a small bow of farewell.

Then he turned and strode away.

Close to home Kate took the lane that led to the back of the house. Though the shop at the front was still open for orders, since her father's death she could hardly bear to go near it. The business was in the hands of the apprentice now and soon the young man would be a master tailor himself. It was hard to predict what might happen then for it was unlikely he would consent to work for his old master's widow for long. Of course, he could ask his mistress to marry him so the business would fall to him by right: it was a common way for an apprentice to make his way in the world, after all, but Kate knew her mother would never consent, her love for her husband sacred and inviolable. Or he might propose to the daughter instead and secure his position through her – Kate had seen the way he looked at her, undressing her with his eyes every time she walked past him. Now her father was no longer there to protect her he had become bolder, and she was careful never to meet his look, never to give him anything he might interpret as encouragement. But today her mind circled on other matters. The fortune teller's words had accompanied her on the journey home, sounding in time to her footsteps, drowning out all other thoughts.

You have witchblood in your veins. Witchblood. From your father most of all.

Opening the back door, she shook her head to rid herself of the whisper. It was absurd, she told herself yet again. The woman was mistaken, a charlatan. It was impossible her father had been a witch. He had been a tailor, happily married, a family man, respected in his community. And yet ... A small thread of doubt wound around her mind. Something secret. Something hidden. A private darkness he never let his daughter share, for all their closeness. Could it be?

She shut and locked the door behind her and listened to the sounds of the house, the sounds of her childhood. She knew every creak and bump, the draw of the chimneys, the rattle of the door to the shop, the sibilant hiss of the tailors' scissors. For a moment she found she was listening for the familiar rumble of her father's voice before she remembered he was gone and had to set her mouth and jaw against the grief.

Her mother would be in the first-floor chamber above the shop at this hour, making use of the morning light at the window to sew. Her eyes were not so keen as they used to be, and for a while they had talked of getting eyeglasses made. But in last few months it had seemed as if their lives were on hold, each day merely survived in numbness through the daily round of household tasks and stitching. There had been no more mention of glasses and now, by tacit agreement, the finer needlework came to Kate. In the daytime, it had proved to be a good distraction from her sorrow, but in the sleepless nights she had sought out other ways to quell her grief, slipping from the house when her mother was asleep, and finding company to flirt with in one of the taverns where she hoped her father had not been known. Gentlemen mostly, easily beguiled by her beauty. The risk of it pricked the sides of her numbness, stirring feeling into her breast. And though the feelings were often bitter – shame, guilt, disgust, fear – they were better than feeling nothing at all, being dead inside.

Voices droned through the wall of the shop – a customer, in conversation with the apprentice – and she cocked her head, instinctively listening once again for her father's tone. Would she never get used to his absence? Blinking, she rubbed at her eyes with a rough sweep of her fingers. Then, swinging the cloak from her shoulders with practised deftness, she threw it over the hook, strode along the hall and up the stairs to confront her mother.

3

THERE IS NO DARKNESS BUT
IGNORANCE

Mary heard her daughter's return: her ears were well-attuned to the noises of the house and she picked up the soft click of the back door latch as soon as it dropped into place. They were noises she would have paid no mind to before, listening instead for her husband's voice, his footsteps, his laugh. With a sigh, she set aside the petticoat she was sewing and stared out of the window at the street below. Two women, neighbours Mary mostly tried to avoid, were gossiping in the street and the children of one of them were teasing a puppy that yapped frantically in distress. Mary felt a brief desire to go down and fetch the boys a cuff across the head but the urge fled almost as soon as it surfaced, and instead she watched the puppy's suffering in silent pity.

Becoming abruptly aware of the cold, she shivered, and drew the thick house jacket closer around her; these days she seemed to feel the chill more keenly. The Dutch winter had always felt more bitter to her than the coldest months in London, though perhaps it was just nostalgia that coloured her memories, for The Hague had never seemed like home in spite of all the years she had lived here. When Toby was alive it had hardly mattered: his company had been everything, so that wherever they were together she was content. Never once had she regretted their marriage, bound together by the secrets they shared and a love that had never dimmed. But since his death her thoughts had begun to wander more readily towards London and to Bankside, its river in her blood, the place she knew and loved the best. In her grief, it seemed as though it was calling her home as a salve for her sorrow, a peace that was waiting to claim her.

In the street below, one of the women raised her voice at the boys, finally putting a stop to the puppy's suffering. The Dutch language still sounded harsh to Mary's ears, and the words had remained reluctant in her mouth. She had never quite managed to master it, though her husband and daughter spoke it as easily as their native tongue.

Toby.

She watched the street and let herself imagine him striding home towards her, the lean, long limbs, the wavy hair, and the changing blue-grey eyes searching the windows of the house for a glimpse of her. But when she heard the door latch rattle behind her and turned towards it, it was her daughter who greeted her and Mary had to remind herself once again that Toby was gone forever, and he would come back to her no more.

Kate's cheeks were flushed from the morning chill and wisps of hair had broken loose from the plait at the back of her head. She had inherited her father's pale beauty – fine features, high cheek-bones. Only her eyes were different – green and wide-set, catlike. And those eyes were focused on her mother now with a light in them that Mary could not read. A question perhaps? Her daughter had drifted away from her since Toby's death – the two women had drowned themselves in their separate griefs, and Kate confided nothing to Mary any more: her thoughts and hopes and dreams were utterly unknown.

Kate sauntered to the hearth. She had learned to wear her loveliness with elegance and grace, Mary realised, though she had no memory of when it changed – it seemed no time at all since her daughter had been a gangly girl, awkward and ill at ease in her skin.

'They were happy with the shirts?' Mary asked, for something to say. There was a tension in the room she found hard to define, an air that threatened trouble.

'Prince Charles thanked me personally.'

'You met the Prince?' Mary smiled. In all the years she had sewn for the royal household she had never once been invited past the threshold of the servants' entrance, though Toby had been welcomed. She had never envied her husband his position there, but her daughter sparked a different, and unexpected, response. 'What was he like?' she asked, to cover emotions she didn't understand.

'Kind,' Kate replied. 'He wants me to sew all his shirts.'

'That's wonderful,' Mary said, and she meant it. A life as a prince's seamstress might open all manner of doors and lead Kate to a different, better life than a tailor's daughter might expect.

Kate crouched to poke more life into the dying fire and threw on another log. The two women watched the flames lick at the new wood before it caught with a crackle. Then Kate stood and swung towards her mother with a question in her eyes, though she hesitated before she brought the words to her lips. Mary waited, both curious and uncertain, and the tension between them seemed to tighten.

Kate said, 'There was a fortune teller in the kitchens at the palace. She read my palm.'

Unconsciously she regarded her hand for a moment before her eyes slid back towards her mother's face.

'What did she see?' Mary asked. She kept her voice carefully casual, but a fine thread of dread was creeping up from her gut, a fear that long-hidden knowledge might yet come to light.

Again, Kate hesitated, running the tip of her tongue across her lips before she answered. 'She said,' she began, dropping her eyes away now, watching the flames, 'that I have witchblood in my veins.'

In spite of herself, Mary's breath came in a sharp snatch and her skin crawled with a sudden chill that owed nothing to the winter damp beyond the window.

'She said from my father most of all.'

Mary swallowed, panic rising. She had hoped she would never have to explain the past to her daughter, trusting they had left it far enough behind them, buried. Long ago, when Kate was small, she and Toby had talked of it sometimes, but as the years had passed she had put it out of her thoughts, allowing herself to believe all that had happened was forgotten. So now no words came to mind and she could think of no explanation for the fortune teller's claim. Kate was watching her, gaze intent and demanding as Mary scrabbled in her head for an answer.

'What fortune teller?' she stalled.

Help me, Toby. Please.

She made a silent plea. In the first weeks after her husband's death she had called to him over and over, hoping for some sign of his presence, a sense that his spirit still lingered, but he had never once answered her, not even in her dreams. And though now she had all but given up hope of ever feeling his presence again, desperation drove her to plead anew.

Please, Toby. Help me.

But the hoped-for answer did not come and she realised she must face this trial alone. Turning away from the accusation she saw in her daughter's eyes, she searched the street below the window for the right words to say. In the lane, the gossiping neighbours had moved away and an oxcart was trundling over the cobbles in their place, its load swaying dangerously as the wheels jolted across the ruts.

'Mother?' Her daughter's voice sounded close by her shoulder.

Mary jumped, startled by Kate's sudden presence close by her side at the window. She hadn't heard her approach. She swallowed, still groping for an answer. It was tempting to deny all knowledge. She could simply dismiss the woman as a fraud, and for the space of three long breaths she considered it before she let the possibility slide away. Kate deserved more than such a lie. Besides, Mary knew from experience that once disturbed the truth had a way of being heard. Kate might believe a lie today but there would be other times, other questions, that might not be so easy to explain away.

'Your grandfather,' she heard herself begin – though why she chose to name Tom before his cousin Sarah, she could not have said. Loyalty perhaps, to the woman who had helped her and set her on her own path? 'Your father's father.'

Kate turned to her mother in surprise. So she had been expecting a denial after all, Mary realised. She could have lied and Kate would have believed her. But now she had opened the box and the lid could not be closed again.

'What about him?'

'He was a witch,' Mary said simply. In the end the words were easy to say. But then, she had never known Tom and he had been dead a long time, so his secrets were easier to betray. Her husband's name, though, she would guard with her life – no one could ever know the darkness the two of them had shared.

'What kind of a witch?'

Mary lifted a shoulder in a half-shrug. 'I couldn't say. But he was hanged for it. Before your father was born.'

For a moment Kate was silent, taking in this new knowledge that must surely shatter her world. Then she rounded on Mary, eyes vivid with fury. 'Why have you never told me this before? It changes everything!'

Mary almost smiled. 'What does it change?'

Kate ignored the question. 'And father?' she asked instead. 'Was he a witch too?'

Mary shook her head. But an image of Toby's book of magic, hidden away in the attic, precious and rare and imbued with a power that was dangerous to wield, pawed at her thoughts for the first time in years. Had he ever consulted it in their life together since they fled from Bankside? Had he conjured in secret, searching for arcane knowledge the same as his father before him? If so, he had kept it hidden from her, and she was glad. She would have been afraid to know, aware that to meddle with the spirits was to flirt with death. They had walked that path together when first they met and people had died because of it. It was one of those deaths that had forced them to flee to Holland.

'No.' She answered her daughter's question. 'Your father was no witch, though the blood was in his veins.'

'And you?' Kate was observing her mother with a new interest, searching for facets she had never suspected till now. 'The fortune teller said the blood came from both sides.'

'A little herblore, as you already know,' Mary said. Learned from Sarah, Toby's mother and Tom's cousin. But she made no mention of the prayers she had learned to say to Hecate under the changing moon nor of the spells they had cast. She had called to the goddess now and then across the years but the connection had waned over time – Mary could hardly remember the last time she had even thought of her.

Kate glared, pretty mouth clamped tight in a sullen pout, disbelief clear in her eyes as her gaze wandered towards her mother's six-fingered left hand. Mary waited, uncertain where Kate would take the argument, though she knew the battle had only just begun.

'Why did you and Father leave England?' Kate demanded. 'What brought you here?'

'A new beginning. A change.'

'But why?' her daughter persisted. 'People don't just forsake a whole life to start anew without good reason.'

'Someone offered your father a share in the business here,' Mary lied. 'It seemed like a good opportunity. There was nothing to hold us in England. No remaining family.'

'I don't believe you.' Kate's arms were folded across her chest and she was glaring out of the window, jaw tight with anger and determination.

Mary shrugged. ''Tis the truth. What do you think brought us here? Do you think we flew on broomsticks? Is that what you want me to say?'

'Tell me about my grandfather,' Kate demanded, swivelling her gaze briefly to sweep her mother with derision. 'I know you know more than you're telling me.'

Mary moved away from the window, depression at the grey winter morning outside settling on her shoulders: Dutch weather, a Dutch street. She crossed to the hearth where the fire was drawing well – the flames were bright and the room was cheerful in its glow. It was a good house, she thought, with its dark wood panelling and the Turkey carpets she remembered choosing long ago with Toby. Happy memories, a life she had never thought to have. She lifted her eyes to her daughter, who was outlined now against the light behind her with her face in shadow, and thought that the girl had become a stranger.

She said, 'His name was Tom Wynter. The story goes that his cousin Sarah was accused of bewitching a young man, and he took the blame to save her.'

'So he wasn't actually a witch, but she was?'

'I've told you – I don't know much about it. What does it matter, anyway? It's ancient history.' She was regretting she had opened the box, aware Kate would never now let it go. But so far she had revealed precious little and she promised herself to say no more.

'What does it matter?' Kate's voice rose in echo.

'Keep your voice down,' Mary snapped. The words would carry to anyone in the shop below. But Kate wasn't listening.

'I have the blood of a witch in my veins – of course it matters. I want to know more. Am I a witch too? Is that how it works? Will the blood find a way to be heard?'

Mary sighed. She was weary, tired of a life without Toby, and it was hard to summon the strength to argue. She wanted to lie down and rest her aching head.

'No,' she said, 'I don't think that's how it works. You have a choice. You always have a choice about the path you follow. Nothing is ever set in stone, whatever the fortune teller may have told you.'

'She told me my future lay in the past,' Kate said.

Mary was silent. She could think of nothing more to say, no wisdom to impart. She wished again that Toby was there – he would have known what to say and Kate would have listened: they had shared a closeness Mary had often envied.

'I need to know about the past,' Kate went on. 'And if you cannot tell me I will find someone who can.'

'Who?' A terrible presentiment crept over Mary's skin.

'The fortune teller,' Kate snarled, and with a swing of her hips she was gone, the door slamming hard behind her, vibrating with the force.

Mary stared for a long time at the empty space her daughter had left behind, and wondered what would happen now.

4

THERE IS A WORLD ELSEWHERE

Kate almost fell down the stairs in her haste to be gone, grabbing at the banister to steady herself as she stumbled, heart pounding in her chest. At the bottom of the steps she lifted her cloak from its hook and strode along the passage to the back door and into the garden where the herbs were struggling for the winter sunlight and the trees were leafless and forlorn. The weeds had been neglected these last few months, and she lifted her skirts free of the wet, boots squelching on the damp carpet of leaves. Then she was in the lane that ran between the rows of houses and striding towards the palace once more.

Her mother was lying, she thought. She had seen the hesitation, the reluctance even to admit as much as she had, so Kate knew without a doubt there was much more to be told. But what? And why had Mary refused to tell? Not so long ago she had thought they were close, but now it seemed she had lived her whole life within a web of deception – her parents with unknown stories, an unknown life. Was it witchcraft that had led them to begin a new life across the narrow sea in The Hague? Had her father been a witch in spite of her mother's denial, true to the blood that flowed inside him?

She paced swiftly, growing warm despite the chill that hung in the air. She could feel the sweat gathering in the small of her back and the trickle down her spine but she hurried on, too impatient to stop and take off the heavy wool cloak, and reluctant anyway to have to carry it. Turning a corner in her haste, she had to sidestep abruptly to avoid a collision with a merchant who was rushing in the other direction.

'Hey! Watch where you're going,' he shouted, though it was as much his fault as hers. She ignored him, simply lowering her eyes and striding on, her mind too full of other thoughts to spare even one for the merchant. She could hear him still railing at her as she walked away but she paid him no mind.

Childish images of witchcraft circled in her mind – the weird old women of half-remembered folk tales, working their dark and dangerous magic. Then she remembered the news of the recent witch-hunts in England, and the scores of poor women who had died on the gallows for their craft. Women accused of consorting with the Devil, giving themselves to him in ecstasy and sin. No wonder her parents had kept their secret close. Would she end the same way, she wondered, her life cut short at the end of a rope?

Shuddering, and her guts heavy with dread, Kate's footsteps briefly faltered. She should go home, she thought, and make peace with her mother, instead of stirring up the secrets of a hidden past. A dangerous past. They had known enough grief already.

But when the great palace loomed before her again she did not pause, drawn onwards by some strange force she could not deny. Fear that she had tarried too long quivered inside her: the fortune teller might not have waited for her to return and she would discover no more after all.

The door to the kitchen was unlocked, and inside, the place was just as she had left it, ripe with steam from bubbling pots, the aromas of roasting boar and venison, the sweet-sour scent of sauces. A host of workers moved in concert, each one's role defined and only the rare misstep. Kate peered through the fug, searching for the figure of the fortune teller and when she spied her at last, still at her place on a stool in the corner, she sucked in a deep breath; she hadn't realised she was holding it.

For a moment Kate hesitated, observing the woman who sat with such stillness, apparently gazing beyond the walls of the palace, undisturbed by the activity around her. She had shed her cloak, and the pallor of her breast gleamed in the firelight above the low-cut dress. Dark silk, Kate noticed, trimmed with lace. She was expensively dressed for a fortune teller, Kate realised, in skirts of fine blue wool with a velvet jacket over her bodice: the robes of a gentlewoman. Kate's innards lurched again – she knew nothing about this woman, and a sense that she possessed knowledge far beyond the reading of palms filtered through Kate's mind, leaving a residue of unease. Her grandfather had hanged for his witchcraft – was the same fate awaiting her? Was it wise to disturb the ghosts of the past? Perhaps her mother had been right to conceal the truth.

For two quick breaths Kate paused, half tempted to turn away, and forget it after all. What did it matter anyway, whose blood flowed through her veins? She was a tailor's daughter, fated to live out her life by the plying of her needle. Nothing would change that, not even sewing shirts for a prince. She should leave, she thought again, and think no more on the fortune teller's words.

She was about to turn away when Isabella's gaze shifted and her eyes caught at Kate's. The look that passed between them quashed all her doubts in an instant – it was a look that offered the world, a look that could not be gainsaid. With a little lift of her shoulders, Kate picked up her skirts and wove her way across the kitchen to take up her place on the stool once more.

'You returned.'

'You knew I would.'

The woman smiled, the stern face softening for the first time. 'I did.'

'How could you know such a thing?'

'You are young and curious. And if your mother wanted you to know about the past, she would have told you long ago.'

Kate swallowed, a sense of trepidation sliding through her. She set her face as best she could, hoping to hide the onslaught of feelings behind a mask. But even as she did it, she doubted there was much she could hide from this woman.

'You wish to know where you come from?'

She nodded, no longer trusting her voice to speak.

'What are you prepared to give in return for this knowledge?'

Kate hesitated. She had not thought till now beyond the knowledge itself. She should have expected there would be a price to pay for its finding.

'I have nothing,' she managed to breathe, lifting her empty hands. It felt as though the ground had shifted under her. She was stepping into a different future and the realisation both scared and excited her.

'Everyone has something.'

'I don't understand.' She felt foolish suddenly, and judged.

'Are you prepared to give this up? This life?' The fortune teller gestured with an elegant hand around the kitchen. A blood-red jewel on one of her fingers caught the light and glimmered. 'Are you willing to leave it all behind to find out the truth?'

Kate's breathing quickened and though she ran her tongue across her lips, her mouth was dry. Could she? She had never thought to have such a choice.

'What would you have me do?' she asked, and the words were hard to form in a mouth that felt like sawdust.

Isabella leaned forward and placed a hand on Kate's wrist. Her fingers were hard and cold despite the warmth of the kitchen, and Kate quivered with her touch.

'Come with me,' she said, 'and I promise you will find what you seek.'

Kate swallowed again, past the lump in her throat, and forced herself to meet the other woman's eyes. They were watching her, waiting, and though Kate wanted nothing so much as to believe in her, her whole body prickled in warning.

'Go with you where?'

'Trust me,' Isabella whispered, as though she were inside Kate's head. 'Trust me.'

For the length of a heartbeat Kate said nothing. She already knew the woman was not to be trusted. Already knew the danger. But in spite of the doubts and the voice in her head that was screaming no, she still heard herself say, 'I will go with you.'

The other woman's face broke into a delighted smile that did nothing to quell the quiver of fear in Kate's veins, nor the sense she had struck a bad bargain. But even so, she could not bring herself to walk away.

'Wonderful,' Isabella purred, rising to her feet. 'Wait here – there is something I must attend to.'

Then she turned and left.

~

Kate waited as she was told. In the heat and bustle no one paid her any mind but it was hard to be patient when the future lay just beyond her fingertips; she yearned to race towards it. Excitement and terror tumbled in equal measure inside her and she had to fight against the urge to pace in the corner, forcing herself to sit and be still, hands clasped lightly on her lap, fingers twitching.

She could scarcely believe the path she had chosen to follow, and her mother's voice, practical and scolding, sounded over her thoughts. Kate's innards lurched again: what was she thinking? She knew nothing of this woman and yet she had placed her fate in her hands. She should go home and make her peace with her mother, she decided, who might yet be coaxed to part with the truth, given time. But still, Kate made no move to leave, unable to bring herself to back away.

Examining her hands, she traced the lines of one with the fingertips of the other, searching for the secrets hidden within them. How could a person tell so much from a palm? Surely there must be some sorcery in it? Or was it guesswork merely, and the woman was a liar and a charlatan? Kate shook her head against the doubts, reminding herself of the truths Isabella had spoken and that her mother had already confirmed. This was her one chance to walk a different road and escape the humdrum life she had been born to – from birth to death as a seamstress, her world bounded by the neighbouring streets, and all that lay beyond them forever unknown to her. More than anything, she wanted to know the world in all its chaos and beauty, and she was willing to take the risk for the knowledge.

Time passed. She watched dinner being served. Great platters of venison and boar, sweet-spiced sparrows, tarts with sugared cream and rosewater, quince cakes and jellies. Soft white bread and spiced wines. The empty plates came back and she remembered she was hungry. Fear and excitement waned to a bored and weary lethargy. Twice, she made the decision to go home after all, and got almost halfway to the door before the desire to know hardened in her blood like a charm that drew her back once more and forced her to wait again.

By the time Isabella returned at last, Kate was sinking into drowsiness. She had dragged the stool closer to the wall so she could lean her shoulder against it, and she had begun to doze in spite of the racket of the kitchen all around her, dreaming strange bright dreams that were forgotten the moment she opened her eyes, leaving just a wispy trail of unease in their wake.

Isabella strode between the kitchen staff, her face stern, and Kate stood up with a slight dip into an instinctive curtsey. She was unsure of the relationship between them now – was she a servant now? A pupil? She should have asked more questions, the voice in her head scolded, before she set her fate in this stranger's hands.

'Forgive me for keeping you waiting so long; there was much to arrange. We sail on the evening tide,' Isabella said, flicking a glance to the windows. The sky beyond was dark, night almost upon them. 'So we must make haste.'

'Sail?' Something akin to panic flared through her body, breath turning ragged, heartbeat quick.

'To London, to find your past.'

Of course, she thought. She should have realised. Isabella regarded her with a long cool look of appraisal, and Kate lowered her eyes, searching the flagstones of the kitchen floor for the strength to simply walk away.

She did not want to go to London, not like this, as a thief in the night.

Casting her mind across the small chamber in the attic at home where she had lived her whole life till now, her gaze slid over the bright counterpane and cushions sewn by her mother. Her brushes and mirror. Two books on herbs, the chest containing her skirts, and the little box that had been a gift from her father when she was just a girl, treasured all these years. In her mind's eye she checked the contents: some beads, a bracelet, a small silver brooch. Her heart turned over with the thought she might never see those things again and for the length of a breath their call was almost strong enough to summon her home. She glanced across the kitchen towards the low servant's door – a few strides would see her on her way, out into the evening, with the fortune teller and all she had offered put aside and forgotten. She swallowed, hesitating as her thoughts roiled with the possibilities – a different future, a life to be lived.

Her mother would be frantic, she thought, but still the knowledge was not enough to make her change her mind – she wanted to experience the world, and fate was holding out an unexpected chance she might never see again. How could she refuse it? She would write, she told herself, when she arrived in London, and set her mother's mind at ease. Or find someone on the quay to take a message.

'I have nothing to bring but the clothes on my back,' she said.

'I have clothes a-plenty that can be altered to fit,' Isabella said, 'and there is little else you need.'

Then, with a nod, she turned abruptly and Kate found herself following her across the kitchen towards the door and out into the bitter night beyond it, as if drawn by an invisible thread.

In the courtyard the air was frigid. A cold mist had seeped between the buildings and Kate's breath puffed in little clouds before her face as she walked. She huddled deeper into her cloak but it made no difference; the chill air still crept inside the heavy wool and made her shiver. Isabella walked beside her and their boots rang on the cobblestones as they strode with purpose towards the docks. She did not allow herself to cast a look behind her.

At the quayside, the ships loomed large in the dark, lanterns casting a dim and eerie light that sent the shadows dancing across the ground. The vessels seemed so much bigger at night, and forbidding. Kate had never been on a ship, though she had often watched them come and go, trailing their possibilities of adventure.

Now, faced with the prospect of the voyage her blood quivered with fear. Was she willing to entrust her life so completely to this stranger merely to learn her family's past? To go all the way to England and put herself so far beyond her mother's reach?

She was truly leaving it all and, in spite of all her hopes of a journey, she had never thought she might leave like this – secretly, in the darkening night at the side of a stranger, with no chance to say farewell to everything she had ever known. The ball of doubt hardened again in her belly. It was not too late to change her mind, the warning voice whispered in her head. She could still turn back, go home, forget it. But she kept walking even so, striding towards her fate, boots slipping on the greasy stones underfoot.

Dark, faceless figures flitted through the shadows on unknown business, and Kate searched among them for someone who might deliver a message to her mother. But all of them moved with purpose, and she dared not disturb a single one of them. She quickened her steps to counter her fears and Isabella slid a glance towards her.

'Which of them is ours?' she asked, gesturing to the ships drawn alongside.

'A little further.'

As they walked on, picking their way between the sheds and boxes and coils of rope, two men lurched towards them out of nowhere. Kate screamed in shock as one of them snatched at Isabella's arm, but Isabella was too quick for him, twisting her body away, nimble and light.

'Bitch!' The man shouted. 'Whores!' They heard him hawk and spit on the cobbles as they broke into a run away from him.

'The docks are not a safe place for women,' Isabella said, as they slowed their pace once again, and Kate cast a glance behind her. The shadows flickered with unseen danger, and men's voices, disembodied, drifted on the air. She had never been afraid of the dark before, enchanted instead by the possibilities it contained. Fear of it had always seemed to her to be a weakness but now she had to set her shoulders and swallow down her disquiet.

'I am not afraid,' she said, and Isabella gave her a smile.

They came at last to a three-masted barque where final preparations to sail were under way.

'The *Fortune*,' Isabella said, slowing to a halt close to a gangplank that rang with the footsteps of men shouldering loads, hurrying. Above them the deck seemed alive with voices, shouts passing from one man to another. 'Come,' she said, and Kate followed her aboard. The men threw surly looks their way – few sailors liked to have women aboard – but there was no time for more than cursory glances, and Kate was glad.

She set her gaze seaward. Far out from the shore in the distance, faint lights flickered, hovering. Other ships, Kate guessed, leaving on the tide, and excitement began to chase away the residue of fear. She smiled at her companion, who was watching her with an appraising eye. They found themselves a place at the rail close to the gangplank, watching as the walkway was cast back to the quay and the ropes were tossed from the mooring posts. Shouts rang out as the sailors leaned into the capstan and the ship began to inch away from the dock. Kate turned to watch the men straining against the slow turn of the wheel as the deck lurched beneath her feet, and tightened her grasp on the rail as the wind snapped in the sails being unfurled further forward. Men clambered over the masts and rigging above her but she paid them no mind, her thoughts shoreward, watching the city slowly diminish, taking on a different aspect. Lights flickered, and the shadows merged together until she could no longer make out the individual buildings. Then a gust of wind caught at her hair and as she lifted a hand to brush it back, she was conscious of Isabella's gaze on her face. It was a look she was more used to getting from a man but she took pleasure in the other woman's admiration, aware of her own beauty. Turning with a smile, she met the other woman's eyes, intense even in the gloom, and suddenly alive with a light that Kate no longer recognised. A flicker of warning flared again through her blood and she shivered.

'You're cold,' Isabella said. 'Come, let's go below.'

Kate left the deck with a sense of reluctance in spite of the chill. The open sea beckoned, ripe with the unfamiliar tang of new-found freedom, and she wanted to laugh with the awareness of the thrust for life inside her: she could have frozen half to death in its contemplation and barely noticed. But the fortune teller had grasped her arm and was steering her towards the stairway as the deck began to roll under their feet. Kate braced the muscles in her legs and belly to keep her balance, and followed Isabella to their cabin.

Inside, it was cramped and airless, shadows stretching and shifting with the rock of the ship, boards creaking. A bed, a trunk, a lantern that swung from a hook on the wall. There was no window and her head brushed against the ceiling. Somewhere in the distance a bell tolled, and now and then a man's half-heard voice drifted through the walls. Someone had left them a tray of simple food. Bread, cheese, smoked fish and a jug of ale, and Kate remembered she was hungry.

They ate, speaking little, but the silence was comfortable enough. There would be time for all her many questions later and for now she was still marvelling in the knowledge of her flight, surprised by her recklessness and savouring the sense of adventure. She closed her mind against the image of her mother's distress and the warning bell that still tolled at the edges of her thoughts. The decision had been made and it was too late now to change her mind. She felt light-headed, and the rocking of the ship only served to heighten the sense of strangeness. It was like a dream, unreal and soon to end, so that she half expected to wake up in her attic bed at home.

'We should sleep,' Isabella said, when they had eaten their fill. 'It's been a long day.'

Kate nodded in agreement. The movement of the ship and the food in her belly had made her drowsy but still, she was reluctant to bring the day to an end. Tomorrow would bring a new reality, when she must face the consequences of her flight in the harsh light of the day. For now, her life seemed full of wonder, a new world opening before her.

'Let me help you,' said Isabella, standing up.

Kate got to her feet and stood, feet braced against the movements of the ship, as the other woman untied the laces of her bodice, their faces close. The taint of an unfamiliar scent clung to Isabella's hair – a bittersweet spice, exotic and intoxicating. She inhaled, and the fortune teller looked up with a smile that Kate could not quite read. But she smiled in reply, enjoying the brightness of Isabella's attention – it was surely a light to savour. Then, stepping out of her skirts, she climbed into the narrow cot they would share. She doubted she'd sleep well: she had slept alone for most of her life and it was many years since nightmares had taken her to the safety of her parents' bed.

From her place in the high berth she observed Isabella as she moved about the small cabin like a seasoned sailor, unworried by the rolling motion of the ship. Kate's eyes followed the fortune teller's movements, watching the fingers that were deft with the ties of her bodice before she laid her skirts and petticoats across the single chair. The shift she wore was of the finest linen and the seamstress in Kate smiled in pleasure at its quality. But Isabella's outline beneath it was clear to see in the wavering light of the lantern behind her and Kate observed her, noticing the narrow hips and slim legs, the small, upturned breasts. Like her own body, Kate realised, boyish and lean. She had always wished for more curves before but now, observing another woman much like herself, she saw the beauty in the clean, lithe limbs, a strength, and she ran a hand across her own flat belly in appreciation.

Isabella finished undressing and climbed into the bed beside her. They could not help but touch, thigh to thigh, shoulder to shoulder, and Kate turned onto her side, facing away. The lantern still burned and its glow swayed across the cabin, shadows looming and falling as the ship rolled and swayed. She was grateful for its light.

As the other woman settled herself at Kate's back in the narrow bed, Kate was aware of the movement of Isabella's legs against her own as she fitted her body around the curves in Kate's, conscious of the press of the other woman's breasts against her back, a hand resting on the muscle of her arm. Briefly she tensed, unused to such contact, before she forced herself to quell her unease and the unexpected rise of anticipation. Where else was Isabella to lie?

'Good night.' The whispered words were close enough to Kate's neck that she could feel the warmth of them against her skin before Isabella turned abruptly away to lie on her back, withdrawing the tantalising promise of her embrace. Despite her misgivings, Kate was surprised to feel the emptiness of disappointment.

She murmured a reply, unsure of her feelings any more. She had never thought to be looked at by a woman the way Isabella looked at her. Had never thought she might bask in such attention. But she had been certain of the pleasure it brought her, the sensation delicious, and a smile caught at the corners of her lips at the thought of it.

It had been the strangest of days, but now, lying drowsy and warm in the soft bed beside Isabella at the start of a new life, she was content to let sleep claim her.

And that night, not a single dream came to trouble her.

❦ 5 ❦

THOSE STRONG KNOTS OF LOVE

Mary waited as suppertime came and went but still there was no sign of her daughter. The tailors closed up the shop and left, and Mary did not notice them go. Not so long ago, she had awaited the end of the work day with eagerness, listening for Toby's step on the stairs, anticipating his smile as he ducked through the low door of the first-floor chamber. It was those moments she missed the most since he had gone, she realised, the small and precious daily things that make up a life together. His head on the pillow next to hers in the morning, his nod of thanks for the cup of ale she brought to him in the shop, evenings spent before the fire, content in each other's company.

She missed him far more than the infants that had come and gone, though their deaths had once threatened to unravel her. But in those days Toby had been by her side and they had weathered the grief together, secure, loved. Now she felt unutterably alone. Her daughter had become a stranger, and there seemed to be nothing to hope for in her life any more but the swift release of death so that she might be with Toby once again.

Standing now at the window, she stared down at the street where the shadows seemed alive in the flickering lanterns that burned at the doorways. Above the rooftops a silver slice of the waning moon peeped from behind scudding clouds but it cast scant light across the scene below. Sarah used to pray to the moon, Mary recalled, dancing in its light. Perhaps she, Mary, should do the same, though God knew it had brought no great good fortune to Sarah. Had she found her happiness in the end? Mary wondered. Was she resting in peace at last with Tom? She hoped so. Whatever the truth of Sarah's relationship with Tom she had only ever been kind to Mary, even when she was just a Bankside whore that Toby had taken pity on.

With a sigh, she turned from the window and went to the hearth. The fire was almost out – she'd paid it no attention all through the hours she had been waiting, her thoughts wholly taken up with worry for Kate. More than eight hours had passed since her daughter fled from the house in a fury and she had not yet returned. She had never stayed out so long before, and Mary's blood quivered with unease. Shivering, she squatted to throw on another log, poking at the half-dead embers, stirring the life back into them, drawn to the brightness and warmth.

The sound of a footstep on the road outside the house made her turn her head to listen but she knew straight away that the tread was not her daughter's. Sitting back on her heels she stared into the flames as they began to lick at the new wood, feeling the heat touch her face before she lifted her head to the window once again. Should she go out and search? Try to find this fortune teller? Or perhaps she should scour the taverns she knew Kate had begun to frequent since her father's death, finding comfort, Mary guessed, in the arms of strange men. A better mother might have been able to stop it but in the throes of her own grief Mary had been powerless against her daughter's defiance, and so she had lowered her eyes away and pretended not to know.

When the church clock three streets away tolled the hour of ten, Mary decided at last she could wait no longer; now that she had made the decision, her movements took on an urgency, fuelled by the sudden fear she had left it too late, that she should have gone hours before. After scrawling a hurried note in case Kate should return ahead of her, she lifted her warmest cloak from the hook by the door, lighted a lantern from one of the candles, and stepped out into the night, where the sudden chill almost took her breath away. Hunching her shoulders, she set out with quick and automatic steps towards the palace.

She had thought movement might help ease her worry, but after the torpor of the hours of inactivity she was seized now with a panic that she had waited too long. By the time she stepped into the square before the Binnenhof she was almost running, sweat collecting in the pit of her back in spite of the cold.

The palace windows were still ablaze with light and Mary was glad. The streets she had passed through on her way had seemed ghostly and forbidding, and the sense of life before her now was a welcome sight. They would still be celebrating Christmas, she thought, the last of the twelve days of revels and festivity. She swallowed, her mouth dry, and set her steps towards the entrance that Toby used to take. For herself, she had never been inside before, though there were many within its walls who wore her needlework. But she had often come this far with Toby for the pleasure of the walk in his company before he left her at the threshold – master tailor to the exiled nobility of England.

The low door stood ajar and the light and smells and clatter of activity within flooded out into the night. She knocked once, and as she stepped inside the biggest kitchen she had ever seen, a wash of heat swept over her. She blinked in the steam and felt the flush of warmth that reddened her face. No one paid her any attention – she doubted anyone had even heard her knock. Everyone was busy.

Taking off her gloves, she let the hood of her cloak drop back. She could feel the line of sweat at her hairline and she wiped at it with her fingers as her gaze travelled over the scene before coming to rest at last on a spit boy who was staring into space as he turned a hog above the great fire. With a deep breath, she crossed the flagstones towards him. He watched her approach without interest, dropping his head in automatic deference when she stopped before him. But he kept the spit turning nonetheless.

'Tell me, boy,' Mary said. 'Is there a woman here who tells fortunes?'

He lifted his eyes then, and she saw the surprise in them. 'The palm reader?'

'Aye.'

He slanted a glance towards the far corner. 'She was here before,' he said. 'But then she left. Dunno where she went.'

'Can you tell me anything about her?'

He shrugged and shook his head, then turned his attention back to the meat he was turning. It was almost cooked, Mary thought, the skin crisp and crackling, a golden glow and ripe with sweet succulence. At another time Mary's mouth might have watered.

'Is there anyone who can?' she persisted.

He shrugged again, having lost interest, and she turned away to look for someone else to ask. Everyone was absorbed in their tasks. She could feel the tension in the air, a sense of haste, and it was hard to find the courage to interrupt any one of them. A servant strode in through another door, handsomely dressed. He paused briefly, apparently waiting for something. Mary approached him and he gave her a brief appraisal as he decided how to react, but she was dressed well enough to command his courtesy and he dropped his head in a nod of recognition.

'Madam. How may I be of service?'

'There was a fortune teller here before. I wish to know where I might find her now.'

'You want a fortune teller?' The derision in his voice was barely concealed.

'No,' she responded with equal disdain. 'I want that particular woman.'

'I see.' His face settled back to neutral. 'I'm afraid I cannot help you.' He gave a curt bow and walked away, and Mary cast a glance across the kitchen, searching for another she could ask. But even as she looked she knew it was futile, for who ever thinks to question a fortune teller beyond asking what fate for you she sees?

She would have come and gone unremarked and no one would know or care where she came from or where she would go to next. She was a diviner of fortunes and that was all.

It was hopeless, Mary thought. She would never find her. But still she asked, desperation lending her courage as she interrupted cooks and servants alike.

Do you know where I might find the fortune teller?

But always the same answer came – a shrug and a shake of the head.

Finally, when there was no one else left to ask, she turned towards the door. She would have to seek elsewhere and find her daughter a different way. Sliding through the gap into the night outside again, she shivered with the sudden chill. She would search in the taverns, she decided, and look for her daughter there. It was a small chance, she knew, but it was the only chance she had.

That night, falling into exhausted sleep after fruitless hours in search of Kate, Mary dreamt of Bankside for the first time in years, and in the dream the place was both foreign and familiar. The long line of whitewashed brothels stretched out exactly as they did in her memory, and at her back the river slapped against the shingle. Torches burned in doorways and windows shed their glow into the darkening night, just as she remembered. But even so, she was intensely aware that everything was different now and she was no longer a part of it. Shivering, her shoulders bare and her gown cut low across her breasts as she had worn it in those days, Mary stepped forward and made with automatic steps for the Cardinal's Cap.

The door was firmly shut when she placed her hand on the handle and she had to fight to shove it open but when, finally, it gave with a lurch, the brothel inside was not the place she remembered. It seemed to be all but abandoned. No fire danced in the fireplace, no candles or lanterns lit the shadows, and in the gloom she saw overturned chairs and empty cups on tables that were grey with dust. A draught from the still-open door sent a tremor through the air, and the room, disturbed, seemed to let off a sigh.

Closing the door behind her Mary looked around, conscious of an unknown presence. Fear caught at her innards and as she half turned to flee, a voice called her name.

A voice from the past.

A voice she once knew as well as her own.

Rosalind.

She swung slowly to face the room once more, peering into the half-dark. Shadows shifted and a new chill settled. She waited, gripped with fear, until her old friend stepped at last into view. Rosalind smiled, eyes bright with humour as Mary remembered her best – the friend she had been before the old man arrived and robbed her of her wits.

Come home, Rosalind said, *'tis time*.

The room spun around her and when finally it settled, it had returned to the brothel of Mary's memory – bright and noisy, lively with wine and ale and the promise of pleasure. At the tables she saw men she recognised – the players, girls she had known, Toby, the sorcerer. And beside the sorcerer at a table close to the fire was Kate, holding the old man's hand. Mary tried to call out, to run towards her ...

She woke with a start, breathless and sweating in the dark. The fire in the chamber had long since gone out, and the chill air bit against her bare skin. But she tipped herself out of bed regardless, desperate for movement to test the limbs that had refused to obey her in the nightmare. Dragging her robe from the side of the bed that used to be Toby's, she slid her arms inside it, clutching it tightly round herself. Then she went to the window and looked out at the night.

Dying torches flickered in their sconces on the neighbouring houses – the night was almost done, but the road was still deserted. Theirs was a peaceful neighbourhood, set away from the roughness of the docks and peopled with families of artisans and tradesmen who slept soundly at night between days of honest labour. It was worlds away from the Bankside she had come from, and though she had always been grateful for the safety of the peace, she missed the liveliness of home, the connection to life in all its raw and risky beauty, a celebration of the miracle of existence, physical and rough. Now, staring down into the empty street, she yearned for that connection – other human beings to touch or to care about.

Toby, she thought, and lifted her eyes to the stars above the rooftops. Toby.

Slowly, her breathing settled and the sweat dried at the back of her neck, but the image of Kate with the sorcerer remained vivid as her thoughts flailed in a futile effort to understand.

The sorcerer was long dead. She had killed him herself and watched the blood spread across the floorboards before she and Toby had fled to begin this new life across the narrow sea. Toby had taken his real father's name, and with their marriage she had taken it too, leaving the names of Chyrche and Sparrow far behind them. They had lived a respectable life all through the years since then, and only now and then had they revisited the past – a word here and there, a shared look that needed no explanation.

So why had the sorcerer stepped back into her thoughts? And how?

The church clock struck the hour, unseen beyond the houses, and Mary cast a wistful look back to the bed she had left, warm and inviting, but she knew she'd sleep no more tonight. She needed movement and activity to stir her thoughts and find an answer to the riddle of her dream. So she dressed hurriedly, stepped out into the passageway and, surefooted even in the dark, the way well known, she went downstairs, threw on her cloak and went out once more into the frigid night.

There was no forest grove nearby where she could go to call on Hecate as Sarah had taught her, so Mary went instead to the little graveyard at the edge of the city that served as the final resting place for the English exiles. The streets she passed along were deserted and she was grateful for that, but the morning was bitter cold, stinging against the skin of her face, lips growing numb as the lantern she carried flickered bravely in the darkness.

Even in the dark, Toby's grave was easy to find. The place was chiselled into Mary's heart – in the first days after his death she had barely ever left it. It was marked by a small headstone engraved with the name he had taken, *Toby Winter,* the name that fitted him best. Kneeling now beside the mound of earth that was all that remained of her husband, she ran her hand across the grass that had begun to grow, the young blades tickling her palm. As a girl long ago she had been afraid of graveyards, but she had learned since then she had far more to fear from the living than the dead.

But still ...

She had dreamt of the sorcerer and of Rosalind, and though she was tempted to dismiss it as the meaningless visions of a mind disordered by worries, she knew it was not so. Did the dead have the power to visit the living? she wondered. Toby would have known, she thought. Toby would have understood how to read it – he had studied such things.

Sitting back on her heels with a sigh, she lifted her eyes to the heavens, though there was little to see there – the moon and stars were obscured by lowering clouds that threatened rain.

Was he up there, with God, watching her now? Or did he dwell in some other realm of the dead? With his father perhaps? Or with the demons he once used to summon?

Hecate, she murmured.

It had been too long since she last called upon the goddess. She should have brought an offering, she remembered, of incense or honey or cake. A gift of love and respect. But she had nothing with her to offer but the pain in her heart and her trust in the power of the goddess that had not waned with the years. She wanted to cast a circle, and call to the quarters as she remembered Toby had done. But she lacked the knowledge to do it right, and so instead she scrambled to her feet, knees cracking with the cold, and raised her arms to the sky as she recalled Sarah used to do sometimes. For a moment the words were hard to find, buried in the recesses of her thoughts, but when they came to her lips at last they issued not from her memory, but from some deep place inside her.

'Great goddess, I worship thee
With my body, my heart, my soul
Help me now as you have done before
Lead me to my daughter – keep her safe from harm
Show me how to find her
And as I stand at the crossroads, guide my footsteps truly.'

She bowed her head. The words had come by instinct, and though her voice had trembled, hesitant in the silent dark, she hoped the goddess had heard.

Then she knelt again at the graveside, a welcome fine thread of peace at her core, and waited to know what she must do.

It was still dark when Mary reached the quayside, the winter dawn coming late.

Come home, Rosalind had said.

At the docks the wharves were already lively, torches and lanterns ablaze as the ships were readied for the morning tide, and the sight of it made her smile in spite of her troubles, a reminder of Bankside, one more call towards home. She walked briskly, alert to the dangers for a woman in such a place – old instincts that had stayed with her throughout the years of respectability. She was aware of the looks she drew, surprise and curiosity to see a well-dressed woman alone in the dark without so much as a maid beside her. There was a time she would have welcomed their interest, rich pickings to be earned. But now her business was different, and she was uncertain. Did she dare to trust the message of her dream? Though a part deep inside her clung to the hope that Kate was still in The Hague and would find her own way home, it was only a small part, because she knew in her heart it was not so. Her dream told against it, and in the hours she had waited at Toby's graveside for Hecate's guidance, the repeated call to return to Bankside had sounded as an irresistible knell deep within her. In spite of doubts that still gnawed, she knew Kate had left The Hague to discover the past as she had promised, and she had gone to London to do it.

Words of English reached her ears from amongst the chatter of the wharf men. Turning towards the sound she saw a three-masted merchantman that was being loaded with a cargo of wine and spices and timber, and she stepped towards it, more confident in her mother tongue. One of the men left off his work and watched her approach. Thick threaded veins stood out in sinewy forearms, the man in his shirtsleeves in spite of the cold. His forehead shone with sweat but he had kind, shrewd eyes, and she trod across the wharf towards him. She had to ask someone, after all, and he seemed as good as any.

'I need a berth to London,' she said.

The man jerked his head towards the ship alongside. 'She'll be sailing on the evenin' tide,' he said.

'Who must I speak to?'

He shrugged, and Mary gave an inward sigh of disappointment, but she waited just in case until he turned away with a small smile of apology and resumed his work. She watched him for a moment, running her eyes across the ship before she turned to look along the quay for someone else to ask, waiting, impatient. Shivering in the cold, she huddled deeper inside her cloak. She should have waited till daybreak, she thought, and called upon one of Toby's associates – men of trade, men with connections. One of them would have been able to help her. But they would have asked questions and delayed her with their kindness and good intentions, and she wanted to be gone before the day was out. She looked up and down the dock in growing desperation. Another ship perhaps? Should she keep on walking?

She had almost decided to walk on when a young man stepped out of the darkness into the circle of the torchlight by the ship. If he was surprised to see a woman on the dock he showed no sign of it, and fine, handsome features opened into a courteous smile. Good teeth, she noticed, and dark eyes that seemed to miss nothing. A young gentleman, by his dress and bearing. A stroke of luck, perhaps? She answered his smile with a curtsey.

'May I be of some service to you, madam?' He spoke in English, and an instinctive ripple of relief eddied through her.

'I hope so,' she replied. 'Is this your ship?'

'She is not, regrettably.' He shook his head. 'But I sail on her on the evening tide. To London.' He cast an automatic glance to the sky, judging the hour and the weather with a practised eye.

'What must I do if I also wish to travel to London? It is a matter of some urgency.'

The man hesitated. Then he said, 'Do you have the proper papers?'

She tilted her head. 'What is it to you?'

He gave a half-laugh and leaned in closer. 'There is a different process, is all.'

'Then, no,' she murmured in reply, 'I have no papers.'

He considered her for a moment and she lowered her head, coy. She had grown unused to such open scrutiny but the light in his eyes was familiar – he was wondering what he might gain from helping her, weighing up her respectability against her need.

'I would be very grateful for any help you can give me,' she said, with just enough of a smile to let him hope. Then she turned to regard the ship once again. 'Is she a fast ship?'

He smiled in return, and she sensed he was in a hurry of his own. 'I certainly hope so. Come with me now, and I will do what I can to aid you.' Then, as an afterthought, he said, 'What is your name?'

'Mary Johnson,' she said, lying out of instinct – she could not have given a good reason why.

'Rafe Tyndall,' he replied, 'at your service.'

She went with him to the Customs House and they found the ship's captain in furious argument with an official who seemed to be enjoying the other man's frustration. As they came upon him, he threw up his hands in surrender and turned so abruptly he almost barrelled into them.

'Forgive me,' he gasped. Then, recovering himself, he dipped his head in a bow. 'Master Tyndall.'

Rafe gestured to the office at the captain's back. 'Problems?'

'Always.' The captain shook his head in exasperation.

Mary waited as Rafe drew the captain to one side and began to talk in a low undertone she could not quite catch. Once or twice the seafarer slid her a glance, and she wondered what tale Rafe was spinning to secure her passage, and what it would cost her in the end. She had surprised herself on the quay, slipping back into old ways with such ease – it had been many years since she had needed to please any man but Toby, who had loved her. But now she stood with her hips at an angle, head tilted and her lips curved in the slightest of smiles as the captain's gaze passed over her in appraisal. She had met his type many times before – too many years at sea and a thirst for simple pleasures on shore.

Rafe, however, was harder to read. He was thirty years old or so, she guessed, and attractive, with dark, intelligent eyes, and a forelock of hair that fell forward over his face. He lifted a hand to smooth it back as she watched him. But she sensed a deeper current beneath the charm – he seemed to her like a man who had secrets, and perhaps a sadness inside him that he wanted to hide.

The murmured conversation came to an end and Rafe beckoned to her to join them. She stepped across and sank into a low and respectful curtsey. When she rose, the captain addressed her.

'Mistress Johnson. Master Tyndall has explained your unusual circumstances and I am willing to grant you passage. We will set you ashore downriver a ways from the city.'

'You have my thanks,' she answered.

He nodded then turned away, and as she watched his broad back diminish along the passage she wondered what tale Rafe had spun to such success.

'What circumstances?' she enquired.

He gave her his most charming smile. 'I said you were in the service of the Prince of Wales. As I am, myself.'

'And you trust him?' Being caught as a Royalist spy carried far greater risk than stealing an illicit voyage.

'Aye,' Rafe nodded. 'With my life.'

'Then I will trust him also,' she replied, though she had yet to determine how far she trusted Rafe. That he was not all he appeared to be she knew without question.

'You have luggage?' he asked. They fell in step beside each other as they found their way to the door. Beyond it, the quay was beginning to lighten, the dark giving way to a slow creeping greyness, shadows shifting into sharper relief. The *Falcon*'s masts were dark against the brightening sky. She was going home and though the thought of it tugged at her heart, Toby's absence from her side for the journey lit the old grief inside her, so that she had to bite her lip against the pain.

'Just a bag.' Mary turned toward Rafe, her face a mask.

'That is all?' He seemed surprised.

She nodded. It was already packed and ready at home, waiting, and it contained everything she needed – a few clothes, a silver-backed hairbrush and mirror that had been a gift from Toby, a few tools of her trade as a seamstress and, of course, Toby's book, sewn into the lining. It was the most precious thing she owned – her husband's link to his father. She would never part with it willingly but it would fetch a good price from the right man if the times became desperate enough.

Rafe bowed. 'Then I will take my leave of you for now. The tide turns at six of the clock. Do not be late. The *Falcon* will sail with or without you aboard.'

She nodded. As yet he had asked for nothing in return. Once aboard, she supposed, he would ask for his payment and, though she knew he was hiding something, it took scant imagination to guess what form the payment was likely to take.

'I will be here,' she said.

Then, with a slight bob, she turned and strode away along the quay, weaving easily through the growing bustle of the morning.

THE UNDISCOVERED COUNTRY

Kate stood on deck as the ship laboured up the river. The crossing had been rough, three days of storm and rain, but she had been unafraid, thrilled by the ocean's power, the plunge and toss of the ship in the foam. She had wanted to go on deck to feel the storm against her face, the untrammelled force of the elements, but Isabella had warned her against it. When, heedless, she had left the cabin anyway she was manhandled roughly back inside by the first mate. Her arms still bore the bruises from his grip and she rubbed at them gently now as the *Fortune* slid sedately upriver with the tide, guided by the pilot who had come aboard at Gravesend. But her gaze was fixed on the riverbank and her first glimpses of England.

A different world, she thought. The land was higher, hillier, greener than the flat city of her childhood, and the sweep of the river enthralled her. It was a power in its own right, broad and deep, and alive with the traffic of a myriad of boats. Lifting her face to meet the low afternoon sun that lay ahead of them, she drew in a deep breath. Even the air smelled different, less redolent of the sea, and she turned with a smile as Isabella came to stand beside her.

'Welcome to England,' the older woman said. 'The land of your forebears. What do you think?'

Kate swept her gaze along the bank. A village was nestled in a copse of trees, a church spire peeping through the bare winter branches, and a cluster of men were unloading barrels and cases of some unknown cargo from a small merchantman that was moored at a jetty. Her own people, she thought, who spoke her mother tongue. Would she feel at home amongst them or be forever on the outside, the curse of the traveller?

'I like it so far,' she answered.

'You will like London more,' Isabella said. ''Tis the greatest city in the world.'

Kate laughed and turned her face forward, peering upriver, waiting for her first sight of the city.

The bustle of the docks in The Hague seemed slight against the hubbub of London. So many craft of all kinds on the water – merchantmen and warships, barges, barques and wherries, leisure boats and tugs, as if the whole of London had emptied to live upon the river. But the shoreline too was alive with trade – she could see signs for chandlers and biscuit-bakers, rope and sailmakers, warehouses, inns and taverns. At Rotherhithe, great watermills churned to make gunpowder, and at every wharf they passed men laboured to unload goods she could only begin to guess at. Kate had never imagined so many people could exist in one place, and she drank all of it in, intoxicated by so much vitality around her. She could hardly wait to disembark to take her place in the midst of it and become a part of this dazzling circus of life.

They stepped ashore at a wharf on the river's south side and in the brief pause before they set off she gazed about her in wonder. Across the press of people and activity bustling all around her, she noticed a young man leaning against a wall and gazing out at the river, a single point of stillness in all the hustle. Briefly, their eyes locked. Then Isabella turned and began to walk away, and Kate swung after her to follow closely through the press, the young man forgotten as she wove between boxes and barrels, ducking under ropes and pulleys, her senses assailed by the cacophony of shouts and gulls, the thwack and rattle of ropes and sails, the grind of chains. Strange scents hung in the air, spice and wine and fruits she didn't recognise above the ranker scent of shit and putrefaction.

The stone quay, so solid underfoot, threatened her balance, her land legs taking time to return after the days at sea, and though she longed to simply stop and stare she was afraid to get lost in the crush – Isabella had told her nothing of where they were going, of what to expect. To find herself alone now would be her undoing: she had not a penny to her name, and not a single friend she could turn to.

Ahead of her, the fortune teller wove easily through the throng and Kate, unused to such crowds, struggled to keep up. She wondered what had become of the trunk she had seen in the cabin but her questions were soon forgotten as they emerged from the stir of the quayside and into a quieter street beyond it where half-timbered houses leaned out over the road. In the shadow they cast, Kate shivered. Puddles scarred the roadway and Kate guessed they barely ever dried – no sun ever warmed these streets – and as the stink caught in her nostrils she had to swallow down the urge to gag.

Isabella was striding westwards, following the line of the river with her skirts held free of the muck at her feet. Kate had almost to run to keep up, but nonetheless it was hard to keep her eyes from exploring all that they passed. She had so many questions but no breath to speak and, besides, the set of Isabella's mouth deterred any hope of conversation. But no matter – she was in the greatest city in the world and her life was just beginning.

They came at last to an ill-kept street where a huddle of beggars stood hunched around a low-burning brazier that gave off an acrid stench. Mangy dogs prowled amidst the mud and refuse, and an old man struggled to propel an empty handcart over the ruts, his forehead shiny with sweat in the cold. The beggars lifted their heads and extended automatic hands in supplication but Kate had nothing to give and Isabella spared them not so much as a glance.

They stopped at a house where a faded sign creaked lightly above the door, and Kate could just discern the remnants of the image of some kind of bird painted upon it. Following Isabella inside, she found herself in a large single room with a fire that was all but out, wooden stairs that led into the gloom above and a door at the back, which she guessed must lead to kitchens and a yard beyond. A small window looked out onto the street but scant light filtered in and Kate wondered if the sun had ever once touched the walls. The place reeked of damp and automatically she shuddered.

The noise of their arrival drew a manservant from the rear of the house. He was middle-aged and unshaven, and though Kate's first impression was of sullen ill humour, his face lit up with obvious pleasure at the return of his mistress. The broad smile transformed him, and she gave an instinctive smile in return.

'This is Nathan,' Isabella said. 'He has served me long and well, and you may trust him. Nathan, this is Miss Winter – she will be staying with us a while.'

Kate nodded a greeting then moved to the hearth and reached out her hands to its meagre warmth. Isabella slid her gaze around the room, as though seeing it through a newcomer's eyes – the damp patches on the wall, the murky light, the taint of mould. But the furnishings were ample – Turkey rugs and cushions, a couch, a table and stools, a sideboard. A single vast wall hanging depicted the serpent in the Garden of Eden. The colours had faded to muted shades and the lower edge of it was spotted with mould. It was a shame, Kate thought. It must have been beautiful once.

'We live modestly here,' Isabella said. ''Tis safer than in more open comfort. The poor wretches you saw in the street are too busy fending off starvation and disease to care about our loyalties. We give them a little bread now and then and they leave us alone.

These days are dangerous for those who have openly supported the King.'

Kate nodded. She had given little thought to the politics of the civil war that had riven England's peace these last years, and though she had served the English Prince in his exile in Holland she had barely spared a moment to consider his plight, such matters beyond her concern. But now it seemed the war had drawn her into its sphere after all – she was in the house of a Royalist in a city she knew to belong to Parliament. No wonder Isabella chose to live in quiet secrecy amongst the poor and forgotten.

Then Kate remembered the fortune teller's choice of words.

We, she had said, *we* live modestly ...

A pull of misgiving turned in her gut. Who was *we*? Silently, she scolded herself for her foolishness, for failing to ask more questions. She had not thought to consider Isabella might have a family, a husband. What would they think of her – a penniless seamstress from The Hague who had left her home and family on a whim? To cover the sudden flush of shame, she crouched to the fire and took up the poker, rearranging the logs so that the fire began to burn more brightly. When she could trust herself to speak again, she stood up and turned to face the room once more.

'It's not what you were expecting, I think.' Isabella smiled and raised an eyebrow in question. 'It was once an alehouse, known as the Wounded Raven.'

Kate could not help but return the smile, though her innards still seethed.

'I can't rightly say what I expected,' she managed to say, 'but no, this was not it.' Then, because she could not help herself, she said, 'Do you live alone? I mean to say ... are you your own mistress?'

Isabella touched her fingers to Kate's hand. They were cold but gentle, and there was a softness in her eyes Kate had seen only rarely before.

'I am,' she murmured.

Kate nodded, heart lightening. Even though she barely understood her feelings, she had no wish to share Isabella's attention nor the warm glow of her regard. She recalled the closeness of their bodies in the narrow cot on the ship, the unexpected pleasure of the other woman's touch, and allowed herself an inward smile. Flicking another glance around the room, her eyes lit upon the servant. He was still standing at the foot of the stairs, waiting for Kate knew not what. Isabella followed Kate's gaze with her own.

'Fetch us more wood, Nathan,' she said. 'The fire is almost out.'

With a curt nod, he was gone.

Isabella's fingers tightened in Kate's. 'He is a good man,' she said, 'but he is very protective of me and you have yet to earn his trust.'

Then she turned away and threw the last remaining log on the fire.

Kate's bed was in a chamber that was colder, darker and dirtier than any place Kate had ever been. She hardly dared to hold the candle aloft, afraid of what the light might reveal lurking in the shadows, and she lay down fully clothed, still shivering under quilts that were putrid with damp. But she let the candle burn – even the bobbing shadows were better than the total dark.

Lying on her back, she stared up into the black above her and wondered what manner of chamber Isabella occupied now along the passage. Was she also sleeping under dank and filthy blankets in a fireless room? It seemed unlikely. Surely there were less unwelcoming beds to be found elsewhere in the house – for why had Kate been condemned to such a berth? A reminder of her place in the household? Moneyless, dependent, a stranger.

For the first time, she allowed herself to ponder the reasons why Isabella might truly have brought her to London, letting her thoughts play across the memory of the days at sea. They had talked and laughed and played cards together in the close warmth of the candlelit cabin, Isabella as close as the sister she had never had. She had let down her guard, and started to trust, lulled by the seeming friendship. Had it all been a pretence? Had Kate's company merely been a distraction from the tedium of shipboard life?

Now, in the reality of this foetid bed, the questions she had refused to consider till now forced themselves into her thoughts. For what purpose was she here? It was not mere generosity, she realised: there would surely be a price to pay for the adventure, and the sudden understanding of it sent a tremor of fear through her blood.

For the first time since leaving The Hague, doubt began to spread its poison.

She should have listened to her mother.

She should have heeded the warning bells in her head.

In the cold room, she shivered. She had acted in haste with her usual recklessness – her mother had always said it would be her undoing. Mary would have told her all given time. But now she was alone in a strange land and subject to Isabella's whims. What had she hoped to discover? All the excitement and desire that had set her on this journey and buoyed her spirits on the voyage seemed to fade into the shadows that hovered in the corners of the room: she wished she had never left the warm comfort of her bed in The Hague where all was known, all was safe. Self-recrimination sidled through her – she had been a fool, and now she was trapped here penniless and alone, and no way to get home.

She had finally begun to drift off into a restless doze when the low creak of the turning door handle startled her awake. She sat up with a gasp, holding the covers in front of her like a shield. The candle was almost out, a guttering stub, and the shadows lurched and danced against the walls like drunken men. The door swung back and she shrank away, fearful. But the figure who emerged from the dark of the passage outside resolved into Isabella, and

Kate let her breath go with relief. She could not have said who or what she had expected to see but her nerves were ragged, stirring her fears.

'Isabella,' she breathed.

The fortune teller latched the door silently behind her and stepped across the room to sit on the edge of the bed. She took Kate's hands in her own. The fingers were hard and cold, and Kate struggled to remember their former gentleness.

'Did you think I had abandoned you?'

'A little,' Kate whispered. Only now did she admit the fear fully to herself. But even through her relief she had lifted her guard again, distrustful, remembering there would be a price to pay. She must be wary, she reminded herself, and tread with care.

'We must be discreet,' Isabella whispered, 'in front of Nathan. He loves me well but he is easily jealous.'

Kate was silent. She had yet to determine Nathan's character for herself, for a servant may conceal many traits before his mistress. But still, it seemed strange to Kate that Isabella should give so much care to the opinion of a hireling.

'Come,' Isabella said. 'My chamber offers more comfort than this. We shall sleep as sisters, as we did on board the ship.' She smiled, and as the candle spluttered its dying flare, Kate saw the shadows cross the other woman's face, darkness in the hollows. 'Quietly!'

They crept from Kate's door along the passage and into a large room at the front of the house. A good fire blazed in the hearth, and many candles burned so that the room was warm and cheerful, the damp and shadows held at bay. Colourful quilts and cushions adorned the bed, and heavy curtains shut out the bitter night and the hardship that lay beyond the windows. In the sudden warmth, Kate shivered, and went to the fire for a moment, reaching her hands to its light, watching the flames leap and dance. Then she turned and took her place under the covers in the inviting softness of the bed.

They lay together as they had in the narrow cot on the *Fortune*, with Isabella's legs pressed against her own, breasts against her back, but she no longer felt the familiar quiver of pleasure the older woman's touch had aroused: a runnel of distrust now belied the gentleness. Despite her drowsiness and the warmth and softness of the bed, the fear still lingered at the edges of her thoughts, shadows that darkened her ease.

Behind her Isabella turned away, fidgeting and restless, as though there was something she wished to say but was uncertain how to begin. Kate rolled onto her back so that they lay side by side, arms just touching.

'What's wrong?' she whispered, with a sidelong glance. 'You're not usually so restless.'

There was a pause. Then Isabella turned her head towards Kate on the pillow, observing her with a look that Kate could not quite recognise. A flicker of fear caught at her once again, and she had to brace against the light in Isabella's eyes.

'Do you dream, Kate?' the older woman asked.

Kate gave a small shrug, surprised by the question and Isabella's hesitation in asking it. Drowsiness forgotten, her mind sharpened, wary again as she sensed the possibility of danger.

'Sometimes. Doesn't everyone?' Instinctively, she made no mention of the nightmares that had once wracked her childhood nights. 'Why do you ask?'

Isabella smiled and turned to stare once more at the ceiling, profile flickering in the golden light. By way of answer she said, 'What do you dream of?'

'I rarely remember.'

'Pity,' Isabella replied, and turned her head on the pillow to observe Kate once again.

Kate was silent. In the pause, her thoughts wandered back unbidden across the years to find the half-forgotten dreams that used to send her night after night to the safety of her parents' bed. She had barely thought of them in years, but the face of the old man who had stalked her was vivid again before her now – intense grey eyes and a leer about his mouth. She shuddered at the memory, and other images she thought she had forgotten began to play at the edges of her mind.

A hanged man, a graveyard, a yew tree, a dog.

She swallowed, confused, and aware of Isabella's eyes intent on her face.

'Are you remembering now?'

In her confusion she was almost tempted to confess all she saw. But some inner core of mistrust stopped the words in her mouth. She shook her head, and Isabella's face grew hard.

'Do not lie to me,' Isabella said. 'I promised to show you your past but if you hide what you know I cannot help you.'

'There's nothing to tell,' Kate insisted. 'Merely blurred images from childish dreams, nothing I can put words to.'

Even as she lied, she wondered why she did so. She had left all she had known behind her and given her life into this woman's keeping in search of knowledge – it seemed absurd to hide the memory of childhood dreams. And yet, some warning force inside her kept her silent: knowledge is power, her father once told her, and she had never forgotten it.

Isabella observed her for two more breaths then rolled out of the bed with a sigh that betrayed her irritation. Drawing her robe around her, she crossed the silent rug to the hearth and crouched to poke at the fire, although it was already drawing well: the flames crackled merrily, heedless of the small drama playing out in its light.

'Go back to your room,' she said, without turning. 'We will talk again.'

Kate hesitated, aware she was being punished. Isabella's bed was warm and soft, and her own was hard and ripe with damp. She wanted to stay.

Isabella stood up and turned from the hearth. 'Go,' she said.

Kate slid from the bed with reluctance and picked up her clothes. With the thought of the cold beyond the door she remembered again her own neat chamber in the attic at home, clean and bright and safe. It beckoned brightly across the sea. Then, clutching her dress before her, she slipped from the room, padded silently along the passage and into the unwelcoming dark of her chamber.

7

MY TROUBLOUS DREAMS THIS NIGHT
DOTH MAKE ME SAD

In the morning Kate emerged from a tangled web of dreams that her mind groped to recover. But the images slid away even as she chased them down, until all that was left to recall was the hanged man from the dreams of her childhood, and a graveyard. She sat up, holding the covers close against the chill. The room was dim in the morning light; the narrow window looked out towards the backs of other houses built close by and they blotted out the sun.

Looking around her chamber, there was no trace now of the shadows that had so frightened her. It was just a damp and tatty room with old furnishings that were chipped and worn, and a much-faded quilt on the bed she could see in the light was badly frayed at the edges. A basin of water and a jug had been set on the dresser and she refused to let herself wonder who had put them there, and when.

With a sigh of reluctance she clambered out of the bed, found the chamber pot beneath it, then dressed hurriedly, skin bubbling as the cold air touched it. Her bodice and skirts were sticky with damp and she wished she had taken the time to bring others: although Isabella had promised her a change of clothes she had yet to make good on her word. The splash of icy water against her face refreshed her a little. Then, squaring her shoulders and taking a deep breath to prepare herself for whatever the day may hold, she opened the door and went downstairs.

The place was empty, and she neither saw nor heard another soul as she wandered through to the kitchen. The house was eerily quiet, as though it were cloaked against the noise of the city she knew was humming just outside its walls, and the silence sent a quiver up her spine.

In the main chamber, someone had left bread and cheese and a jug of small beer on the sideboard, and she ate it standing up, examining the room as she did so. In the dull morning light she could see that the furnishings were no longer so fine as they once had been, chips in the dark wood of the sideboard and the chairs, cushions and rugs wearing thin. It seemed the war had not been kind to Isabella. A Royalist, paying the price for choosing the losing side, she supposed, and wondered if the Prince of Wales, living in comfort at the Binnenhof Palace, understood the sacrifices made on his behalf. Then she wondered which way she would have fallen herself if she had needed to make the choice. It was easy to support the King from the safety of The Hague, harder amidst the harsh realities of war.

With a grimace at the bitterness of the ale, she drained it down regardless. Briefly, she wondered where Isabella might have gone and when she would return, but the thought slid away almost as soon it arose. Without Isabella watching over her she was free for a while, and the knowledge of that freedom blossomed in her chest as excitement. She was alone for the first time since she had left the palace at Isabella's heels, and with a quick glance once more upstairs to be sure, she gave herself a smile. Then, fetching her cloak from where she had left it hanging, she swung it across her shoulders, fastened it tightly at the neck, and stepped out through the front door, locking it behind her with the key that had been left on the sideboard.

The street outside assailed her senses. It was alive with racket – the knocking of hammers, shouting, wheels on mud, the grind of some kind of machinery she could not see. A dog was barking with regular insistence, and somewhere close by a small child began to wail. The stench almost brought her to her knees and she was half tempted to turn back inside to the peace behind her. But she had not travelled so far to sit inside and wait for permission like an obedient child, and so she forced herself forward, treading carefully through the rutted mud, lifting her skirts clear of the filth that littered the street. No one paid her any mind as she picked her way over the channels of dirt, too busy with their own concerns. An old woman sat on a stool before a smouldering brazier, and her gaze never strayed from the flames, as though she might find the answers to the mysteries of the universe if she could only stare for long enough. Kate couldn't tell what it was she was burning, only that it gave off an acrid smell.

In the clear morning light, she could see more clearly the true poverty of the neighbourhood. Crumbling tenements that were black with mould and grime, windowless; beggars in swathes of rags and barefoot, men with missing limbs, children glassy-eyed with hunger. She had never seen such desperation before, and the sight of it appalled her. Was it the war that had brought so many so low? This was her world now too, and the fear that she could end her days in such want and desperation began to threaten the curiosity that had led her here. With a shudder, she quickened her pace, seeking escape. Her past seemed unimportant now, her witchblood an irrelevance.

Winding through the maze of lanes, she remained wary. Blank eyes watched her pass, hands held out in automatic desperation. Ragged children tugged at her skirts but she shooed them away, wishing she had coins to give. The streets all seemed the same – filthy, rank, dark, and just when she had begun to believe that all of London was rotten, she spilled out of the maze at last and onto a wide main thoroughfare that was lined with inns and shops and well-to-do houses. A press of horses and carts and weary-looking travellers were headed towards the river, and she realised she had stumbled onto the street that led to the great bridge across the

Thames and the city of London itself. She watched, considering if she should fall in with them, but when a rough-looking man with bad teeth and a pockmarked face leered towards her she twisted away in sudden fear and headed south, in the opposite direction.

She kept walking, hoping he had not turned from his path to follow, and only when she was sure he was not behind her did she slow her steps and start to take in all that was around her – the row of inns, the shops, and more people than she had ever seen in one place in her life. She stayed wary, unused to such crowds, and mistrustful.

Seeking a quieter road, she turned off the main street on a whim into a lane that ran alongside one of the inns. It was narrow and overshadowed by the buildings either side of it, and as soon as the High Street behind her faded into silence, a trickle of foreboding crept over her skin, prickling. She had been safer with the crowds, she realised, and instinctively she flicked a glance behind her. There was no one she could see but the feeling that someone was following was hard to shake off and so she quickened her footsteps, careful not to slip on the icy ground.

The way narrowed still further, high walls on either side until it was only just wide enough for her to pass through; a bigger man would need to turn his shoulders. But the light at the end of it beckoned and by the time the lane tipped her out into the street, she was almost running. Stopping abruptly, she squinted in the sudden bright light, a low sun warming the road. When her eyes had adjusted to the change, she looked about her.

She was standing in a broad street that ran north to south. Buildings of all kinds lined both sides – traders mostly, their shop fronts open to the day. It was a more prosperous neighbourhood than the one she had come from, and the hammer and clatter of tools and voices drifted across the morning. Half-timbered houses nestled between the workshops, and across from where she stood, a young servant girl was kneeling to scrub a stone step. Kate observed her as the girl paused and sat back on her heels to wipe her forehead with a soapy hand. The two women locked eyes for a heartbeat until Kate slid hers away, embarrassed to have been caught watching. Hurriedly, she turned north and began walking again.

She had not gone far when she found herself outside a graveyard. Her footsteps slowed of their own accord and her breathing quickened – she had never much liked graveyards, fear of them fuelled by her nightmares and a visceral dread of what they may hold. Her thoughts flitted to the memory of her father's grave in The Hague where the headstone was still bright and new and the grass had not yet grown across the mound. A wash of grief crashed like a wave in her guts so that she had to rest a hand on the gate of the graveyard to steady herself against the desire to howl out loud with sorrow.

Not here, she scolded herself. Not now.

Forcing herself to dry-eyed attention, she ran her gaze across the unkempt collection of graves before her. The place was familiar to her somehow, as if awaking a half-forgotten memory, and she hesitated, frowning as she ransacked her memories to track down the recollection. Then the shadow of her dreams fell across her thoughts, and she remembered. Here, she knew without a flicker of doubt, she would find the grave of her nightmares. Here was buried the hanged young man. Trepidation rippled through her blood, and her fingers tightened on the rotting wood of the gate, knuckles white. What force had brought her here? She wanted to run, and the rush of longing for the safety of home that billowed through her almost took her breath away.

For long moments she waited as the urge to flee warred with her curiosity. Her innards churned and her throat was dry. How could this place be before her now in reality, when she had seen it so many times in her dreams? Some strange magic she did not understand. Casting another glance behind her to reassure herself she was alone, it was still hard to brush off the suspicion she was being watched. Then, obeying an instinct she would have preferred to ignore, she slid through the gap between fence and gate and into the yard within.

Inside, she saw at once that it was a resting place for the bodies of the poor and unloved, the sinners and thieves. The graves were unkempt and overgrown, and few bore any marker to say who lay beneath. But as she wound her way between them away from the road, a sense of tranquillity descended, a sense of lives lived, and souls at rest with no more hardships to face in this world. The rapid patter of her heartbeat began to slow as she wandered amongst them, sidestepping the thistles and clumps of nettles that caught at the hem of her skirts.

The morning was bright and cold with a watery sun that rested low above the rooftops, and she let her feet guide her as they chose along the ill-kept tracks while her gaze searched across the scattered graves for the path she used to follow in her dreams. Then a bank of cloud rolled in front of the sun, and a sudden chill crept once more across her skin, a sense of foreboding deep in her bones. Had she been followed after all? She scanned the graves around her, peering through the gaps, but there were few places where a man might hide and she could see nothing but the mounds of earth and weeds, the brambles and bushes against the wall. She was about to persuade herself she was imagining things when a movement caught at the edge of her eye, something shifting near the furthest wall where the thicket was most overgrown. She turned towards it, holding her breath. Saw it again – a dark shape, indistinct. It was too small for a man, and she froze, aware once more of the rapid patter of her heartbeat and the dryness of her mouth. The chill of the morning was quite forgotten in her fear, until finally the shadow emerged from amongst the weeds.

It was a dog.

She almost laughed with relief until she realised it was the exact same dog that used to appear in her dreams: black and powerful, with sombre yellow eyes that were regarding her now. The laugh died in her throat, but it was not exactly fear that replaced it – she sensed the animal meant her no harm. Combing her memory, she recalled the dog in her dream had shown her the way, taking her where she needed to go. Was it here to guide her now?

She took a step towards it. Then another. The dog lay down and rested its great head on its paws, tail thumping gently on the grass. Kate picked her way through the weeds until she was close enough to touch. Squatting down, she held out her hand and the dog lifted its nose and sniffed at her fingers before it turned its head away with a deliberate movement. Kate followed the animal's gaze towards a yew tree against the wall that stood close by and saw a small headstone there, just visible amidst the weeds.

She stepped towards it, holding her skirts free of the nettles and grass with one hand, and when she reached it she saw the block of granite marked an overgrown grave. Surprised by the presence of a headstone, she crouched to brush the dirt away with her fingers, grit catching in her fingernails, cold and damp. When at last she could read the name that was engraved there, her heart seemed to stop in her chest.

Tom Wynter, she read. *Died 1607.*

Her grandfather. The man who had hanged as a witch.

She ran the tip of her tongue across her lips – they were cold and growing numb in the chill of the morning.

Was Tom Wynter the hanged man who had haunted her dreams? Had he led her here? He must have, she decided. How else could she have discovered him? In all of London's maze of streets and lanes, how else would she have found her way to this very spot? The thought of it made her smile – the connection reaching through the generations. Perhaps she would find her answers after all. And without Isabella's help.

Lifting her head, Kate noticed a matching headstone beyond Tom Wynter's – the same dark granite, overgrown with weeds. She moved towards it and pulled at the tall grass until she had cleared it enough to make out the name. Her fingers ached at the toughness of the stems.

Sarah Chyrche. Died 1632.

The grave of his cousin? The girl he had died to protect? Perhaps. Kneeling between the two graves, Kate wondered what she should do with this new knowledge. She was grateful for it, amazed that she had found so much so soon, but uncertainty gripped her now. Briefly, she closed her eyes and let her mind's eye linger on the visions of her dream. Slowly, the hanged man's face sharpened into focus, and for the first time she saw the likeness to her father. The pale eyes, the high cheekbones, the wave of hair. But the eyes before her now spoke of knowledge from beyond the grave, unknown depths she could not hold. She shivered, acutely aware of his presence, as if he were there in flesh and blood, and abruptly, she opened her eyes.

'Tom Wynter?' The name left her lips as a whisper, unbidden, and a part of her felt absurd, talking to an image from a dream. 'Grandfather?'

Instinctively, she reached out, and as soon as her fingertips brushed the soil of the grave, a wash of feelings roiled through her in a riot of emotion that almost felled her; she had to brace against it to stop herself from tipping.

Connection, grief, passion, belonging, regret.

All of these things swirled like a storm in her blood but it was the connection she felt most of all, her soul bound to the power she had touched. Her vision began to darken, and as her body seemed to fall, weightless, her hand jerked of its own accord away from the grave.

Tom Wynter, reaching out to her from the realms of the dead?

She was aware of the sound of her breathing in the silence of the graveyard, ragged and shallow. Glancing towards the road, she saw a couple of young women in gaudy gowns talking together close by the wall. One of them was telling the other a story, her hands drawing pictures in the air as she spoke. Most likely, they hadn't even seen her. Kate turned her attention back to the grave. Did she dare to touch it a second time? Twice, she reached out her hand again and withdrew it at the very last moment, afraid of the force that awaited. Then, with a sense of trepidation, she lowered her palm once more to the grass and dirt that covered Tom Wynter's body and braced as the same feelings flooded through her. But this time she was ready, and she welcomed them in so that they did not overwhelm her as they had before.

'What is it you would tell me, Tom Wynter?' she murmured, and though she received no answer, the sense of connection pulsed sweetly like a letter from a faraway, long-missed home. Sitting back, she let her hand slide away from the earth atop the grave and breathed deeply, gazing around her to bring herself back to this morning, this place, anchored in her waking world.

Was she losing her mind? It was impossible that these half-recalled images from long-ago dreams should be here before her in reality now. But the connection still hummed in her veins, a new and precious knowledge that ran deeper inside her than thought. Was this the promised key to her future?

Turning from her contemplation of Tom Wynter's grave, she scanned the graveyard behind her once more. The women in the gaudy dresses had gone. But there was danger in her shadow now, she was sure of it, and she needed to be wary. She began to shiver, the morning chill creeping inside her cloak, and her feet were numb with the cold as she stumbled to get up. But still, she wished she could have stayed longer at his graveside, even though she could find no words to explain all she felt, all she wanted to say.

'I will come again,' she whispered at last.

Then, turning, she wandered slowly from the graveyard and into the street beyond its gate.

8

ONE FOOT IN SEA AND ONE ON SHORE,
TO ONE THING CONSTANT NEVER

Mary was early to the wharf. The day was bitter cold, and a freezing mist curled around the masts so that the ships loomed ghostlike from the fog, and the calls of the men as they worked sounded far off and disembodied. She shivered, moving gently from foot to foot, toes growing numb. Restless, she let her eyes wander along the quay. Torches made little headway through the mist, and here and there she glimpsed the bright spark of a brazier. But the dock was alive with activity – men, boxes, ropes, sails, livestock, all shifting in a complex dance as the ships were made ready for the turning tide. The *Falcon* strained gently at her moorings, her masts lost in the clouds that shrouded her. Men went ceaselessly to and fro, engaged in crucial but unknown tasks, and a sliver of excitement kindled inside her. She was going home, and though she had learned across the years to live with the ache of missing it she was glad, in spite of her fears for her daughter. She only hoped it was the right decision, and that her dream and her call to Hecate weren't leading her astray. Shaking her head against the doubts, she peered again along the quay into the shifting mist, searching for the figure of Rafe Tyndall amongst the shadowy forms that peopled the dock.

Each minute seemed to take an age before she heard the

church bells on the breeze, tolling the hour. He was late. Then, finally, just as she was beginning to despair, a tall figure emerged and her heart gave a little skip in the moment before she remembered that it was not Toby she awaited but another man, whose intentions she did not trust. But when Rafe stood before her at last she was glad enough to see him – she had no other plan to fall back on if he had failed to come.

'Mistress Johnson.' He bowed in greeting, and she dropped into a curtsey in reply.

'Master Tyndall.'

'Shall we board?'

She nodded and he bent to sweep her bag from the cobbles at her feet, swinging it easily over a shoulder. Then he offered her his other arm and she took it, the cobbles slippery, the gangplank unsteady. But she felt ill at ease, as if she were being unfaithful – for all the men she had bedded in her life she had only ever walked arm-in-arm with Toby.

Two sailors nodded a greeting and stepped aside to let them pass. Mary's boots slipped on the steep incline of the gangway and she found she was glad of Rafe's arm after all. From the deck she followed him down the steps to the tiny cabin he told her they would share.

Observing the single narrow cot she understood – it was as she'd expected it would be, and inwardly she sighed – she had thought those days were over. A lurch of guilt lifted inside her. Her husband only six months in the ground and here she was again, using her body for trade. But, she reasoned to herself, it was only one man and really, what other choice did she have?

She waited as he stowed her bag beneath the bed, tucking it safely away so it wouldn't shift with the toss and roll of the ship. She was aware that this was no simple transaction, and she was unsure of the rules he expected to play by. In her old life, she had been a good judge of men, but this one she could not quite read.

It was warm in the cabin and a lantern swung gently from a hook, throwing shadows that shifted across the floor. She remembered the last time, the only other time, she had boarded a ship. She had been fleeing England with Toby, and Kate had still been an unknown possibility inside her. So long ago, her daughter a grown woman now – the thought of it made her feel old.

Dropping her gloves onto the table she gave Rafe a smile. He was observing her and there was a light in his look she knew well, a hunger alight in his eyes. She met the look with a tilt of her chin but, even so, she was flattered that he wanted her – perhaps she was not so old after all. He smiled and inclined his head in silent question, and she thought again that he was really quite beautiful – something otherworldly about him, a charisma that was hard to resist.

He held out his hand towards her as if inviting her to dance and when she took it, his fingers were strong and cold against hers. They stood for a moment, an arm's length apart. Then he said, 'It is a small cabin but the bed is yours alone, if that's what you wish. I can sleep in the chair.'

She was surprised into silence by her misjudgement of him. He was more of a gentleman than she had given him credit for, and she gave herself a wry smile. She had learned to judge men at the bawdy house – perhaps not all men could be read so easily.

'However …' His fingers tightened on hers and drew her nearer to him, letting the sentence hang.

She said nothing, struggling with her feelings. The ship gave a sudden shudder against the quay, and Mary almost stumbled, held steady only by the strength of Rafe's fingers. She wanted him, she realised. Beyond the need to pay her way, desire for him flared through her. Since Toby's death she had thought she would never feel such things again, and a sense of herself as an unfaithful wife rippled through her.

'I am a widow,' she said.

A flicker passed across his eyes that was hard to read in the candlelight, but it was gone in a moment – he hid his feelings well.

'I understand. But perhaps it's time to love again.' He drew her in close to him, so that her breasts brushed against his shirt, and she was aware of his warmth, the strength of the muscles beneath the clothes. For three long breaths, she hesitated, until he tipped her chin upwards with a curled finger and placed his mouth on hers.

With the kiss, all her reservations slid away, her body giving in to the pleasure of his touch. His mouth was warm and gentle, and the taste of him was sweet. She raised her hands to unfasten the cloak at her neck, and his hands met hers to help so that they fumbled together for a moment, tangling, making them laugh.

Dropping her hands away from the clasp, she let him peel the cloak away, shivering as the cool air touched her skin. He lowered his lips to brush the side of her neck and she tilted her head away, trying not to recall the caress of Toby's mouth against her body, Toby's hands on her shoulders, trying not to compare, still unwilling to admit she desired this man who was not Toby. But the feeling persisted, insistent despite her protests. Toby was dead, she reminded herself, his cold body dragged from the sea more than six months since. She was a widow now and she must manage somehow. How else was she to find her daughter and make a new life for herself?

Rafe began to untie the laces of her bodice, fingers deft and practised, searching inside to find her breasts. Letting go of the memory of her husband's touch, she surrendered to the pleasure of the other man's embrace, liking the warmth of his body as it pressed against her, the brush of his fingertips across her nipple. Her breath caught and quickened: she had forgotten the excitement of a new man, the anticipation of unknown pleasures yet to come. But in spite of the pleasure, it still felt like a betrayal.

A sudden knock at the door startled them from their caresses and they stepped quickly apart, still breathing hard. Mary's heart hammered in her chest as she turned her body away from the door and began hurriedly to retie her bodice. Rafe swept a palm across his hair, took a deep breath, and in two strides he was at the door, drawing it open just wide enough to put his face to the crack.

'Yes?'

'The captain wants a word, sir.' A boy's voice, soft and barely audible. 'As soon as you can.'

'Tell him I'll be right there.'

'Yes, sir.'

Rafe closed the door and turned back into the cabin with a smile. They locked eyes, and though she could still see the handsomeness in the fine, dark features and the strong muscles of his body, the desire she had felt for him just a moment before had already ebbed away. Silently, she said a prayer of thanks to the cabin boy for interrupting them. In spite of the temptation and the brief bright flare of desire, she knew she was not yet ready to love again, whatever Rafe had said.

She returned his smile.

'Duty calls.' He tilted his head towards the door, and Mary watched him run his hand across his hair once more before he turned the handle and disappeared out into the passage. For a moment, she stood and regarded the door, unsure what to think. Would he expect to resume their caresses on his return? Perhaps. But she knew now that he was not a man to force her against her will, and she allowed herself a small sigh of relief. She would remain faithful to Toby after all – a respectable widow, her honour intact.

With nothing else to do, she lifted herself up onto the narrow bed, lay back into the surprising softness of the pillows, and let the gentle rock of the ship lull her into a restless doze.

She woke abruptly when the latch of the door clicked open and shut again and she heard Rafe's boots on the boards. Disorientated, she sat up abruptly and swung her legs over the edge of the bed. How long had she slept?

Rafe crossed the small cabin and slid into the chair at the table, then turned to face her.

'Was everything all right?' she asked, to cover her confusion. 'With the captain?'

'Aye. A matter of business, merely.' He made a small gesture to the cot with his head. 'Did you sleep?'

'A little,' she replied. 'It's like being rocked in a cradle.'

He gave a small laugh. 'I always sleep well aboard ship,' he said. 'I think I missed my calling as a sailor.'

She smiled and the silence between them stretched, but it was not uncomfortable. He seemed in no hurry to resume where they had left off when the cabin boy knocked, and she felt no trace of the tension that had sparked between them before. Perhaps he had sensed her change of heart; she hoped so.

'So,' he said, after a while. 'What business takes you to England in such a hurry?'

'A personal matter,' she replied with a nonchalant shrug. Her feet swung loosely above the floor like a child's. However much she liked this man, instinct kept her silent: it was in her nature not to trust.

'Am I not to know?' He made a show of being offended, a half-smile at the corners of his mouth.

Mary shook her head.

'Even after aiding you as I have, in your moment of need?'

'Even then,' she replied, with a laugh.

He held her eyes for a moment more then swung away from her towards the table. Within moments he seemed already absorbed in a book and some papers he had taken from his bag, her presence apparently forgotten. Mary shuffled back on the bed and, with nothing else to do, she observed him again with a dispassionate eye. There was something a little untamed about him, she decided, the vital spirit of his youth still undimmed. He should have been at play in the brothels and gambling dens of Bankside, she thought, instead of running secret errands for an exiled prince. But then, perhaps such work fed a sense of adventure, a desire to be at the heart of great affairs. Some men thrived on danger, she knew, though she would never understand it. She had lived through enough dangers in her life to be grateful for the peace that safety offered.

She shuffled back onto the bed and lay down again, gazing up at the wooden slats of the ceiling above her head. She had no intention of sleeping again, but when the ship began to draw away from the quay, her thoughts were lulled by the movement and as she drifted away, her last waking thoughts were of Kate, and the search that lay ahead.

Rafe settled himself at the table and took out his books and papers. He was aware of the woman lying sleepy in his bed and the memory of her warmth and the taste of her lit a pleasant heat in his guts. He had been surprised by her willingness – as a respectable widow, he had thought she would guard her honour with more care. Ah, who was he to judge? Both of them alone on a journey – what harm if they sought pleasure together? But he had sensed the change in her on his return from the captain's cabin, as though she was having second thoughts. The coyness had faded from her smile, and there was no more invitation in her eyes. Perhaps the memory of her husband had caught at her conscience after all, and they would share no more caresses. It was a shame, but he couldn't blame her for that.

He leafed through the book on the table before him but his attention failed to stick: he was too conscious of Mary's presence, her soft warmth, the creamy skin. He turned to observe her. Her face was peaceful in repose, the lines of wariness that creased around her eyes in her waking hours smoothing out in sleep. Her hands rested lightly on the pillow before her face, and it was only when he had been watching her a while that he noticed she had six full fingers on one hand. He started, surprised he hadn't realised before – it was rare such things escaped his notice. A common man might believe she belonged to the Devil, and a brief image flickered through his mind of Mary sporting naked with her master. He gave himself a wry smile. If there was a hell, he would surely meet her there.

Perhaps she sensed his gaze on her face because after a moment her eyelids flickered open, and the wariness returned abruptly to her face. Rubbing a hand across her eyes, she sat up and swung her legs over the edge of the bed to face him again.

'How long was I asleep?'

'A few minutes only.'

She said nothing but looked about the cabin, and he noticed that she cradled her left hand in her right, as though to hide it. Despite her age, she was still a handsome woman. He guessed she was in her forties, but her body was still lean and strong, and her hair tumbled fair and thick about her shoulders, loosened from its fastening and mussed by sleep. As if reading his thoughts, she reached up to gather it in her hands, plaiting it deftly with practised ease. When she was finished, the braid hung neatly over one shoulder to lie against her breast.

'What are you reading?' she asked.

'This?' He flicked a casual hand towards his papers. 'Just an old book I came across in The Hague.'

She tilted her head with interest and reached out to take it so that she could examine it more closely. Out of no more than courtesy, he supposed, the habit of polite conversation, and after a moment's hesitation, he passed her the book. He watched as she ran her eyes across the pages, flicking lightly through them, pausing here and there to let her attention linger on some passage or picture that interested her.

Then she handed it back to him, and her face was as still as a mask.

'You're an ... astrologer?' she asked. Her tone was light, but he heard a note of trepidation in the words, and he was surprised she had understood so much. The text was in Latin and Greek, and the symbols were arcane and hard to read, even for him. He had been studying it a while.

'You can read it?'

'I recognise some of the pictures.' She lifted one shoulder in a shrug.

'How so?' His heartbeat quickened with interest.

'My husband knew something of the art,' she offered. 'He had a book with pictures such as those.' She gave a careless gesture of her head towards it as though it was of no significance to her, and Rafe realised he must tread carefully – she was already on her guard.

'Do you happen to remember its title?' he asked, keeping the tone conversational, mildly curious, despite the rapid patter of his heartbeat in his chest. For although the book did indeed contain some mention of astrology, the pictures she had recognised were of sigils and symbols of alchemy. The volume in his hands was a grimoire, a collection of magical texts he had bought in secret from a man who had smuggled it overland from the East, and it had cost him almost everything he owned to obtain. Its possession would brand him a heretic if the wrong people came to know of it, and its mere existence could cost him his life. It was a rare text, and few men ever owned them. Who had her husband been, to possess such a thing?

'I don't recall the title.' She shrugged again. 'It was just some old book. About the stars.' She gave him a rueful smile as if to say such things were beyond her understanding. But he knew it was a lie, and he studied her for a long moment, wondering how best to answer. She had surprised him more than once, and he was on the back foot now, struggling to appraise her anew.

'He told you nothing more of it?'

'No. He was interested in the art of astrology for a while, and so he studied sometimes in the evenings after his days at work.' She met his gaze with open innocence and he had to quell his surprise. It was not an object of casual study, after all, but a discipline of lifelong learning. Scholars and sorcerers both, dedicating whole lives to the art.

'What happened to it?' he asked. 'Do you recall?'

'I cannot rightly say,' she replied. ''Tis many years since I saw it last. Perhaps he sold it.'

'I hope he got a good price for it. Such books are very rare and often of great value,' he said. 'Do you know how he came by it?'

'I believe it was his father's,' she said.

He said nothing, and he was certain she knew far more than she was telling. He observed her for a moment and cast his mind back across the stories he had heard in all the years of his studies, sifting the fact from the fiction, the truth from the fairy tales. Could it be the fabled book of magic that men whispered of in taverns? Cursed and powerful, its whereabouts unknown these last twenty years or more? A book men would kill for. A book men had died to possess. It was possible. The rumours spoke of it last on Bankside; but Rafe had once heard that many years ago it had made its way to The Hague. He regarded Mary, who was watching him now with a small smile on her lips, her head tilted. He returned the smile, but he was sure that behind that innocent face there lay all manner of secrets, and he would need to be clever to discover them.

9

YOUR BAIT OF FALSEHOOD

Kate found her way back from the graveyard with little difficulty, an unerring sense of direction that had served her well her whole life. Illicit childhood expeditions, and more recent secret forays to taverns far from home – she had always known her way. Even now, caught within the web of the dark and stinking lanes of a strange city, she did not once mistake the road back to the nameless street where her new home stood, windows blank and dark, the brickwork black with dirt.

The front door was unlocked and when she stepped inside, the fire was bright and burning well. Isabella was standing before it, reaching her hands to its warmth. Uncertainty coiled through Kate's body at the sight of her as she recalled the other woman's anger and her banishment back to the cold and damp. She said nothing, waiting to know which facet of Isabella was before her now, and the not-knowing set her on edge, pulses quickening.

'I knew you would find your way back to us,' Isabella said with a smile, as though genuinely pleased to see her. They were friends again, apparently, and Kate wondered if her transgression had truly been forgiven or if the fortune teller's warmth was just another game she was playing. 'Did I not say so?' She turned and spoke to Nathan who was coming through the back door with an armful of firewood. He slid an uninterested glance over Kate and nodded, then went to the fireplace.

Nathan set down the timber and withdrew, disappearing out to the passage which led to the kitchen. Kate could smell the aroma of cooking. A stew, or soup perhaps, she hoped. The cold morning had made her hungry. She took off her gloves and slid her cloak from her shoulders before she crossed to the hearth to stand with Isabella before the heat of the fire.

'Where did you go?' Isabella asked lightly, as though nothing at all had passed between them in the night. She must tread warily, Kate reminded herself. However friendly Isabella chose to be, she must remember the streak of cruelty underneath.

'I found a graveyard,' she replied, dismissing it with a shrug. 'Not far from the High Street.'

Isabella observed her with interest, shrewd eyes alight. 'You found your way to the Cross Bones? How very interesting.'

'There was a dog.'

'Ah,' Isabella breathed. 'So I was right.' She slid her eyes back to the fire. 'And you followed it? The dog?'

'It was just there, at the graveyard,' she answered. 'It surprised me. I thought someone was watching me.' It was instinct to keep her new-found connection to herself. Though she had travelled all this way on Isabella's promise of knowledge, some nascent force inside her chose to keep Tom Wynter to herself. His influence, perhaps? A link being forged through the generations? Her blood had hummed with awareness of the past, and she could still sense his presence, hovering near.

Tom Wynter.

She sounded his name in her head and felt it resonate inside her. It took effort to keep the smile from her face.

Isabella sighed. 'I hope you'll tell me the truth, Kate. I cannot help you if you keep things from me. And remember, I will know if you lie. I've looked into your past and I can read you like a book.'

It sounded like a threat but Kate smiled her most compliant

smile and nodded. 'Of course,' she said. 'I came with you to learn. You have much to teach me and I am a most eager pupil.'

Isabella regarded her a moment longer, as if considering whether or not to believe her before she decided to smile in return.

'Good,' she said, 'then come with me.'

With a swing of her skirts she swept towards the stairs, her hem a whisper on the boards beyond the edge of the carpet. Kate followed, regretting the growing distance from the fire and the possibility of soup. It was cold on the steps and she wondered where they were going as they passed the row of closed doors along the upstairs passage, past her own room, past Isabella's, to another staircase that climbed into the dark. She grasped the rail and lifted her skirts free of her feet, following the swish of Isabella's gown just before her as her eyes struggled to adjust to the gloom. At the head of the stairs Isabella halted. Kate heard the grating of a key in a lock and when the door creaked open on hinges that needed to be oiled, a square of light spilled across the landing. Blinking in the sudden brightness, Kate stepped through the door behind Isabella and found herself in a spacious attic that stretched the whole length of the house. Generous windows at the front stood open to the sky, higher than the roofs across the road so that the watery light of the winter morning soaked the room.

In the centre of the attic was a large oak desk and all around the walls, rows of shelves were covered in books and jars and oddments and fragments of unknown things. Shells and feathers and painted boxes, carved wooden icons, pots, twigs and pine cones, curled-up papers, rocks and pebbles, pieces of coloured glass that flared in the sun. Paintings hung in the spaces in between the shelves – semi-clothed bodies in shocking poses. No wonder Isabella kept them behind a locked door. A heady scent filled the air, utterly different from the musty damp of the rest of house. Sage and frankincense. Cinnamon. Lemon. Herbs hung to dry in bunches from the roof beams, and close to the fireplace was a dark wooden settle spread with bright embroidered cushions. Inhaling deeply, she searched to name the taints of the other herbs and spices but the mix was overwhelming and she couldn't pick it apart any further. A narrow bed that had been recently slept in stood against the wall in one corner. But in spite of all its wonders and the brightness of the day that streamed in through the windows, an underlying sense of something awry made her suppress a shudder.

An image of the hanged man from her dreams flickered briefly in her thoughts.

Tom Wynter.

His blood in her veins.

'Welcome to my workshop,' Isabella said, with a grand gesture to all that surrounded her. 'Do you like it?'

'It's wonderful,' she replied, and meant it. In spite of her unease it was surely a place to explore, treasures to be found. She crossed the rug to examine one of the pictures. An Oriental couple in sexual congress. A second man behind the first, naked and engorged. Awaiting his turn with the woman? Or about to enter the man? She had never seen such images, never imagined that a man might paint such intimacies. Her belly contracted, her breath quickened.

'From the East,' Isabella said, airily. 'Where Christianity has yet to reach.'

'A heathen view of sin,' Kate murmured. She could not tear her eyes away.

There was another, beside it. Two women, one with a large-nosed mask tied to her waist, about to penetrate the other, their mouths open with desire. Isabella came to stand next to her.

'That's my favourite,' she said, and laid a hand on her shoulder. Kate flinched, on edge, and Isabella laughed.

Kate dredged up a smile, and the shadow that hung across the place seemed to lengthen.

'They are extraordinary,' she managed. 'I never knew such pictures existed.'

'They are very rare and very precious.' Isabella leaned in closer. 'They belonged to my father.' Then, more briskly, 'We should begin our work.' She turned away from the paintings and took a stool at the desk, gesturing that Kate should pull up another beside her as she cleared a space amongst the scattered papers and books that sprawled across the surface. Dust motes filled the air and Kate cleared her throat.

'Do you know anything at all of witchcraft, or of magic?' Isabella's tone took on a businesslike edge, different from her usual throaty murmur, and in her fingers she began to mould a piece of wax.

Yet another side to her, Kate thought, one more facet to observe.

'A little herblore, only,' she said.

'To heal?'

'And to harm. My mother taught we should know all the properties of a plant. Even a poison may heal when used rightly.'

'Your mother sounds like a wise woman.'

'She is,' Kate replied, and shrugged away the twist of guilt that sidled through her. Mary would be beside herself by now, searching and desperate for her missing daughter. She would be fearing the worst, Toby's death still fresh and raw. She should write to her, Kate thought again, and set her mind at ease.

'What is that you're making?' she asked, gesturing to the soft wax that Isabella was forming into a figure.

'This?' The older woman looked down at her hands, as though surprised Kate would ask. ''Tis a poppet.'

'Whose?' she risked. Her heartbeat quickened with the fear her curiosity would awaken Isabella's anger. And another fear that ran deeper, not yet acknowledged, that there might be a doll that bore her own image.

'A woman who owes me something.'

'May I see?'

Isabella picked up the figure and placed it into Kate's outstretched hand. It was still warm and soft against her palm and the limbs were not yet complete.

'What will you do with her when she's finished?'

'Call upon the spirits to make her pay, then bury her in some unclean place.'

Poor woman, Kate thought, and dared not ask what it was that she owed. She handed the doll back to Isabella, who continued to shape it between her fingers, deft and precise, even as she looked up to talk to Kate.

'Tell me more about your family,' she said. 'I'd like to know.'

Kate hesitated, as though to share the details of her parents was some kind of betrayal. Then she said, 'My parents settled in The Hague before I was born. My father was a tailor.' She paused, the words still hard to form, the memory still raw and painful. 'He died half a year since,' she managed to say, 'and they dragged his body from the harbour one morning. No one knows how it happened, no one saw a thing.' She had to force her thoughts away from the image the words brought to mind.

'Unfortunate,' Isabella said, but she offered no condolences. Perhaps she had not mourned her own father much. 'And your mother?'

Kate hesitated, conscious of how little she knew of her mother's past, a closed book. Poor beginnings, Kate had always supposed, that Mary was ashamed of or wanted to forget. Maybe she had been disowned, for the disfigurement of her hand. Kate recalled the childhood taunts against herself for her mother's six fingers. *Child of the Devil*, they had called her, *Satan's spawn*. And when she was older the boys had asked if they could come and watch one night, while her mother coupled with the Devil.

She said, 'My mother never spoke of her family. I know nothing of them.'

'And you weren't curious enough to ask?'

She shrugged. Her parents' history had never seemed important before. Till her father's death, her thoughts had always looked forward, searching for something better, hoping for escape. But now she understood the past contained the future, and she had been a fool not to question it. There was a silence that was heavy with a meaning Kate could not quite grasp and to break it she said, 'How did you learn your magic?'

Isabella gave Kate an indulgent smile. 'Witchcraft is innate. A gift from the goddess. But magic – that's a different thing altogether.'

She nodded, though she hardly understood. Was it witchcraft that had connected her to Tom that morning in the graveyard? Or was it something more simple – the spirit of her ancestor reaching out from the past? She was no longer certain what she believed, but with every beat of her heart she grew surer that Isabella was not to be trusted.

She said, 'Why are you helping me? What does it matter to you if I come into my own as a ...' she stopped. It was still hard to label herself as *witch* – it was not a title to carry lightly. Words have power, her father had told her, and she knew the name of *witch* could bring its bearer great misfortune. She thought again of Tom Wynter and his cousin, the price he had paid. And all the others who had died for their claim to the word in recent years.

Isabella sat back on her stool, placing distance between them. 'You do not trust me.' It was not a question.

'I trust you,' Kate was quick to answer, though even as she said it she knew it was a lie. Admiration, perhaps. Desire for approval, knowledge, friendship. But even in the unquenchable roil of all those feelings, she knew she dared not trust. 'Only I wonder why you would choose to bring me here and teach me, when I have so little to give you in return.'

Isabella smiled then, her face softening into the features of a different and gentler person. Another facet.

'You remind me of myself,' she said. 'But you have no one that can teach you, as I had. And it is the way of the world that one generation takes the next in hand – I have no child to whom I can pass on my knowledge. Who then will carry it forward? Should I leave no legacy behind? Should all of my skill and learning die with me? That is not what I wish for. Not at all. So I have chosen you, dear Kate, to be my successor, to teach you what I know so that all I have learned and done does not go to waste.'

It was a pretty speech, and Kate was half-tempted to believe it. She wanted so much to trust this woman who had selected her out of all other women to take under her wing, and she was eager to harness the gift Isabella had glimpsed in her palm. But the doubts still flickered and they had been fanned by Tom Wynter's presence at the edge of her awareness.

'I'm honoured,' she said, with a self-conscious smile, 'and grateful. I am sure I have a great deal to learn.'

'Indeed.' Isabella tilted her head in teacherly approval – Kate as an obedient pupil, willing, acquiescent. 'Shall we begin?'

10

THIS BLESSED PLOT

The ship's captain set Mary ashore a few miles downriver from Bankside – a row boat in the dark that dropped her into an unknown place. She was aware of the presence of the hulk of the ship at her back as the boat rowed away, and Rafe's presence aboard it. A slight twinge of regret sidled through her for what might have been, for she had spent the nights of the voyage sleeping alone and they had said their farewells as friends. She did not expect to see him again.

The night was lit only by the merest sliver of moon, and the stars were all but hidden by a shifting ragged veil of cloud. As the row boat's lantern diminished, the night settled around her, enclosing her in its mantle. It was silent on the riverbank, just the plash of oars as the boatman rowed back to the ship to reassure her she was not alone in the world. She had never been anywhere so silent and so dark. Her whole life she had lived in a city, surrounded by a press of people, their presence close by, connected.

Guide me, Hecate.

Then, with a shake of her shoulders and a determined tilt of her chin, she set her footsteps onto the path alongside the river to make her way towards London, towards the place she still thought of as home. Walking through what remained of the night, she followed the snaking road westwards in the still, cold air. She saw no one, though twice she glimpsed the silver flit of a fox, eyes gleaming, and once she heard a man's voice raised in song that drifted across the fields from far away. The sound made her smile, glad to know she was not entirely alone after all.

Slowly, unnoticed at first, the sky began to give up the darkness, soft grey creeping over the heavens as the earth turned its face to meet the sun. The road at Mary's feet shifted into clearer focus, and the trees and hedges all around her started to reveal their shape. Birds sang to welcome the day and she was aware of an awakening all around her, a change in the vibration, a coming to life.

With the first flicker of the sun behind her, she found a fallen log to sit on and opened the little parcel of food and drink she carried. She had left her belongings on the ship in Rafe's safe-keeping to be delivered to the Cardinal's Cap, all save the book, which she had slipped inside her bodice. She had been alarmed by his interest in it and though she could think of no good reason for him even to suspect that she was carrying it, she dared not take the chance. It was safer with her, where she could be sure of its whereabouts.

She nibbled at the dry ship's biscuit without appetite and wet her mouth from the bottle of ale. Then, needing to rest a while, she took out the book to examine it.

Through the years in The Hague she had barely thought of it, its presence locked away in memories she had not allowed herself to visit. Now, running her fingers across the soft smooth leather of the cover, the past began to bubble to the surface. The brothel. The church. The first meeting with Toby. Then Judith stepped across the recollection – Toby's first, brief wife, married only for the child she carried, and dead soon after at the hands of Alexander as he lusted for the book that Mary held now in her lap. It was hard to imagine that so small a thing could incite such desire – in her hands it lay inert, a simple book. Ancient, perhaps, and valuable for that, but nothing more than a collection of scrawled rituals and symbols, bound in age-worn covers of leather. But Toby had told her once that he could feel the power it possessed each time he touched it, its force vibrating, latent and dangerous.

She opened it to the first page and read again the two names that were inked on the flyleaf.

Tom Wynter.

Toby Chyrche.

Her fingers lingered on the letters of her husband's name.

Toby.

She formed the name on her lips and smiled as the letters blurred with tears. His passing had left a hole inside her she knew would never fill, a void at her centre. Shutting the book with a snap, she dragged a hand across her eyes to clear them, packed up the remains of her meal, and set off once more on her way through the lightening morning. The time for grief was past.

Bankside had changed. The long row of whitewashed brothels that once faced the water had given way to more sombre colours, and the painted signs that used to beckon so brightly to those who came to seek their pleasure by boat had long since disappeared. Apparently the Puritans had done their work well, though she guessed the old trade had simply learned to be more discreet. It would take more than Puritans to bring it to an end – men would always find a way to seek their pleasure and there would always be women with few choices in life but to offer it.

Mary ran her gaze along the row, remembering. The Castle on the Hoop, The Little Rose, The Cock, The Unicorn, The Flower de Lyce, all so vivid in her memory, had given way to chandlers' shops and a ropemaker, a pie shop, a cooper, and what looked to be warehouses. A few of the old places had remained as taverns and inns and she smiled to see the Cardinal's Cap amongst them. A rusty sign swung in the morning breeze, creaking gently as it always had. She had grown up within those walls, become a woman, and it was at the Cardinal's Cap that she had first met Toby. For a moment she hesitated, fearful of what might wait behind its door, but she had not come so far to give up now, so with a deep breath and a tilt of her shoulders, she set her steps towards it.

The door opened with a shove, and she halted a moment on the threshold to let her eyes adjust to the gloom after the brightness of the morning outside. When her vision had settled she saw the place had barely changed after all – a shabby alehouse with scattered tables and chairs, and an unmade fire that was grey and cold in the hearth. It was early yet and there were no customers, but the wooden staircase still led up to the passage and the rooms where the girls used to do their business. Did they still? Or had the Puritans rendered it a respectable house these days? She gave herself a wry smile: it was hard to imagine that Bankside could ever be restored to virtue.

Beyond the stairs a counter had replaced the hatch where they used to fetch the ale, and it was littered now with empty jugs and cups. Old habits flickered in her fingertips – the madam would not have permitted such a mess in her day. No one had slept till the place was clean, no matter the hour.

She stepped forward and brought her fingers to rest on a table by the window. Toby had sat there once and watched her, she recalled, waiting for her attention. It seemed like only yesterday. Taking her hand from the table, she held it in the other as though nursing the memory within it, then with a surge of determination she wove her way between the chairs and tables towards the apartment at the back where the madam had lived.

Stopping at the door, she paused briefly, hand lifted ready to knock, memories rising. So many times she had stood here, and the same slight rush of nerves whispered over her skin that she had always felt before this door, summoned to her mistress. With a smile to her old self, so long ago discarded, she brought her knuckles to the wood and rapped hard. The knock was loud in the quiet passage but nothing seemed to stir beyond the door, so she rapped again, harder this time, fist thumping.

She waited. Finally, she heard the scuff of feet and stepped back, nervous now of who might be about to stand before her. Then the door opened a fraction and a woman's face, bleary with sleep, appeared in the gap.

'Who is it?' the woman said. 'Who is there?'

'My name is Mary Sparrow,' she replied, using her old name by instinct, stepping back into the person she used to be, 'and I come as an old friend.'

The door opened wider and the woman stepped forward. She was loosely wrapped in a brightly coloured robe, her hair messed and awry. Her eyes were puffy with sleep but there was no mistaking it was Rosalind.

'Mary? Mary Sparrow?'

'You called me to come,' Mary said. 'I dreamt of you.'

Rosalind's face creased into a smile and within a moment the two women were embracing, holding each other tightly. Tears pricked in Mary's eyes – she had never thought to see her friend again, and though she had journeyed here on the hope of her dream, doubts had torn many times at her certainty.

Rosalind took her hand and they went together into the room behind the door. Mary's gaze flicked over the walls – the same exotic wall hangings that she remembered, though they were faded now and shabby, and the same cushions that had once been bright and cheerful seemed only to serve as a reminder of better times. But she was overjoyed to see her friend, and she took a seat on the bed.

'May I stay here?' Mary asked. 'I've nowhere else to go.'

'Of course,' Rosalind answered. 'And there's work if you need it. There's always work, no matter how hard the Puritans try to reform us.'

Mary nodded but said nothing. She would work if she had to, but not before. Lifting her eyes, she examined her friend. The years had not been kind – the thick dark hair that had been Rosalind's pride and joy was streaked with bands of grey, and her body was puffy with fat. But the eyes were bright with life, and a seeming wisdom within them that was new to Mary.

'I'm looking for my daughter,' Mary said. 'Kate.'

Rosalind drew her robe tighter around her. She nodded towards the fireplace. ''Tis cold,' she said. 'The girl doesn't light the fires till later.'

'I've been walking,' Mary replied. 'I am warm enough. But I would take some food – I've not eaten in a while.'

Rosalind got up from her chair and went to the door. Mary heard her slippers as they scuffed along the hallway towards the kitchens at the back and followed her friend in her head. Every detail was clear in her memory – the passage, the crooked door, the scrubbed table where she used to sit to take her meals – and she was troubled to realise the overwhelming sense inside her now was that she was home where she belonged.

She ate the bread and butter and ale that Rosalind brought. Good English bread, softer than its Dutch counterpart – she had forgotten how much she once missed it. Rosalind sat on the bed and watched her, and there was a quiet companionship between them, an affection that ran far deeper than words. They had grown to womanhood together and been the best of friends till Alexander had come amongst them, leaving a trail of hurt in his wake.

'He's back,' Rosalind said, as though she had read Mary's thoughts.

Mary lowered the hunk of bread in her hand back to the plate.

'He can't be,' she replied. She had killed him herself, and watched the blood drain out of him. His cold dead eyes had followed her in her dreams for years.

'He's here, close by, somewhere,' Rosalind insisted, voice low and tremulous. 'I can feel it.' She slid her eyes away to gaze at the unlit fire, unwilling to meet the question in Mary's look.

Mary took another mouthful of bread, chewing slowly, think-ing. Then she said, 'What happened that night? What did he do to you?' When he had left Rosalind terrified and trembling, she meant, and robbed of her wits. Even now, all these years later, her friend still carried the taint of it, a fearfulness – the vivacious girl Mary had loved had gone for good that night, replaced by a shade of the woman she had been.

'He sent me to a shadow realm, a darkness,' Rosalind whispered, with her eyes still focused on the cold ashes in the hearth.

She had never once said the words before, though Mary had asked her again and again in the months that had followed. Mary waited for more, holding her breath. But Rosalind was silent and in the quiet, she heard the noise of movement on the floorboards of the chamber above – one of the girls moving to and fro with quick, light footsteps that still carried through the ancient timbers.

'And now?' Mary said when it became clear her friend would say no more.

'Be careful,' Rosalind replied. 'He wants revenge.'

Mary swallowed, fear prickling over her skin. She had not thought to face the sorcerer again. She had thought that battle was over. And now she was alone, without Toby to help her.

'And Kate? My daughter?'

Rosalind shook her head. 'I have no connection to Kate. But perhaps ...' She trailed off.

'Perhaps what?' Again, she waited for Rosalind to speak, hopeful for any scrap of word about her daughter, but again, Rosalind said nothing. Silencing her frustration with a deep breath, calling on all her reserves of patience, she turned away instead and loosened the laces of her bodice at her front.

Rosalind stared as Mary drew out the book.

'I need you to keep this for me. Somewhere hidden, somewhere safe.' Her eyes tracked the walls. This had been the madam's chamber once, and she knew for sure there must be some clever place for concealment, a secret pocket beneath the floor perhaps, or a hidey-hole in the wall.

'I don't want that here,' Rosalind said, still staring. 'It was his, wasn't it? The sorcerer's?'

'Yes,' Mary admitted with a small nod, 'and it would be safer hidden with you than with me.'

Rosalind sucked in a quick gasp of air and lifted her eyes to meet Mary's. They were wild with terror.

'I have nowhere else,' Mary breathed. 'No one else I can trust.' She held the book in her hand – small and inert, it was all but impossible to believe the power it contained. But she understood her friend's reluctance nonetheless. 'On its own,' she said, 'it's quite harmless.'

Rosalind said nothing, and for a long moment Mary feared she had asked too much. Then, with a sigh, Rosalind got up from the bed, squatted down and rolled back the threadbare rug. Mary watched, peering at the uneven floorboards as Rosalind reached for the knife beneath her pillow, slid the blade into one of the joins and lifted the board from its place. Beneath was a spacious cavity where Mary could see other neatly wrapped packages; briefly, she wondered what other treasures Rosalind was keeping safe, and for whom.

She held out the book but Rosalind shook her head. 'You do it. I'm not touching it.'

Mary dropped to her knees before the opening and tucked the book neatly along one edge. It fitted perfectly. Then she took the wooden board and fitted it back into place.

'Will he come for it?' Rosalind asked, still kneeling.

Mary swallowed as she lifted herself back and away. 'He's dead,' she replied.

But a new doubt had begun to gnaw at her certainty, and the words sounded hollow even to her.

11

IF THIS BE MAGIC, LET IT BE AN ART
LAWFUL AS EATING

'We must call upon the Shadow, to connect to the witches of the past.'

Isabella was slowly pacing the length of the attic and Kate watched from her place at the desk. The room was warm with a good fire burning in the hearth, and they had dined well on sweetly herbed pigeons and rice boiled in cream. The rich French wine still sang in her head, and she was comfortable and drowsy.

They had spent the afternoon in study, and she had learned how to cast a circle and call to the guardians; the fundamentals of the correspondences; a witch's tools – a knife, a chalice, candles – white for purity, red for the blood of life. They had spoken too of demons and sigils and the planets, and most of all they had talked of Hecate, Guardian of the Crossroads and Keeper of the Keys.

'We must raise the spirits of your ancestors to inherit the knowledge that has gone before.'

Kate was silent, and the presence of Tom Wynter flickered at the edges of her thought. A sign, perhaps?

'Are you willing?' Isabella swung from the hearth where she had stopped her pacing, and fixed her pupil with eyes that flashed green, catlike, in the flickering light. Kate had to hold her nerve against it – she felt exposed and unready beneath its glare.

'Of course,' she said. Fear chased away all thoughts of warmth and comfort, and the sleepiness of the wine was forgotten as her heartbeat quickened with excitement, new knowledge beckoning. An unexpected power seemed to pulse in her veins. She would have gone with anyone who offered her this, she realised, need rising inside her.

'I am willing.'

~

The lane was tar-black when they stepped through the door, and Isabella's torch seemed barely to pierce it, giving just enough light for them to find the road before their feet. Kate cast a look skyward. There was no moon, no stars, and the heavens were full and low above the rooftops.

They went south, away from the river, and Kate was aware of its flow at her back. Her mother had sometimes spoken of the Thames with a wistfulness that had made Kate roll her eyes – who could be so sentimental about a waterway? But now she was beginning to understand. The river was the sacred centre of it all and the life at its edge was precarious and raw. Did Father Thames still watch over it? Did he still inhabit the deeps? As a child, her father had told her stories of water nymphs and goddesses and the magic of the moon-led tide – she wished now she had listened more closely.

In the black and wretched lanes they were wary, senses alert, ears tuned for closing footsteps, a man's whisper, the rustle of a cloak. But her fear of the dangers of the night could not dampen the brightness of her spirit. Her soul was open to all that was around her, influences seen and unseen, and there was a power in the very earth she walked across. She had never felt so alive.

They emerged from the maze unscathed onto the High Street, which was lively with folk spilling in and out of the taverns and eateries. Torches blazed at the doorways of the houses and shops in between, and she picked out the lane beside the inn where she had turned to chance upon the graveyard. What power had drawn her there, when so many other roads had beckoned?

She kept close to Isabella, unsure where they were headed. She had received no answers to her earlier questions, and for now she chose to set her mistrust aside, following her mistress with a willing and curious heart. But she was conscious of the eyes that tracked them as they walked. Idle men, deep in their cups, and no less dangerous than the lanes they had just left behind. Slowly the bustle around them began to dwindle as the road led away from the bridge. They passed houses where chinks of light showed at the edges of curtains, and Kate's fears began to turn inside her again, stirring a disquiet about what the night ahead might hold.

Finally, the road tapered to a track, the mud frozen and rutted underfoot, and the torch became their only light as the fields and heathland stretched away on either side of them, lively with the rustle and calls of creatures of the night. A fox barked, and from somewhere close by the sudden croak of a toad made Kate flinch in startlement.

The road seemed long, but after a time she began to sense the forest that loomed up ahead of them, her senses alive to the snap of twigs and the play of air amongst bare branches, the hoot of an owl. When, finally, they reached the line of trees that marked the woodland's border, she stopped mid-stride to gaze up at the great branches that towered into the sky, bowing above her head. A hornbeam, perhaps, or an oak? In the dark it was hard to tell, and the torch offered little help as Isabella stepped under the canopy. But in the heartbeat before Kate hurried to follow, she had the surest feeling she had been here before. Running a few strides to catch up with the light, her fears seemed to fall away. Somehow, the place was known to her, and the path was unexpectedly famil-iar. She was meant to be here, she knew, and when a fallow deer bellowed in the distance she wanted to laugh as her own spirit rose in answer.

They followed the path for a while, winding deeper into the woods until the other woman stopped so abruptly that Kate almost tripped in surprise. Isabella turned slowly, holding the torch high so that the shadows flickered into the branches overhead.

'Here,' she said, and her voice sounded strange in the silence, out of place. 'At the crossroads.'

Kate lowered her eyes to the earth at their feet. They had halted where the track split into two separate ways that wove deeper into the forest ahead. In her mind's eye she followed them and the same lingering sense of familiarity touched her once more. Shaking her head in confusion, she knelt to unpack the little basket they had brought while Isabella began to pace out a circle. One by one, Kate laid out all they needed neatly on the cold dark earth.

Blankets.

A chalice, a knife, candles.

A flask of wine.

Incense of pine and mugwort.

Charcoal.

'I call on the guardian of the East – may we partake in the mysteries of the air!'

Isabella's voice rang loud in the silent dark as she called to the guardians of the quarters for protection, dipping the torch as she did so to light each of the candles Kate had set out.

'I call on the guardian of the South – may we partake in the mysteries of the fire!'

The flames seemed to rise and flare in answer to the summons, and heat stirred in Kate's blood. She stood up.

'I call on the guardian of the West – may we partake in the mysteries of the water!'

She became aware of Tom's spirit somewhere close by, guiding and protecting her. Was it his memory of this place she had glimpsed? His knowledge that filled her now?

'I call on the guardian of the North – may we partake in the mysteries of the earth!'

With the circle complete, Kate felt again the same stirring of connection she had known at the graveyard and it filled her as a surge of power through her veins, her whole body vibrating with energy and power. Until now she had doubted, still half expecting to discover that the promised witchblood was a lie and there was no such thing as the Shadow. But as she wheeled slowly to dip her head and acknowledge each guardian spirit in turn, their presence was undeniable – each one felt, seen, and heard. All her doubts faded into the ether as her own spirit awoke, and she moved as if in a dream, conscious thought suspended.

In the centre of the circle, she lit the remaining candles, and their flames flickered bravely against the dark. Remembering all Isabella had taught her and the preparations they had made, she began to strip down to her shift, shivering as the night air whispered through the linen. Winding a blanket across her shoulders she knelt. Then she watched as Isabella, too, undressed and knelt beside her. In the faint candlelight, lithe limbs gleamed pale beneath the flimsy fabric, muscles taut and boyish. For the length of a heartbeat, Kate was distracted, but there was no conflict within her – the nascent desire she felt for Isabella was at one with the rise of her spirit and the surge of connection in her blood. She barely noticed the cold.

She sat quietly, allowing her senses to open to the night, and she was acutely conscious of all that was around her: the wool of the blanket beneath her knees and the cold, dark earth it lay upon; the touch of the winter air on her skin, hairs rising in the cold; the soft murmur of the trees, and the faint light of stars hidden high above them.

After a while, as though at a silent signal, they turned to face each other, knees just touching. In spite of the cold she felt the sweat break out along the runnel of her spine. It was hard to breathe.

'Speak now,' Isabella murmured, and took Kate's hands in hers. A rush of heat lit between them, centred at her breast.

'Guardian of the Crossroads,' she called out. *'Keeper of the Keys, Spirits of this place. I call on you now to open the doorway and light up the path that leads to the memory of the Shadow. Reveal to me my*

heritage and protect me on my journey, I honour you now with an offering of wine.'

She raised the chalice to her lips and the sip of wine she took felt like molten light inside her. Wonderful, powerful, the sense of belonging beating through her blood like a drum. Beyond the circle's edge she sensed a shimmer in the dark as the outline of a woman's form emerged for a heartbeat as a blessing.

Hecate.

Dark eyes glimmered. Hands outstretched.

She was magnificent, and Kate bowed her head, overawed to be in her presence. She passed the chalice to Isabella, and when she raised her eyes again, the goddess had gone. But the trail of her presence remained as a shimmer in the dark and Kate gazed after her, unable to tear her eyes away.

The spell was only broken when Isabella touched her arm with a light brush of her fingers and Kate started, surprised by the other woman's presence. In her communion with the goddess she had quite forgotten about Isabella. Drawing her thoughts once more to the circle she remembered the rite Isabella had taught her and all the steps they must follow for its success. But still, it took a great effort of will to drag back her attention – care for Isabella paled against the onslaught of feelings for the goddess. Beautiful and terrible, they all but consumed her, and in the aftermath she was trembling. All the world around her seemed to breathe with life. Every leaf and branch, the dirt beyond the blanket, every mouthful of air was imbued with the spirit of magic, and her whole being roared with the joy of being alive. If this was witchcraft she wanted more of it, heedless of all the many risks it carried.

Turning reluctantly away from her contemplation of the remaining shimmer in the dark, she faced Isabella again. The other woman was watching her and though the light in her eyes was impossible to read, Kate no longer cared. She was brimming with her connection to Hecate, her body light as air, and Isabella had no more power to disturb her.

The two women embraced in celebration of the rite, and the

coolness of Isabella's skin was exquisite against hers. Her breath lifted. She was alive to everything the world had to offer, every sensation, every pleasure, and she wanted it all. Kate tipped back her head and laughed out loud, and the sound seemed to echo off the branches of the trees. Her blood seemed to sing with life, and she wished the night could never end.

Finally, slowly, Isabella shifted away, and got to her feet. Kate watched her as she paced the edge of the circle she had traced, dismissing the guardians, and thanking them for their protection. Then, with a sudden shiver, remembering at last the chill of the night, she got to her own feet and dressed hurriedly, her skin stinging now with the cold, her fingers numb.

But in spite of it her blood was still humming with power, and in the darkness, she smiled.

12

STEW'D IN CORRUPTION

In the morning, the sun was high and bright at the window by the time Kate woke and she turned her head towards it, wondering that she had woken so late – it was a rare day she slept through the rising of the sun, whatever the season. Rolling onto her side, she drew the covers closer round her against the chill of the room – a cold that seemed to infuse her bones, impossible to shift in this house, even when the fires were roaring. After they had returned from the forest she had lain awake most of the night, dozing only in bursts of fitful dreams, and now, staring into the morning, she sifted through the traces of the shadows they had left behind.

With an effort of will, she threw back the covers and rolled out of bed, dressing hurriedly, shivering, fingers fumbling with the ties. A faint scent of warm bread caught in the draught that curled around the door, and her stomach growled. She splashed her face with the icy water in the jug and wished she had a looking glass – she hadn't seen her own reflection since she left The Hague.

When she went downstairs the main chamber was empty and the fire was almost out, embers pulsing. With a shiver, Kate crouched to poke it back into life, throwing on another log that cracked and sparked as the heat took hold. When it began to burn at last, she turned to the sideboard where bread and jam and cheese had been laid out and helped herself, eating quickly in her hunger, not even bothering to take the food to the table.

After she had eaten enough, she climbed the stairs towards the attic with a slow and reluctant tread. She was uncertain which of Isabella's many facets she would meet this morning. They had walked home from the crossroads in silence, in spite of the rite they had shared. Then, imbued with the joy in her new-found connection, Kate had barely cared. But now, in the cold light of the morning, she cast her thoughts back across the night, and Isabella's silence took on a more sinister aspect. The briskness of her stride and the hard set of her mouth. Her refusal to so much as spare Kate a glance. For whatever the fortune teller might have claimed, Kate knew she would never welcome a power that could rival her own. Not for the first time, she wondered what game the other woman was playing. What gain for her to nurture the power of Kate's witchblood?

On the last few stairs, voices from the other side of the attic door slowed her steps, prompting her to move in silence. She crept forward with a hand against the wall to steady her, head tilted towards the conversation. The walls were thin and though the voices were low and discreet, the words carried easily.

'For what purpose did you bring her here?' Nathan's tone was impatient. It was a strange way for a servant to address his mistress, she thought. Was there something more between them? A secret history? There was a pause and Kate held her breath, waiting for the answer to the question she had only just asked herself.

'She is connected to my father ...' Isabella stopped abruptly, as though she had been going to say more but had thought better of it.

'You said she has witchcraft in her blood.'

'I did,' Isabella answered. 'And I was right. If she can harness it she will wield great power. I saw the possibilities last night when she felt its call within her.' The praise was grudging, but Kate's lips curved in a smile of pleasure nonetheless. 'But that is not why I brought her here and I must take care lest she comes into her own too quickly. First, I must shape her to my will.'

There was another silence and footsteps on the boards. Isabella, she guessed, pacing back and forth. Kate flattened herself against the wall and prepared to run if the steps came too near to the door.

'Then why?' Nathan's voice was unnervingly close, but still she could not tear herself away.

'Her family took something from my father.' She growled out the words and Kate's skin prickled with fear at the threat contained within them. 'Something very precious. So we must be patient and let her lead us back to it.'

'Is that why you take her to your bed?'

To Kate's surprise Isabella let out a laugh. 'Are you jealous?'

There was no answer.

'Dearest chuck, you have no need to be jealous. She comes to my bed, yes, but we sleep as sisters and nothing more. I need her to trust me as I sculpt her to my will, moulding her as I mould the waxen poppets on my desk. Soon she will give me what I want, for it must be given willingly. Then I will need her no more and she will be as dust beneath my feet. What I share with you, Nathan, is something altogether different. You know my heart.'

Kate heard the scuffle of feet on the boards and Nathan's low groan of pleasure. For two more breaths she waited. But the conversation was at an end. In fury, she flung open the door and stepped inside the attic. Isabella was on her knees in front of Nathan. His breeches gaped open, and her mouth was around his cock, but at the sound of the juddering door she turned her head, languid, unhurried, a smile on her lips.

'Have you come to join us?' she asked, tilting her head to one side. Her fingers stroked the tip of Nathan's cock and he shuddered, his hands gripping the edges of the desk behind his hips, knuckles white. But his eyes never left Kate's face, and her innards writhed at the lust she saw there.

Kate stared, groping vainly through her mind for the words

she needed. 'As dust beneath your feet, you said,' she managed to whisper.

Isabella let go of Nathan and got to her feet. He waited and slid his own hand inside his breeches, watching as she stepped towards the door before he wet his bottom lip with his tongue. Kate's hand tightened on the handle of the door. She was breathing hard, her chest tight and painful.

'Oh come, Kate,' Isabella said. 'Don't be such a child. You always knew I had reasons to bring you here. And surely you're not shocked!' She flung out an arm in a careless gesture towards Nathan. 'This is Bankside. And I know well the desires that lurk in your heart. Come.' She held out her hand for Kate to take. 'Join us. It will be fun.'

Kate shook her head and backed away. The thought of Nathan so much as touching her made her skin crawl.

'This is your home now.' Isabella said. 'Where else can you go?'

'Anywhere but here,' she whispered. 'You're poison.'

Then she turned and fled.

❧ 13 ❧

A ROOTED SORROW

Though the Cardinal's Cap was officially a tavern now instead of a brothel, there were still girls available for those men who knew to ask. Old hands mostly, who remembered from the days before the Puritans took over – out-of-work actors, gentlemen, gamblers laid low by parliament's curbs on pleasure, and other sundry Royalists who came to lament the times they lived in and drink to the health of the King. But even still, they mourned and toasted in undertones and took their pleasures discreetly. Bankside could no longer openly celebrate its debauchery, and though Mary had only ever wanted to leave it she realised she regretted the change. The place had lost its reckless vitality, where life was raw and wild, all things possible and nothing forbidden. People were frightened now to follow their desires and to dream – you could see the disquiet in their eyes. That the streets were safer and more orderly these days Mary did not doubt, but it seemed as though the joy in life had been diminished.

She shared Rosalind's bed as they used to do when they had lived like sisters. The upstairs rooms were mostly empty now with fewer girls living in, but those beds held memories Mary preferred not to visit. So she lay curled amongst the quilts and blankets that had once been Madam's, and listened to Rosalind's breathing. It was good to hear it and know that in the years Mary had been away her old friend had found her way back from the Shadow, although it appeared she would never again be the carefree girl of before. Perhaps it was the sorcerer's death that had set her free. It was no wonder then, Mary thought, that the threat of his return left her panicked and afraid. Alexander had taken from them both.

But in spite of it all Rosalind had done well for herself. She was the madam now, running the house for the sea captain who owned the place. Mary remembered him from the old days when he had been one of Madam's favourites, but he had long since given up his ship for a less perilous life ashore. She doubted he would remember her – a respectable gown and a cloak of expensive wool belied her humble, sinful beginnings, and few men ever took the trouble to look any deeper.

By the time she fell asleep, the tavern was quiet and settled beyond the door and the fire had sunk low in the hearth, the last embers pulsing with a faint rosy light that followed her into her dreams.

In the morning she woke disorientated, sitting up abruptly in the darkness and taking a moment to remember where she was. It was not yet light – the sun rose late at this time of the year – but a slight warmth lingered in the room from the fire. Beside her, Rosalind was sleeping, her breathing regular with the soft, small snores of the deeply asleep that made Mary smile – it was a sound that took her back to earlier times, when their lives had still been before them and they had shared their dreams.

Getting up, she dressed quickly, silently, finding her clothes in the gloom with practised ease, lacing herself in. Despite the early hour she was hungry and old habit led her out and down the passage to the kitchen at the back. There was bread and butter and a hunk of cheese in the pantry as there had always been, and a flagon of watered wine on the table. She settled herself on the bench and helped herself. She had never thought to sit here again, and the unexpected return to the past stirred another sudden wave of grief for Toby. All the years she had spent with him since she had left this place were as smoke now, nothing more than a memory. Tears pricked behind her eyes and she blinked to force them down. It was strange, she thought, how the sorrow swept in so abruptly, unseen, to fell you like a blow from behind. Her whole body hurt with want for him.

All appetite gone, she pushed the food away, but she sipped at the wine with a grimace as she fought against the grief. She knew it would come again but she had no time now to indulge her tears – she had a daughter to find. Draining the last mouthful of the wine, she felt the little kick of its courage inside her. Then, with a deep breath of resolve she strode back to Rosalind's room, took her cloak from the peg on the back of the door, and went out into the still-dark morning.

On the quayside she halted to breathe in the familiar rank scent of the river. Even at this hour the waterway was busy, alive with the plash and creak of oars and the slap of sails, ropes twanging. Men's shouts drifted disembodied across the tide and far below her she heard the shush-hush of the waves on the shingle. Lights bobbed, seemingly suspended in air, ghost-like, and the dark hulks of ships loomed black against the dull predawn grey. For a moment she could imagine she had never left, tied to the Thames, its water running in her blood. She was a child of Bankside, and though she had loved the life she had made with Toby, grateful for it every day, this place where she was standing now was where she truly belonged.

Lifting her head to the breeze, she felt the loose strands of hair lift and fall against her face as she watched a wherry draw in to land at Goat Steps. The glow of its lantern sent shadows cavorting across the shifting water and two young men, apprentices by the look of them, stumbled onto the quay. Returning from a night of pleasure, she guessed, and about to struggle through a day at work. She smiled at a plight she understood, and quelled an old instinct to call out to them. She watched them stagger away, perhaps to a beating from their masters for their drunkenness. Some things would never change, whatever the Puritans believed.

Downriver, the bridge had opened its gates at last and the waiting traffic had begun its roar. Wheels and boots and hooves, shouts and laughter combined into the familiar hubbub. Mary listened for a moment. Then, setting her shoulders to her purpose, she strode off to begin her search for the fortune teller who had stolen her daughter.

She went first to Borough Market, and the overripe stench of meat and fish and rotting vegetables disturbed long-forgotten memories of illicit adventures on rare escapes from the orphanage, when the stink and clamour had offered a life of possibilities away from the harsh and barren severity she was used to. As a girl, she had always been drawn to the market, a new world, and she had taken a beating more than once for spending time amongst the market stalls, watching and listening, fascinated, when she should have been elsewhere, working. As soon as she was old enough she had run away for good, finding a home running errands at the brothel where there was more to eat and fewer beatings.

She gave the small girl she had once been a wry smile and slid between the stalls as she used to, though the traders treated her differently now in her well-to-do gown and fine wool cloak. No one winked or joked and a part of her was sorry. She no longer belonged to this world and the life she had left it for was over.

A weary-looking woman selling baskets was setting up her stall and when Mary hailed her she looked up from her work with surprise. Her thoughts must have been a hundred miles away. The two women exchanged a smile and Mary cast her eyes across the baskets as though looking to buy. Then she said, 'Have you happened to see a fortune teller here? A palm reader? I heard there was one hereabouts.'

The woman's eyes narrowed. 'You want a fortune teller?'

Mary tilted her head in assent and a thread of unease rippled through her. In the brave new world of the Puritans, telling fortunes was frowned upon, she remembered. She would have to tread with care. 'Do you know of her?'

The woman shook her head and turned away to rub at some imagined flaw on the handle of the nearest basket.

'Thank you,' Mary offered, but the woman's gaze remained steadfastly averted and Mary backed away.

She asked others and always met the same response: distrust and reluctance. But she persisted. A palm reader was a rare enough thing that she would be remembered, and though she could be anywhere in London Mary's gut held her to search first on Bankside. A baker's boy strolled past and she bought a pie from his basket, standing by the river to eat it. The pastry was warm and flaky, sticking to her lips. Then, as the morning wore on she began to trawl the taverns, asking the same questions again and again and turning aside the strange looks she attracted with a haughty glare that dared anyone to challenge her.

By midday she was exhausted, and not a single person had told her anything that might help. The flush of nostalgia and the pleasure of forgotten memories had long since palled, and when she returned at last to the Cardinal's Cap with aching feet she was jaded and depressed. Weaving between the tables of drinkers, she ignored them all, and she closed Rosalind's door behind her with relief, shutting out the world beyond it.

What had she been thinking? That she would simply find this woman in a morning, and bring her daughter home? She crossed to the hearth and poked more heat into the fire, throwing on another log, reaching out her hands to its warmth. She had not noticed how cold the day was and with the sudden realisation, she shivered.

Later, when she had eaten a little and rested, she took her leave of Rosalind and set out again, heart steeled, hope ebbing low.

Have you happened to see a fortune teller here? A palm reader? I heard there was one hereabouts.

Each time she asked the question drew the same response. A shake of the head and an unease that she had asked. She went from taverns to tailors' shops, chandlers, ropemakers, drapers and book-sellers, and every other shop she passed in between.

It was a bookseller who suggested she ask the watermen. 'They see most people come and go,' he told her. 'And everyone must cross the river sometime.'

She thanked him – it was the first kind word she had heard all day – and as she turned to leave his shop her eye fell on a small stack of playscripts by the door. Despite her urgency she reached out a hand to examine them. On the top was a copy of *'Tis Pity She's a Whore*. She flicked through it, remembering the players who had come to the brothel.

'They're going cheap,' the bookseller said behind her. He was an old man with a kind, tired smile. 'No one wants playscripts any more, now the theatres are all closed.'

''Tis a pity,' she said. 'I used to like the playhouse.'

'Aye,' he agreed. 'But there are greater things to mourn at present than the death of the playhouse.'

She nodded and turned again to the scripts. The next one she came to was *The Tragedy of Macbeth*, and she swallowed, remem-bering its darkness – the witches and the madness, and the sorcerer who had watched her in the midst of it, malevolence dripping from his smile. Shivering, she went to put it back but the book-seller said, 'Take it. Take it as a gift. You seem as though you have need of a little good fortune today.'

She swallowed, half tempted to throw it back on the pile and run, but it seemed ungrateful when the man was showing her a kindness. And perhaps it was meant to come into her possession after all, perhaps it was the work of Hecate.

'You're very kind,' she said, 'and I thank you.'

'Go carefully, my dear, and find your fortune teller.'

Mary smiled and gave him a small curtsey. Then, with the little script clutched to her chest beneath her cloak, she stepped out into the darkening afternoon.

14

THE SHADOW OF A DREAM

With nowhere else to go and her blood running hot with fury, Kate made for the Cross Bones graveyard. A grey sky glowered, backlit by a pale blinding sun that rimmed the edges of the clouds with gold. She drew her cloak hood closer over her face to shield her eyes against it and the ground was hard and sure underfoot. Her thoughts were filled with an image of Isabella she could not shake away – kneeling in front of Nathan, his breeches gaping open, and the leer on his face as they beckoned her to join them. She spat onto the road beside her as she strode but the bitter taste remained and her whole body ached with disgust.

At the gate of the graveyard she paused, her breath leaping hard in her chest as she ran her eyes across the uneven rows of mounds. It was a desolate place to end your days – unkempt, crowded, shunned. A couple of young children in rags were kneeling at a new-dug grave not far from the fence, a brother with a comforting arm around a smaller sister. Orphans now, she guessed, fending for themselves in a hostile world. She could barely imagine how a child might face such a future – until now she had never known hunger or want in her life. It crossed her mind that she should have been more grateful for her own beginnings, and she brushed aside the flicker of the desire to go home. She had set upon her path and the only way to go was forward.

The gate caught on the dirt when she pushed it with her hand, sticking, and she had to jam her shoulder against it. Squeezing through the gap, she picked her way along the overgrown paths, skirting the children, and when she reached Tom's grave she dropped to her knees, touching her fingers to the dirt in greeting. The sense of connection glimmered in her veins, and she sat back and allowed the sensation to ripple through her, lifting her face to the cool light of the winter sun that dappled the grass.

She was still in awe of his sacrifice – he had given his life to save his cousin's. Would she ever love anyone so much? She hoped so, but her spirit still yearned for experience, a life to be lived, as his must once have done – a whole lifetime surrendered out of love. Opening her eyes, she rested her hand again on Tom's grave and this time her body flared in warning. She swivelled abruptly, eyes sweeping the expanse of tangled weeds and uncut grass, the untended mounds. The children had gone and she was completely alone, but the sense of menace still lingered as her gaze scanned the scene before her over and over, searching for the source, finding nothing. Then, at last, she saw the man at the gate, and she shrank back between the headstones.

The man sidled through the gap and paused for a moment, his gaze running over the sweep of the graveyard as though he were looking for something, or someone. Searching for the resting place of someone he'd loved, Kate told herself. But even as she thought it she knew it wasn't true. She was too far away to see his face, but she could make out he was more neatly dressed than most who came to this place and it took only a moment more to realise it was Nathan.

Looking for her? she wondered. Why?

She hesitated, torn with indecision. Then she remembered the leer on his face, his cock in Isabella's hand, and the warning tingled brighter up her spine, terror in her veins. Very slowly, she reached out to touch the stone at Tom's head.

'Help me, Tom,' she murmured. 'What should I do?'

The answer came as a shout that echoed in her head.

Run!

But there was nowhere to run to. Nathan was threading between the graves, heading towards her. How had he known where to look? How had he found her? Her palms were slick with sweat and she wiped them on the wool of her skirt. Then she shifted out from behind the tree, unwilling to let him know she had been hiding.

He was almost upon her.

'Nathan.' She dipped her head in greeting, preserving the civilities, though her mouth was chalky with fear and she could barely get the words to her tongue. 'How did you know to find me here?'

'Miss Winter. It is my business to know where you go.'

'You've been following me?'

'Aye.'

Isabella must have sent him in search of her.

'For what reason?' she managed to ask, tone light, an attempt at a smile.

'My Lady has plans for you. She won't like it if you go astray.'

He moved closer and fear slid to panic as Kate recognised the light in his face as lust. Would he dare? she wondered. Or had Isabella sent him precisely for this purpose? He took another step towards her and she shrank back, slipping once more behind the yew tree and along the wall, away.

'You can't escape,' he said. 'Your witchcraft won't help you now.'

Briefly she lifted her eyes heavenward, trying to recall the power she had raised only hours before when she had felt as though the whole world were hers. But she heard no answer this time, and the knowledge of her weakness as a woman before this man enraged her.

Nathan was advancing, confident that she was cornered, and she read for certain now the intention in his eyes. When he began to drag at the buckle of his belt she reached for the little knife she kept at her waist, backing away, the small blade held out before her with a shaking hand. He cast a derisory glance at it and laughed, his mouth widening, wet with saliva. Like a dog, she thought, drooling. Her eyes scanned all around her, desperate for some way out, but there was a wall behind her, a line of half-dead brambles, and Nathan stood between her and the gate.

He grinned when she stumbled backwards on the overgrown grass, a thistle catching at her skirt as her feet felt their way around the graves. She kept her eyes on his – he was enjoying the chase, lust feeding on her fear as he inched closer towards her, almost within reach. Then, with a sudden leap, he lunged, knocking the knife from her hand and grabbing her wrist, fingers vice-like, dragging her down.

Another moment and she was pinned to the earth, her body under Nathan's. All her senses were filled with the sour scent of him as he fumbled to lift her skirts, trying to still her kicking legs. She struggled, free hand lashing out wildly, and though she managed to catch him a blow across his face it was not enough to save her. Her skirts were above her hips, her legs bare to the winter morning, and in a heartbeat more he would be inside her.

Then she remembered the knife. She hadn't seen where it fell but she reached out both hands and desperately searched the ground around her, fingers scrabbling through the overgrown grass and weeds until finally, finally, they closed upon the handle.

Nathan was taking his time, enjoying the moment of conquest as he knelt between her legs, cock in hand, ready. She waited until he leaned his weight forward, and as the tip of him brushed against her, she lunged at him with all her strength so that the knife blade slashed across his cheek.

For a moment he froze, incomprehension written in his face, before he reared up and away from her with a howl of rage, fingers searching for the point of pain. Kate scrabbled to her feet, and though a part of her wanted to stay to watch him suffer, instinct drove her to run. She was at the gate in a moment and squeezing through the gap into the road.

Two housewives with baskets on their arm stopped their conversation to look at her, but she paid them no mind, footsteps leading her away from the graveyard. She gave no thought to where she was running as she twisted this way and that through the maze of lanes, but some unknown force must have guided her footsteps, because by the time she slowed, breathless and sweating, she realised she was on the quay by the river just above the bridge. She paused for a moment, hands resting on her knees, bent almost double. Her breathing was ragged, her heartbeat a rapid drum in her chest, and she could feel the sweat in a trickle down her spine in spite of the chill wind that was blowing off the water, whipping the tide into peaks. She smoothed back a strand of hair that had blown loose from its fastening and watched as a wherry pulled in at the landing stage to deposit a pair of young gentlemen in fine dark velvets onto the shore. They stopped to look at her as though wondering if she were on offer, but she stared them down with such a look that they exchanged a glance and a shrug and went on their way.

The afternoon was already starting to close in when her wandering brought her to the church at St Saviour's. The dark tower loomed up into the evening but the golden light behind the windows spoke of warmth and welcome. At least it would be place to rest a while out of the wind.

She pushed open the door and the sweet voices of the choir at Evensong filled the great Gothic arches that soared above her. The candle flames flinched in the sudden draught and one of the worshippers turned to look as the wind blustered through the opening. But no one else seemed to notice her, entranced by the music. It was nothing like the worship Kate was used to in The Hague where they prayed in a whitewashed hall – spoken psalms, open confessions, and the earnest, ardent prayers of exiles. She was astonished by the beauty of it and it spoke to her in a harmony of sound she had never heard before. For the length of the song her worries were forgotten, the music like a salve. Moving away from the door along the wall, she closed her eyes, listening.

But the service was almost over. The music finished and the spell was broken by the shuffle of feet on the flagstones and the chatter of the worshippers as they greeted friends and exchanged the gossip of the day. She stayed close to the wall, easing her way around the congregation as they made their way towards the door while she searched for a hidden corner to rest and gather her thoughts. Behind the choir, she found a small chapel where no candles burned and only a little light from the rest of the church could enter, shedding a soft warm gloom across the stone. She cast a quick look behind her. No one was looking, no one had seen her. Gratefully, she stepped inside, sank down with her back to the wall, rested her shoulder against one of the columns, and tried to think what to do next.

Her belly had begun to turn in on itself with hunger and nerves and her mouth was dry – she had neither drunk nor eaten since breakfast. Overhead, the bells began to strike the hour, the mournful tones vibrating through her, and she wrapped her arms around herself against the cold that crept from the ancient stones as she began to doze, drifting in and out of a restless slumber, exhausted from the sleepless night and the fear and emotion of the day.

She was beginning to sink deeper into her sleep despite the cold and her hunger when the sound of footsteps in the nave startled her from the encroaching oblivion, and she shifted closer to the column, nestling in its shadow. Her heartbeat was loud in the hush as the last toll of the bell faded into silence, and she could still hear the footsteps moving to and fro beyond the choir, apparently without any purpose. But they were coming closer, and she held her breath. A memory of Nathan's weight on hers at the graveyard pressed against her thoughts, and the fear that he had followed her again shuddered through her in a wave. There would be no escape from him in here.

A figure appeared in the archway that led into the chapel from the nave. His form was little more than an outline against the light behind him but from his shape and the quick, light movements, Kate judged he was a young man, probably the curate doing a final check of the place before he turned in for the night. She shrank further back against the column and for a moment it seemed he had not seen her, half turning to go, when some instinct made him pause. Her breath stopped as he ran his eyes across the chapel once again. This time he saw her and started in surprise.

'You, girl!' His voice was terse with shock. 'What do you do there? Come out where I can see you.'

Kate unfurled from her hiding place and stood up beside the column. Her feet and hands were numb with cold, and she held the stone beside her, unsteady on her feet.

'What are you doing here?'

'Taking shelter from the cold. 'Tis bitter outside.'

He hesitated. 'You cannot stay.'

'I have nowhere else to go,' she told him.

'Go back to wherever you have run away from,' he said. 'You have a master? A father?'

She swallowed and said nothing.

'Then you do.' He nodded. 'That is where you must go. 'Tis your God-given place in the world. You must honour it and obey those that have rule over you.'

'I will go,' she said, for what good would it do to argue? Then she wondered if this was what he had entered the church to do, to serve the poor and rough in a congregation of whores and players, gamblers and thieves. Or had he once nurtured hopes for a better parish, and the chance of advancement? The thought of it made her smile.

He stood aside to let her pass in front of him on her way back to the nave. 'God be with you, child,' he murmured.

Her boots echoed in the silent church, and she took a side door that was standing open to the night. Outside, the wind had dropped but the chill was bitter still. The darkness flared with scattered torches and braziers, shadows moving amongst them, and the sweet scent of woodsmoke filled the air, reminiscent of winter nights in The Hague, walking with her father on some unknown errand. A simpler time, she thought, with innocent pleasures, when she had known nothing of witchblood and the ghosts of the past. She pulled her cloak tighter around her and drew up the hood.

Standing in the lea of the wall, surveying the night before her, she weighed up her choices. The hour in the church had been but a stolen moment, a brief lull in the nightmare her life had become, for there was nowhere else she could go except back to the Wounded Raven. The memory of Nathan above her at the grave-yard seemed to slice through her innards and her whole being recoiled; she had to swallow down the bitter taste of vomit rising from her gut. She would rather starve, she thought, than face him again. But as she stood in the shadow of the church wall she wondered if that were really true. It was a thing people said, but faced with the prospect of death in cold reality, Kate knew she did not have the will to let herself die when a chance of life remained. She supposed she would end up back there by the end of the night, because she would surely freeze to death otherwise. It would be a bed, at least, however damp and unpleasant, and there would be food and the warmth of a hearth. But even so, she feared the cruelty to come, remembering the smile on Isabella's face when she turned from her place on her knees before Nathan and the leer on Nathan's mouth. She shuddered. She no longer cared to discover what Isabella wanted from her – the price of the knowledge was too high to pay.

Still undecided, and still reluctant to trace her steps back to whatever awaited her at the Wounded Raven, she clutched her cloak more tightly around her and ambled through the dark towards the river. Standing by one of the landing stages, she cast her gaze across the water. It was lively with boats, their lanterns bobbing wildly. Wherries and pleasure boats, tugs and merchantmen. Half a dozen men were unloading a cargo of barrels from a boat that bobbed in the current, straining at its ropes, and the tide slapped against its hull in quick relentless waves. On the far shore, the city of London loomed – the towers of St Paul's a darker mass against a velvet sky, and a myriad of lights flickering brightly. She wondered if she might find better luck in the city itself but the bridge was already closed for the night and she had no coins to catch a wherry.

She sighed and turned from the water to let her gaze wander across the row of buildings that faced the water behind her. Taverns and inns rubbed shoulders with various shops and work-shops, houses and shacks, and before them the street was lively with people. Young couples walked together, discreetly holding hands, and a group of poor-looking women crouched around a brazier, hands outstretched to the warmth. Life going on all around her, untouched by her sorrows, oblivious.

Taking a deep breath to settle her thoughts, she ran her eyes across the buildings, searching for some kind of inspiration. She was homeless, penniless, a long way from all she had ever known, and the flicker of desire for home began to burn more brightly inside her. Tears prickled behind her eyes, and she blinked, forcing them down. Crying would not help her now. She had been a fool. What had she been thinking when she agreed to follow Isabella? How could she have been so trusting? She should have heeded the warning bells that had sounded in her head. She should have listened to her mother, who had chided her for her whole life about the trouble her recklessness would one day lead her into. She sighed, and tried not to think what her father would say if he could see her now. But still, she thought, in spite of everything, she was glad to have found Tom Wynter and awoken the connection to the witchblood in her veins. Perhaps her father would not think so badly of her – after all, it was his blood she had inherited. His witchcraft that ran inside her.

She let her gaze run across the row of buildings again. Perhaps she could find work at one of them, as a maid or a cook or a servant? Perhaps her skills as a seamstress might serve her well? She had sewed shirts for a prince, she reminded herself. That must surely count for something. But the day was almost done, darkness closing in – she doubted anyone would be hiring a seamstress at this hour.

She read the names of the taverns. The Crane. The Horseshoe. The Swan. The Cardinal's Cap. The Bull's Head.

Her attention wavered at the last one and lingered on the sign that hung above the door – a great black bull with sharp white horns – and the image pricked a memory.

Rafe Tyndall at the Binnenhof in The Hague.

Though want for him that night had almost turned her inside out, she had barely spared him another thought since, her attention all wound up with Isabella. Now, she recalled his words with perfect clarity.

'*If you should ever find yourself in London, Miss Winter, and I can be of service in any way, leave a message at the Bull's Head on Bankside. I would be pleased to aid you in whatever way I can.*'

The Bull's Head was before her now. How strange that of all places in London, she had found herself at his door. This must be the famous Bankside, she realised, that the English exiles in The Hague had talked about sometimes. It must surely have been something to see before the Puritans closed it all down, enforcing their joyless creed of the fear of God. But now it seemed very ordinary – nothing more than a busy river dock, with the usual shops and warehouses, taverns and workshops.

She drew in a deep breath, hesitant to trust her luck to the word of a gentleman she barely knew. But really, what other choice did she have? In all the press of humanity that teemed in the lanes of Southwark, there was not one other soul she could lay claim to, not one other person who might care if she lived or died.

Except for Isabella.

For three more breaths she turned back to gaze at the water, drawing strength from the relentless roll of the tide. Then, with a whispered murmur to Tom for his protection, she squared her shoulders, headed across the cobbled quay, and went through the door of the tavern.

15

O SHAME, WHERE IS THY BLUSH?

Inside, the Bull's Head was much the same as the taverns Kate had haunted now and then after her father's death in The Hague, searching for she knew not what as she flirted with unknown men, while the danger of it pricked the numbness of her grief into feeling. A low and tobacco-stained ceiling hung above scattered groups of men drinking or playing at dice. She kept her hood raised, hiding her face – she had no desire now to draw attention to herself. Her gaze swept the room. Men's heads turned towards her, and a girl in a low-cut gown gave her a friendly smile before turning her attention back to the man she was dallying with. Kate hesitated on the threshold, in half a mind to back away. This place seemed to be more than a tavern, even to her untutored eye. But with an effort of will she forced down the temptation to flee – she had nowhere else to go, and Rafe Tyndall was her only hope.

A young man who sat alone at the hearth was watching her. He was dark-haired, with eyes that were almost black, but there was an open liveliness in them that was attractive – you could tell from his face that he was kind. Could he see the rapid rise and fall of her breathing? Her mouth was dry with her nerves, but he seemed familiar from somewhere and she rifled through her memories to place him. Their eyes met, and she remembered: she had seen him on the quay when she had just arrived, taking her first steps onto English soil. He had held her gaze just the same way then, she recalled, dark eyes searching hers, and even that brief moment of familiarity seemed like a lifeline to her now. They regarded each other for two more breaths, before he beckoned her towards him with a small movement of his head. She needed no second invitation and when she reached his table, he stood up.

'I saw you before,' she said. 'You were on the quay.'

He nodded. 'Walter Clun, at your service.'

'Kate Winter.'

He gestured for her to take a seat and she cast a brief glance across her shoulder as she slipped into place.

'Ale?'

She nodded, and he raised his hand to one of the girls to bring another cup. When it came, he poured and watched her as she cradled the cup carefully between both hands, taking small and tentative sips. It was watery and bitter but still it was welcome, and she was almost overwhelmed by his kindness. Relaxing a little, she let the hood slide back from her head and gave him a small smile of thanks.

'What brings you to the Bull's Head?' Walter asked. He did a sweep of the place with a look. 'It's no place for a young woman alone.'

'I'm looking for someone,' she replied.

'May I know his name?'

'Rafe Tyndall.'

For a moment he said nothing but she saw the disconcertment on his face as if her words had caused him worry or pain, and he was wondering how best to answer her. His gaze on her face was intent and it was hard to look away.

'He told me I might find him here,' she clarified, and swallowed, running the tip of her tongue across her lips. 'Do you know of him?'

He leaned forward on the table, resting his weight on his forearms so that his head was close to hers, and his reaction lit a spark of panic inside her. She swallowed it down, forcing herself to be calm. 'Is there nowhere else you can go?' he murmured. 'This is not a safe place for you.'

Tears pricked at the backs of her eyes and she blinked them away, furious with herself for her weakness. She had not come here to cry before strangers. She shook her head. 'I ... did a foolish thing,' she whispered, 'and now I am alone.'

'Perhaps I can help you.'

She hesitated. He was young, she realised, just a little older than herself, and from his garb she guessed he was some kind of artisan – an apprentice perhaps? She doubted he could offer much in the way of assistance. What harm though, she thought, to share her troubles? Mayhap he knew of someone else who could aid her, who might give her work or a roof above her head. And she was curious, too, to know his objection to Rafe Tyndall.

She said, 'A week ago I was a seamstress, an *émigré* tailor's daughter in a well-to-do house in The Hague.'

His eyes brightened with interest. 'I've been to The Hague,' he said. 'A troupe of us a while since, acting for the English exiles there.'

'You're one of the actors that came to the palace?' In spite of everything, she was delighted by the connection. 'My father told me about it. He was there. When he came home, he acted out parts of the plays for my mother and me. It was wonderful!' Her spirits lifted briefly with the memory of when her father was still alive, in better times. But the recollection cut abruptly away to the horror of the truth – her father dragged from the water pale and bloated, with seaweed in his hair. She gave an inward shake of her head to rid her mind of the image. 'But that was a long time ago, in a different life.'

'I am an actor,' he answered softly. 'Though we play only rarely these days. The Puritans don't allow it.'

She took another mouthful of the bitter ale to give herself a moment to steady the onslaught of emotion, and barely heard his words. He was waiting for her to go on with her story, but despite the temptation of his kindness, the desperation of her situation forced her thoughts along a different track.

She said, 'Where will I find Rafe Tyndall?'

His eyes slid away and seemed to search the floor for an answer before he lifted his head to look at her again.

'Leave,' he whispered. 'Leave and don't come back. Forget about Rafe Tyndall.'

She stared at him and her heart contracted with dread. What did he know of Master Tyndall?

'This is a brothel, Miss Winter. Rafe Tyndall's brothel. If he asked you here it can only be for one thing. He means to make of you a whore.'

Comprehension swept through her in a wash of fear that leached her skin of its colour: she could feel the blood draining away. The voices in the tavern seemed to ebb into silence, the outside world a blur. What had she done? Her mind scrabbled for an answer and in the moment of hesitation, she saw Rafe Tyndall on the stairs.

'Go!' Walter urged.

But caught in her indecision she remained motionless at the table. For where could she go? Back to Isabella and Nathan? Onto the streets outside? Even the church had failed to offer her a refuge. The tavern was warm and cheerful and the night beyond its doors was bitter. Better to take her chances here with Rafe Tyndall, she decided, than freeze to death on the street. And perhaps, after all, Walter Clun was not to be trusted. She gave herself an inward smile. Before she met the fortune teller she had thought herself a good judge of people. Now she no longer knew who or what to trust in.

Rafe saw her straight away and there was no mistaking the delight and surprise in his smile. He made his way across the tavern, and nodded a brief greeting to Walter when he reached them. In spite of what Walter had just told her, her heart turned over at the sight of him – the sweep of his hair and the clear dark eyes that were wide now with the unexpected pleasure of her presence. He seemed to look right inside her, her soul bared before him, and in the roil of her feelings Walter's warning faded out of mind.

'Miss Winter.' He bowed, and she rose from her stool to curtsey before him. 'Well, this is a surprise.'

From the edge of her eye she saw Walter's scowl. He was hunched over the table now, gripping his cup of ale between both hands and staring into it as though he might divine the secrets of the world within its depths.

'It is an honour and pleasure to see you here. Truly.'

'You said I could find you here,' she said. She held Rafe's eyes with her own, and though her chin was tilted in challenge, he met it with a smile that left her defences in tatters.

'I did,' he agreed. 'Come, and you can tell me how I may be of service.'

Then he slid a glance to Walter. 'We have the Cockpit Theatre,' he murmured, and slid Walter a key.

Walter nodded but he did not look at Kate again, despite her pause to take her leave of him. When it was clear he would not raise his head to wish her farewell, she followed Rafe between the tables and up the wooden stairs towards a gallery beyond.

❧ 16 ❧

THE DARK BACKWARD AND ABYSM
OF TIME

'Westward ho!'

The watermen's shouts seemed to beckon as Mary retraced her steps to Bankside, and she stopped at the steps that led to the landing stage. The winter afternoon had given way to the dark and the chill bit hard, wind gusting off the river where the tide seemed to swirl and eddy. She took the stairs with care in the gloom and thought that she must be getting old. Once she would have pattered down without a second thought, sure-footed and heedless of the risk.

The boatman waited, watching, his face ghoulish in the shifting light of the lantern that swung on its pole in the stern. 'Westward?'

She shook her head. He waited, rubbing his hands together. It was an unforgiving time of year for the rivermen.

'Have you happened to see a fortune teller?' she asked. 'A palm reader? I was told the watermen would know.'

He stared as though uncertain whether to respond at all and she waited, half expecting he would simply row his boat away without another word. Then he said, 'Get in,' and she obeyed, taking his hand to steady herself as the boat swayed and rocked beneath her.

He was older than first she had thought, lines on a careworn face, and she thanked him as she took a seat on the wooden slat, arranging her skirts, cloak drawn tight around her against the cold. He started to row, upriver, straining hard against the tide, and she was aware of the lean strength of his body beneath the layers of clothes. She knew the type – wiry and strong but hungry – and, ashamed to find herself imagining him naked, she slid her gaze away to track the shoreline, torches flickering at doorways, shadows dancing.

He said, 'How well d'you know Bankside?'

'I used to know it well,' she said, without turning her head from the shore. 'But I've been away for many years.'

The boatman followed her gaze. 'You'll find it much changed.'

Mary turned her head to look at him again. 'There used to be theatres.'

'Aye, there did,' he agreed, with a sigh. 'But no more. 'Tis a pity.'

She nodded her agreement then turned to let her gaze wander again to the bank, trailing over the buildings that lined the water – houses, tenements, warehouses, shops, a tavern or two all clustered cheek-by-jowl, and the tide lapping at their heels. They would be damp inside and chilled by a cold that no fire could ever chase away. But even so, she thought she could live on the water and be happy. She had missed this river and, in spite of everything, it was good to be home.

The boatman steered towards Falcon Stairs and a small tremor of apprehension rippled through Mary's blood that she dismissed with a lift to her shoulders, a hardening of her jaw. The steps led to many places, she reminded herself, not just to there. They drew alongside, and the wherry shifted to and fro on the tide, unsteady as the boatman called out to a boy who was loitering in the hope of some task that might pay a penny or two. The boy ran down the steps and the boatman spoke to him in an undertone that Mary could not catch above the splash of the water against the steps.

'He'll take you.' The boatman reached out a hand to help her stand and she took it, grateful for his steadiness as she stepped onto land. She turned back and gave him the pennies she had been holding ready. He nodded his thanks.

'I thank you,' she said, with a smile. But he had already dropped back to his place, oars in hand, the wherry drawing quickly away from the steps. She watched it go for a moment, riding swiftly now with the tide, then turned to the boy who stood beside her. He looked up, expectantly. 'Shall we?' she said.

He turned without a word and she followed him away from the river through the maze of lanes that threaded between the shamble of buildings, and with each corner they turned, her heart tightened a little more in her chest, dread spreading through her limbs so that her feet felt heavy, each step hard to take. When they made the final turn she stopped and the boy, sensing she was no longer pacing one stride behind him, halted and turned back.

'It's that house there,' he said, pointing.

She swallowed and nodded. The street was as dark as she remembered, the buildings towering into the evening so that the ground was murky black. An old woman sat before a brazier that threw out a weak and pulsing light, and a single torch flared at a doorway. Mary passed her tongue across her lips. Her heartbeat was rapid, her mouth dry.

'It used to be an alehouse,' the boy said. 'My pa told me. It was called the Wounded Raven.'

'I remember,' she replied, and the words came out as no more than a whisper. The sorcerer's house. The place where she and Toby had killed a man. She shivered, though she was sweating beneath her cloak from the walk. The boy waited for his coin, watching her. She fumbled in the pouch she carried at her waist and the child's hand closed tight around the penny she gave him before he disappeared into the darkness, footsteps light and fading rapidly.

Voices carried to the street from behind the doors and windows of the houses – an argument flaring, a woman's shout and a man's low growl in response, threatening violence. In

another house, a child began to wail, and along the lane somewhere two cats were squaring up for a fight, yowls echoing off the
blackened walls.

Mary flicked a glance into the darkness. The woman at the
brazier watched her with mild curiosity. Mary drew in a deep
breath to harden her resolve, set her shoulders once more, and took
a step towards the house. Thin curtains fluttered at the filthy
windows and betrayed the flicker of candles that burned behind
them. Someone was home. She lifted her fist and knocked hard,
and when no one answered she knocked again, her knuckles loud
against the rotting timber. Her heart was thudding and all the
words she had been turning over in her mind to say when she
found the fortune teller at last failed to come to mind now.

She waited. Knocked again.

Finally, the door opened a fraction and a man's face appeared
in the crack. A recent scar shone vivid and red across one cheek,
and it was hard to look away from it.

'What do you want?'

'The fortune teller,' she replied. 'I was told she is here.'

The door opened wider and the man drew back to let her
through. She stepped inside and her gaze was drawn of its own
accord towards the wooden staircase just beyond his shoulder. She
knew where it led. The memory of the attic was vivid and unwelcome in her thoughts. Did the bloodstain still mark the floorboards or had the years scrubbed it clean? Dragging her eyes
downward to the room before her, she saw the old alehouse was
now the main chamber. A good fire burned in the hearth and the
room was cheerfully furnished with rugs and cushions, a table and
sideboard stacked with plates and mugs. But there was a chill in
the air nonetheless, a dark and cold the fire did nothing to dispel.

The servant gestured for her to enter and she stepped away
from the stairs and towards the fireplace.

'Sit,' he commanded, 'and I will fetch my mistress.'

Mary watched him disappear up the stairs and stood with her
back to the fire, enjoying the heat on her legs. She heard voices up

above, carrying through the walls and floorboards. Then two sets of footsteps, thudding on the stairs. She braced, and waited.

A woman emerged from the gloom. Slim-hipped and boyish, she was pale, with hooded, catlike eyes. She was almost beautiful, Mary thought, like an imperfect rendition of Kate's loveliness, but she carried some unseen taint that marred her beauty, some quality about her that Mary instinctively distrusted.

'Good evening,' the woman said.

'Good evening,' Mary answered. She was still uncertain of her course but she knew by instinct that honesty would get her nowhere – this woman was without either kindness or pity. 'I was told you read palms,' she said.

The woman tilted her head with a small smile of assent, and there was a moment of silence before she turned to the servant who had remained at her shoulder.

'Bring us wine, Nathan. Then leave us.'

The servant bowed, and the woman invited Mary to a stool at the fireside. She sat with reluctance: she felt safer on her feet, but she settled herself, adjusting her skirts with care and watching as the other woman drew another stool close. The fire was warm on her cheek – she could feel the redness rising. They waited for the servant to bring the wine and it seemed to take a long time. In a silence broken only by the crackle of the flames, Mary was aware of the knocking of her heart and the dryness of her throat.

Eventually the woman said, 'How did you hear of me?'

'A waterman,' she answered.

The woman nodded, apparently satisfied. Then Nathan returned at last with a jug and two cups. He poured and placed the jug to keep warm on the hearthstone before handing a cup to each of them.

'To good fortune,' the woman said, and drank. Mary watched for a moment, then sipped at her own. The warmth was welcome in her chest, and the taste was sweeter than her own recipe – some spice she did not recognise. But she felt no ill effects and so she took another mouthful before putting her cup down on the small table by the side of her stool. The fortune teller was studying her every movement, cat's eyes intent and watchful, and Mary was careful to keep her thoughts hidden. It was years since she had needed to practise such deception but old habits die hard, she thought, and the years of early training had served her well. She could still wear a mask as well as any.

'So,' the woman said finally. 'You wish me to read your palm.'

Mary nodded.

'And what is it that you want to know?'

Mary swallowed, uncertain. Then she said, 'I want to know if my future lies on England's shores or across the narrow sea.' The words came without premeditation, a true desire that surprised her. She had planned to ask about Kate.

'Give me your hand.' Drawing her stool closer, she opened Mary's offered palm: her right hand, the one with five fingers. The left remained curled and hidden on her lap. For the first time, the fortune teller's gaze left off its study of Mary's face, dropping instead to examine her hand as she ran her fingers lightly across the skin, tracing the lines. Her face was set still in concentration.

'Now give me the other,' she said, and Mary unfurled her left hand slowly, stretching it out with reluctance. She had never had her fortune read before and she was afraid of what six fingers would mean – as a child she had believed she belonged to the Devil.

A tension fell as the fortune teller took Mary's disfigured hand, a silence that hung heavy in the room. Beside them the fire popped and roared, the heat burning fierce against Mary's cheek. She waited, barely daring to breathe, until finally the woman raised her eyes. Mary met the gaze with determination, fears forced beneath the surface, hidden. But the other woman was adept at deception also and Mary could not read what she saw there beyond the flicker of a new hostility.

'Your future,' she said at last, 'is hard to determine. There is darkness in your past and it haunts you still.'

Mary braced against the memory of the place, images tumbling in her thoughts – the sorcerer, Toby, the ritual, and the cold hand of death that reached out and held her briefly in its grasp. It was so long since she had allowed herself to think of it and the memories surged now from the buried recesses of her mind.

Kate, she thought. What was Kate's part in all of this?

'My daughter,' she heard herself say, and the fortune teller drew in a quick and almost imperceptible breath.

'What of your daughter?'

'She met you in The Hague. At the Binnenhof.'

The fortune teller raised her head at that and Mary was uncomfortably aware of her hands on her lap, still in the other woman's grasp, sweating. She should have said nothing, she realised too late, and kept her cards closer to her chest. They held each other's eyes for a long, long moment, until the fortune teller dropped her gaze away with the touch of a smile at the edges of her mouth.

'I know nothing of your daughter,' she said.

Mary ran her tongue across her lips. Perhaps she was mistaken after all and this was not the woman she sought. What proof did she have? But they were seated now before the hearth at the Wounded Raven, the sorcerer's shadow cast long, and knew that she was right.

'You lie,' Mary said, rising to her feet in a swift movement that brushed the fortune teller's hands from her lap.

The woman smiled and gestured around the room with an upturned hand. 'See for yourself,' she invited. 'You'll not find her here.'

'Where is she?'

The fortune teller got up from her stool and said nothing. But she reached a hand to Mary's arm and gently drew a loose hair from where it had caught on the sleeve. Mary's eyes followed the movement and though a warning bell tolled inside her she said nothing, her thoughts still searching for her daughter.

'I will find her,' Mary said. 'And if she has come to harm ...'

The woman tilted her head, waiting for the end of the sentence.

'... if she has come to harm at your doing, I promise you, you will pay.' It was not a threat she made lightly – she had killed before, fighting for her life and for Toby's, and she wouldn't hesitate to kill again to protect her daughter if it ever came to that.

The fortune teller must have read the truth in Mary's words, because she turned away and squatted to the fire, poking at the logs though it was already drawing well. Mary allowed herself a small smile of victory.

'I wish you well in your search for her,' the woman said. 'But I think we are finished here.' She looked up and got once more to her feet, smoothing out the front of her skirts with elegant fingers. 'Unless you still wish me to read the fate in your palms?'

Instinctively Mary clasped her hands together before her. But she hesitated nonetheless, half tempted by the offer. For who amongst us does not desire to know our fate? Then, remembering the woman had already lied to her face, she shook her head. 'I will discover my own fortune,' she said.

'As you wish.' The woman dipped her head in a cursory nod of farewell and turned once more to regard the fire.

Mary waited another heartbeat more, watching, before she swung away. Then, at the door, she looked back.

'What name do they call you?'

'Isabella Last,' the woman said. 'And you, they call Mary Sparrow, do they not?'

'My name is Mary Winter,' she answered, setting her face again, pulses quickening. How could she know?

She swung away and yanked open the door and though the air in the lane outside was rank with the stench of poverty and want, she gulped it greedily. The woman at the brazier cast an idle eye in her direction before returning to the wool in her hands. Mary drew her cloak close around her against the evening's chill and, the way still familiar even after all these years, set her footsteps back along the lane towards the tavern at the Cardinal's Cap.

17

THIS THING OF DARKNESS I
ACKNOWLEDGE MINE

Kate took her leave of Walter with reluctance. How could she have been so stupid? How could she have been so blind? But even after his warning, a small part of her kept up hope as she followed Rafe Tyndall along the corridor towards his quarters. She could feel the desire for him rising in her gut, warm and treacherous. Briefly, she cast a look back towards the head of the stairs, towards Walter. He had been kind, she thought, and she had been in sore need of kindness.

At the end of the corridor Rafe unlocked the door and she followed him into a large and richly furnished sitting room. Velvet upholstered chairs were scattered in no apparent order across thick Turkey rugs, and paintings on the walls hung in heavy gilt frames. But in spite of the opulence, the light was dim and a stale taint coloured the air, as if the windows had been closed for too long. He turned to face her.

'Please, take a seat. Wine?'

She shook her head. She was still woozy from the ale on an empty belly and she needed her wits about her. Did Walter have the right of it? Did Rafe intend to set her to work in the brothel? Looking at the man before her now it was hard to believe he was the owner of a bawdy house, with his sad dark eyes and fine chiselled features. In her imagination, brothel-keepers were rough and greedy, men of violence; he hardly seemed to fit the mould. Taking a chair beside the unlit fire, she shivered and drew her cloak more tightly around her. Rafe poured wine for himself and settled in the chair across the hearth from her.

'Your good health.' He lifted his glass in toast once again.

'And yours,' she replied, with a tilt of her head.

He took a mouthful of his drink and they regarded each other across the expanse of the fireplace. It was Rafe that broke the silence.

'What brings you to the Bull's Head, Miss Winter? It is a surprise to see you here so soon. How may I be of service?'

She hesitated, aware she was at his mercy, and she struggled to find the perfect words to explain her plight.

'I find myself in a difficult situation,' she began, and he nodded, encouraging, the smile in his eyes that could undo her in a moment. The familiar heat lit in her belly once more, even as she tried to tamp it down. How could he still conjure such a response when she knew him for what he was? Some kind of sorcery, perhaps? Her thoughts flitted to Isabella, sensing a compelling darkness in them both.

'I travelled to London with a companion but she was not all I thought her to be, and now I find myself quite alone.'

'So how may I be of help?' He raised a questioning eyebrow.

'I need somewhere to lodge,' she answered, with all the dignity she could muster. It was hard to keep the tears from her eyes and the tremble from her voice. 'And work. You have seen my skill with a needle – I thought perhaps you could help me find work as a seamstress.' She looked up at him and trailed off with a sniff, tears threatening to fall. She clamped her jaw against the emotion and wiped at her eyes.

'You have no need to fear me, Miss Winter,' he said, gently. 'I don't know what Walter led you to believe but I am no monster.'

She was silent, not trusting herself to speak.

'Did he tell you I would set you to work in the brothel? Is that what he said?'

She nodded, and when the tears welled this time she could do nothing to prevent them.

He shook his head with a wry smile. 'There is something of the Puritan in Walter,' he murmured. 'A chaste streak that disapproves of the brothel and my interest in the trade.'

She looked up at him then and wiped at her tears once again with her fingers, hope kindling and a question in her eyes. Her voice was still too hard to find.

'I have never yet forced a girl to work against her will, and I never shall,' he said. 'Though I have little enough to offer you, I will aid you as best I can.'

His kindness unravelled her, and she began to sob in earnest. All she had been through, and it was Rafe Tyndall's kindness that had brought her to tears. She shook her head against the tumult of emotion but it did no good, and she was aware of Rafe in the chair just across the hearth from her, watching with concern in his eyes. After a moment, he got up and fetched her a glass of wine that she took with a trembling hand. Then he crouched before her and squeezed her other hand with his, looking up into her face.

'Tell me about this companion who abandoned you,' he said.

She took a mouthful of her wine, and though her breathing was still ragged and uneven, when she tried to speak at last she found her voice had come back to her.

'I was such a fool,' she said. 'This fortune teller offered me the world, and like an idiot I believed her.'

'The fortune teller from The Hague?' His voice was low and there was an edge to it she had not heard before. Her skin prickled in warning. 'Isabella Last?'

'Yes. Do you know her?'

'Our paths have crossed,' he offered, with a tilt of his head that suggested there was far more to tell. 'What did she offer you?' It was more than a casual question, his eyes intent on hers, and fear crawled through her once again.

Kate hesitated. He would think her insane if she told him the truth, that she had fled her home and her family on the promise of discovering her witchblood. In those words it sounded like the delusion of a madwoman even to her own ears. But he was waiting for her answer, her fingers still held tightly in his, and when she raised her eyes to meet his, she knew she would end up telling him all of it, an invitation in his look that was impossible to resist. Taking another mouthful of wine, she tried to settle her breathing, and Rafe lifted a hand to wipe away a tear that had lingered on her cheek. For a heartbeat, she thought that he would kiss her. His touch was delicious and her breath caught again, but this time it owed nothing to her weeping.

'Tell me,' he urged. 'I will not judge you.'

'It will sound like the fantasy of a disordered brain,' she murmured, shaking her head.

'No matter.' He smiled and ran the backs of his fingers across her cheek. She inclined her head to meet the touch and took a deep breath. She was just about to begin her tale when there was a knock at the door.

He rolled his eyes and gave her a rueful smile that made her laugh. 'The actors are at hand,' he said, 'Stay, and we can talk later. You are most welcome.'

He got up then and as he went to the door, she turned in her seat to watch the actors arrive. An assorted group of men spilled through, lively in conversation, and one of them was Walter. They exchanged a small smile. The others settled on the seats that were clustered around the hearth, and Rafe looked to her.

'Could I trouble you to go to the kitchen,' he asked, 'and fetch us wine and meat? The girls will know what to get. And get someone to come and light the damn fire. It's cold enough in here to freeze the Devil's balls.'

One of the other men laughed, and Kate hurried to do as he had asked. On the stairs she paused to let one of the girls go past, leading an old man by the hand, and the girl raised her eyebrows in greeting. Kate gave a small smile in reply then slid her eyes away.

Would she soon be doing the same? Taking unknown men to bed, her body no longer her own? Or was Rafe telling the truth when he promised to help her? She knew his own interest in her was unfeigned – she had felt the spark of desire that passed between them in The Hague. But she was learning that people were not always what they seemed; in spite of his claims, Rafe Tyndall was a brothel-keeper on Bankside, and working girls were his business.

By the time she returned from the kitchen with a tray that was laden with cold meats and bread, cheese and radishes, the fire was already burning and the room was cheerful in its light. There was much laughter between the men and when she poured wine for them all, they paused in their conversation to raise a toast.

'The King's Men,' one of them said, and she flicked a glance to Walter, who lifted his glass with the others. 'Long may they play.'

Then, 'Thoughts, gentlemen, on our choice of play?'

She set the plates on the sideboard then stepped away to settle herself on a stool at the edge of the circle of men. She sipped at her wine and its warmth in her blood was comforting.

'Walter here wants to do the Scottish play. Dealing as it does with the death of a rightful king.'

There was a rumble of dissent. One of the men said, 'Times are hard enough without inviting misfortune.'

Kate flicked a curious glance to Rafe, who turned to her with a nod and a smile as if he had felt the weight of her look, before he spoke to the player again.

'You played in the first production, did you not, Master Lowin?' he said.

Lowin nodded. ''Tis a cursed play,' he said. 'I swear Master Shakespeare woke something evil that very first time, and always I dread the worst when we play it.'

'Tell us the story of the curse again,' Rafe said, and Kate was glad – she wanted to hear it too.

Lowin looked around the table, as though undecided whether or not to recount the tale. Then he sighed, took a draught of his wine and refilled it from the jug. Finally, he began.

'Will – Master Shakespeare – was warned not to play it. The seamstress, Sarah, foresaw ill-fortune, but Will wouldn't listen. 'Tis a good play, after all, and he was proud of it. So we began to learn it. But accidents happened. Burbage broke his arm, and the youth who was to have played the lady began to lose his mind.'

'How so?'

'Sarah's cousin seduced him.' He smiled to himself, remembering. 'Ah, Tom Wynter – he could have lured the Virgin Mary herself into bed. Such charm and beauty in a man I never saw before nor since.'

Kate held her breath and her insides felt as though they had turned to water.

'But the youth,' Lowin continued, 'was wracked with guilt and said it was the doing of witches, that Sarah and Tom had used witchcraft against him. It fell out badly for the two of them in the end – Sarah was accused and tried, and to save her, Tom took the blame.'

Kate's heart seemed to stop in her chest and the room began to swim around her, the edges darkening so that she had to brace herself to stay upright. Her thoughts tumbled over one another with this new knowledge, impossible to pin down.

Tom.

She called out to him in her mind and felt his answer as a growing certainty.

'There were rumours too that Tom had bedded his cousin. Certainly they were close and the times were different then ... it would not surprise me.'

'What happened to them?' Kate heard herself asking in the pause that followed.

Lowin turned to her in surprise, as though he had forgotten she was there.

'Tom Wynter was hanged as a witch,' he said. 'And his cousin married her father's apprentice. There was a child, I believe, that might have been Tom's, but Sarah stayed away from the playhouse after that and I never saw her again.'

'It's a sad story,' someone said.

'It is indeed,' Lowin agreed. 'And that's why we are not playing Macbeth.'

There was a ripple of agreement around the table. Only Walter mumbled in dissent and Kate understood his disappointment – she too wanted to know this play that had wrought her grandfather's death. An image of the pauper's graveyard nudged at her thoughts – the grave next to Tom's. Sarah Chyrche, his cousin. His lover also? She curled her mind around it, searching for answers, feeling her way towards the truth. Had her father been the child that Lowin mentioned? It seemed a possibility.

Rafe turned to her again. 'Are you all right?'

She must be wearing her emotions too plainly on her face, she thought, forcing her lips into a smile. She nodded, but her limbs still felt like liquid. It had seemed no more than a tale told by a fireside till now, a story of long ago, despite the connection she had felt and the ritual she had done. But Tom had swung from a rope for his witchcraft, and her own sudden fear of dying the same way seemed to pulse now through her blood. She slid her eyes away from Rafe's gaze. However much she liked him and needed his help, she had not yet learned to trust him.

As the silence lengthened, Rafe's attention shifted once more to the players. They began to talk again of their choice of play. *The Tempest*, she thought she heard them say, but she was no longer listening, her thoughts turning instead on the hanging of Tom Wynter – the story John Lowin had told. She refilled her cup and sipped at it. She was unused to drinking more than a little and her head began to grow light, the edges of the world becoming softer. So this was how it felt to be drunk, she thought, and she liked it.

She half listened to the men's talk, plays and parts and plans, until the hour grew late and the men slowly drifted out into the dark with a promise to meet again the night after next to begin their rehearsals. Walter was one of the last to leave and though she saw the glimmer of regret in the nod of farewell he gave her, she paid it little mind. When only she and Rafe were left, she waited, breath quickening, uncertain. He turned towards her, giving her the privilege of his full attention, and the room was bright in the light of it. She felt exposed beneath his gaze, as though he could see right through her to all the secrets she was holding inside. It was hard to keep her eyes on his, and she saw herself as she supposed that he must see her – a foolhardy girl who had run away from home and thrown herself on the mercy of the first man she found to help her.

They were standing close before the fireplace, the embers pulsing low, and the room was warm. Kate could feel the sweat in the hollow of her back. Voices, thick with drink, skirled in snatches from the tavern below, and now and then footsteps sounded in the passage beyond the door. Rafe was watching her with a look in his eyes she could not meet, uncertain what it was she saw there. She recalled the touch of his fingers against her cheek, and the almost-kiss, and even as she took another mouthful of wine, she cursed herself for not keeping a clearer head.

He reached a hand towards her and she took a step to stand nearer beside him. Her head spun with the movement, and she grasped at his fingers until the dizziness lessened.

'Forgive me,' she whispered. 'I am unused to so much wine.'

'There is nothing to forgive,' he replied.

He was very near to her now, her skirts brushing against his legs, and his face was close enough for her to kiss if she simply chose to lift her head. She was aware of his warmth and hardness, the naked man beneath the clothes and the blood that beat inside him. Her breath lifted in her chest, want for him suffusing her. The familiar taint of mistrust flickered through her insides, but she no longer cared if she should trust him or not: desire overrode all else.

Slowly, she raised her head to look at him. Rafe's fingers tightened in hers and the moment hung, their lips no more than a whisker apart, until finally he lowered his mouth to hers and kissed her. All her senses were filled with his touch, overwhelming, so that she felt as though she were drowning, no more air to breathe.

She would do anything at all that he asked of her, she realised, and the prick of fear from that knowledge only served to fuel her desire. His lips swept across her neck as he drew her into his embrace, and with one hand he pulled at the laces of her bodice. Her legs threatened to fold beneath her.

Did he suspect she was still a maid? Did he care? For all the men she had flirted with in the taverns in The Hague, she had never let one get between her legs, aware that a woman's virtue in this world was her most valuable possession. But here, on Bankside, she was untrammelled. She was alone, adrift amongst strangers. Who was there to judge her? No one would either know or care if she was a maid, and she had no strength to resist. She would give him her virginity and willingly, for she had come to learn that life was short and full of risk, and this chance might not come again.

Rafe's fingers found their way beneath the loosened bodice to caress her breast, and her own hands moved eagerly to drag at the buckle of his breeches. His breath stopped as her fingers found the warmth of within and began to stroke it.

'Slowly,' he murmured, and her hand halted in its movement, uncertain now. Should she admit to her innocence? A part of her longed to warn him so that he might lead her more gently into knowledge, but he was a man who was used to whores; would he even want her if he knew the truth of things? She suspected not, and so she kept her silence. 'But please, don't stop ...' he said. Then he smiled at her and she laughed, finding her confidence again, his cock warm and hard against her fingers.

Rafe let out a sigh of pleasure and they stood for a moment, face to face, and though her bodice gaped open and his cock brushed against her skirts, she felt no shame at all in front of him. How could it be a sin to give this man her body?

'Do you trust me, Kate Winter?' he asked, rubbing the tip of his thumb across her lower lip.

'I want you,' she answered, and that much was true.

He laughed. 'Then you shall have me.' She held her breath as he stripped her bodice away from her shoulders and arms, and untied her skirts so that they fell in a pool at her feet. She stepped out of them, and he lifted her shift over her head. Standing before him in only her stockings, she shivered, in spite of the warmth of the fire. Did he like what he saw? She hoped so. Briefly, she caught his look, and when she saw the hunger in his eyes she knew the answer.

But still, old habits of modesty made it hard to resist the urge to cover herself before the appraisal of his gaze.

He stepped closer once again and ran his fingertips across her skin – her shoulders, her breasts, her belly and hips, her thighs and the soft triangle that lay between them, admiring. Her back arched in response to his touch, skin burning with sensation, her belly on fire. Then he lifted her, his hands tightly gripping her hips, and lowered her onto him. A burning pain sliced through her and she cried out, but he held her firm and as he began to thrust inside her, the hurt curled and spiralled into an unfamiliar pleasure. She had never suspected such conflicting impulses could feed on each other and excite the senses so exquisitely; in spite of the pain she had no desire for him to stop, and she held him tightly, pressing hard against his back with her legs to draw him deeper into her, as if they could become one being if he could only go deep enough.

Too soon, he finished with a shudder and a small cry, and buried his face in her neck as he lowered her slowly to the ground. Her legs were unsteady when they first took her weight, and she leaned herself against him for support. Then, without a word, he took her hand and led her through to the bedroom.

Later, Rafe lay on his side and let his fingertips trail across the perfect skin of her back and shoulders. She really was very beautiful, he thought, and in spite of the instinctive desire her beauty had aroused in him, he realised he liked her more than for the possibility of an idle fuck, their union containing the promise of something even sweeter yet to come. He saw in her a trace of himself as he was in his youth – reckless, with a hunger for life she could never satisfy.

Her eyes were closed now, and for the first time she was peaceful in his presence, though he knew he had yet to fully earn her trust. Ah, who could blame her? He was the keeper of a bawdy house, after all, and she was a penniless girl who had run away from home with a fortune teller. And until tonight she had been a maid, although he hadn't realised until the blood was already on her thigh. Strange that she had chosen not to tell him. Had she thought he would turn her out of his bed if he had known? He allowed himself a small smile. Perhaps he would have at that – he was not the scoundrel that Walter had painted him; he was just a man fallen on hard times, doing his best to make a living. But he was glad he had not been faced with the decision – it was no small thing to take a woman's virtue in a world where her value depended on it.

Lying back, he let his mind wander over all he knew of Isabella Last. The fortune teller had haunted the English exiles in Calais and The Hague for as long as he could remember, inhabiting the edges of society and searching for he knew not what. Once, spurred by boredom and wine, and against his better judgement, he had let her read his palm. He had known it was a mistake as soon as her fingers touched his skin, her spirit reaching into his to search for hidden truths, forging a dark connection. He had been naked and exposed before her with nowhere at all to hide, and he had snatched his hand away before she even uttered a word. Afterwards, he had met the disdain in her gaze with false bravado when she pronounced he had a blighted soul and that his wife had known it, before he stumbled away, bruised and in pain. How could a person read another so easily? Reach inside and touch their deepest core? That she was dangerous, he doubted not for a second: her offer to Kate must surely have concealed a darker purpose. But what could she possibly want from an exiled seamstress from The Hague?

Turning his head on the pillow, he saw that Kate's eyes had opened, and she was watching him, eyes alert and wary once more. He let his face soften into a smile. One day, he hoped he might see trust in that gaze. Trust, and perhaps even love, though he was reluctant to admit it. After all, he barely knew her. But even so, she had touched a note in him that had not been played for far too long. Perhaps the time for grief was over.

'What did the fortune teller promise you?' he asked again.

Her whole body tensed and her breathing quickened. She gave a small shake of her head. 'It doesn't matter.'

'She must have brought you here for a purpose. What reason could she have?'

'I don't know,' she said too quickly, and though she barely moved, he felt her withdraw from him, and the intimacy between them receded into the dark.

Sorry for the change, he turned again on his side to face her and propped himself on an elbow. Her eyes, almost black in the candlelight, tracked his movements, untrusting.

'Perhaps I can help,' he offered.

With a sigh she lowered her eyes away. He touched his hand to her shoulder, the skin smooth and cool beneath his fingertips.

'Tell me,' he coaxed.

'I ...' she began, and licked her bottom lip with the tip of her tongue. In spite of his desire to know what she had to tell him, her lips were very tempting and he had to quell an urge to kiss them again. 'I am Tom Wynter's grandchild,' she whispered, 'and I am connected in some way I do not yet know to the fortune teller's father.'

For three breaths he said nothing, startled by the confession of her heritage. How strange that they had talked of Tom Wynter only that night, though the actors had known only part of the story. For there were other rumours that surrounded Wynter's death, beyond the accusations of witchcraft and seduction, beyond the fact of his sacrifice. As a student at Oxford, he had heard the scholars and alchemists whisper that Wynter had conjured with the aid of a book that was coveted above all others. A book of great power, the rumours said, imbued with the magic of ages, and missing for almost two generations. Was it for the book that the fortune teller had brought Kate Winter here? For her link to Tom Wynter? Perhaps.

'Tell me what you know,' he said.

She was silent, and he thought she would tell him nothing more until abruptly she sat up and drew the quilts tightly around her, hugging her knees close to her chest. He waited, watching as she seemed to straighten out the story in her head: had she decided to trust him after all? He hoped so. If Isabella Last wanted something from her she was in danger, and it was better she shouldn't face it alone.

Finally, finally, she began to speak, and he listened as she poured out her story in fits and starts and circumlocutions – meeting the fortune teller at the palace in The Hague and her mother's evasions, the connection to Tom Wynter at the graveyard, Isabella's attic, and the servant, Nathan, who had tried to rape her. He listened to all of it, without comment, without questions, but when she had finished he knew there was far more she had not yet told him.

'Did Isabella speak of a book?' he asked.

She considered for a moment. 'No,' she replied. 'But I did overhear that I have something she wants, something whose power I don't yet know.' She looked up at him once more and the dreaminess that had coloured her eyes as she told her story had given way to the more familiar flicker of wariness and challenge. 'What book?'

Should he tell her? Did she have a right to know? For the length of a breath he hesitated, surprising himself by his unwillingness to give up the secret. But she was connected to it by blood and inheritance and her life was now at risk because of it.

'A book of magic,' he said, at last. 'A book of spells and rituals from all parts of the world that men have killed and died for.'

He paused. She was watching him now with an intensity he found almost disturbing.

'It's different from other books of its kind – it has a magic of its own. The very pages are redolent with the power of the men who wrote on them, and it's said that in the hands of its master, it hums.'

And it was reputed to contain rituals for summoning demons through the power of sex, he thought, but did not say so.

'She thinks I have it?' Kate frowned, bewildered.

'Tom Wynter owned it once.' He shrugged. 'Some say that the spirits he conjured from it brought about his death.'

'He died to save his cousin.' Her defence of Tom was instant. 'To save her from the gallows.'

Rafe nodded in agreement. 'Aye, he did. But perhaps what came before was not so simple.'

She thought about this for a moment before tilting her head as if in acknowledgement of the possibility. Then she turned to him and he saw the familiar challenge in her eyes that he was beginning to love so well. He waited.

'How do you know so much about it?'

He gave her an equivocal smile. 'I have studied a little magic myself ...' He trailed off with a shrug and hoped she would accept it, half-truth though it was.

She said nothing but he knew it would not be the end of the conversation. She was too bright, too curious, and though he longed to protect her from knowledge that could only put her in more danger, he guessed he would end up telling her all of it. As he had with Ellen, he thought, whose face was becoming harder to recall with the passing years since her death. He tried to summon her image before him now – the shrewd pale eyes that disappeared when she laughed and the rosebud perfect mouth; for a fleeting moment he recalled her with startling perfect clarity. She had never been as beautiful as Kate, for sure. Not on the outside. But she had possessed an inner light for Rafe that through their years together had chased all of his darkness away, and he missed her still.

When he raised his eyes to look at Kate again, she was watching him with a frown of question in her eyes.

'What were you thinking of? You were miles away.'

'I was thinking about my wife,' he said, because he could think of no good reason to hide it from her. 'She died in the war. She and our son.' For once he wanted to be honest so that they might begin to build a trust between them.

'Did you love her?' Kate asked, and he smiled then, pleased that she should care.

'Yes,' he replied, 'very much.'

They were silent a while, both alone with their thoughts, until she turned to him again and lay her body close to his, her legs across his, her breasts against his ribs. Then she trailed her fingertips across his chest and belly and groin until they came to rest at his cock, teasing lightly. She was learning fast, he thought, and a moment later he had rolled his body over hers and was kissing her again.

When he was sure that she was sleeping, her body pressed soft against him in the bed, Rafe forced himself out of the comfort of the quilts, shrugged on his robe and padded barefoot from the room. The last embers of the fire were still pulsing in the hearth and the main chamber was warm as he dipped a candle into the glow to light it. Once it was lit and the flame began to flicker bravely in the dark, he left the warmth with a slight sigh of regret and went out into the chill of the passage.

The place was quiet. The last customers had left and the girls were sleeping now alone in their beds. Fingering the key in his palm, he made for the little door at the far end of the gallery. Then, with another glance behind him to make sure no one was watching, he slipped the key into the lock, turned the handle, and stepped through the opening. Another door, concealed within, opened on a narrow flight of steps that led upwards.

Locking the door behind him, he climbed the stairs on silent feet. His shadow bobbed alongside him in the light of the candle, then stretched across the floor of the attic, misshapen and monstrous, until he lit more candles and the room began to glow golden in their light, shadows flickering gently against the sloping roofs as he ducked beneath them.

He sighed with pleasure. He loved this room and he had been away from it for far too long – it was his sanctuary, and when he had discovered it by chance after the brothel had come to him in a game of chance, he had raised a prayer of thanks to whatever gods or spirits watched over him. It was almost perfectly hidden and, though he knew its discovery could take him to the gallows, he could think of no place safer for his work.

He let his thoughts wander back to Kate, asleep now and at peace, and wondered what strange impulse had prompted him to offer her his protection in The Hague. Some strange intuition? A glimpse of what was to come? He had never been gifted to see the future before; even his dreams were of the past, nightmares of loss and blood and war, and his helplessness in the face of it.

When they parted in The Hague, he had doubted their paths would ever cross again. She was just one more seamstress that served the royal household, existing for the Court only in the clothes her hands could make, invisible.

But now she was sleeping in his bed on Bankside, and he was half in love with her already. Did she feel the same? He hoped so. For a moment his task was forgotten, images of Kate rippling through his mind – her laugh, her spirit, the challenge in her look that delighted him. The softness of her body wrapped against his. The close, slippery welcome of her maidenhead. For all the women he had bedded in his life, only Ellen had ever touched him inside the same way as Kate. Was it love? Perhaps. He realised he was smiling to himself and if he had had a place to walk to, there would have been a new and welcome spring in his step.

With an effort of will he set aside the warm pleasure of his thoughts and turned his mind towards the task ahead of him. He needed to know his part in Tom Wynter's story, to know his connection to Kate and the fabled book of magic. He had no doubt that he had a part to play, but he had yet to discover his role. And he was eager to find out, aware of the power of their enemy and the quick march of time against them. Quickly now, impatient to begin, he started to gather up all the things that he needed.

Within a few minutes, he was inside the chalked circle that took up half the attic floor. In the centre the polished steel mirror stood propped on a stand that he had fashioned from a branch of yew. It had been a gift from his wife as a talisman for protection when he went away to war, and during the long months apart from her he had found some solace in the work, whittling the small piece of timber into the likeness of a dagger. A perfect stand for the mirror, it had stayed with him all through the years of conflict, and though he was half tempted to ascribe his survival purely to good fortune, a part of him held to the protection offered by the little branch of yew. Pity was, Ellen hadn't kept it for herself and the boy. In the end, their need for it had been greater than his own.

Now, he placed a candle at each of the cardinal points and three more to stand sentinel around the mirror before he traced the line of the circle's edge and began to murmur the words of protection.

'Gabriel, archangel and guardian of the West, may your blessings descend in the name of EL.'

To the North.

'Auriel, archangel and guardian of the North, may your blessings descend in the name of ADONAI.'

To the East.

'Raphael, archangel and guardian of the East, may your blessings descend in the name of Alpha et O.'

To the South.

'Michael, archangel and guardian of the South, may your blessings descend in the name of Emmanuel.

I beseech Thee, O Lord God, that Thou will deign to bless this

Circle, and all those who are therein to preserve us from evil and from trouble: grant, O Lord, that we may rest in this place in safety through Thee, O Lord, who livest and reignest unto the Ages of the Ages. Amen.'

The words, though softly uttered, seemed loud in the silent room, and when he was finished a deeper quietness seemed to descend. Closing his eyes, he bowed his head, waiting for his breathing to settle and his heartbeat to slow. He had attempted this ritual only once before, many years ago, but the time had not been right and the place not secret enough, so it had been impossible to focus his thoughts entirely as his teachers had taught him during those long nights of study in Oxford. But he refused to let the memory of that failure disturb him tonight. He needed to understand the connections and his place in the story unfolding now on Bankside: Tom Wynter's story, still revealing itself, as his spirit refused to go to its rest.

Rafe knelt before the mirror and tied his thoughts to his breath. Slowly, he became aware of the hum of night-time Bankside beyond the attic walls – the close press of humanity, the thud and splash of traffic on the river, and now and then a man's voice, raised and drifting on the breeze. He exhaled a long deep breath and it came out as a sigh. Letting his thoughts soften and meld with all that was around him, his heartbeat began at last to slow and his breathing gentled. Then, when his mind had finally quieted, he opened his eyes again and gazed into the mirror.

The conjuration he had learned was very strange, a form of Latin he had never studied, but he had memorised the words by heart, and now he spoke them three times out loud as the ritual demanded.

'Iclis, piclis, ticlis moves baruch cortex garyn ruent hismuie haruel fuganes furtym fermal farus cornalis bosuo zelades pasapa phirpa tirph. You who are God, Alpha and O, make this mirror grow until it is sufficient for my sight.'

He waited, focusing his gaze on the polished steel surface as it seemed to glow and waver before his eyes, deepening, inviting him in.

'*By God, and by the three children, Sydrac, Mysaach, and Abde-nago, and by the three magi, Caspar, Balthasar, and Melchior, and by the three patriarchs, Abraham, Isaac, and Jacob, I ask of you for understanding...*'

He waited, barely breathing, shoving aside the doubts that threatened to crowd his thoughts. Nothing. He closed his eyes, just for a moment, and sensed the movement of the air in his chest, the soft rise and fall of the muscles. When he opened them again and stared once more into the mirror, the depths of it began to fill with swirling billows of cloud. He watched, straining to make sense of them, to discover images or thoughts or words within the fumes. Then, very slowly, the smoke began to disperse, thinning and fading to form the image of a young man, tall and handsome, with sad eyes that spoke of realms known only to the dead.

'*What do you wish to know?*'

The man's voice seemed to echo in his head, as clear as if he were standing right beside him now in the attic, and Rafe was abruptly aware of his own body as a corporeal, mortal being. He could feel the flow of the blood as it passed through his veins, each beat of his heart, the air that rose and fell in his lungs, and though he had prepared the questions in his mind before he started, now that he was actually faced with a spirit, words failed to come. He searched his thoughts, desperate, afraid to anger this being he had summoned.

'I ... wish to know,' he finally managed to stammer, and his voice sounded loud in the silence, 'my part in the story of Tom Wynter's book.' It was not what he had planned to say but when the answer came he knew he had asked aright.

The voice said, '*The book's sojourn with the Wynters is almost done, and it grows impatient to find a new master.*'

'And Isabella Last?'

'*The book left her family's possession long ago and it has no desire to return. Find the book and your part will become clear to you.'*

'Where is it? Can you tell me that?'

'*The widow has the key.*'

Then, without warning, the figure receded back into the smoke and Rafe lifted his fingers to the mirror, reaching, as if he might call the spirit back with his touch. But when his fingertips brushed against the cold polished surface all they found was hard steel that glinted now in the candlelight and held no trace of the depths within.

18

'TIS IN MY MEMORY LOCK'D

In the half-dark lane outside the Wounded Raven, Mary crossed to join the old woman carding wool at a low-burning brazier. Warmer outside, the woman told her, than the dampness within the house. Mary smiled and held her hands out to the fire. The day was drawing in and night was on its way, though it was but halfway through the afternoon. It had taken all her willpower to make herself return.

'I've seen you before,' the woman said. 'Years ago you came here, when the place was still an alehouse and the old doctor had the room upstairs.'

'You have a good memory,' Mary replied. 'I came only twice.'

'I see everything,' the woman said, 'though my eyes are not what they were. I've spent my whole life in this lane.'

Mary tried not to think of the want and squalor a life lived here would entail – her own poor beginnings seemed plentiful in comparison.

'What can you tell me of the woman who lives there now?'

The woman coughed, hacking up a gob of brown spittle that she hawked into the brazier where it sizzled, and when she spoke again her voice was rough.

'A widow. A gentlewoman with a single manservant. Fallen on

hard times, I would say, her family's fortune lost in the war. 'Tis no place for gentlefolk, here. But then again ...' She stopped and coughed again.

'But then again?' Mary prompted, when the silence grew long.

'She wasn't born to money. I see behind the mask and I would say she's in her rightful place.' The old woman spat again, this time to the ground, and Mary cast her eyes across the front of the building, considering.

Then she said, 'Has there been a young girl here these last few days?'

For the first time the old woman lifted her face, and Mary saw the grime that was etched in the lines, the red and haggard eyes. Had she once hoped for more than the fates had dealt her? Did she still?

'Aye, there has.'

'Do you know where I might find her?'

The woman lowered her eyes to the wool in her hands, absently straightening the lengths.

'She's been gone the last couple of days. Run away is my guess, and for that I wouldn't blame her. It's a cursèd place.'

Mary's heart turned in her chest. 'May I ask of you one more thing?' she said.

The woman nodded.

'If anything changes, or if the girl returns, can you get word to me at the Cardinal's Cap? There will be a sixpence both for you and the child who brings the message.'

'Of course,' the woman answered. 'But she has flown and I doubt I'll see her again. Pity. 'Tis rare for me to look on such beauty.'

'I thank you warmly for your time, and I bid you good day.' Mary dipped her head and her boots crunched in the dirt that covered the lane as she walked away, her skirts lifted clear with one hand. She had come too late, and now she must begin her search again.

She went back to the Cardinal's Cap; though it was officially a tavern now, to her mind it remained a brothel. The roar of voices drifted out to her on the quayside – the long winter nights had always been good for business – and when she ducked through the low door, the wall of sound and heat enveloped her. She stepped into it and from old habit cast her gaze across the drinkers, but seeing no one she recognised, she loosened the cloak at her neck and wove easily between the tables towards the room she shared with Rosalind at the back.

'Mistress Johnson.'

From within the cacophony she heard the name she had given Rafe Tyndall at the quay in The Hague. A chill rippled along her spine – she had not thought ever to see him again. What did he want with her now? With a shiver of unease, she recalled his questions about Toby's book.

'Mary.'

She set her face into a smile, then stopped and turned towards the voice that had spoken. Rafe was seated alone at a table that stood almost under the stairs. How had she not noticed him before? He was smiling towards her, an invitation in his eyes, and though all she wanted was to be alone with her thoughts, she found herself settling onto the stool beside him while he called out for more ale to the harassed boy who was serving.

'Your things arrived?'

She nodded. He had sent on her bag as he had promised and she was grateful, but she wished she had not had to tell him the place where she was lodging. For all that she enjoyed his company there was something about him she did not quite trust, a latent darkness she feared to rouse. She breathed deeply, forcing herself to recall his kindness in securing her a passage, then slid once more into the woman she thought she had left behind long ago.

'They came yesterday,' she told him. 'You have my thanks.'

He dipped his head. 'I am glad to be of service.'

The boy brought a tray with a jug and another cup. Mary poured herself some ale, and refilled Rafe's. It helped to have something to do.

'And what brings you to the Cardinal's Cap tonight?' She turned her best smile towards him.

'Looking for you.' He made no effort to conceal the interest in his eyes and she gave herself a wry, inward smile. Once, she would have welcomed his attention – a handsome young man with money to pay, and it was hard to remember she now had a choice to say no. But in spite of that knowledge, she remained wary, guard in place. She sipped at her ale and waited for him to speak.

'You seem distracted,' he said.

She had lost her touch, she thought. 'I am tired, merely,' she replied.

'Ah.' He topped up their drinks from the jug. 'The demands of your errand. How goes it?'

She had told him nothing of her purpose in London, despite his curiosity and charm. 'It's in hand,' she offered. 'Though not yet finished.'

'And still, you do not trust me, Mistress Johnson.' He tilted his head with a smile that was hard to resist. 'Why so, when I have proved myself so honest?'

'I trust no one,' she answered, with a smile of her own. ''Tis safer that way.'

He slid his eyes away, considering for a moment, before he met her look once again and lifted his cup.

'To trust,' he said, 'and success in your endeavours, whatever they may be.'

'I can drink to that.' She tapped her cup to his with a small clink and drained it off. The ale was doing its work, a warm sweet wooziness seeping through her limbs, a softening of her thoughts. She should slow down, she thought, and keep her wits about her. She was here to find her daughter and not to flirt, however pleasant that might be.

The door opened with a flush of winter air that made her

shiver and she looked towards it with an instinctive brief half-hope of seeing Toby, as she once used to do. Then she remembered that Toby was dead, and the hope twisted once more into grief. She dropped her eyes to the cup in her hand to hide her sorrow – she should have drunk less ale.

'Why here?' Rafe was asking. 'Why would a well-to-do woman such as yourself stay in a place like this?' He gestured around the tavern with a sweep of his arm and she lifted her head to follow the movement, trying to see it with his eyes. The low ceiling beams dark with age and smoke, the cracked flagstones and wonky tables that were blotted with age-old spills, the rough men that drank at them, laughing with the whores.

One of the women caught her eye and winked, and Mary smiled in return. She turned her gaze to Rafe. He was watching her, trying to piece the puzzle together, and she liked that he could not understand her. It was power of a sort, that she might yet have need to use.

'I was born not far from here,' she said, which was the truth. 'And I like to be close to the water.'

'You're not afraid? 'Tis a rough place.'

'There are dangers everywhere,' she replied, with a shrug.

He studied her a moment. Then he said, 'Your husband was from here also?'

She kept her head lowered away, so that he could not see into her eyes. But she could feel the intentness of his gaze, and under-stood the question was not just idle curiosity. Why should he care about Toby?

'Yes,' she said. 'Why do you ask?'

She waited, and for the length of a heartbeat he hesitated, as though he were not yet quite decided on what he wanted to say.

He wanted the book, she thought again, just as Toby had. She was certain of it now. She had been careless on the ship to mention it: she should have held her tongue. But how could she have known of his interest in it? Was every man whose path she crossed connected to its fate? It appeared so. She thought of it now, tucked away under the floorboards in Rosalind's room, almost within spitting distance. Could he sense it? she wondered. Did he know it was here? Though it would serve any man who possessed it, Toby had told her, to steal it from another was to flirt with death. So who was its master now? She suppressed a sigh. She should have left it in The Hague to find its own destiny.

'He was a tailor, like his father before him. They had a shop in Narrow Lane.' In her nervousness she was speaking quickly and telling him too much, she knew, even as the words tumbled from her lips.

'What took you to The Hague?' He looked at her across the rim of his cup, and the depths in the darkness of his eyes unnerved her.

'Business,' she managed to say. And though she was aware he was still waiting, watching her and hoping for more, that was all she gave him.

They drank in silence for a while, observing the other drinkers, the whores moving deftly between them with jugs of wine, their shoulders bare and their gowns cut low enough that a single movement might just uncover a breast. Once, she had worn her gowns the same way. Until she met Toby and her life took a new and unexpected road. Because of the book, she thought, her own fate tied to it also.

One of the girls was laughing with a middle-aged man – some kind of shopkeeper, Mary guessed. She had swung out of his reach as he tried to grab her with a meaty hand, and as she made for the stairs she paused just long enough to swing her skirts up over her back and reveal the white cheeks of her arse. The man, who had hesitated until then, got up from his stool so suddenly it tipped over with a crash, and then he was running across the floor towards her, chasing her up the steps. The woman shrieked, laughing, and Rafe turned to Mary with a smile.

'Why would you stay at the Cardinal's Cap?' he asked again, and this time, the question was more direct. 'When there are so many other inns to choose from? This is a low place and if it were to be raided you would be taken in along with all the doxies. Why would you run such a risk?'

Had he guessed? she wondered. Had she somehow given herself away on the ship? Perhaps good women refused to share a cabin with a stranger. Perhaps only old whores took such risks.

'You ask a lot of questions, Master Tyndall,' she replied. 'My business is my own, as I told you before.'

'Forgive me,' he said quickly. 'I meant not to pry. I'm curious merely.' He gave her his most charming smile and in spite of herself she felt her defences weakening. 'I am just trying to piece together the puzzle that is Mary Johnson.'

'I'm not so much of a puzzle.' She took a mouthful of her ale, and observed him. 'I'm sure you have me all worked out already.'

'Perhaps,' he conceded. 'But I'd like to be certain. How about I tell you what I know of you so far, and you can tell me if I'm right.'

'And if you're wrong?'

'I'll stand you dinner. But if I'm right, I get to take you to my bed ...'

Mary let out a startled half-laugh. It was an unexpected bargain.

'... to finish what we started on the ship.'

Briefly, she recalled the flare of desire that had sparked between them that very first day of the voyage. Colour flooded her face and throat; she could feel its heat across her skin. She turned away, hoping he would not notice, and when she lifted a hand to her neck it was hot to the touch.

He gave her a smile. Charming, courteous, tempting.

She hesitated. Now that she was once more under the roof at the Cardinal's Cap, her marriage seemed to be no more than a fading memory. With Toby she had been a different woman – loved, honest, respectable. But here on Bankside her old self had begun to simmer to the surface again and she could think of no good reason to refuse him. He was very handsome, after all, and she liked him.

'I accept,' she said.

He sat back against the wall and folded his arms across his chest, waiting, a slight smirk on his lips as he appraised her anew. Mary sat up and preened herself in the light of his attention, playful. The boy brought them more ale and she poured for them both. Her head was beginning to grow light, the edges of the world around her softening, and for a moment she recalled her old life, when ale was a salve against the pain and hardships.

'Mary Johnson is not your real name,' he began, and she laughed. 'You aren't quite sure why you gave me a false name – to protect old secrets, perhaps?' He sat forward, and as she felt herself undressed by his gaze, body and soul naked before him, she understood the game had changed and she had been a fool to accept the challenge.

'You came back here,' he continued, 'because you once called the Cardinal's Cap your home. You were a girl like her.' He gestured with his head towards one of the whores, who was standing with an arm draped across a young man's shoulders, her breasts in line with his face. 'You met your husband here in the brothel and you served him as a whore until, united in some strange adventure, your husband took you away across the narrow sea to The Hague.'

Fear threaded through her, coiling upwards from her belly. How could he know such things?

'You are connected in some way to Tom Wynter and I think the book of magic you spoke of on the ship once belonged to him.'

Instinct urged her to run from this man who knew too much, the secrets of a life she thought she had put behind her laid out bare. But where could she go that he would not find her?

'What do you want with Tom's book?' The words left her mouth before she could stop them, and she clamped a hand to her lips before they could betray any more. She could have denied it and called him a liar, but now she was caught and the lid that had kept the past in place these last eighteen years was starting to come loose.

'Am I right?' he asked.

Mary said nothing, panic running in her blood. She reached for her ale and almost spilled it by the trembling of her hand. When she had replaced the cup on the table, Rafe caught her wrist in his fingers. She froze against the urge to yank her arm away from him. What did he want with her?

'You have no cause to be afraid of me,' he said, so softly she was barely sure she had heard him aright. 'I wish you no harm. But I have some part to play in this story,' he went on, 'and I am trying to understand what that might be.'

'What part?' she demanded. Though his grip was gentle, his hand on her wrist was warm and strong, and she wished he would let her go. Her eyes flicked across the tavern, searching for aid, but there was no one that would help her, no one that even noticed her.

'I don't yet know,' he answered.

She remembered their bargain, and he had surely won the bet. Mistrust ceded to fear, memories of the sorcerer bobbing to the surface. She recalled her dream of Kate in his company. Then Isabella Last trod across her thoughts. Was it for the book that the fortune teller had brought Kate to London?

'Do you have it?' he asked, when she said nothing. 'Do you have the book?'

She shook her head, and he let go of her arm with a sigh of exasperation. 'I wish you no harm, Mistress ... whatever your name is, and I would help you if you'd only let me. There are others who seek the book who will stop at nothing to get it.'

Isabella, she thought.

'Your connection to Tom Wynter has put you in grave danger.'

'I have no connection to Tom Wynter,' she lied. 'I know only what others have told me.'

He was silent, still watching her with those eyes that seemed to read her soul, and she kept her gaze lowered away from him. Then she said, 'Well, Master Tyndall, it appears you have won our bet. Shall we?' She wanted it over with – the desire she had felt for him before had receded to the same dull resignation she used to bring to her work, and become a duty, nothing more.

Rafe's eyes flicked across her, appraising, and she got to her feet, impatient now, but he gave a small shake of his head.

'It was a jest, merely,' he said, 'and I've no wish to take something that's not freely given.'

She inclined her head in acknowledgement. 'Then I thank you, Master Tyndall, and wish you good day.'

It felt good to walk away from him.

Rafe watched her go, enjoying the swing of her hips as she wove between the tables and through to the rooms behind the tavern. He could imagine her here, as she must once have been, with the sweet bow of her lips and the strange six-fingered hand.

One of the girls, still young and fresh, caught his eye across the room and tilted her head with a question in her eyes. Briefly, he considered it, but if he wanted a whore there were girls at the Bull's Head he could have for free. Across the years since Ellen's death, he had often taken comfort that way, reluctant to invest anything more of himself in a woman than the quick release of a fuck. Until he had met Kate, whose beauty had unsettled him in a way he thought he had forgotten, dismantling the walls he had erected to protect himself. With her reckless lust for life, she reminded him of the man he used to be long ago, before the war began. Before Ellen and his son were killed.

Gazing into the space that Mary had left behind her, he drained the last of the bitter ale with a grimace, still trying to fit together the pieces of the puzzle. Then he counted out the coins to pay, put them on the table and got to his feet.

On the quay outside, a wherry was docking at the landing stage and a party of gentlemen were preparing to step ashore, seeking Bankside's illicit pleasures. They carried themselves warily in muted colours, aware of the risk of it. Rafe clutched his cloak around him against the chill that swept off the river, and lowered his gaze away from them. The mirror had told him that the widow had the key and he knew she understood far more than she was telling him: he had seen the flicker of surprise and fear in her eyes that he had guessed so much. But he hadn't meant to frighten her, for without her trust he was powerless to protect her.

Casting a final glance across the water where the watermen were pulling hard against the turning tide, he wheeled abruptly and strode along the cobbles towards the Bull's Head.

Towards Kate.

She would have spent the day on the costumes for the play, her skilled hands teasing new beauty from the collection of well-worn garments that made up the company's wardrobe. She already seemed to have made the Bull's Head her home, her place at Rafe's side barely questioned, and in spite of the bitter cold the thought of her lit a welcome warmth inside him. When he shoved open the door and stepped into the brothel, he realised he was smiling.

❦ 19 ❦

A GREAT PERTURBATION IN NATURE

Mary slept late, adapting to the hours of the tavern as though she'd never had any other life at all – the early mornings of the tailor's shop seemed to belong to a different person, a different world. The curtains were bright with the morning light behind them when she woke, and she lay on her back staring up at the beams of the ceiling where the ancient wood was blackened with age and smoke, and there were cracks along the grain. Beside her, Rosalind was still deep in sleep, breathing softly, eyelids flickering with her dreams.

Mary's own dreams had been filled with foreboding, though she could barely recall the details, images flickering half-seen through her mind. A graveyard. A fear of drowning. A growing darkness. The sorcerer's influence, she knew, coming back to haunt her after all these years. She had always supposed it had ended with his death. She gave herself a wry smile – she should have known better.

She thought of Rafe and the game they had played in the tavern. For all his charm and courtesy, his unexpected knowledge of her past had frightened her: she had not thought he would see beneath her lies so easily. He knew she had the book, that much

172

was certain, but how far he was prepared to go to possess it, she could not say. She shuddered, memories of the Wounded Raven rippling through her blood – it had been so much easier to be brave with Toby at her side. For the length of a breath she found herself longing for the safety of The Hague she had left behind, before she remembered there was nothing for her there any more. No husband. No child. No life at all – only memories.

Rosalind sighed in her sleep and shifted position, one hand tucked neatly under the pillow. Turning back the covers gently so as not to disturb her friend, Mary slid from the bed and, as she began to dress, she caught her reflection in the looking glass on the wall. She stopped before it, angling her shoulders this way and that to see herself better, running her hands over the lines of her bodice. Skilfully sewn dove-grey silk with delicate lace and a modest neck-line, it was a gown for the person she used to be across the narrow sea, a well-to-do tailor's wife, respectable and demure. She should alter it, she thought, lower the neckline, get rid of the lace. She was a worthy tailor's wife of The Hague no more, but a denizen of Bankside. And though God knew the place was full of all sorts from everywhere, she felt an urge to reclaim her beginnings, proud to belong. Rosalind would have laughed to hear her and Mary allowed herself a smile at her own recollection of how desperate she had once been to leave it. But in those days she had been a bawd, earning her bread on her back each night, and she had come to understand that it was not the place she had hated so much as the life she had been forced to lead. She finished dressing, moving in silence so as not to awaken the still-sleeping Rosalind, and stepped into the passage that led out into the tavern.

It was not yet mid-morning and the place was deserted, though the servant girl had already swept the place clean and laid out the fire in readiness. From the hidden kitchens at the back of the place Mary could hear the clatter of the cook at work, the thud of the cleaver on the board. The scent of broth drifted through, meat and sage and rosemary, competing with the stench of stale ale and sweat that never left the place, no matter how long the doors and windows stood open, nor how much incense they burned.

A light knock at the door startled her from her thoughts, and she wove between the tables and chairs to open it. A young boy in a tattered set of drawers and a cap that was too big for him stood on the step.

'I got a message,' he said, 'for ...' He looked her up and down, '... for the lady that came to the Wounded Raven.'

'That was me.'

He nodded, then closed his eyes briefly to remember the words he'd been told to say. 'She's not been back,' he said, 'but a gentleman came to visit early this morning.'

Mary drew in a slow breath to calm her quickened heart. Rafe? Perhaps, though she dared not imagine what his purpose might have been.

'Thank you,' she managed to whisper, but the boy just stared.

'She said you'd give us a sixpence.'

Swallowing, Mary struggled to focus her thoughts on the boy. Her mind was churning with uncertainty, and he had to say it twice before she heard him.

Perhaps it meant nothing. Perhaps it was only some poor fool seeking to have his fortune told. But she would go there, none-theless, and discover what it meant for herself.

'Here,' she said, reaching to her belt for her pouch. She gave him a coin, and he looked up at her expectantly.

'And the other one?'

'Can I trust you to see it safely home?'

'It's for me grandam. She'll box me ears if I don't give it her.'

Mary smiled and placed the other coin in his grubby hand. Then she said, 'Wait here,' and, turning, she stepped back inside to walk swiftly to the kitchen. The cook looked up in surprise but she ignored him and cut off a hunk from the bread that had come from the baker that morning. It was still warm, and the crust broke easily in her fingers. When she returned to the door, the boy's face brightened at the sight of the gift.

'Make sure you save some for your grandam,' Mary said, and he nodded gravely, holding the bread as though it were a long-lost treasure. Then she sent him on his way, and as she watched his small back get lost along the quayside, her heart turned in pity for the want in his young, poor life. She doubted he had ever known a belly that was full.

Mary fetched her cloak and went out into the morning. A weak sun lit the edges of the clouds but the day was grey, and she had to walk with care not to slide on the greasy cobbles underfoot. Shivering, she hunched her shoulders inside her cloak and was grateful for the extra warmth of the modest neckline – perhaps she would keep it after all. At the water's edge she stopped, looking down at the shingle as a wherry approached the steps, rocking with the turn of the tide. The oarsman strained to bring the boat alongside and the gentleman passenger stood up inelegantly, waiting for the best moment to step ashore. Mary turned away to gaze upriver, watching the river traffic as she pondered the possibilities, undecided.

Then, making a decision at last, she ducked back inside the tavern and made for Rosalind's room, searching for paper, quill and ink. Her friend was still peaceful in sleep, and Mary crept around her until she found what she was looking for. Taking it through to the tavern, she sat at a table close to the window where the light was best and where, she remembered again, Toby had once sat to watch her. She shook her head to clear it of the memory – she needed to think. Words had never come easily and there was so much she needed to say. In the end, she scrawled a brief few lines that wished Kate well and gave her the address at the Cardinal's Cap.

She would leave the letter with the woman at the brazier, she decided, and trust in fate. Folding the paper, she returned to Rosalind's room in search of wax to seal it, and this time Rosalind stirred at the sound of the latch on the door. Mary halted, sorry to have woken her, but her friend smiled as she sat up and stretched, a glimpse of the girl she had once been lighting eyes that were mostly sad now, and full of cares.

'You're up early,' she said.

'Not so early,' Mary laughed. Then, 'A messenger came. I must go again to the Wounded Raven.'

'Kate is there?'

'No, she isn't. But there was a gentleman there, and I'm afraid that time is running out.'

She had said nothing of Rafe Tyndall to her friend, reluctant to place more cares on the other woman's shoulders. But the knowledge of his interest had spurred her into action – she could not just sit by and wait.

Rosalind noticed the letter in Mary's hand. 'There's wax in the drawer there and my seal. I'll fetch a candle.'

Mary crossed to the desk and slid onto the stool; when Rosalind returned with a candle she had lit from the kitchen fire, she affixed the seal with inexpert fingers, wax dripping onto the paper. She cursed her incompetence – she had rarely needed to send letters before.

'I'll walk with you there,' Rosalind said.

Mary turned on the stool. 'Are you sure you want to?'

''Tis safer with two of us,' her friend said with a shrug and a smile that did not reach her eyes. 'And I am weary of being afraid.'

For a moment Mary said nothing, biting gently at her lip. Then she raised her eyes to her friend.

'I would welcome your company,' she said. 'It will be like old times.'

They strolled arm-in-arm as they used to do as girls, and more than one man clocked them with an admiring glance. They were both still handsome women and they moved with a confidence that came with their knowledge of it. They passed a couple of young merchants who stopped to stare. One of them, egged on by his friend, called out to them.

'Where can we find you again? We have money to spend.'

'We cost more than you can afford,' Rosalind laughed, and they walked on, aware of the two men staring at their backs and swinging their hips just a little bit more than they had before. But in spite of their levity, their steps slowed as they wound deeper into the maze of narrow streets that led to the sorcerer's house. Memories of the darkness seemed to settle on Mary's shoulders, pressing down, and when they reached the end of the lane Mary turned to her friend.

'Would you prefer to stay here? I can go on alone.'

Rosalind hesitated, casting a frightened look into the alleyway.

Mary squeezed her arm. 'Wait for me here,' she said. 'I hope not to be long. And if you leave before I return I will understand.'

Her friend gave her a grateful smile and drew back quickly, relieved to go no further. Mary returned the smile but her heart was thumping, and the sweat was slick at her hairline as she turned the corner into the gloom. The lane was deserted – there was no brazier, no old woman, no ragged children, not even one of the mangy dogs that prowled the street. Mary swallowed and came to a halt, staring up at the house, the faded sign hanging still and unmoving in the morning damp. Lights burned in the attic, the flicker of candles and flame, and a new and sudden terror began pulsing through her.

With an effort of will, Mary lifted her fist to bang on the door. To her surprise, it swung open with her knock, and a chill that was deeper than the winter morning seeped out through the opening. For a moment she froze, fighting down the temptation to turn and run, back to the safety of the Cardinal's Cap and away from this place. Then, girding herself with thoughts of Kate and a whispered word to Toby, she squared her shoulders and stepped inside.

In the hearth, a low fire smouldered and a fine haze of smoke hung in the air, but it offered no warmth. The room was empty,

the remnants of a recently eaten meal strewn across the table –
crumbs and dirty dishes, the last crust of a loaf of bread. There had
been a servant when she came before, she recalled, but she saw no
sign of him now. Then, with a hand on the newel post and gathering her courage, she set her foot on the bottom step and began to
climb.

There were more stairs than she remembered and by the time
she reached the topmost landing her legs were aching and her
breath was short. She paused outside the attic door to recover, and
to find the will to resist the urge to flee.

Kate, she reminded herself. You must do this for Kate. But the
memory of the last time she had been here and the horror of what
had lain beyond the door filled her. She gave a small shake of her
head as though to dislodge the image, but she could not shake it
free.

Toby, she called. *Give me strength.*

For the very first time since his death she saw the image of his
smile in answer, and just a glimpse of it was enough to propel her
forward. Without pausing to knock she put her hand on the
handle, pressed it down and flung back the door.

The room was just as she remembered it. The great desk still
stood in the centre, littered with books and papers and jars of
things she couldn't name. The narrow cot where Alexander had
tied her still stood against the wall with the same faded quilt across
it, and the half-recollected scent of it touched her nostrils now,
damp and mould. She swallowed, dragging her eyes away. But
there was no circle chalked on the floor, and no jewelled dagger,
and she let out the breath she was holding.

Isabella turned from her contemplation of the fire and smiled.

'Ah, Mistress Winter. You answered my summons.'

The floor beneath Mary's feet seemed to tilt, and she had to
brace to keep her balance. She said nothing, her thoughts still
groping to understand.

'I'm surprised you did not think to question the old
woman's loyalties, when she all but lives on my doorstep.'

Isabella gestured towards a stool at the hearth, but Mary remained by the door, preferring to be on her feet with escape close at hand.

'What do you want with my daughter?' she managed to ask, her mind still whirling. 'What is it you think she can give you?'

Isabella said nothing but crossed to the desk and settled herself on a stool, taking her time to arrange her skirts and the books to her liking, before she picked up a piece of wax she had been moulding into the shape of a woman. Alexander had sat just so, all those years ago, Mary recalled.

'Or is it me you want? Was it me you wanted all along?'

Isabella's mouth curled into a mirthless smile. 'You begin to understand at last.'

Mary was silent, still trying to fit the pieces together, beginning to realise she had walked into a trap.

'Your daughter is both innocent and reckless,' Isabella said. 'But she is young yet and still has much to learn. For myself, I've enjoyed leading her astray; tempting her away from the safety of her life with you in The Hague and introducing her to the ...' She circled her fingers in the air and smiled. '...to the *delights* of Bankside. I predict she'll not remain innocent for long.'

'You're a monster,' Mary breathed, so low she wasn't sure that Isabella even heard her.

'She was grateful for the chance to stretch her wings,' Isabella said. 'To flee the constraints of a virtuous life. It's funny, how the urge to sin can run in families ... my own father, of course, liked both girls and boys. My mother used to claim that he'd swive anything with an arsehole.'

Mary stared. 'Your father was Alexander. The sorcerer.'

'And you killed him.'

'Yes,' said Mary. 'Just there.' She pointed to a spot on the ground between them. 'I stuck a point in his balls and watched the blood drain out of him. It must have been the Devil's own job to clean the stain from the boards.'

Isabella hissed, and for the first time Mary saw a crack in the cold composure, flecks of anger glinting at last in the green of her eyes.

'So now I will have my revenge, and reclaim from you the book you stole.'

Mary shrugged. 'I stole nothing,' she said. 'What would I want with a book? I'm just a whore, remember? My skills lie elsewhere.'

'Chyrche took it.'

'Toby is dead.'

Isabella swung a strand of hair back across her shoulder and gave Mary a flirtatious smile.

'I know.' She sighed. 'He wouldn't tell me its whereabouts either.'

Mary felt herself begin to sway and reached a hand to the door frame to steady herself. She should have known his death had been no accident, but in her grief and her loneliness she had not allowed herself to think it.

'Tell me where it is,' Isabella said, 'and I will lead you to your daughter so you can both scuttle back to your little shop in The Hague to live out your dull and pointless lives, though I would hazard a guess it might be too late to save her virtue.'

'I don't have it,' Mary said, with a shrug of helplessness. Toby had died to keep the book from this woman's hands and if she had to, she, Mary, would do the same. 'I can't help you.'

Isabella hissed again. 'You're lying. I know you are. And I will get it in the end,' she said, 'one way or another and you, I promise, will be sorry for it.'

'Perhaps,' Mary said. 'But remember, I managed to kill your father even as he held the book in his hands, so I am not frightened of you, Isabella Last.'

Isabella gave a short, low laugh. 'Then you are more of a fool than you seem.'

A creak in a floorboard right behind her spun Mary round to look, and she found herself face to face with the servant, mere inches away. She could smell his sour breath and see the pock marks in his skin beneath the stubble. The cut on his cheek had begun to fester, livid and starting to putrefy. Sarah would have made a compress of yarrow and chamomile, she thought, to stave off the infection, and an unexpected surge of grief for Toby's mother filled her.

'Show Mistress Sparrow to the door,' Isabella ordered. 'She has finished her business here.'

The servant nodded and Mary followed him down the steep wooden stairs, eager to be gone. For all her bravado, terror pulsed in her limbs, and it was all she could do to stop herself from running as soon as the door slammed shut behind her. She found Rosalind still waiting where she had left her.

'Dear God!' her friend said, as soon as she saw her. 'You are pale as death. What happened?'

Mary struggled for words but none came, her thoughts and lips disconnected as the edges of her mind seemed to blacken. She shuddered, a cold that was born somewhere darker than the morning reaching into her bones, and she held fast to Rosalind, desperate for her warmth and life, her own blood seeming to blanch and sicken.

'We should go,' Rosalind said, and wrapped an arm around Mary's waist when her legs threatened to buckle. Mary staggered, barely able to put one foot before the other, her body refusing to obey her mind. Fear spiralled through her, memories of Rosalind losing her wits at the sorcerer's hand all those years ago. This was Isabella's doing, she knew. But how? How? She began to shake, and Rosalind held her more firmly against her own body, taking more of her weight.

Forcing her eyes to focus, she stared at the shops and houses, the tenements and people that they passed, but all of it was blurred and shadowy and grey, as though all warmth and colour had been sucked out of it. Spasms wracked her body – the same pitiless cold she had known only once before, when the fingers of death had reached out and almost claimed her. Her wrist began to burn with the memory of its grasp.

It seemed a long journey home and by the time she fell at last into Rosalind's bed, she could do nothing but curl in upon herself, shivering and tearful, her mind groping to latch on to some meaning beyond her pain and her terror. But her thoughts were mired in darkness, and all she knew for sure was that some demonic force was dragging her to Hell.

Her last coherent thought was to wonder how she would save her daughter now.

20

THE PLAY'S THE THING

In Rafe's quarters they had pushed the furniture back against the walls and Kate was watching the players rehearse. The needle in her hand had ceased its movement and the linen shirt lay forgotten on her lap.

Rafe as Prospero, a different man, transformed in his magician's robes. She wanted to laugh in delight at the illusion, and by the time Walter as Ariel entered the scene, all thoughts of the world beyond the play had been quelled – Prospero's island was the only reality now.

> 'Not a soul
>> But felt a fever of the mad, and played
>> Some tricks of desperation. All but mariners
>> Plunged in the foaming brine and quit the vessel,
>> Then all afire with me. The King's son, Ferdinand,
>> With hair up-staring—then like reeds, not hair—
>> Was the first man that leaped; cried "Hell is empty,
>> And all the devils are here."'

Kate's belief in Prospero's magic was absolute. Rafe was pale-faced and beautiful in the fine silk robes, with a shimmering cloak that caught the candlelight and seemed aflame. She could not prise her eyes away from him, and a sense she would only later recognise as envy bristled in her thoughts – to make oneself anew and inhabit the soul of another was a gift she could only dream of. No wonder they took such risks to play, in spite of the laws against it. No wonder people still braved the danger to watch. This was magic indeed, a spell that was woven in words upon a stage, and the Puritans were right to fear it.

~

In the early hours of the morning after the rehearsal, Kate startled awake from terror-sick dreams, sweat-drenched and sobbing, heart drumming in her chest fit to burst as she sat up in Rafe's bed, eyes searching the dark in desperation for something, anything, familiar to hold on to and moor her to her waking life. But the visions of her nightmare still clawed at her thoughts, vivid and persistent.

Beside her Rafe stirred, woken by her movements, and without a word he drew her into his embrace. She sank against the warmth of his body, the anchor she was searching for. She held him with all her strength, pressing him close, as her own body was wracked with sobs.

'Hey,' he murmured, and stroked her hair, his lips brushing against it, vital and welcome. 'It was a dream, is all. You're safe. I'm here, and you're safe.'

She wrenched herself free of him, breathing hard.

'It wasn't just a dream,' she whispered. She had never been so sure of anything in her life. 'My mother is in danger.' Her gaze scanned the darkness again, but this time she was seeking an answer to the questions that hammered in her mind. 'I don't understand.'

'What did you dream?' Rafe asked, taking her hand between both of his, caressing her fingers with his own.

She shook her head, unable to form the words she needed, her breath still ragged and uneven. Rafe slid from the bed, drew back the curtain to let in the faint light of the city, and went to the sideboard to pour them both wine.

'Drink this,' he said, handing her a glass. 'It will calm you.'

She sipped at it. He was right. The wine was cool and smooth against her throat and warm in her chest. Slowly, her breathing began to settle and the clamour of her heartbeat to quieten. He waited patiently beside her and when she thought she could trust her voice again, she told him what she had seen.

She had heard her mother calling out for her in the darkness, she said, desperate and afraid.

She had been powerless to search, her limbs stayed by some dark magic that even in the dream Kate knew had begun with Isabella.

Then, in the very last moment before she woke, she had found her, but she was deep underwater as though trapped at the bottom of a well, and Kate did not know how to save her.

'I don't understand,' she finished. 'My mother is in The Hague.'

'No, she isn't,' he said, and his voice was no more than a whisper. 'Your mother is at the Cardinal's Cap tavern, just along the way here.' He gestured with his head. 'Barely a stone's throw away.'

She stared. 'You know my mother?'

Rafe let out a long breath, and his eyes tracked the lines of the quilt across the bed as though he were trying to decide what to say. Kate waited, thoughts tumbling in a new confusion: she felt unmoored again, adrift.

She had held on to the image of her mother at the house in The Hague as if to a lifeline – an unchanging reality, a place of safety, home. Something to cling to. Something real. A place to return to. Now Rafe was telling her that Mary was here on Bankside, and that he had known of it? How could that be?

'She followed you here,' he said. 'I met her on the ship from The Hague, but it was only two days ago that I made the connection. She had told me nothing of her purpose till then, and never mentioned your name to me once.'

Kate was silent. Of course her mother had followed her. When Kate failed to return home, Mary would have searched for the fortune teller, and left no stone unturned. She would have learned of their flight to England and boarded the next London-bound ship herself. She should have realised, Kate thought now, that her mother would do anything to protect her daughter and keep her safe.

She raised her head to look at the man before her. He was watching her and his eyes flickered with the fear of her anger but she did not care. What other secrets was he keeping? What else was he not telling her? He lifted his hand to caress her face but she jerked her head away from his touch.

'Why didn't you tell me?'

Again he hesitated, as though trying to decide how much to say.

'Don't lie to me!' She slapped her hand against the muscle of his arm, her fury fanned by the fear the dream had kindled.

'I'm not lying,' he protested. 'I haven't lied to you. I've been trying to work things out, to understand how all of this is connected. Please, Kate. You must trust me.'

'I don't trust you,' she replied. 'I don't trust you at all.'

How could she have been so taken in? She had imagined she was in love with him, this man to whom she had given up the prize. Once or twice in idle moments she had allowed herself to daydream of a whole life together – marriage, children, a lasting love. How could she have been such an idiot? Walter had tried to warn her but she had refused to listen, letting her feelings, her desires, betray her. And now, in the words of the pastor at the church in The Hague, she was *a fallen woman*.

Sliding back from him across the bed, she began to gather her clothes from the floor where they had dropped them in the heat of their passion. In the cold room she started to dress. Despite the dark, she could hear the beginnings of the day beyond the window.

The lone voice of a man hailing a wherry at the landing stage drifted through the morning, and the wheels of a cart trundled across the cobbles just outside.

'Where are you going?' Rafe asked, reaching for his own clothes.

Briefly, she let her eyes graze across the whiteness of his body as he lifted the shift to put it on, observing the smooth hard muscle, broken here and there by the scars of war that were livid and red even in the gloom. Then she turned her head away, enraged to be so distracted.

'None of your business,' she snapped, tugging at the laces on her bodice, tying them tight with fingers that trembled with cold and fury.

'Kate, please.' Rafe came to stand before her, touching his fingers to her arm. 'Please. Bankside isn't safe for you alone. If your mother's in danger, then so are you.'

She snatched her arm away from his touch. He had lied to her. He had known her mother was at the Cardinal's Cap and had not told her, and she no longer trusted a single word he said.

'Leave me alone!'

Rafe let his arm drop, and though she saw the hurt in his eyes, it made no difference. She needed to find her mother, and she would do it alone. With a final pull on her bodice, she jammed her feet into her boots, and walked out of the room, laces flapping.

Outside, on the quay, she huddled deeper into her cloak. The dawn was still an hour or more away and the night was bitter cold, its tendrils curling inside her collar, beneath her skirts. She walked to the water's edge, breathing in the damp salt scent, hard and fresh in her lungs. She shook her head to try and clear it of the jumble of thoughts inside, struggling to make sense of it.

But as she turned to face the row of buildings that looked out upon the river, to search for the Cardinal's Cap amongst them, a small smile curled the edges of her lips because, in spite of her fury with Rafe, she was overjoyed to know that her mother was nearby, and that very soon she would find her.

THIS SUPERNATURAL SOLICITING

Rafe stood at the window and watched from the window as Kate gazed out across the river for a moment before she turned away to find the Cardinal's Cap, striding along the cobbles with her cloak held tight around her against the cold, her hair, still mussed from the night in his bed, catching in the breeze that blew off the water. He didn't blame her for her anger – he should have told her, he thought now, even when he hadn't been certain. But he knew for sure that he was not the only one keeping secrets – there was plenty she had not yet told him, and he was eager to know more about the witchcraft she had barely even mentioned.

She was Tom Wynter's grandchild, his blood in her veins. Witchblood? He let his thoughts wander back across what she had told him of her dream – the gift of foresight was rare and strange, a skill withheld from ordinary men. What other powers did she possess? He had not thought to ask. But had she learned yet to harness them? However deeply the blood ran in her veins, it was all but useless without the proper skill to call upon it.

Kate disappeared from his view and as he let his gaze rest on the space she had left behind her, an unexpected memory flickered through his thoughts: his wife in the first days of their marriage, setting out the bowl of water on the kitchen table as she prepared to scry, the air heavy with smoke from the bundle of sage in her fingers. Though he had not thought of it in years, every detail of the room was clear in his mind; the morning light at the window and the block of sun that fell across the floor. The bundles of herbs hanging from the rafters, drying. The pot that bubbled gently on the hearth, and the squabble of the chickens beyond the back door. Even her face was perfectly drawn in his mind. They had been so full of hope for a life together, he remembered, and on an impulse she had decided to scry. She wanted to know how many children they would have, she had told him, if the fates would be kind and bless them with a family. How long had they been married then? A few weeks at most. They had been so much in love, and nothing else had mattered. Sorrow curled through his insides. It was hard to recall the taste of such innocence – he had been a different man in those days, as yet unscarred by grief and war, a man he could barely remember.

He hauled his attention back to the scene beyond the window, hoping Kate had found sanctuary at the Cardinal's Cap with her mother, but he feared for her all the same. Isabella would still be on the hunt – she had lured Kate to London on the promise of her connection to the book, and if she had found her in The Hague, she would surely find her again on Bankside.

But perhaps Kate had merely been the bait, he thought then. Was it Mary the fortune teller wanted? Mary with her knowledge of the book, alone on Bankside with no community to protect her at her back. Another piece of the puzzle slotted into place.

Idly, he let his mind turn over the possibilities. For all he knew, Mary could have left the book behind in The Hague. He tried to picture it, the precious pages stowed away safely in an attic some-where and awaiting Mary's return. It seemed unlikely. It was too valuable a thing to be left so unattended, and however innocent Mary may pretend to be, he knew it was only an act. She under-stood both its risk and its value, of that he was certain. Was it hidden away at the Cardinal's Cap, a few minutes stroll from where he stood now? The thought of it curled in his gut, tempting. He couldn't deny that he wanted it – what man who knew of its power could say any different? But he was aware that for all the knowledge it offered, it rarely brought good fortune to its masters, and an unease trickled through him: the warning of Kate's dream was hard to shake from his shoulders, and Tom Wynter's death flickered in the background of his thoughts.

He raised his gaze from the quay to look across the river where the city was just starting to come to life in the grey of the early morning. Wheels and the tread of boots sounded on the cobbles, and from somewhere along the row he could hear the faint clank of a hammer. A man's voice called out another's name in irritation and a woman's high tone replied.

The unease spread to his limbs as a physical ache, a tension in his jaw. He rubbed at his jawline with his fingers, searching to alleviate the pain, but it made no difference. He should not have let her go, he realised. While he was standing at the window staring at the morning like a fool, she was striding into dangers he doubted she was skilled enough to face alone. He had failed to protect his wife and child, leaving them to meet their fates without him, and he didn't plan to lose Kate the same way. He swung away from the window. Then, dressing hurriedly, heartbeat quick, and afraid now that he had tarried too long, it was only moments before he was thudding down the wooden staircase, across the tavern, and out onto the quay beyond the door.

Kate found the Cardinal's Cap with ease, just a few doors along the row from the Bull's Head. It was still closed for the night with the door shut hard against her, and though she hammered on the timber until her palms and knuckles were sore with the effort and her face was streaked with tears of frustration, no one answered. Behind her, the morning was beginning to lighten, the darkness giving way to a dull streaked grey that gleamed on the water. She slammed her fist against the door again for a final time, then almost jumped at a voice close by.

'They're closed, lovie,' a woman said.

Kate turned, and dragged a hand across her eyes to wipe away the tears she could no longer hold back.

'So I see.'

'What's so special about that one then? What of the others?' The woman smiled with a lopsided grin, and Kate saw the paint on her face, the low-cut, much-repaired dress. The woman's chest was raised in goose bumps with the cold, but she seemed oblivious.

'There's someone here I need to see,' Kate replied.

'Dumped you, did he? That's men for you.'

She shook her head but she had no energy to explain. Besides, who would believe her?

'There's plenty of taverns would take a girl like you,' the woman said then. 'You a maid?'

'What is it to you?' Kate answered, face growing hot, as though the woman had caught a glimpse of the nights she had spent with Rafe, the truth of her.

'Just trying to help, m'dear,' the woman said, turning away. 'Just trying to help.'

Kate stared after the woman as she ambled away towards the market, watching her exchange a comment and a laugh with two young gentlemen who had just stepped off a wherry at Goat Steps. It was early in the morning for pleasure-seeking, she thought. But perhaps they had not yet been to bed.

Stepping away from the door with a final glance across the front of the building, Kate turned and wandered to the water's edge, shoulders hunched against the cold: she hadn't thought to find herself outside with nowhere to go in the gathering dawn; she had thought to find her mother. Now, with the doors barred against her, she began to doubt Rafe's story. Surely if her mother were there she would answer. Surely no one could sleep through the racket she had made.

On an impulse she swung round once more to face the row of buildings behind her, eyes scanning the strip of assorted shops and workshops and taverns. Despite the Puritans' edicts, men of all sorts still haunted Bankside in search of their pleasure, the streets spilling over with drunkards and whores – it was a rough part of town. So why on earth had her mother chosen to come to the Cardinal's Cap? Of all the places in London she could have stayed – respectable inns, safer streets – why would she choose to stay here amongst all the sinners and thieves? It made no sense to her at all.

With her back to the river, she let her gaze wander again along the row of buildings, wondering what she should do. But as she waited, still trying to reach a decision, the door of the Cardinal's Cap was dragged open, and a young boy slid through the gap on his way to perform some errand. Goading her chilled limbs into movement, Kate hurried across the quay towards him before the door closed on her again.

'Good morrow,' she hailed him, and the boy turned in startled surprise, stopping abruptly in his tracks to stare. 'Do you live here?' She gestured with a hand, and he followed the movement with wide eyes before he nodded. He was poorly dressed, in a much-mended shirt and hand-me-down breeches that were too big for him, but he seemed well fed, so perhaps they kept a good house, and the people were kind.

'May I enter?'

He shrugged, as if to say it was nothing to do with him one way or the other, and stood back to watch as she went past him. Inside, she paused, taking a moment to let her eyes adjust to the dim light after the brightness of the morning outside.

The place was much the same as the tavern at the Bull's Head. An empty fireplace, a low ceiling, scattered tables, stools and benches, and a stale smell of ale and old food. A tavern or a brothel? It was hard to say. A set of wooden steps led to a gallery upstairs with rooms leading off it, and at the back was a counter. Instinctively, she made for the corridor beside it that led to the rooms behind.

At the rear of the building she found a kitchen where a fire was already burning. A middle-aged maid with tendrils of hair working loose from her cap had just set a bucket of water on the hearth. She turned at Kate's approach but she showed no surprise at a stranger in her kitchen: perhaps she was used to it.

'Forgive my disturbing you,' Kate said. 'But I'm looking for my mother, Mary Winter. I was told she was here.'

The maid gestured with her head towards the door that Kate had come through. 'I couldn't tell you,' she replied. 'You need to ask Madam. The door in the passage. But I'd guess she'd be sleeping now. We keep odd hours here.'

'Thank you,' Kate said, with a nod of her head. She turned, and with a few strides she was standing before the door the woman had told her. She hesitated, her heartbeat quick with nerves as the image of her dream flickered at the corners of her thoughts and the memory of the seeping darkness crept through her. She shivered, and it took a moment to gather the courage to knock.

She waited. Nothing. She knocked again, then pressed her ear to the wood and heard only silence. But on the third knock, the door opened a fraction and a woman's face, bleary with sleep, pressed close to the gap.

'Who is there?'

'Kate Winter,' she replied. 'I was told my mother is here.'

The door swung open wide. 'God be praised!' the woman said, and stood back to let Kate in. But she closed the door sharply behind her and drew the bolt across it.

The room was bright and cheerful with warmth – a low fire pulsed in the grate, and candles were set all about on every surface. Cushions and wall hangings lent colour to the air, but her gaze was drawn straight away to the figure of her mother in the bed, curled up like a child, her face still. For a moment, Kate thought she was sleeping, until she saw her eyes were open and staring blindly before her.

She ran to the bedside and crouched, taking her mother's hands in her own. In spite of the heat of the room, they were frozen, and Mary showed no signs of recognition of her daughter, no sign she knew anyone was there at all, her gaze blank and lifeless, skin slick with fever. Kate looked up to the other woman.

'What happened?' was all she could think of to ask, and the chilling world of her dream slithered again in her mind, its call stronger now.

'The fortune teller,' the woman said. 'She sent her to the dark. I know what that's like: I been there myself, many years ago.'

Isabella, Kate thought, and passed the tip of her tongue across her lips. But why?

The woman sat on the edge of the bed and rested a hand on Mary's leg, gently, as one would on a sleeping child. 'Can you help?'

'I don't know,' she murmured, rubbing her mother's hands between her own, hoping to force them to warmth. Her mind was racing, scrabbling for answers that seemed to rise and fade before she could grasp them fully. Images and memories circled through her thoughts as she chased desperately after them, trying to hunt them down. Isabella, Nathan, the attic. The graveyard, her dream, Tom Wynter. They seemed to whirl in no apparent order, a tangled web. Remembering all that Isabella had taught her she closed her eyes and listened to the soft whisper of her breath in the rise and fall of her chest as she tried to connect to the thread of the air that gave her life. But the clatter of her heartbeat refused to ease, and the memory of her dream crowded out all other thoughts. All that filled her mind was the image of her mother deep underwater, and no way to reach her.

She balled her fists, infuriated by her inability to tease apart the knotted threads of her thoughts, to find the path she needed. How could she undo the fortune teller's magic? How should she even begin?

Hecate, help me. Show me the way.

She sat back on her heels for a moment with the plea to the goddess echoing in her thoughts, but she heard no answering whisper, no kindling light to guide her. She was aware of the other woman's anxious gaze on her face, and though she had a hundred questions to ask of her, they would have to wait. How long could a person languish in the Shadow? How long could she survive?

Panic threatened as a prickle beneath her skin and she forced her breathing to slow to counter the rising fear. Her thoughts skittered this way and that, searching for some glint of knowledge to hold on to. What use was her witchblood if she had not the knowledge to use it?

A sudden knock at the outside door made her flinch in shock. A man's fists, pounding hard. Her heart seemed to turn over in her chest, fear a hard ball inside her. Her mother's friend, whose name she would later learn was Rosalind, crept to the chamber door and listened. Her own fear was etched in deep lines across her face. They exchanged a look and Kate shook her head in answer to the unspoken question.

A moment's hesitation, then Rosalind went out into the passage and crossed the tavern floor. Kate half followed, one hand still on the door. But from where she stood she could see the door, and she waited, mouth dry.

'Who is there?'

'Rafe Tyndall.' His voice was hard and clear even through the heavy timber, and the sound of it sparked a slew of emotions in Kate she could not even begin to unpick. When Rosalind turned to Kate in question, she nodded, words too hard to find. The older woman slid back the bolts, and then Rafe was striding towards her through the semi-darkness of the tavern.

'Kate!'

In spite of everything, she had to bite back a smile. Whether or not she could trust him, her delight in his presence was a feeling she could not deny. How could her body betray her so easily? How could her emotions be so at odds with what she knew in her head? He had lied to her, she forced herself to remember, and she was no longer a maid. They stood together for a moment of awkward silence until he made a gesture towards the passage behind her.

'Is your mother here?'

She nodded. 'She is in the Shadow and insensible to the world – the fortune teller sent her there.'

'I can help,' he said. 'We can ask the spirits to guide us.'

She hesitated. 'I must do it alone,' Kate whispered, instinct guiding her words. It was her inheritance, in her blood, the battle begun in her grandfather's time.

'Do you know how to save her?' He reached for her hand, wrapping his fingers around hers, cold and hard, and there was no memory of the pleasure they had given her in their touch. 'Do you know what you must do?'

His grip tightened on Kate's hand and she had to brace to withstand the fierceness of his gaze as he searched her face. Tears pricked at her eyes. She had thought to go to Tom Wynter's grave to seek his help, but beyond that, she could not say – she had no knowledge of poppet magic nor how to undo Isabella's spell, and with Rafe's blunt question, she felt the full force of her ignorance. She had barely started the journey of her witchcraft, her witchblood only just beginning to rise – what could she do alone against the magic of the fortune teller?

She shook her head, furious with her ignorance, her inability. She didn't want to need him. But her mother's life hung in the balance, and for all the power of the witchblood that ran in her veins, she did not know what to do.

'Is the book here?'

Rosalind took a sharp intake of breath that was loud in the silent room, giving him his answer, and though his fingers remained wound with Kate's, Rafe turned his attention towards her. The older woman shot Kate a frightened glance that she did not know how to answer. The silence hung in the room.

'Let me help you,' Rafe urged. 'Let me help you unlock your power and find what you must do.'

She said nothing, wondering how he understood so much when she had told him so little, and her eyes swept across the room, searching for answers to all the questions that circled in her mind.

'And then,' he went on, 'then you can do alone what you must to bring your mother back.'

Kate moistened her lips with the tip of her tongue, considering. It was tempting, but dare she trust him again? She brought her gaze back to his face. He was watching her intently, and his eyes were dark in the gloom, unknowable depths contained within them. His fingers tightened on hers, and she remembered again how much she loved him. What choice did she have? If it would empower her against Isabella's magic, she could do nothing else. Reluctantly she nodded, and with her answer, his mouth twitched into an almost smile of relief.

'What must we do?' she asked.

'We need the book,' he replied, and doubt rippled through her once again.

'Why?'

'Because it contains a power to rival the fortune teller's,' he said. 'Because we need all the help we can get to counter the force of her magic. She is a powerful witch, but perhaps together and with the book, we can find a way to defeat her.'

She sensed the truth in his words, but still she was reluctant to put the book into his hands. It was a precious and dangerous thing that her parents had kept hidden away and safe all these years. And yet, she could not deny her own growing desire for it, for the possibilities it offered. She raised her head towards Rosalind, who was watching them both, her face pale with terror, eyes wide.

'Do you have it?' she asked, and when Rosalind gave an almost imperceptible nod in reply, she said, 'Fetch it.'

'I'm not touching it,' the older woman replied, and a shadow seemed to pass across her. 'But I can show you where it's hidden. But only you.'

Kate followed her into the room where Mary still lay unmoving in the bed, eyes open and gazing blankly into space. Kate kept her head turned away, and any lingering doubts ebbed into the chill of the morning. Rosalind crouched to shift the rug and lift up the floorboard, then pointed to the package that was neatly tucked away, almost invisible against the wood. If Rosalind had not shown her, Kate's gaze would have passed right over it as if it didn't want to be found. She lifted it out and felt the weight of it in her hands. It was heavier than she expected, and though she wanted nothing more than to unwrap it straight away from its covering of cloth and let her fingers rifle through the pages, she was aware of Rosalind, backed to the wall as far as she could get away from it, and Rafe, waiting just beyond the door. She flicked a glance to her mother's still form in the bed and then, with a nod of thanks towards Rosalind, she got to her feet and went back out into the tavern to join Rafe.

They went to the Bull's Head, and she followed Rafe through the locked door at the end of the gallery to find herself in an attic she hadn't even realised existed. A small, shuttered window above a desk let in a dull gleam of light, and books were scattered on every surface. A shelf held an array of items – a globe, an hourglass, a dagger. Feathers and crystals, jars of all shapes and sizes and colours, and cleverly wrought instruments of brass whose purpose she could not even guess at. Ducking beneath the low sloping roofs, her eyes straining to see through the gloom, she stepped carefully around the lines of the circle that was chalked on the floorboards and refused to allow thoughts of Isabella any room in her head.

'Welcome to my study.' Rafe smiled. 'Come, sit.'

They drew up stools to the desk, and Kate laid the book in the space that Rafe cleared for it amongst the mess of papers and books. For a moment, both of them hesitated, caught in the excitement of anticipation. Then, remembering the vacant stare of her mother's eyes, Kate reached out and carefully unwrapped it. It lay before them, inert as any other book. With its dark faded cover, the leather worn smooth from centuries of handling, it exerted a strange fascination. They both went to open it together, their fingers meeting, and a charge ran through her, though whether it was from the touch of Rafe's hand or the contact with the book, it was hard to say. They laughed, awkwardly, and Rafe withdrew his hand with reluctance as Kate opened up the cover.

Two names were written in fading ink on the flyleaf.

Tom Wynter. Toby Chyrche.

She slid her fingertips across the letters, searching for a connection, and found herself wondering why of all the men who must have owned it, only Tom Wynter and her father had thought to inscribe their names within it. Flicking a glance towards Rafe, whose attention was intent on the book, she began very slowly to turn the pages. She was aware of him sitting close beside her and his close concentration on the words before him, her presence apparently forgotten. Written mostly in Latin, she recognised letters of Greek and Hebrew too, and other scripts she did not know. Symbols, some of them familiar from Isabella's attic, were scattered throughout, and now and then, she paused in her turning of the pages to look more closely, though there were none she could understand. She slid another glance towards Rafe, who was rapt, his breath quick with excitement.

'Can you read any of it?'

He wheeled towards her, startled, as though he had quite forgotten she was there. 'Some,' he replied. 'But not enough to perform any of the rites without study.'

She said nothing but kept on turning the pages, hoping still to find something they could use, a rite that would arm them against Isabella's magic, or some instruction on how to break the spell on Mary. Panic began to thread through her limbs – perhaps the book was worthless to them after all. How then could she save her mother? In spite of the rise of her power, she was still no more than a fledgling witch, and the knowledge of her impotence enraged her. She began to flick through the pages more quickly, and she was a little over halfway through the book when she came upon a rite that was written in a different hand. She paused as she realised the words were in English. She stopped, barely breathing, and ran her gaze across the page, struggling to read the tiny writing.

A rite to ask the spirits for whatsoever thou wilt, she managed to make out.

A rite for two people to perform together.

As her eyes tracked down the page, a sweep of understanding shuddered through her. Magic born of the union between a man and a woman. A moment of bliss that has great power in the realm of the spirits. She turned to Rafe, who had lifted his hand to rest it on the page, as though he might absorb the words more clearly through his fingertips. After a moment that felt like an age, he turned to meet her look, and she saw her own excitement and eagerness mirrored in his eyes. Though urgency for answers tapped in her blood, her mother's fate hanging in the balance, it was hard to deny the rising desire inside her. And yet, a sense of danger lurked at the edges of her thoughts. It was dark magic, she reminded herself, that had brought about Tom Wynter's death. She swallowed and imagined the constriction of the rope around her neck, no more breaths to come.

'We'll keep looking,' she said, turning the page. 'There must be others in English.'

Gently, he reached out his hand to stay the movement of her fingers, before he turned back to the page in English. Her own hand was trembling.

'There is no time.' He lifted his head towards the window as though gazing towards her mother, trapped in the Shadow at the Cardinal's Cap. 'Perhaps there are other rituals in here that will also serve, but we have found a rite to help us, and it's in English, simple to decipher. There are no strange requirements, nothing we need except my body and yours, some charcoal and candles, and a circle in the dark.' He nodded towards the circle that was chalked on the boards, and she followed his gaze, her eyes tracing its lines and the symbols around its edge. How many times had he conjured here, she wondered. What other books did he possess to have such arcane knowledge? *I have studied a little*, he had told her, but she knew now it was another lie. This was the workshop of a man who had spent many hours at his craft, and the realisation both reassured and frightened her.

'Will it work?' she asked. 'Will the spirits tell us what we need to know?'

'If the book is as potent as it's claimed to be.'

He must have read the doubt in her eyes because he turned his body fully towards her on the stool, and touched his fingers to her chin, so that she lifted her head to look at him.

'What other choice do we have?' he whispered. 'How else can we set your mother free?'

Briefly, she wondered why he should care so much about her mother, but there was no time for such musings now and, whatever his motives, she was grateful for his aid.

'Are you willing?' he asked, with a nod towards the book.

'Yes,' she murmured, wondering even as she said it if she would come to regret her decision. 'I am willing.'

He gave her a small nod of acknowledgement, and they both turned back to study the book more closely. The words seemed to lift and blur before her eyes, impossible to pin down, and she wanted to cry in frustration. But after a moment, Rafe lifted his eyes from the page and faced her again.

'We must bathe,' he said. 'I'll fetch fresh water from downstairs. Gather candles and charcoal, and lay out a blanket.' He stopped when her gaze travelled to the circle that was chalked on the floorboards: he must have glimpsed her hesitation. 'We have no choice,' he said softly, laying a hand on her arm. 'How else will you discover what you must do?'

She lifted her head, and when she met his eyes with her own, he was looking into her as if he would read her soul.

'You must trust me in this,' he whispered.

Her heart turned over in reluctance but she knew that he was right. Swallowing, her whole body was alive with the sense of his nearness and her fear of the rite to come: it was hard to set aside the doubt. She gave him a small smile in answer and then he was gone, his boots pounding on the wooden stairs.

When he returned a few minutes later with the bowl and jug of water, he set them down near the window. 'Come,' he said. 'Let us bathe.'

Casting a glance across the blanket and candles she had set out within the circle, she got to her feet and went to him at the wash-stand. He was stripping off his doublet and shift, pulling off his stockings, and she let her gaze wander across the muscled body, tracing the lines of the scars that marked the pale skin. Her breathing quickened as he stepped out of his breeches and he was before her, naked and beautiful. The memory of the night turned her insides to water – the taste of him, and the warmth of him inside her. Rafe paused as he reached for the cloth to wash himself and turned to her with a half-smile.

'You too,' he said.

She lowered her head away, embarrassed, and shy now to undress before him – it had been different in the night. But there was a purpose now beyond the consummation of their desire, her mother's life at stake. Turning slightly away, she began to pull at the laces of her bodice, fingers deft, and by the time she was undressed, Rafe had finished his ablutions. He poured more water into the bowl, dipped the cloth and wrung it out. Then, ignoring the hand that reached out to take it from him, he stepped close to her and began to sponge her skin. The water was cold and she shivered, goose bumps rising as he passed the cloth across her shoulders and back, lifting one arm and then the other to wash her flanks. She was aware of his closeness behind her as he squatted down to sponge her buttocks and thighs, the cloth passing gently between them, taking her breath away. She almost stumbled when he stood again and wiped the cloth across her breasts, her belly, her quim. Her nipples hardened, though whether it was from cold or desire she could not have said. Her whole body seemed to be on fire, and when Rafe finally let the cloth slide back into the water and took her hand, she was barely breathing. They stood for a moment of connection, and she braced her soul against her fears of what was to come.

Rafe led her into the circle, and she knelt on the blanket as he told her to do while he paced out the perimeter, calling to the angels to protect them – the ritual magic of the ancients. It was a different art altogether from the witchcraft that ran in her veins but it was no less potent for that. The candles flickered, and ghoulish shadows danced against the rafters of the sloping roof. Closing her eyes, she let Rafe's words fill her like the passage of a favourite piece of music, vibrating deep in her core. They drifted in and out of her consciousness, a caress.

'Gabriel, archangel and guardian of the West…

… Michael, archangel and guardian of the South …

'I beseech Thee, O Lord God, that Thou will deign to bless this Circle, and all those who are therein to preserve us from evil and from trouble …'

She waited, and though the air was cool against her skin she was warm with a fire that burned within her. Rafe turned to face her and she could not tear her eyes away from the beauty of his body – the clean, lithe limbs, the pale smoothness of his skin. The flames inside her licked more keenly, sharp-edged with the darkness of her fear.

Tom Wynter had used this book that lay on the blanket before her.

Tom Wynter had died at the end of a rope.

Rafe knelt close behind her and placed a single kiss on her shoulder blade. Then he whispered for her to go onto all fours. Barely breathing, she did as he bid her, and a moment later she felt the scratch of charcoal tracing lines across the small of her back. Rafe was still mumbling words she could not catch, but the fire within her flared and lifted as the lines became the shape of a sigil, a call to the demon who owned it like a brand that burned right through flesh and bone and into the core of her being. The shape of it consumed her until it was almost all she was aware of, her soul enslaved to this sign on her body.

But some small part of her remained alive to the touch of Rafe's thighs against hers, one hand grasping her hip, as the other guided his cock between her legs, brushing the tip of it against her, testing, until at last he slid inside her with one hard thrust, and the fire within her roared with pain and ecstasy.

Rafe began to murmur the incantation, moving in time with the rhythm of his words. Half-heard, they washed over her ...

'I conjure you ... by the virtue and power of His divine majesty .... and by the innumerable powers that you and your superiors possess ...

I conjure you in the name of Tom Wynter, who controlled you once, and in the name of the Holy Father, and all His marvellous works; by the heavens, by the earth, by the sea, by the depth of the Abyss, by the winds and the waters of the sea ... by this act of bliss that calls you forth ...'

The room went black, the candles extinguished, and the heat that had raged so brightly inside her was snuffed out in a moment to be replaced by the cruel chill of an ice she thought would be her end. How could any living soul survive such brutal cold? Her eyes scanned the dark, searching desperately, and though there was nothing she could see in the blackness, she knew beyond doubt that they were no longer alone. She could sense the demon lurking beyond the circle's edge, and the cold breath of the deathly realms that trailed it.

'I welcome thee, great Lord ...'

Rafe hailed it, welcomed it, and commanded it to help them. It gave a low rumble in reply that in her terror she could not make out.

'Ask your question.' Rafe's whisper was close to her ear, and through her fear, her body still burned with the pleasure of him moving inside her, faster and deeper, their union the power that had drawn the demon from its realms of death.

It was a moment before she could find her voice, her tongue

sticky in her mouth. She swallowed, searching her mind for the right words to say. Then she said, 'Show me what I must do to save my mother from the Shadow. Give me the tools I need to free her.'

There was a moment of silence. Rafe's movements quickened, ecstasy building alongside her fear, fire and ice in her veins, until she climaxed in an explosion of light that burned in the likeness of the sigil that was traced on her skin. Her body shuddered and pulsed, and her mind brimmed full with a sudden wash of images.

A forest clearing. An ancient yew tree standing sentinel.

Tom Wynter with a key in his hand.

A seeping darkness.

And within the fabric of that darkness, the threads of her mother's life holding her in an icy embrace that chilled her to the bone.

The visions began to falter and fade, and from somewhere that seemed very far away, she heard Rafe dismiss the demon. He was still moving inside her, quickening.

'Hold on to whatever it showed you,' he murmured. 'Realise it, send it out into the ether, make it real.'

His fingers dug hard into her hips, and his thighs were slick with sweat against hers. Beyond her body the memory of the visions still hovered, and she raised her eyes towards it briefly, tucking it surely inside her mind so that she would not forget a single detail. Then ice melted into flame once again, the fire of the sigil meeting the heat of her desire as Rafe reached his finish at last.

Afterwards, lying in Rafe's arms on the blanket, Kate barely noticed the cool of the room, still burning with the memory of the rite. Rafe propped himself up on an elbow and trailed his fingers across her breasts and belly, along the inner edges of her thighs, and she was surprised by the new lift of desire inside her, want for him again spreading through her limbs. He bent his head to kiss her, and his lips were soft and warm and moist. Gentle. Loving. Not the fierce bright need of before, their only purpose now the pleasure of their touch.

But however much she wanted him, there was no time. Her mother's life hung shuttered in the dark, and Kate needed to be gone. She lowered her head with a small and sorrowful shake and they moved sadly away from each other, still reluctant to break the magic of the moment. But Rafe, understanding, got to his feet, and she let her eyes feast on the pale, strong beauty of his body as he dismissed the guardians of the circle.

When they were dressed and warm again before the fire in Rafe's quarters, he asked what she had seen. She took a sip of her wine before she answered. The last passions of the rite had begun to ebb and she was weary. The sigil on her back pulsed dully, and she wondered how long she would bear its imprint, if she would ever be free of it.

'Tom Wynter has the key,' she said. 'Tom will grant me access to the darkness.'

'And then?'

'I don't know,' she replied, with a shrug. 'But the goddess will guide me. I know she will.'

'And you'll go tonight?' She could hear the trepidation in his voice.

'I must. And I will go alone – I thank you for all you've done but you cannot help me any more.' She took another mouthful of wine, warm and soothing against her throat, and shivered again. But the memory of the furnace that had inhabited her during the rite burned fierce and hot inside her.

'I should come with you,' Rafe was saying. 'Surely it is safer with us both.'

She smoothed down the front of her skirts and swung her head towards him. 'This is witchcraft, Rafe, not the magic you are used to. You have no weapons against its power, as I do. No witchblood you can call on. Besides, you're needed at the Cockpit – they cannot do the play without you.'

He sighed in reluctant agreement.

'I know you only want to help, but I must do this alone,' she said, 'I'll go to the Cross Bones at dusk and meet you at the Cardinal's Cap when it is done. Then, together, we will decide what to do about Isabella Last.'

He said nothing, but only took a drink of his wine and stared into the flames, as though he would read the answers in their depths.

22

LET'S AWAY TO PRISON

Rafe left Kate at the Bull's Head with reluctance. A last embrace, and words of courage whispered in her ear. Would it be the last time he saw her? For all the latent power of Kate's witchblood, Isabella was a formidable foe, and fear for Kate trailed at his heels. Shaking his head to rid his mind of the thought of it, he threaded quickly through the crowds that had gathered on the bridge as travellers hurried this way and that to beat the closing of the gates.

There was nothing more he could have done to help her, he told himself. The rite they had done had given her the knowledge she needed and he could do no more, but his spirit still chafed as he stepped off the bridge and into the city, winding his way through the darkening afternoon towards the theatre. The others would be waiting for him as they readied for the evening's performance, anxious and fretting. He should have been with them all day – pacing out the scenes, measuring the distances for the stage, last-minute rehearsals. He imagined their increasing dismay at his absence, for they had no other actor to call upon to play the part without him.

'Good of you to join us at last,' John Lowin observed with a shake of his head, when Rafe finally stepped through the door. 'We had all but given you up for lost.'

'My apologies,' he replied, with a dip of his head. 'I was delayed.' Then he hurried through the empty theatre towards the tiring room behind the stage to change into Prospero's robes.

A little later, as the first of the playgoers trickled through the doors and began to take their seats, Rafe peered out from the balcony above the stage to watch. It was a wealthier crowd than he was used to – courtiers, merchants, and gentlemen with their ladies in fine-coloured silks, jewels glinting in the light of a myriad of candles that burned against the walls. This audience preferred the indoor comforts of the Cockpit to the uncertain weather of the old playhouses on Bankside, and they relished the risk of their small rebellion against the Puritans. The whole theatre echoed with the hubbub of voices and boots, chair legs scraping on the boards, coughs, and the rustle of fabric as people shifted and fussed, greeting friends, getting comfortable. He marvelled at how so many people knew to come when they had passed the word so discreetly. John Lowin's work, he guessed, with his network of contacts built over all his years in the business of plays. He admired them for coming. In these days it took courage to defy the rules – parliament's punishment was swift and severe.

The seats filled quickly, and when every one was taken and still more people were standing at the back behind them, the boys who had collected the entrance money closed and barred the doors. Then, with a nod to the youth who handled the props, Rafe left his vantage point in the balcony and hurried down the stairs to await his entrance in the tiring house. The first clap of thunder came just as he reached it, and the first players strode out upon the stage.

The audience gasped at the sudden crash and shifted in their seats, worldly cares abruptly forgotten. Another clap, and though he had known it was coming, Rafe too, flinched at the sound, his nerves on edge. Briefly, he sent a thought towards Kate. She would be at the graveyard now, facing Isabella in some unknown way he

could not imagine, and he had to struggle to bring his mind back
to the world of the play that was just beginning on the stage
beyond the tiring room curtain. It seemed to have lost all its power
to enchant him, and the realisation saddened him. Time was when
the realm of the playhouse's magic had offered him the world.

'Boatswain!

Here, master. What cheer?

*Good – speak to th' mariners. Fall to't yarely, or we run
ourselves aground. Bestir, bestir!'*

But the first lines had barely even been uttered when a sudden
mighty crash at the doors at the back of the theatre silenced the
players mid-speech. Beneath his make-up Rafe felt the colour leach
from his face, and the illusion of the play's world was shattered in a
moment. The actors were actors no more, but a haphazard group
of dazed men in costume, startled into sudden wariness. Rafe
swung a glance to the others as first one soldier then another
stepped through the doors into the theatre, and he saw his own
fear reflected in their eyes. Though they had all known the risks,
they had still hoped to escape the authorities' notice. Did the
sheriff not have more important matters to concern him when the
fate of the King hung in the balance? He thought of King Charles
in a gaol cell, awaiting certain death. Would the players meet the
same end? There would be no clean blade for the likes of them to
sever their heads from their neck. No, they would be dropped
from a gallows, to kick and struggle as their last breaths were
choked from their bodies. They would die as Tom Wynter had
died, and he suppressed a shudder at the prospect, schooling his
face to calm defiance. They were actors, after all, and perhaps this
would be their greatest role.

Women in the audience began to scream, getting to their feet
in panic. Stools and benches tipped and fell as the crowd milled,
their exit blocked by the phalanx of guards. Men's voices rose in
shouts, and scuffles began to break out as soldiers tried to lay hands

on those who would evade them. On stage, two of the players turned to flee, heading for the door that led from the tiring house, but more troops had filled the space behind them and there was nowhere for them to run. They stopped, trapped, as the soldiers stepped forward to apprehend them.

'You are under arrest!' A voice boomed above the riot. 'By order of Parliament.'

The audience hesitated and a small group close to the door made a run for it. On the stage, soldiers marched forward and began to grasp the players one by one. Instinctively, Rafe struggled against the grip of the man who held him until a pike was lowered, forcing him to stillness though the rage still seethed, heartbeat hammering, fury in his blood. All of them resisted, all of them fought, until one of the soldiers, growing frustrated, backhanded Rafe across the face. He fell like a stone and he stayed down for a moment, wiping the blood from his mouth as he struggled to suppress the desire to retaliate, to launch himself to his feet and set upon the man who had struck him. From the audience, a woman's high wail of fear carried above the disquiet, eerie and unsettling.

A rough hand hauled him back to standing. He could taste the metal of the blood in his mouth, and when the man's grip tightened around the muscle of his arm, it was instinct to jerk away. But another soldier moved in on the other side of him so that he was trapped between them. The audience began to quieten with the realisation that they were not the ones in danger, but they wavered still, caught in the indecision of their fear. Then a couple of merchants in thick black velvets near the back turned and began to run, breaking the spell. The whole audience pressed towards the door, pushing and shoving, voices rising once more in anger and fear and pain as feet were trampled and skirts ripped in the crush. Rafe watched them go for a moment before the soldiers began to lead the players away, boots loud on the boards as they tramped their authority in unison. Risking a glance behind him, Rafe saw that a few of the guards had remained behind, searching through the props and costumes in the tiring house, gathering them up.

Stealing them, no doubt, a wardrobe that had once clothed Shakespeare and Burbage and Edward Alleyn. He spat a gob of blood onto the stage, and one of the men who held him tightened his grasp, forcing Rafe's shoulder up into an unnatural angle that spasmed with pain.

'No more misdoing from you,' the man growled, and Rafe could only acquiesce as he was led out with the others into the winter night, the bitter chill biting easily through the fine linen robe that was all he was wearing. All of them, taken in the clothes they had been wearing on the stage: Simon, in Miranda's skirts that swayed as he walked, and John Lowin in a silk and velvet robe that dragged in the dirt behind him.

23

WE KNOW WHAT WE ARE, BUT KNOW NOT WHAT WE MAY BE

On her way to the Cross Bones Kate skirted the market, oblivious to the dangers that lurked in the darkening passages, and when a rough hand grabbed at her arm she was so startled that she lashed out instinctively, bringing her hand hard against the man's face, sending him reeling in surprise. He swore and lunged after her but she had picked up her skirts and run before he fully regained his balance. She could hear him yelling, and the words *dirty whore* echoed off the buildings.

In the bustle of the High Street she felt safer. The road was vivid with life – travellers making a last-minute dash for the bridge and the bright conviviality of the inns and taverns spilling out into the street. Beggars patrolled, rich pickings to be had, and a one-legged man plucked at her sleeve as she passed.

'I lost it fighting for the King, miss. Can you help an old soldier?'

'I'm sorry,' she murmured. 'I have nothing to give you. I wish I did.'

He must have seen the truth in her face because he touched his forehead in respect and said, 'Bless you, miss,' before limping away on a rough-fashioned crutch to try someone else.

It was quieter on Red Cross Street, with few people abroad,

and the graveyard was silent and shrouded in the growing gloom of the dusk. At the gate Kate paused, heaviness seeping through her limbs, remembering the last time she had come here. Instinctively, she looked behind her, head tilted to listen, but she could hear nothing but the soft whisper of her own breath and far-off voices that carried in drifts on the wind. A woman's high laugh blew past her in a snatch.

Swallowing, and holding the vision from the rite in the centre of her thoughts, Kate put her shoulder to the gate and shoved it open wide enough to slip through the gap. Then she paused and scanned the darkness as her eyes picked out the squares of inky black and the paler grey that marked the way between them. In her mind's eye she could see the yew tree beyond that marked her grandfather's grave, and she trod softly towards it, setting down each foot with care in the gathering dark, hoping she had remembered aright. But her memory served her well, and when she reached the grave she sank to her knees beside it.

'Help me, Tom.'

Her whisper sounded loud in the silence.

'The spirits told me that you have the key to save my mother. Will you help me?'

She waited, eyes closed, seeing the image of him in her mind as he had come to her in the vision, pale as mist and beautiful, with blue-grey eyes that gazed from realms beyond the living. Such charm and beauty as he had never seen, John Lowin had said. But now, with his form once more before her thoughts, she noticed for the first time the dark welts on his neck, scars from the rope that had taken his life, and when she opened her eyes again she knew that he was with her – she could sense the ghost of his presence in the darkness.

'You must call on your power,' she heard, 'and walk in the Shadow.'

She was silent.

'You doubt me.'

'I am afraid,' she whispered.

'There is much you do not yet understand. But my blood runs in your veins. Trust me.'

Kate touched her hand to her own neck, imagining the tightening of a rope and the slow restriction of her breath, the final gasps for life. Instinctively, she reached towards the headstone as though to wipe away the hurt, and her fingertips brushed against something smooth and cool just beneath the surface of the earth at its base. Something that had not been there before. She scrabbled to uncover it, her fingernails filling with cold dirt and grit until she had prised it free from its hiding place. She held it up and examined it. It was a poppet, the wax figure of a woman, pale and lifelike. She ran her fingertips across the tiny face and remembered Isabella moulding the shape of it in the candlelit attic, the cold glimmer in her eyes as she caressed the soft wax to form the woman's body. A woman that owed her something, she had said.

Mary, Kate realised now. Her mother. To be buried in some unclean place. Here, she had meant, at the Cross Bones, where the souls of the sinful and the damned were laid to rest. Her hand closed around it.

'What must I do?'

'You must journey to the Shadow and bring Mary home. She still has a part to play. But make haste. Time is short.'

Kate scrambled to her feet and stood for a moment beside the grave. Taking long slow breaths to calm herself, she reached deep into her being to unearth the knowledge and the courage she needed. For what seemed like an age she felt only the weight of her ignorance and the fear that she would fail. How could she defeat so powerful a witch, when she had learned so little? How could her inexperience possibly match Isabella's lifelong knowledge? It was a most unfair battle, and the shadow of despair threatened to fall. She fingered the poppet, almost paralysed with indecision.

Trust. She heard Tom Wynter's voice once more. Let your witchblood guide you. It will lead you truly.

Closing her eyes, she let his voice envelop her, surrounding her like a caress. Then she tied her thoughts to her breath as Isabella had taught her, and slowly she began to feel the first light shimmer in her blood, a soft thrum that ran in her veins. Her hand tightened around the poppet as the vibration began to well, rising into the beat of a drum, power surging through her.

She opened her eyes and, to her surprise, Tom was there before her, beautiful and pale and smiling, real and bright as day. Bowing his head in a nod of satisfaction as Kate gave herself over to the instinct that was running now in her blood, he faded once more into the night. She smiled in return, glad for the reassurance of his presence. She was not alone, after all, and the knowledge of it lent her courage.

Tucking the poppet into her bodice to keep it safe, she began to search the ground around her, hunting for sticks and branches to fashion a circle. Working quickly now, surer of herself, she laid the sticks end to end to encircle the tree and the grave. Her fingers stiffened with the cold, fingertips blackened with soil, and the wood became harder to hold but she barely noticed, intent on her task.

When the circle was complete at last she stood in its centre, and she was aware of the hum of her blood, imbued once again with the spirit of magic, roaring with connection to all that is, was and ever will be. She paced the edge of the circle, but her feet barely seemed to touch the ground, her whole being buoyed by the call of her witchblood. The same surge of power ran through her as on that night at the crossroads when she had first set eyes on Hecate: she was a witch of ancient blood, brim-full of her ancestors' knowledge. And as she turned to each quarter to call to the guardians, the words came to her lips with surprising ease: it was as if she had known them all her life.

'*I call you, spirit of the air, guardian of the East, to watch and protect us ...*'

When she had called to each of the quarters, she felt safer within the circle of their protection. Then she laid out the candles she had brought and, with a flick of her fingers, conjured them into light. Amazed by this power she hadn't known she possessed, she almost laughed with delight as she knelt again by the grave. She still had no clear understanding of what was to come but she trusted now to Tom's presence and the instinct that resided in her blood to show her the way.

'*Maiden, Mother, Crone,*' she called out. '*Guardian of the Crossroads, Keeper of the Keys.*

I call on you now to open the doorway and light up the path that leads to the Shadow.

I have nothing to offer but the courage in my heart and the love I bear my mother.

Guide me to her. Let me free her from the fortune teller's grasp.'

She waited, hoping she had done right. Questions arose in her thoughts and she pushed them aside – there was no time for doubts. She needed to be certain and strong, to feel the pulse of her witchblood.

'*Show me what I must do.*'

'Trust.' She heard Tom's voice close beside her. 'Do as you must. Hecate will guide you.'

Slowly, the silent dark began to come alive. At the edges of her vision she glimpsed shapes like the shadows that haunted the corners of the Wounded Raven. Pale lights hovered in the air, glowing, and between them glimmered eyes that watched her, the eyes of no earthly creatures. A mist rose, curling its fingers through and around the shadows, and from somewhere close by there came the high-pitched call of a screech owl. Kate closed her eyes and shuddered, terror in every fibre.

Forcing herself to open her eyes, she saw a new light. A curious glow glimmered in the trunk of the tree before her as though she were seeing firelight through a crack in a door. The tree from her vision, she realised, the gate to the Shadow. It welcomed her, drawing her in. A world within the tree? She reached forward, tentative fingers brushing the bark to touch the warmth, and with the movement she began to tumble into blackness.

Over and over, falling, the endless descent of nightmares. She opened her mouth to scream but no sound emerged, and though she flailed her limbs in desperate search of something to grasp, her hands found only the air, fingers curling but touching nothing. The fall seemed to last forever and when finally she landed, unhurt, she found herself in a world that was like nowhere she had ever been in her waking life – a forest of darkness with ash underfoot, trees without leaves, gnarled and dead, and above her a sky that pulsed, blood-red oozing through cracks in a dark haze of smoke. Fear gripped her innards as she realised it was the world of her childhood nightmares, where the old man had stalked her. Her mouth was gritty and the taste of the air was acrid. Was this the Shadow? The realm of her forebears? It was not as she had imagined it. How could such a foul place be the source of a witch's power? Then she remembered that she was in a world of the dead and the departed, a memory of the past. It was the realm of spirit, an otherworld, home to the gods, demons and ghosts – it was no place for the living.

'Tom?'

There was no answer, and her spirit quivered with the realisation that now she was alone. Perhaps he could not follow where she had gone. Perhaps he did not want to. Lifting her gaze to take in the desolation before her, her eyes lit on a movement a little distance away.

A shadow that shifted. Eyes in the dark.

As above, so below.

Calling on every last ounce of courage in her heart and drawing herself upright, she lifted her chin, eyes skyward.

'*I am a witch of ancient blood,*' she said, and wondered if the Shadow would hear the tremble in her voice. '*And I claim rite of passage in the Shadow.*'

Dark shapes flitted through the trees around her, and she waited. She should have brought an offering, she thought. Wine, or honey, or blood. But she had not even a knife to cut herself. The shapes seemed to swarm closer, settling into human shapes, dark-robed, pale-faced. Eyes flashed red through the gloom.

'*I come naked,*' she said, surprised by the words she found on her tongue, *'with nothing to give but all that I am – my blood, my heart, my spirit. It is yours. All I ask in return is for the spirit of Mary Winter to be returned to the world of the living.'*

A whisper flickered all around her, like a breath of wind through winter branches.

'In her stead, I give you this poppet.'

She held the wax doll high above her head in both hands, and wheeled very slowly so that the spirits on all sides of her could see its form, though she guessed they saw with eyes that needed no direct line of sight. The whisper seemed to flicker closer, filling the air with the echo of its hiss, until all her thoughts were suspended in its vibration. The drum of her witchblood threatened to fall away, fear dragging once more at her limbs, but in spite of it she forced her arms to remain aloft and her feet to still keep turning, the poppet bargain still defiantly in play. Her head began to pulse with the din of the voices that filled it, pain like a band around her temples, deafening, until her body began to sway, giving way before the onslaught. What did they want from her?

With one last mighty effort of will, she found the strength to ask again.

'Will you set Mary Winter's spirit free?'

The hiss diminished, as if shocked into quiet by her words, and she waited, barely breathing, the poppet still held tight in her hands. Her arms ached with the effort of holding it up, but slowly she realised the doll was softening between her fingers so that the shape of the woman was becoming blurred and indistinct in her hands. Wax began to drip through her fingers, warm as it ran across her skin, and she lowered her arms and held out what was left of the poppet before her. The liquid dropped to the ground at her feet until nothing more of it remained beyond a memory of its warmth against her skin.

'I thank you,' she said, and the words that came to her lips seemed to issue from somewhere deep inside her – the instinct of her witchblood. *'I wish now to depart this place. I thank you for*

letting me pass. Show me how to return to the realm of the living, and I will trouble you no more.'

Nothing stirred. A deeper silence breathed through the forest, and Kate's innards contracted in sudden terror that she was trapped – that the Shadow had taken her spirit in exchange for her mother and the poppet had meant nothing after all. She waited, heartbeat quick, mouth dry. Then, she began to wheel slowly once more, eyes searching the gloom for she knew not what. Behind her, alone amongst the dead and ashy trees, she saw a vast and ancient yew she had not noticed before. How could she have missed it? A gnarled and knotty trunk with heavy branches that bowed to the ground to meet a carpet of needles that covered the earth at its roots. Hope sparked. It was a beacon of life and light, bright with the ancient sap of ages – she had only ever seen such majesty in dreams. She stepped towards it, reverent and in awe as she placed her palm against one of the branches, feeling the living warmth against her skin.

'Take us home,' she whispered. 'Great and ancient yew. Take us home.'

She stood back and waited, running her eyes across the folds of bark, hollows unnumbered, until a small glimpse of light flickered between the roots, growing like a fire that has just been lit and shedding a glow that seemed to spread, inviting. She watched as the source widened, a door opening, beckoning until, without making a conscious decision to go, she found herself stepping through.

Then, nothing.

❦ 24 ❦

SICK IN THE WORLD'S REGARD,
WRETCHED AND LOW

Kate woke startled, disorientated, unsure of her whereabouts. She stared about her then shivered, suddenly aware of the cold. She was at the Cross Bones, she remembered, kneeling as she had been when she entered the Shadow, and Tom's grave was beside her. Above her, a narrow moon was close to setting, shadows long across the cemetery. Mary was nowhere to be seen and Kate hoped her mother's spirit had returned to her body. Was she waking up now at the Cardinal's Cap, surprised and wondering how she had got there? There was so much Kate needed to ask, a whole story waiting to be told.

Around her, she could see the outline of the protective circle she had made. She must open it, she thought, and dismiss the guardians who had kept her safe. She turned, following the edge of the circle with her eyes for a moment, before her blood seemed to freeze with foreboding. Her breath quickened as her eyes searched the darkness of the graveyard. Another moment, and she saw him.

Nathan, his pale face just visible in the dim light beyond the circle's edge, was watching her.

Her breath left her body in a gasp as dread swept again through her veins. She stumbled to her feet, legs numb from the cold and refusing to move, but even as she staggered, she kept her gaze pinned to him. He was observing her, an odd smile on his face, and though her first fear was that he would try to force himself on her again, it took only the length of a heartbeat to realise he had a different plan. She followed his gaze as it traced the line of the circle and, with a surge of horror, she understood.

He meant to denounce her as a witch.

Instinctively she raised a hand to touch her neck, remembering the welts on Tom's throat where the rope had burned as it choked the breath from his body. She shuddered, the chill of terror colder than the winter night, reaching deeper inside. Nathan stepped forward into the circle, heedless of its sanctity, and though Kate made to run, her legs and feet failed to respond, half-frozen. He grabbed her arm, fingers vice-like on the muscle. She would have more bruises come morning. Then he leaned in close and she could smell the sour ale on his breath.

'Think you could get the better of me, eh?' he murmured. 'You're just a girl.'

She fought against his grip and twisted her head away from him but he tightened his hold, wrenching her arm with a vicious jerk that sent a spasm of pain through her shoulder.

'But they'll hang a girl just the same, you know. If she's a witch.'

She fought again, refusing to give him the satisfaction of her submission, and he dragged her closer against his body until all her senses were suffused with the stale unwashed scent of him, the putrefying cut on his cheek. Unlaundered clothes and damp, ale and tobacco, and underneath it all a taint of something sweeter she recognised as the smell of Isabella.

'I've sent a boy to the constable,' he said. 'So enjoy your last moments of the sky above you, earth beneath your feet. Not long till you're swinging from a rope and then eternity in Hell.'

Kate struggled again against his hold but his grip was firm. Unable to free herself from his grasp, she spat instead into his face. Enraged, he didn't even pause to wipe the spittle away before he brought his hand across her cheek, striking her to the ground.

She could taste the blood on her lip, but she smiled up at him regardless, pleased to have goaded him in spite of the punishment she knew was to follow. He grabbed her hair and hauled her back to her feet, and she yelped with the pain of it tearing at her scalp as he gripped her jaw between the fingers of one hand and, tipping her face up to look at him, placed his mouth on hers. She fought to free herself as his tongue forced its way into her mouth, and he dragged harder at her hair until she was forced to be still. He gave a low laugh, let go of her jaw and reached to her skirts, ravelling them up to search out the flesh of her thighs and the soft triangle between them, his fingers hard and rough against her skin.

'Touch me there and I'll curse you,' she spat. 'You'll never tup anyone again.'

It was not a curse she knew how to do but it had its effect – he understood the power of magic well enough to be afraid, and he let her skirts drop once more to the ground.

Men's voices and the sound of running feet turned him away from her to peer into the dark. But he kept his hold on her hair and she had no choice but to submit. Torches and lanterns approached, bobbing in the cold air as the flames twisted through the dark, and the pale shadows from the moon faded as the lights came closer. Nathan watched and waited, and in the pause she called to Tom in her head.

Help me. Or I will meet the same end as you.

Have faith, she heard. *Trust.*

Then the guards were upon them and she blinked in the brightness of the torches, the men's faces in shadow behind the flames. Nathan showed them the circle and she saw the hatred in their glances towards her. Though she drew some satisfaction from their fear of her, she knew it would do her no good in the end. Ignorance brings out the worst in men – witches had died agonising deaths all through history because of it.

Two men approached her, looking her up and down, appraising. She saw the disgust in the eyes of the older one, sweat on his upper lip from the exertion of the run to arrest her, and the open curiosity in the face of the other.

'Ain't you never seen a witch before?' the older man said.

He shook his head. 'I never thought they'd be so young and pretty. Thought they was all old and wrinkled.'

'The Devil is cunning,' the other man said. 'Don't be fooled. She's rotten underneath. There are no words for the perversions that pretty face is hiding.'

Kate said nothing but gave the young man a small smile. She saw him fight the temptation to return it, a young man's natural reply to a pretty woman, but when he grasped her arm as he was told, his grip was still pitiless. Then, between them, the two men dragged her out of the circle and across the graveyard towards the gate. On the way, she managed to cast a single look behind her towards Tom's grave and the yew tree, where she thought she saw a wisp of the image of her grandfather's ghost. But she may have merely imagined it, the hopeful vision of a frightened mind. For all her bravado on the outside, she was shaking in her core.

They half dragged, half carried her to the Justice of the Peace, and Kate fought them all the way so that when they arrived and the Justice's housekeeper opened the door they threw her with relief to the hall floor at her feet. The old woman stifled a scream of startlement as she leaped back, and Kate looked up to see a lined face staring down at her in horror. She would have thought a Justice's housekeeper would be more used to such things.

'Is your master home?' The constable's voice rang loud in the quiet house.

'He is,' the woman replied. 'I will fetch him.' She slid an uneasy glance at the prisoner before she swung away, skirts whispering on the rush mats that covered the flagstones. Kate rubbed at one knee where she had landed before the young guard helped her once more to her feet. She gave him a small, grateful smile for his kindness and saw the flush across his cheek. But she kept her head tilted away from Nathan, who stood watching her with malice in his eyes. A shudder ran through her – he would see her dead if he could, and with every breath she felt the noose at her throat draw tighter.

The housekeeper returned. 'This way.'

Kate let the young guard guide her along the hall to a large room at the back of the house where a great fire burned in the biggest fireplace she had ever seen. A coat of arms hung above the mantel, three foxes and a chough on a background of gold and blue. Shelves full of books and ledgers lined one wall, and behind a great oak desk sat the Justice. He was younger than she had expected, with dark curls that hung to his shoulders, and pale, intelligent eyes beneath mobile brows. He was no Puritan, that much she could tell from the fine velvets he wore, sable grey, and a little spark of hope kindled inside her – her prettiness must surely be in her favour with such a man. But still, her fate hung in his hands and if she read him wrong her life would be forfeit. Lowering her eyes, she was careful to seem demure before him.

'What have we here?' He sat back in his chair, fingers steepled before his chest, contemplating her.

'A witch, sir,' the constable replied. 'Caught in the act of summoning. In a circle in a graveyard when we found her.'

The Justice tilted his head, interested. 'And who accuses her?'

Nathan stepped forward. 'I do.'

'Of what, exactly?'

Nathan lifted a hand to the knife wound across his cheek.

'This, your lordship,' he said, voice wheedling and subservient, a tone she had not heard from him before. She glared at him with contempt. 'It has not healed, just as she promised. It festers. She cursed me because I would not lie with her.'

The Justice turned to Kate. 'Is this true?'

She shook her head, not trusting her voice.

'Speak, girl,' the Justice demanded.

'It is not true,' she said, lifting her eyes to meet her questioner for the first time. He held her gaze for a moment, and though she saw intelligence in their depths there was little kindness, and the flicker of hope guttered in her belly. She couldn't think how best to play this game that offered her life as prize.

Tom, she thought, but this time she heard no answer.

'Yet you were found within a circle in a graveyard, were you not?'

'I did not curse this man,' she said. 'I've done harm to no one.'

'Then what were you about at the Cross Bones, my dear? What game were you playing?'

'I was visiting my grandparents' graves. I ... I ... hoped for their counsel ... it was a foolish attempt ... I have never done such a thing before.'

The Justice let out a long sigh. 'And who were your grandparents?'

'Tom Wynter, sir. And Sarah Chyrche.'

'And your parents?'

Kate hesitated, and for a moment she felt herself begin to sway with fatigue and fear. Tightening her muscles, curling her toes, she forced herself to stand straight, to think.

'My father is dead,' she said. 'And my mother ...' How could she explain? She said, 'I left my mother in The Hague.'

The Justice observed her, apparently alert to her weariness and her hesitation. He said, 'And you travelled from The Hague for the purpose of finding your grandparents?'

'I travelled in the service of a lady, sir. As her maid and seamstress.'

'How know you this man?' He gave a lazy gesture of his hand towards Nathan, who ran the tip of his tongue across his lips. Like a snake she thought. Venomous.

'He is also in the lady's service.'

'I see.'

'She killed her father, sir,' Nathan said then. 'So that she might follow me to England.'

The Justice considered this, the steeple of fingers tapping against his lips. Then he rose to his feet in one languid movement.

'All of you, out,' he said. 'Except her.' He pointed a long finger towards Kate's chest with a movement that seemed to arrest the beating of her heart. She swallowed, held her breath, and waited as the others shuffled out of the door. The door clicked shut behind them and the Justice rounded the desk to lean his hips against it just in front of her. She kept her eyes lowered, wary.

'What is your name, girl?'

'Kate Winter, sir.'

'Well, Miss Winter, I can tell you I believe not one word of the tale you have told. You were found inside a circle of magic in a graveyard at night, and whatever fantastic story you may concoct for the reasons, the facts are plain. You were engaged in an act of witchcraft. Do you deny it?'

'I harmed no one, sir,' she pleaded. 'I only wanted the counsel of my grandparents.'

'You knew how to cast a circle, knew how to raise their spirits, and yet you claim it was not witchcraft?'

Kate sniffed, blinking back the tears that threatened behind her eyes. She would hang, she thought, as Tom had hanged, and the rope would snuff the breath from her body. She touched a hand to her neck, conscious of its fragility.

'Prison for you now, my dear.' He peered into her face and she turned her head away. 'And we will talk again before your case goes to the Grand Jury. I'll hear the truth before they hang you. You have my word.'

Circling the desk once again, he resumed his seat and drew a sheet of paper towards him. She heard the nib of his quill scratch out the words that held her fate, and risked a glance towards it as he finished, sprinkling the salt, shaking it dry. From the side of her eye she saw him fold it with meticulous care and affix his seal. Then he crossed to the door and summoned the constable back into the room.

'Take her to the Marshalsea,' he said. 'Here is the warrant.'

The young guard slid his hand under her arm and nudged her forward. She resisted the urge to struggle, for what good would it do here, now? She had fought his grip all the way from the graveyard and it had availed her nothing. She must save her strength, she realised, and think of another way to save herself. So she let him lead her from the room, and walked beside him, obedient, all the way through the chill winter night till they reached the vast dark door of the prison.

Outside the Marshalsea the guard kept his hand on her arm as they waited. She turned to look at him. He was very young, she thought, younger than her, and too callow for such work – his innocence would not last long. Then the great door was wrenched open with a clunk of iron as the bolts were shot back. He bundled her through the opening, and when the door slammed shut again behind her she flinched, startled, drawing close to him out of instinct – clinging to warmth and life as she tasted the foetid air of the prison. He didn't push her away as she expected and she was grateful. She wondered if he had been inside before, and if it frightened him too.

'This way.' The gaoler held up a candle, and before he turned away she saw the grime in the lines of his face, teeth black and rotting. Blinking back her tears as she was borne forward through a maze of corridors that rang with human misery, she shuttered her mind to the horrors she could imagine behind each door they passed. Now and then a wail sounded, like an animal in pain, and at one door she heard the pounding of a fist against the iron, slow and monotonous, hopeless. Her spirit shrank inside her, curling into a ball in her guts – this was the rest of her life, this place of misery and despair. Until she swung from a rope, this would be her world. She tightened her hold on the young guard's arm until at last the gaoler stopped at a door ahead of them and began to search methodically through the bunch of keys that hung at his waist.

Finally, he opened the door with a squeal of wood on stone that cut through her mind, and then she was cast through the opening and thrown to her knees onto filthy straw. The stench almost made her heave, and by the time she recovered her senses the door had been locked behind her and the men's footsteps had receded into silence.

The cell was almost black, lit only by the flickers of a torch in the passage beyond the small, barred opening in the door, and a missing brick in the wall high above them that led to the outside world. In the darkness she was aware of other bodies, other souls in fear and pain. Shadows lurked at the edges of her vision – the ghosts of those who had gone before, she supposed, doomed to haunt this place. Trembling, both with fear and the bitter cold, she waited for her eyes to adjust, picking out the living shapes as best she could. No one spoke. No one acknowledged her, and she shuffled towards a space by the wall, drew her knees up to her chest, and curled into herself.

Then she lifted her mind towards Tom once again and begged him silently for help.

25

THE SPIRITS OF THE DEAD MAY WALK
AGAIN

Mary woke in the bed she shared with Rosalind at the Cardinal's Cap, sleepy-eyed and still drowsy. For a moment she floated in the in-between, savouring the laziness before the sudden recollection of the night startled her awake. She could hear the bells at St Saviour's striking the hour, the chimes drifting in snatches on the breeze. Her mind followed their toll above the murmur of Bankside but she didn't think to count them till it was too late. The laughter of a woman echoed closer at hand along the passage outside the door, and for a single breath she thought herself back as a girl again in the brothel, working. Then she remembered she was a different person now, and the memory of the night tumbled into clearer focus through her mind.

The cold, the dark, the Shadow.

The terror that had pressed around her heart.

The sense of sinking under water, and no light to show her which way to swim to save herself.

How had she returned home? What power had saved her?

She sat up abruptly in the cold room. Images played like a nightmare in her thoughts, making her wonder if she had merely dreamt it, the Shadow nothing more than the imaginings of a brain overwrought with too much grief and worry. She swallowed, clutching the quilts to her chest against the chill. The fire was almost out, and the pulsing embers threw out a weak orange light. In its glow, the room seemed to be the most wondrous place she had ever been – no watching eyes, no shifting shades of death.

Sighing with relief to be home, she forced herself out of the warmth of the bed and, taking up her clothes from where someone had laid them neatly on the chair, she stood before the dying fire to dress, shivering.

It had been no dream, she thought, as she drew the laces tight across her chest. She had been cast into a realm of death, and now she was free. But how? She took a deep breath to quell a rising sense of panic. Then another, but it made no difference. Something inside her was alive to some new danger she did not yet know.

Kate, she thought again. Where was Kate?

Finishing her dressing with fumbling fingers, she ran her hands across her knotted hair and stepped out into the passage to meet the roil of sound and warmth from the tavern. Rosalind saw her as soon she appeared, keen eyes missing nothing that passed within the tavern walls. Giving a coy curtsey to the young man she was flirting with, she crossed to the mouth of the passage in a few quick strides, face bright with a smile of relief and concern.

'You've returned,' she breathed, taking Mary's hand in her own. 'Kate did it. God be praised.'

'Kate?' Mary replied. 'She is here?'

'Aye. She came with her man to find you. They took the book.' She gave a slight shrug, and Mary's innards turned over with fear. Kate had saved her and put her own life in danger. But where was she now?

'Oy!' A man's shout made Rosalind turn her head to scan the room. 'Where's my ale?'

'Be patient, sir – I will bring it to you anon.' She swung back to her friend, squeezing her hands in an urgent plea.

'Be wary, walk with care. Alexander's shadow stalks this place again.'

'I must find Kate.'

'Mistress!' The man's drunken voice roared again. 'My ale, if you please!'

'Go to him,' Mary said. 'I will return soon.'

Rosalind nodded and, replacing her best hostess smile, she took the jug from the boy who had brought it at last then sashayed between the tables to deliver it to the roaring man. For a moment Mary watched her. Then, remembering she had neither eaten nor drunk for she knew not how long, she turned back down the passage towards the kitchen in search of sustenance. When she had filled her shrunken belly with some wine and a little bread and cheese, she slipped her cloak across her shoulders and sidled through the tavern to the door, avoiding the reaching hands with a skill learned long ago.

Outside on the quay, the night was bitter-cold and dark with cloud. There were few people about although the river was still alive with traffic – lanterns bobbed through the gloom. Mary gathered her cloak closer to her throat. Then, with a quick glance back along the row of buildings, she lit a torch from the one at the door, and bent her steps along the quay towards the closed-up market, senses tingling and wary. Few lights flared at these doorways and it seemed a long way between them.

Hurrying through the dark-lit passages, she passed two beggars sitting huddled together for warmth in a doorway and wondered why they hadn't found a more sheltered spot to spend the night. A drunkard was leaning against a wall, vomit splattering at his feet. The acid stench hung in the air, and though she held her breath as she passed it made no difference; she could smell it anyway and had to swallow down her own rising bile. These were not her streets any more and she no longer moved with the same confidence she used to; fear pricked at the back of her neck as she cast glances around her, vigilant for danger. Turning a corner close to the High Street, she had to pull up short to stop herself colliding with a man who had a whore against the wall. His bare arse was pale and round, quivering.

'Watch where you're going, bitch,' he snarled, leaning towards her. As she shrank back and away, startled, she caught the whore's eye. The woman winked and Mary answered with a smile before she half ran, half walked to gain the comparative safety of the High Street. Here, at least, little had changed in her years away and the edge of her fear began to dull. The place still bustled with travellers who were biding their time till morning – drinking, eating, exploring, wheeling and dealing. She stepped carefully through the refuse that littered the cobbles and gave a ha'penny to a beggar child who tugged at her skirts as she passed.

By the side of one of the many taverns, she turned off the High Street and cut through the inn yard. A gentleman and his lady were dismounting from horses that were slick with sweat at the end of their journey, and the man's eyes followed Mary as she slid past them, aiming for the lane at the back. It was darker here, and lonely, and she quickened her steps till she came out at last onto Red Cross Street, hurried across the road, and finally stopped at the gate to the Cross Bones.

As both a girl and a young woman she had hated this graveyard, sure she would spend eternity here amongst the thieves and the sinners, and for years it had haunted her, beckoning. She almost smiled at the recollection. She had thought her marriage to Toby had saved her from such an end but fate was strange that way: some destinies are meant to be fulfilled however far we think we have outrun them.

Placing a hand on the latch, she took a deep breath for courage. Beyond the gate the dark night deepened and the shade of the Shadow still flickered in her thoughts, half-remembered as a darkness in her blood.

Guide me, Hecate, she whispered. *Keep me safe.*

Then she lifted the latch, opened the gate with a shove, and stepped through.

Within a few yards, the path petered out and she lifted her skirts clear of the weeds as she trod across the grass. She wished Toby were with her – another living soul as a buttress against all the spirits of the dead she could feel in the air around her as a presence, a silent murmur. The one person who knew her heart. Somewhere here long ago, Toby had buried the child that slid from his first wife without ever drawing breath, and in all their years together he had never spoken of it once, a private grief that he carried locked tight inside of him. Tightening her shoulders, Mary lifted her chin and forced herself to bravery.

The graves were at the back wall as she remembered he once had told her, sheltered by the sacred yew that Sarah had planted to protect Tom's grave. Its presence drew Mary now towards it and the headstones beneath glimmered in the light from the torch in her hand – Tom and Sarah, lying side by side in death as they had lain in life. Mary knelt between them, reached her fingers to the mounds on either side. Could they sense her presence? she wondered. Did they know she sought their help?

She spoke first to Sarah, calling on their friendship and affection, precious as a mother's love. They had shared long hours in each other's company, and though Sarah must have wished for someone better than a Bankside whore for her son, she had never once been unkind.

'Can you hear me, Mistress Chyrche? Are you there?'

Silence.

'Sarah. I call on you to help me now as you used to do in life. I cannot do this alone. Please, I beg of you, if you can hear me come to me. Help me.'

She waited, briefly hopeful, but no answer came and tears of frustration pricked behind her eyes. She had no one else to turn to, no other path to try. Toby was lost to her – she had long since exhausted herself in the effort to reach him. Perhaps he was with Sarah now, mother and son together at peace in their realm of death, and beyond the power of the living to disturb. A part of her hoped so – they had earned their rest. But the survivor in her, the mother of a daughter in jeopardy, needed aid, and so she turned instead towards Tom, a man she knew only by his reputation. Reckless and wild, eager for life in all its chaotic glory, and a capacity for love that knew no bounds. Would he help her now? For the sake of his grandchild? Would he even hear her call?

'Tom? Tom Wynter? Do you hear me?'

She laid the palm of her hand on the grass that covered his grave. Did she have the power to speak to the dead, to summon a ghost? Or had desperation made her mad? She remembered Toby's study, the book, the rituals, learnèd words of Latin. Alexander had made it his life's work to master what she was hoping to do now, armed only with a desolate heart and a connection to the past.

'I have no skills to summon you, Tom Wynter, nothing but my love for my daughter, and a wish to bring her home. She is your grandchild, the daughter of the son you gave to Sarah. The sorcerer's power lives on in his daughter, and Kate is in danger. Please, I will give you anything I have, all of me, if you will come to me now and help us.'

Her whispered words seemed to hover in the silence. She wondered if the spirits were mocking her. Feeling foolish, driven by need, she tried again.

'Damn you, Tom Wynter – this is your doing. Toby, Kate, the book. All of it. All of it comes back to you.'

Another silence.

Beyond the peace of the graveyard, she was aware of the hum of the city at the edges of her perception. Men's voices raised in laughter drifted from the road and, further off, a dog was barking in unending monotonous repetition. She sighed. She had failed, she thought, and her daughter was still lost to her. What more could she do? Then, on a sudden impulse that came from she knew not where, she heard herself say, 'I will let the book go when this is done, and the river can take it where it will. Then perhaps you will be free of it and you can go to your rest at last. But before then I need your help. Please.'

She began to weep with desperation, and she could do nothing to stop her tears. All that had gone before, all that she and Toby had survived, meant nothing now in the face of Kate's danger. She wiped at her eyes with a gloved hand but other tears fell quickly to replace them, hot against her chilled skin.

'Please, Tom,' she whispered. 'I beg of you. Please.'

'Don't cry.'

The voice sounded close and she spun to look behind her, sure she was no longer alone. But the darkness all around was still and unmoving, and no living person disturbed the quiet.

'I am here. What is it I can do to help?'

Mary scrubbed at the tears, blinking her eyes into focus, searching the dark for a sight of him. She wanted to see him, this father of the man she loved, and though she could feel his presence as if he was standing right before her, she saw nothing but the darkness.

'Speak.'

The words tumbled from her lips as though she were afraid he would leave before she had told him all. She recounted all of it, right from the beginning. Her first sight of Alexander all those years ago when he addled Rosalind's wits. Toby's study with the sorcerer and his first wife's death, the rituals, the book, Sarah, Alexander's death, and now Kate and Isabella. It was a long tale to tell, but she did not falter.

Tom listened, so silently she doubted more than once that he had come to her at all. When she finished at last, she waited for his answer, peering into the night, still hoping for a sight of him.

'I will do what I can,' he said at last.

Then, briefly, he shimmered into form before her, and he was so like Toby in all his pale, lean beauty, it took her breath away. One more heartbeat and he was gone, and the dark seemed to draw closer around her. She waited for a moment, just to be sure, then stumbled to her feet, legs numbed by the cold. Drawing her cloak closer around her, one hand holding up her skirts, she turned away from Tom's grave and set her footsteps towards the road, barely breathing in her hurry to be gone. Only when she had latched the gate behind her and was once more on the road, did she dare to breathe again.

❦ 26 ❦

THOU SHALT HAVE JUSTICE, MORE
THAN THOU DESIR'ST

Kate had been in the prison cell some hours and perhaps it was morning, for the door opened with a gleam of light from the passage that fell across the straw, and a woman set down a tray with a jug of water and some bread before backing hurriedly away. The door shut with a clang and a scrape of the key behind her. As the other women in the cell moved towards it, Kate hesitated until a voice said, 'Have your share, girl. There's little enough and the others will take it if you do not.'

Kate shuffled forward and took a piece of the bread, though her stomach recoiled at the thought of it. The water was brackish and she felt her gorge rise in protest, but she kept it down by force of will – she had no wish to starve to death, for as long as she was alive some hope remained, however small. Then she returned to her place against the wall, and the woman who had spoken came to sit beside her. They sat in silence a while but it was comfortable and instinctively she felt the woman was a friend.

'What were you taken for?' the woman asked at last.

Kate smiled. It was good to hear a human voice, a reminder of the world of life beyond the prison walls where people passed the time of day in idle conversation.

'Witchcraft,' she said. 'You?'

'Whoring.'

'From Bankside?'

'Aye, all my life.'

'Do you know of a place called the Cardinal's Cap?'

'I know it,' the woman said. 'It used to be a brothel, same as all the others, but it's more respectable now, on the outside at least. There are still girls to be had, though, and rooms to take them to.'

It still seemed an unlikely place for her mother to lodge, but she supposed it hardly mattered any more – the only place Kate would go from here was to the gallows, and she would not see Mary again.

She said, 'What will happen to you?'

The woman shrugged. In the dark it was hard to guess her age but from her voice she seemed to be only young, perhaps just a little older than Kate. One of the girls she had seen at the Bull's Head perhaps? She had thought only of the horrors of the trade itself when she had turned over the possibility in her mind. She hadn't considered the punishments.

'They'll flog me at the cart's arse and let me go. It won't be the first time nor probably the last.'

Kate gave a shudder in the dark. 'That's horrible.'

''Tis a risk of the business.' Then she said, 'But witchcraft ... that's a different matter. They'll hang you for that, no matter if you're guilty or not. Once you're accused they'll have you.'

Kate touched her fingers to her neck once again, imagining the rope drawing tight, the sudden struggle for breath. Would it hurt? she wondered, or did the terror annihilate the pain?

'You were unlucky to be caught, now that Hopkins is dead.'

Matthew Hopkins – the Witchfinder General, whose infamy had travelled even as far as The Hague, his zeal for hunting witches matched only by his lack of pity. She said nothing; the whore seemed inclined to talk and so she listened.

'But in times of war people are afraid and they seek a cause for their misfortunes. 'Tis easy after all to point the finger at some poor woman and claim she dances with the Devil. Hopkins might be dead but the fear remains. In a world where even the King's head is not safe upon its shoulders, what justice for the rest of us?'

'None,' Kate agreed, though she had given little thought to the matter till now. 'None at all.'

The door squealed open and Kate jumped, startled.

'Winter! Come with me.' The gaoler peered into the gloom, keys rattling in his hand. 'Hurry up, woman! I haven't got all day.'

Kate scrambled to her feet and as she did so the woman grasped her hand.

'My name is Maggie,' she said. 'God be with you,' and though Kate knew she meant it kindly, it felt like a curse. She followed the man into the passage and through a labyrinth of corridors and steps until she found herself in a low-ceilinged room with a window that looked out on the street. There was no furniture but a single table and a stool and she guessed no fire had burned in the hearth in living memory. Shivering, she wrapped her arms around herself under her cloak as she stood by the window and drank in the view of the outside world. The pale gleam of the winter sky was a gift after the darkness of the cell.

The door opened and she turned to see the Justice of the Peace with a young man at his heels, carrying a notebook and quill. For her confession, she assumed. She swallowed, afraid, and cast a final glance to the sky.

Goddess help me. Give me courage.

Then she turned again to face her accuser. He was murmuring now to the clerk, though she knew he was still watching her, making his assumptions. She set her face to neutral, and waited. The Justice finished his conversation and slid himself smoothly onto the stool. The young man stood at his shoulder, awkward with the book balanced on one hand, ready to scribe with the other.

'So,' the Justice said at last. He seemed less at ease than he had in the comforts of his own home and she took some satisfaction from the fact he must share the deprivations and the cold, even for a little while. 'Tell me, Kate Winter, how you first came to be a witch?'

'I am not a witch,' she replied. The denial sounded weak even to her own ears. The magic circle told against her, and though she had saved her mother's life in the bounds of its protection there was no denying its purpose now.

He sighed. 'We both know that isn't true, don't we?'

She said nothing.

'After all, we have witnesses to your spells.'

'You have witnesses I made a circle,' she corrected him. 'Nothing more.'

The clerk's nib scraped on the paper.

'We have the word of your victim.'

Nathan, she thought, getting his revenge. Did Isabella know? Of course she did, Kate realised. This was her doing. She and Nathan, in league together. Her thoughts tumbled over one another, trying to unravel the connections. And nudging at the edges of her mind was always her fear of the noose. She wished there was a stool for her to sit on – the sleepless night was beginning to tell and it was hard to stand straight.

'I must make a report,' the Justice said, 'for the Grand Jury. And I will recommend you for trial with or without your confession. There is enough evidence to convict.'

'Then why am I here?'

'To find the truth, Miss Winter,' he snarled, standing abruptly, startling the clerk at his shoulder. 'To find the truth.'

He rounded the table and stood before her, and when she kept her head lowered, observing the fine leather of his boots, he grasped her chin and lifted her face to his.

'I'm not fooled by your beauty, girl. I know it hides a wicked heart and a soul you have sold to the Devil.' She could see the spittle in the corners of his lips and smell the remnants of wine on his breath. 'I will have women search you for witch marks. I have no doubt what we will find.' He let her jaw go. 'I will see you again.' Then he strode from the room and the clerk gazed after him, stunned for a moment, and uncertain.

'You should go after him,' she said. 'Unless you prefer to stay with me?' She gave him a wry smile and he almost ran, forgetting the inkpot in his haste. She picked it up and turned it in her hands, wondering what use she could make of it. Cupping it in her palm to hide it, she turned once more to the window and let the winter light fill her veins before the gaoler came and fetched her back down into the dark.

~

The days passed uncounted, numberless, and only in her dreams was she free. She dreamt of Rafe, of his beauty and his love, and the brief shared promise of a future together. She had no regrets that she had given him her innocence; she would have been sad to die still a maid. At least she had known what it was to love, and it was the memory of those precious moments she had spent with him that she clung to now to sustain her through the waking days, when fear lay across her shoulders and cast shadows on her heart. Now and then, she was hauled from the cell to face questions or examinations, and she bore the rough, probing search of the women searching for witch marks with open resentment: remorse and confession would gain her nothing.

The women were making the most of their task, enjoying their importance. Standing naked before them in the same cold chamber where the Justice had questioned her, she could not stop herself from shivering as she cast her eyes to the morning sky beyond the window, forget-me-not blue and clear, and wondered if she would ever walk below the heavens again.

They examined her in turn, peering closely, running their chilled, hard fingers across her skin. When they could find no blemish, they made her lie on the table and spread her legs.

'We know the Devil likes the secret places best, hiding in the sinful dark.'

241

Kate kept her head turned towards the window, averted from the prurient malice she had glimpsed in the women's eyes, and held in her hatred as the women searched. Calloused fingertips brushed her thighs and parted the folds between them, and she tensed when the woman slid a finger inside.

'Don't pretend I'm the first to enter here,' the woman hissed. 'Whore!'

In the end they found a single tiny mole beneath her breast, and they were pleased with their discovery; evidence, they said, that she had suckled some creature of the Devil.

'Have you no moles yourself?' she spat, when the woman's fingers lingered. The woman lifted her eyes. A Puritan woman, Kate thought, in her black starched dress and white collar, her mouth turned down in permanent disapproval of the human condition. Joyless. Judging. Though she had been eager enough in her exploration: Kate had seen the ill-hidden lust in her face when she probed her victim's hidden places. 'Shall we search you too?'

The woman's eyes flickered for a moment, fearful, and Kate bit back a smile.

'So you do have them,' she said, leaning closer so the other woman at her back would not hear. 'Does the Devil come to you at night to suckle? Or are they just marks on your skin, same as mine?'

The woman sprang back as though Kate had burned her.

'I am a godly woman,' she hissed. 'Unlike you, witch! Get dressed.'

Kate shrugged her arms through the sleeves of the shift and took her time to retie the ribbon. It was good to be in a room with a window that looked out on the day – a reminder of a world still turning beyond the prison, and a life she doubted she would see again. The woman waited with her arms crossed over her breast as she dressed, impatient, until she was finally finished and the guard dragged her back to her cell.

～

The night before the trial for her life Kate did not sleep, no escape into the freedom of her dreams, no brief moment of liberty when she woke in the morning before she remembered. But she called both to Tom and to Hecate in her thoughts, asking for help and for courage for all that was to come. She was unsure if either of them heard her, but even to know they were there in a realm beyond this world gave her some small comfort. She was not alone, after all, and this earthly life was not the end of things.

She wanted it done with; the fear of the rope at her neck haunted her every waking thought, and once it was finished she would be free of it. She had endured all the many questions and examinations, the hunger and dark privations of this cell, and she was weary of it all. Many times, she had been almost tempted to confess, simply to stop the endless questioning, to be allowed to rest. But always the words caught in her throat as though the rope that would soon tighten about her neck was already in place, choking her into silence.

They came for her early, and even though she had waited with impatience all through the night she was still not ready when the key ground in the lock and the door scraped open on the flag-stones. With the trial before her at last she remembered how much she wanted to live after all.

'Winter!'

Her legs were unsteady as she got to her feet, a tremor in the muscles she had to grit her teeth against. She had vowed to herself from the first that she would never let them see her fear and as she drew herself up straight, forcing her muscles to stillness, a little of her old spirit returned. She remembered her journey into the Shadow and – though it seemed like a different person had inhab-ited her then, fearless and brave – she heard the words repeating in her head.

I am a witch of ancient blood, and I have the power of the Shadow in my veins.

She was shackled for the journey and chained to the other pris-oners who faced the same ordeal. Eight human souls staring death in the face, their fates to be decided in a few short minutes before the court, and they kept their eyes averted from one another, reluctant to see their own fears reflected in other eyes. Chained and manacled, it was hard to move in concert with the others, her arms jerked this way and that by the prisoners either side of her so that by the time they reached the court, her wrists were rubbed raw and bleeding. Outside the building a throng of people milled, lively with excitement as if the proceedings to come were an entertainment, like a fair or a play. Their callousness appalled her, the cheapness of her life to them.

Have courage.

Tom's voice sounded in her head, and she could have cried with gratitude.

I am with you.

She lifted her eyes from the ground for the first time on her journey, aware of the kiss of the breeze on her face, the wide sky above her, pale grey with clouds that teased the day with brief glimpses of blue behind them. Then the column lurched forward and she was dragged up the steps into the courthouse, where the crowd's excitement echoed off the stone walls and high ceiling in a cacophony that seemed to vibrate her whole body. She was borne forwards as the mob surged in. Did these people have nothing else to do today? Was the courthouse always so? She searched the faces in hope of seeing Rafe or her mother but she saw no one at all that she knew. She had expected no different, for how could they know that she was even here? But their absence hurt nonetheless – she would have liked to see a face amongst the others that looked at her with love instead of judgement.

The prisoners awaited their turn from a narrow enclosure close by the wall, to be unshackled one by one when their names were called. The judge arrived and as a hush rippled through the crowd she observed him, hoping for marks of kindness and seeing none. The spectacle began with a call from the clerk and the first prisoner was manhandled to the dock where he stood, pale and dirty, his young face shiny with sweat and fear. Kate's breath quickened, heart knocking so loud she heard nothing of his crimes. But she heard the reading of the sentence, the casual dispatch of a man's life with no more than a few minutes' thought. She wanted to rail in protest, but fear kept her silent.

The morning seemed long and it was hot in the courtroom from the press of people. Her bodice stuck to her back, sweat in a rivulet down her spine, but still she found that she was shivering. Beside her, and attached to her arm by a chain of cold iron, an old man was bent double with a cough that racked his whole body, blood on his lips. A tea of comfrey and lavender would have eased the pain of it, Kate thought, though it was too late for that now. Another, more permanent cure awaited him and her blood turned to ice at the thought of it.

But she was aware of Tom's presence somewhere close by, and the knowledge she was not utterly alone steadied nerves that were threatening to unravel. He had faced the same, she knew, and by choice to save his cousin. She could hardly imagine such a capacity for love, the sacrifice.

Finally, the guard knocked the bolt from her manacles and as she rubbed her bleeding wrists, his fingers closed around her arm and shoved her to the waiting dock, where he stood beside her, threatening, as if she might try to make a run for it. She slid her eyes across the sea of faces that were watching in one last futile hope for a glimpse of a friendly face but she did not find one. Then she turned her attention to the judge who held her fate in his hands. Now that she was facing him she could see he was an elderly man with a lined, sad face, and a mouth that turned down at the corners. Her heart seemed to weigh more heavily as he observed her – she saw no pity in his gaze, only judgement. She stood up straighter.

'Kate Winter?'

'Yes, your honour.'

The judge looked her over once again and she saw the distaste in his eyes, as though he had been offered a rotting piece of meat to buy. A clerk read out the indictment, a murmur she did not understand. Then the judge asked her how she pleaded.

'Not guilty, sir,' she answered, and her voice sounded as though it came from another person.

'Culprit, how will you be tried?'

'By God and my country.'

A murmur rippled through the court before the clerk's voice brought them once more to silence.

'If any can give evidence or can say anything against the prisoner, let him come now for she standeth upon his deliverance.'

Kate waited as Nathan shoved his way through the throng to the front. He kept a hand to his face to conceal the knife wound she had inflicted, saving the sight of it, she supposed, for his moment of triumph. Nathan placed a hand on the Bible to swear and Kate would not have been surprised to see the holy book shrivel under the weight of the lie of his oath. When he took his hand from his cheek and opened his mouth to accuse her, she braced. There was an audible gasp from the court at the festering wound that ran across the side of his face, oozing with putrid pus, yellow, swollen, the bruising still purple. The infection had spread to his neck, a red stain spilling under his collar. Isabella's handiwork, she knew, to make it so.

'Her doing!' he told the court, pointing. 'Her curse. A simple scratch that will not heal. It pains me. I cannot sleep. If I would not lie with her, she said, she would make sure no other woman would ever look at me again. She is a whore and a witch ...'

He rambled on, half-crazed with pain and infection and hatred. But Kate saw the malice in his eyes – he was the fortune teller's creature and under her spell. Would Isabella heal the wound when this was done, Kate wondered, or would she simply let it fester until he died of it now that his purpose was served? Without help, it would surely be the end of him. She scanned the sea of faces that filled the court, searching this time for Isabella. Had she come to witness Kate's fate? To wield her power to destroy? Perhaps that's why Tom stood sentinel beside her – Kate could still feel the chill of his presence and was grateful.

Nathan's voice held the court's attention.

He had seen her at the graveyard.

She had stood within a circle and danced with the demons she had summoned.

She had bared her body on unhallowed ground, alive with the spirits of those the Devil claimed for his own.

He had watched as she knelt before the Devil's member and took it in her mouth.

He had seen the Devil ride her.

And he had heard the words she used to curse him. *You will never tup another woman again!*

The whole court hung on his every word.

When at last his litany ended, she was allowed to answer him.

'You lie,' she said. No one had told her she would be permitted to reply to him, and she searched her mind in desperation for the right words to say, her life hanging in the balance. 'All of it. Lies. It was just a simple cut I gave you.'

'It matters not how you cut me,' he spat back. 'Look at it now! Does it look like a normal wound to you? Is this how a simple knife cut heals?'

A murmur of agreement sounded like a buzz across the room. She saw the jurors nodding their heads in accord and her heart shrank inside her with the sudden understanding that there was nothing she could say to sway them. No matter what she said they would believe a man's word over hers, because the life of a woman mattered less. But she kept her shoulders straight – she refused to be bowed before these men who were judging her, who had already made their decision. She could feel the hostility of their attention as they appraised her, and she knew they hated her all the more for her beauty. They wanted their witches old and ugly, a more predictable world. For how could they know to avoid the Devil, when he came to them in a package so pretty? Her very existence threatened their confidence as men: they could never now see a beautiful woman and trust that she belonged to God. Always the fear would lurk at the edges of their thoughts that perhaps the Devil had bought such beauty for himself, to lure good men into his arms. So she would pay no matter what she said – they had already condemned her, and all the rest was just a show. The gathered throng had been right; the trial was mere theatre, and she was simply an actor with a part to play, the script already written.

'Your wound is your own doing,' she said into the hush. 'It is none of mine.'

''Tis unnatural,' he answered, 'the work of witchcraft. I have sworn it. I am a man of good character, faithful servant to Mistress Last.'

Nathan stepped down, and the men who had arrested her gave their evidence in turn, all of them speaking of the circle she had fashioned around the graves, her strange state as she knelt within it, the yew tree that gleamed with an unearthly glow. The Puritan women told of the witch mark they had found. She half listened: it barely mattered what they said. The verdict was already destined, and she could feel the noose begin to tighten against her throat.

Courage. Tom's voice whispered in her head. *All is not yet lost.*

She lifted her chin, struggling to trust in his words though she could see no end for herself but the gallows. A physician was called to confirm the unnatural festering of Nathan's wounds: such a putrefaction he had never seen in all his years of practice. It was like to be the death of him, he pronounced, and a hideous, painful end.

Good, she thought. 'Twas no more than he deserved.

The physician spoke at length, too, of Nathan's good character. Kate wondered how much Isabella had paid him to bear false witness and risk his soul.

Then it was over and the judge was addressing the jury.

'Good men of the inquest, you have heard what these may say against the prisoner; you have also heard what the prisoner can say for herself. Have an eye to your oath, and to your duty, and do that which God shall put in your minds to the discharge of your consciences.'

She held her breath, although she knew the outcome had never once been in doubt. The whore in her cell had been right – a witch accused was a witch to be hanged. As the hubbub of the crowd grew louder, the jurymen talked amongst themselves and she could see they were all agreed. One or two of them cast looks her way, and she balled her fists at her sides, trying to contain her fear and her rage as after only a moment's deliberation, they pronounced her guilty. The crowd cheered and hooted, and she was led to the bench. The judge looked down on her, and now that she was facing her death, she saw at last a kindness in his eyes.

'I am bound to ask if there is any reason you should not be sentenced to death for your crime.'

Mutely, she shook her head. Her voice would not pass the constriction in her throat, and though she could think of plenty of reasons she wanted to live, there were none amongst them to persuade the judge. She watched as he placed a black handkerchief on his head, and though she saw his mouth was moving she did not hear the words that came from his lips. She was too busy struggling to draw the breath through her throat, as though the noose had already tightened around it.

She would die at the end of a rope after all, just as her grandfather had died before her.

But Tom had died to save his cousin's life. She would die for nothing.

NOW MY SOUL'S PALACE IS BECOME A PRISON

In her dream Kate searched for a way out of a house with many doors, but the passages were a maze and though she tried every door, turning each handle and rattling, all of them were locked. Like the palace in The Hague, she thought, with such long corridors, all brightly lit with candles. There were no windows, no people: nothing but row upon row of doors she could not open.

She quickened her pace, a sense of urgency creeping into her steps. She needed to leave, to escape some unnamed danger, and so she hurried from door to door, panic rising as a heat in her chest. She shook each door in frustration. Surely one must open? Surely she couldn't stay here forever?

Turning another corner, she found herself at last in a passage that was different from the others. There was a window to the outside world along one wall, and when she stopped to look out she saw a well-tended garden, dappled and pretty in the morning light, with a river beyond it that was bordered by reeds. As she watched, a boat pulled in and a man climbed out of it onto the steps of the jetty.

Tom Wynter – tall and pale and beautiful.

She banged on the window, but her fist made no sound on the glass and he did not hear. She tried to shout, her voice a silent cry.

Sliding her hand away, she gazed out through the glass in disappointment, and the reflection in its surface shifted into focus. She flinched, startled. For it was not her own face staring back at her but the face of Isabella, and she was laughing.

Beyond the window and the reflection that was not a reflection, Tom had turned from the boat. He had seen her at last and he was waving, beckoning her towards him. Without pausing for thought, Kate hurled herself through the glass, shattering the image of Isabella into a thousand pieces, and as she ran towards the jetty, she could hear the echo of a dying scream. Tom's fingers were cold against hers when he took her hand to help her into the boat, but with his touch she felt safe, fears forgotten.

She looked back as they rowed away from the shore and saw that the house she had escaped from had gone. There was no trace of it any more, only a bright winter sky that was lit with a cold, pale sun.

Kate woke, surprised to find herself once more in the dark of the cell, shivering with cold. Beside her Maggie lay curled on the straw, breathing lightly, and against the far wall she was aware of the other two women who had barely spoken a word in all the days she had been here. One of them was watching her, eyes glinting in the reflected glow of the torch in the passage.

'You was dreaming.'

Kate nodded.

'What was you dreaming of?'

'Escape,' Kate said, and the woman laughed.

'The only escape for you is at the end of a rope.'

But Kate was no longer listening, her thoughts trailing back across the dream as she sought to unravel the message it contained. Isabella would be the saving of her. Isabella was the key. But how? She let her mind drift back once more across the dream, searching for answers. She was aware of the woman, still watching across the cell, but she no longer cared. Better the eyes of the living than the shadows that lurked at the edges of her mind, waiting for her spirit to join them.

Think, she told herself. Think.

Tom had shown her a key – a boat, a window, a reflection.

A reflection that shattered. A dying scream.

Understanding began to glimmer. She remembered the poppet Isabella had made of her mother – a likeness fashioned to heal or to harm – a reflection, if you will, of a person's essence. She must make her own poppet, she realised, though she knew no spells to utter, no magic to call upon to give it life. But the message of the dream had been clear, and perhaps the rest would come to her in time.

Though Isabella had fashioned her dolls from wax, a figure wrought of cloth would surely do as well. It was the thought behind the making that mattered, the intention. She recalled the rough dolls she had made as a child – lengths of cloth folded and tied with ribbons to form the shape of a person. Her mother had shown her how to make them, and as a girl she had spent hours using cut-off scraps of silk and linen and wool. Now, lifting the hem of her skirt, her fingers found the linen petticoat beneath. The fabric was damp and gritty with prison filth, and she smiled to think of Isabella's poppet made of such stuff.

The cloth was surprisingly easy to rip, and her hands were deft with a seamstress's instincts, folding the fabric over and over on itself and binding it into shape with strips she used her teeth to tear. A little body, arms and legs, a head and neck. She thought of Isabella as she worked, recalling the shattered image, the echo of the scream, binding her intention into each fold she made, every turn of the cloth.

Words of power found their way into her mind as a silent spell.

I cast you, Isabella, into this poppet – no more are you free to wield harm against me.

Your evil will come back to you, one time, two times, three.

The doll was no bigger than her palm when she finished, and

she laid it on her hand to examine it. Its blank white face gazed back at her, expressionless, and Kate remembered the pot of ink she had stolen. Scrabbling behind her in the rotten straw by the wall where she had hidden it, her fingers closed around the little pewter jar. It was beautifully crafted with engravings she could not quite make out in the gloom, and she hoped the clerk had not suffered too greatly for its loss – he had only been doing his job after all, and she wished him no harm.

Opening the stopper, the faint scent of the ink began to colour the foetid stench of the cell, a sweet blend that smelled of blood and claret, and conjured the memory of her father's office behind the shop in The Hague. Selecting a piece of straw from the floor and dipping it into the ink, she dabbed at the poppet gently, straining to see in the dim light as she gave the doll eyes to see and a heart to beat. Then she daubed a single 'I' for Isabella on its belly and, with a thin line of black across its throat, she brought it to life, binding it to Isabella.

Your evil will come back to you, one time, two times, three.

Then she tucked it inside her bodice between her breasts, keeping it close to her heart. She was aware of it always, throbbing with its own cold and steady beat, and though she was uncertain of the way that it would save her, she trusted to the Shadow and to Tom that when the time came she would know.

'Was that a poppet you made?' Maggie wanted to know.

'Yes,' Kate admitted, for what possible harm could it do her now to declare herself a witch? 'Of the woman who put me here.'

'Last chance for revenge, eh?'

Kate smiled and said nothing. But in truth, she cared little for the thought of revenge – she wanted only to be free.

❧ 28 ❧

SUSPICION ALWAYS HAUNTS THE GUILTY MIND

In the evening, the tavern at the sign of the Cardinal's Cap heaved with the press of bodies. The warmth was stifling, the air ripe with the stench of unwashed men and tobacco. It was strange how some days the whole world seemed to be abroad and seeking their pleasure on Bankside. Near the fierce-burning hearth, Rosalind was entertaining a group of middle-aged men in their cups. They were merchants by the look of them – dark grey silks, shiny shoes – men with money to spend, and the table was littered with jugs and platters. One of the girls had draped herself across the man who seemed to be their leader; her breasts were level with his face and his lips almost touched the pale soft skin.

Mary sat talking of old times with a couple of sailmakers who remembered how Bankside used to be in the days before the war, reminiscing over a jug of claret about the theatres and pleasure gardens, the riotous pursuit of amusement in all its forms. None of them spoke of the darker side of those times, the depravity and cruelty that had dwelt alongside the merry-making. They had been better times, they insisted in the flush of their nostalgia, when a man was free to love and dice and revel as he wished. Perhaps they were right, Mary thought, for certainly the realm was no happier beneath the Puritans' heel, with all the joys of earthly pleasures proscribed.

'To the past,' they toasted, and she lifted her cup to theirs.

St Saviour's bells had already struck twelve before the crush began to dwindle, and once it began, the drinkers seemed to flow eagerly away into the night as though called by some unknown voice to their homes. But as the tables emptied the door swung open to admit a final crowd. It was late and it was tempting just to turn them away. She cast a glance towards Rosalind, who shrugged with a rueful smile. Then she saw that Rafe was amongst the newcomers when he paused at the door to sweep his gaze across the tables, searching. She watched, waiting for her daughter to appear beside him. They should be together. Rosalind had said that Kate went with him to work their magic to bring Mary back from the Shadow, and in the long days since then she had waited every moment for Kate to return, afraid. Rafe, too, seemed to have disappeared, no sign of him at the Bull's Head along the way when she sent a boy to ask. But the knowledge that they were together had gone some way to assuage her fears, for surely a girl must be safer in the protection of a gentleman. But here he was now, alone, and fear for her daughter blossomed again in her gut.

She set down the jug she was holding with deliberate care and took a step towards him. Her movement caught at his attention and he turned to her with her own question in his eyes, so that she knew at once Kate was not with him.

'Is she here?'

'I thought she was with you.'

His eyes closed briefly in disappointment and frustration, and behind her Mary heard Rosalind greet the men.

'Gentlemen. What brings you here so late?'

'Wine,' one of the men said, 'and warmth.'

The group clustered at the hearth, and in the brief glance she slid towards them, Mary noticed for the first time the grime that was etched into their faces and their clothes. They were filthy and reeking, and it took her only a moment more to recognise the

stench of prison, the smell stirring memories of her own imprison-
ment. She could still recall with vivid clarity the pain of the hunger
and the fear, and the relief when it was over at last.

'You've been in gaol,' she breathed.

'We were arrested in performance, taken in a raid at the
Cockpit a few days since.' He trailed off with a shrug. She
wondered how she had not heard the news.

'So where is Kate?'

They stood in awkward hesitation until Rafe began to sway,
struggling to keep his feet.

'Eat,' Mary commanded, and guided him to a place at the table
by the hearth with the others. He was no use to her half-dead with
hunger.

At Rosalind's word, the boy had brought warm spiced wine,
and mutton boiled with onions and ginger: the men fell on it as if
they'd barely eaten for days. Perhaps they hadn't.

'Did they treat you ill, in prison?' Rosalind asked, with a coy
tilt of her head, flirtatious.

'They took all our costumes,' one of the older men replied.
'Every last one.'

Mary said nothing. It seemed to her a small price to pay – her
own experience of gaol had ended with rape and a whipping, and
the scars still formed a lattice on her back.

'That was your punishment?' Rosalind pressed, incredulous.

'A heavy fine,' one of the men scowled. 'And a warning that
next time we would not get off so easily.'

He raised his cup in the direction of the oldest man among
them, so that Mary guessed it was his purse that had released them.

She stood to the side of the hearth and enjoyed the heat of the fire
while she waited for Rafe to eat his fill. It didn't take long, his belly
shrunk from the days of starvation, appetite dulled. She drew up a
stool beside him and he turned to her.

'I will go to the fortune teller,' he said, 'and find out what I can. But first I must wash and change out of these reeking clothes.'

'Come,' Mary said. 'You can wash through here.'

She led him to Rosalind's chamber and left him there while she sent a boy to the Bull's Head to bring fresh clothes as he had asked and another to fetch hot water. By the time she returned, he was all but naked before the fire, his shirt and breeches in a heap by the door, rank and blackened with the dirt of the gaol. Even smeared with prison grime, there was still a beauty in the lithe, strong limbs, the clean lines of his chest and shoulders. She set down the bowl of water and a cloth, and forced herself to look away as he began to sponge the dirt from his skin.

He would be a good match for Kate, she decided, a man who could meet the girl's headstrong will with both gentleness and strength. A sliver of guilt for her own brief feelings trickled through her, but did not linger long. Kate's life was in danger, and the niceties of courtship would have to wait. Once, Rafe paused in his ablutions to look up at her with an expression she could not read, and she turned away altogether then, leaving the room to fetch some fresh water.

In the kitchen, she leaned her hands on the table and let out a long slow breath, a myriad of emotions tumbling inside her she could not even begin to unravel. But most of all, it was fear that suffused her, a quickening of her breath and heartbeat, an ache in her limbs. Shaking her head, she remembered Tom's promise to do what he could, but now she wondered what help he could possibly be? What could a ghost do against the power of a witch like Isabella? Despair began to curl around the fear, and in her distraction she failed to hear Rafe come into the kitchen behind her.

'Don't lose hope,' he murmured, as though he had heard her thoughts. She turned to face him, then lowered her eyes away – he was still half-naked, his upper body glistening with damp. 'Kate has come into her power – she will not give up easily.'

The door slammed open and the boy barrelled in with a bundle of clothes in his arms that he half spilled, half threw across the table. Rafe snatched them up and began to dress, and when she thought she had given him long enough, Mary shifted at last to look at him.

'Do you know where to go?'

'Aye. The Wounded Raven. I remember when it was an alehouse.'

'As do I.' She gave him a small smile, and wondered how much of the story he knew. 'Take great care. She is cunning and ruthless, and I would not trust a single word she utters.'

'Our paths have crossed before,' he replied, with a nod of acknowledgement at her warning. 'Many years ago. I know well of what you speak. Trust me, I will be wary.'

Mary swallowed, trying to calm the rising sense of panic, the fear that he too would be ensnared in Isabella's web and it would fall to her to rescue them both.

'Godspeed,' she murmured. 'I will wait for you here. Send word as soon as you can.'

He bowed his head in farewell and then he was gone, and she was alone once more in the kitchen, waiting.

29

FOR WHO SO FIRM THAT CANNOT BE
SEDUCED?

The winter chill outside was like a slap in the face after the warmth of the tavern and Rafe shivered, drawing his cloak closer around him. For seemingly endless days in prison he had known only the bitter misery of cold, hours spent wondering if he'd ever know warmth again or if he would end his days in foetid wretchedness, heat and comfort nothing more than a memory from a half-forgotten dream. He had made a vow to himself that if he ever walked free from the gates of the gaol, he would never again take a good fire in his hearth for granted.

Now, he went to the water's edge and stood for a moment on the quay, still in awe of the broad sky above him and the rank scent of the river. The tide was out, slapping lightly at the shingle below, and a lone wherry was struggling to make headway against the tide, its lantern swaying. Across the breadth of the river, the lights of the city burned and hovered in the shadows of St Paul's, and downstream the towering buildings on the bridge blotted out the gradual lightening of the eastern sky where the rosy fingers of the coming dawn crept unseen behind its bulk.

He should have brought a lantern, he thought, remembering the maze of lanes that encircled the Wounded Raven, for even at the height of midday those alleyways were shadowed and darksome. In the small hours of the night, they would be black as pitch. It was a low sort of place, he recalled, where he had gone sometimes with youthful friends seeking out the murkiest depths that Bankside had to offer, an adventure into lowly places. The memory almost sparked a nostalgic smile until he remembered that every one of those young men he had drunk with were dead and gone now, killed by Puritan swords and muskets – of that group of students, only he was still alive. He shook his head at the thought of it: such a waste of young lives, men with everything to live for, their futures beckoning and bright with promise. As if in sympathy with their fates the scar along his flank began to throb. It had been the worst of his wounds, and for weeks he had been wracked by feverish dreams as he hovered in the space between life and death, until God in his wisdom chose at last to spare him. He had recovered with agonising slowness, and now and then the wound still pained. He had not gone into battle again.

Until now, he thought. A different kind of battle, to be sure – no sword or musket, no cannon fire to tear the limbs to shreds, but no less dangerous for that. He knew the risks: he remembered the last time he had encountered Isabella, many years before when Ellen and his son still lived, and she had seemed to reach inside him and touch his core. The curl of fear she had kindled then coiled once more in his gut. She was a potent enemy, and he would need all his wits about him. Taking a deep breath and straightening his shoulders to gird himself, he turned from his contemplation of the river and began to walk along the shore.

A single torch at the door of the Wounded Raven threw monstrous dancing shadows against the walls in the lane. No one was abroad yet, the place still sleepy with the night. He paused at the corner and passed his gaze across the scene before him. It was just as he remembered; a poor place, mired in misery. The tenements were shuttered and dark and only the rats were astir, sleek and fat, their shadows flitting at the edges of his vision. He had found his way there with surprising ease: even in the darkest of the lanes he had not mistook the way, though his steps had slowed as he began to draw close. And now that the place loomed before him, he felt the ball of dread grow weighty in his guts, a memory of the last time his path had crossed the fortune teller's. But Kate was missing and he knew without a shadow of a doubt that the woman at the Wounded Raven had some part in her disappearance.

For Kate, he thought.

Then, with a lift of his shoulders and a deep breath that did little to dispel the unease inside him, he strode across the lane and began to hammer on the door. The household would be asleep at this hour, he guessed, and it would take time and patience to rouse them from their sleep. So he was taken aback when he heard the footsteps inside after only a moment, and the sound of the bolts shooting back. He waited until the door opened a fraction and a man's face appeared at the crack.

'Who's there?'

'Rafe Tyndall. I would speak with your mistress. Is she home?'

'I'll see.' The servant's face withdrew and the door closed again. Rafe waited once more, aware of the quickness of his breath and the sweat that was pooling in the runnel of his spine in spite of the cold. He did not have to wait long before the door swung open, and the man invited him in. As he stepped inside, he was conscious of the door being locked up behind him and, fresh from gaol, the noise made him shudder, memories of his prison cell surging through his thoughts.

Inside, he saw that the room that used to be the alehouse was the main chamber now, and furnished with once-fine furniture and wall hangings. The man gestured towards the hearth where embers still smouldered, and he crossed towards it. Now and then the ashes pulsed brightly with the memory of last night's fire, and though the place was warm after the chill outside, the air was tainted with a scent of something rotten. Something more than the damp and must and refuse that was common in these old buildings. Something darker he could not quite name. He swallowed down the bile that rose in his throat.

'There is wine if you would like it,' the servant said, with a jerk of his head towards the sideboard.

He nodded his understanding but refrained. He would take nothing from the fortune teller's hands, untrusting. Then, as the servant began to light the candles that were spread about the room, Rafe noticed the gash across his cheek. Festering and putrid, it reached down across his neck, and Rafe recognised the stench as gangrene. He turned his eyes away – he wouldn't like to bet on the man's chances of living much longer.

The servant shuffled to the hearth and threw on another log, squatting awkwardly to poke the fire back into life. Idly, Rafe's gaze followed his movements as he waited for Isabella to arrive.

He heard her before he saw her – the rustle of silk on the stairs that led up into the dark – and a moment later she stood before him. She was clearly fresh from her bed: her hair was braided loosely, hanging across her shoulder, and she was wearing a fur-collared bed robe that she held tight shut across her front like a shield.

'What brings you to my house as such an ungodly hour, Master Tyndall?'

He took a deep breath. He had rehearsed all the possibilities for this conversation on his way and had decided directness was the best approach. He knew she was skilled at playing games and he preferred not to indulge her.

'Where is Kate Winter?'

Isabella gave a half-laugh and he saw the beauty in her smile. He was sure she had used it well and often. 'You do not know?'

'I do not know or I would not be troubling you at this hour.'

She let out a dramatic sigh and he had to quell his irritation. She was enjoying making him wait.

'Is that so?'

He inclined his head in answer, and she turned to the sideboard. 'Wine?'

'No, thank you.'

She poured some for herself and held the cup in both hands so that the robe gaped open to expose the naked body beneath. He could see the outline of her breasts and her belly, the dark triangle of hair, the long, slim thighs, and felt an unwelcome lift of desire. Tensing his jaw against it, balling his fists, he lowered his gaze to the rug that lay on the ground between them, composing himself before he raised his head and trained his gaze to remain on her face.

'Where is she?' he asked again.

'I'm surprised your paths didn't cross these last few days.' She smiled pleasantly, as if they were friends exchanging snippets of news, and though her beauty was beguiling, he was conscious of the current of corruption that rippled underneath. She had led Kate from the safety of her home, and sent Mary to the Shadow, and who knew what other evils she was capable of. 'At the Marshalsea,' she continued. 'You didn't see her there?'

'She's in prison?' It was not an answer he had been prepared for and shock made him blurt his response without thought. 'For what?'

'Witchcraft.' Isabella laughed brightly. 'It's really quite amusing. She tried to save her mother and was taken in the act. I was at her trial today though I took care she did not see me – she will hang come Tuesday.'

Rafe was silent but the pound of blood in his ears was deafening. The image of Kate in a cell like the one he had just left behind sickened him – the cold and misery, the hunger and the fear – and he could think of no way to save her. She would die as Tom Wynter had done, swinging at the end of a noose.

'I was planning to visit her this morning, to say my farewell. Perhaps you would like to accompany me to the prison? I doubt they'll let you in, but I can carry a message. I have ... contacts.'

'I'm sure you do,' he managed to murmur. It came as no surprise to learn she kept a network of people who were in thrall to her, beguiled into doing her bidding, and he wanted to slap the smugness from her face.

Kate, he thought. How could he set her free?

'If you would care to wait while I dress, we could go together?' She inclined her head with a coy and flirtatious smile, and it was hard not to look as the front of her gown gaped a little wider with her movement, showing one breast, the nipple dark and hard. She would be a passionate lover, he found himself thinking, nothing taboo, and the same unwelcome ripple of lust rose through him. She waited, still watching him, as if appraising his reaction to her provocation, and he knew that if he chose he could bed her there and then.

He hesitated, caught briefly in the net of her enchantment, desire flooding his limbs as heat that rose from his groin and his belly. He wanted her with every fibre of his being, an all-consuming passion, dark and dangerous. How had she ensnared him so utterly? She placed a hand on her hip, drawing back the gown to reveal the pale smooth sweep of her belly, the line of her flank and thigh, and an image in his mind of those limbs entangled with his own hollowed out his breath. He was finding it hard to breathe, limbs growing heavy.

Isabella laughed. 'Do I frighten you, Master Tyndall? I rather think I do. Perhaps you prefer the innocence of maids to the challenge of a woman of … experience?'

Lust ripened into hatred and he balled his fists once more against the rising urge to lash out and make this woman pay for all her many sins, known and unknown. That she left a trail of destruction behind her wherever she trod he did not doubt – the world would be a better place without her. But still … She had access to Kate in her prison cell, and that might yet prove to be of use.

'Get yourself dressed, Mistress Last,' he managed to say, calling on the wash of his hatred to stave off the power of her charm. 'And we will go to the prison.'

She dropped into a curtsey of mock obedience to his order. Then, with a flounce of her robe that showed off the full length of her thigh, she turned and walked away from him.

He waited, rage simmering and barely under his control. The servant cleared the ashes from the fire and set it anew and Rafe watched him, observing the unsteady movements, the unnatural brightness in the man's eyes. The fever would overwhelm him soon, Rafe guessed, and he would die a hideous and painful end. He wondered that Isabella, with all the powers of witchcraft and magic at her fingertips, had done nothing to relieve him – even he, with only an old soldier's knowledge of healing, knew that a compress of rosemary and honey might have helped. But perhaps it was too late for him now. And perhaps, too, she had her reasons for letting him die.

Finally, when he had begun to think that she would not return after all, he heard her footsteps on the stairs, but he only allowed himself to look towards her when she crossed the floor to greet him again.

'Shall we?'

He nodded his acquiescence and took in the transformation with a glance. She was wearing a blue wool gown trimmed with lace that set off the pallor of her complexion, and her hair was swept back from her face and held in place with a fine net of pearls. There was no trace left of the temptress of before: she was every inch a goodwife of the middling sort – nothing in her life to hide, and the transmutation was remarkable: she looked like a different person altogether. When she had donned her cloak and fastened it securely at her neck, Rafe followed her to the door.

Outside, the day was beginning. A pale light seeped through ragged clouds that were just visible through the gap between the buildings overhead, and the lane was already lively with people. Two women sat spinning wool beside a brazier and a chicken pecked in the dirt at their feet. A woman, heavy with child, dragged at Isabella's arm, begging for alms, but the fortune teller shrugged her away with a venomous look that made the beggar shrink back in fear; in the lea of a doorway, an ageing whore was servicing a customer, his arse bare and jiggling. Rafe slid his eyes away. He had preferred it in the dark when only the rats were abroad to bear testament to the lane's seedy poverty.

Isabella strode at speed, her stride matching his, and it seemed to be no time at all until they stopped before the great wooden doors of the Marshalsea. The ancient brick walls loomed high and dark above them, and the timber of the doors was rotting with age. Rafe shuddered. He knew what misery lay within, and he had to swallow down again the bile of his hatred for the woman at his side. For the first time since they had set out from the Wounded Raven, Isabella turned to him and spoke.

'Do you have a message you would like me to deliver?'

'Aye,' he replied. 'You can tell her not to give up hope, and that I have not forgotten her.'

The fortune teller looked him up and down, as if appraising his response and finding it wanting. She gave a curt nod in answer that told him his message would go undelivered: he had thought as much. Then she turned away and began to hammer on the dark and heavy oak.

30

WE CANNOT CROSS THE CAUSE WHY WE
WERE BORN

In the grinding cold and dark it was hard to grasp the passing minutes of her life, and as the hours rolled towards her execution, her trust began to waver. Would she hang after all, as Tom had done? All the years to be denied her, all the love and joy she would never know, stretched out unclaimed before her. Tom must have waited in a cell like this for his death too, counting down the precious minutes of his life. Had he paced as she did, imagining the feel of the rope around his neck, the last moment of awareness before the breath was stopped? She measured the day in the quarter-hours the church bells struck beyond the walls. St George's, Maggie told her, with bitterness in her tone, a godly church where Puritans had worshipped long before every church became a Puritan church, devoid of ritual or colour.

The bells had not long tolled the hour of eight when Kate heard boots in the passage beyond the door. When they halted outside the door to her cell, she stopped pacing. The key scraped in the lock and as the door screeched open, she turned to see, expecting only the shapeless form of the woman who brought the ale and dry bread she would have to force past her lips to get down. But it was the gaoler who stepped through the opening instead, broad shoulders and bristled head filling the narrow space. Her heart tightened, the ache of fear spreading in her limbs – had he come for her already? Had she mistaken the day? She touched a hand to the poppet hidden at her breast and held her breath. Then she saw the gaoler had brought a visitor, a woman's form half hidden behind him, and she breathed again in the moment before she realised the visitor was Isabella, and the blood seemed to stop in her veins.

The fortune teller's face was almost covered by the hood of her cloak as she slipped out from behind the gaoler and stepped into the cell. The man waited as she handed him some coins, which he took with a bow of his head that was at once both curt and obsequious. Then he left them, and the door shuddered shut behind him with a clang.

Kate drew herself up, hand still on the poppet. This was her chance, her only chance, and her heart beat quick with fear. She had thought she would know what to do.

Help me, Tom. Please. One last time.

Isabella's eyes wandered over the confines of the cell. She seemed at home, untouched by the ghosts of misery that lingered at its edges, the darkness. She was a creature of the night, Kate remembered, and the shadows were her natural habitat, but she still carried with her the freshness of the outside world, a breath of sweet air and the now-familiar scent of cinnamon and lemon. Stepping forward, she slid back her hood, and beneath it her hair was neat and pinned, a respectable woman – one of her many facets.

'Good morning, Kate,' Isabella said, as though they were meeting by chance in the street. 'Are they treating you well?'

Kate made a gesture with one hand that took in the cell. 'As you see.'

Isabella stepped in closer and, though Kate's instinct was to move away, to put distance between them, she held her ground.

'What do you want?'

The fortune teller smiled. 'I can help you,' she said.

'Why would you do so when it was you that put me here?' She

was aware of Maggie, rising to her feet by the wall with sudden interest.

'It was Nathan did that – I had no part in it.'

'You lie.'

Isabella sucked in air with a sharp hiss that seemed to echo off the stones. Her fists balled and unballed, mouth tight with the effort of self-control.

'You may believe what you wish,' she breathed, 'but I am here to offer you my help.'

Kate said nothing. The poppet grew warm at her breast and she could feel its tremor against her skin.

'Or you may remain here and die. Is that what you want? To swing from a gallows? I believe it is a painful death.' Isabella slid a glance to Maggie, close now at Kate's shoulder. 'I can save you, Kate,' she whispered, 'but I need the book to do it.'

Ah, Kate thought. At last.

'The book?' she asked. 'What book is that?'

'Your father's book.' Isabella's tone was impatient, and she glanced towards the door.

At the mention of her father, Kate's thoughts slid back in time to an image of the house in The Hague, and her father adjusting the eyeglasses she had teased him about when he read in his chair in the long winter evenings, legs stretched towards the warmth of the fire. It was hard to imagine he might have used the book as she and Rafe had done, calling spirits from other realms.

'The book Tom Wynter stole from my father,' Isabella spat. 'The book of magic your father took from mine, when he and your whore of a mother murdered him. Where is it? Tell me.'

Kate drew in a long breath – she hadn't known about the murder.

'I can save you,' Isabella repeated, more urgently this time, and with another glance to the door, 'but only if I have the book.'

'I can save myself,' Kate replied, drawing the poppet from her bodice.

Isabella took a step back and for the first time Kate glimpsed the light of fear in the other woman's eyes. She smiled, and words she had not searched for drummed inside her mind. She raised her head and spoke them aloud.

'*I am a witch of ancient blood, and I call on the power of the Shadow to bind Isabella to take my place.*'

Though her voice was no more than a whisper, the words rang through the cell, the air vibrating in their wake.

'*I call upon the dark light of Hecate and the ghost of Tom Wynter to see it done.*'

She held the poppet out before her in both of her hands and in her mind's eye she saw the shattered image of her dream – Isabella's form in a thousand pieces.

'*As I have seen it, make it so.*'

She pressed her thumbs against the poppet's breast and watched with satisfaction as the real woman seemed to stagger, struggling for balance. Maggie reached out a hand, and Isabella snatched her cloak away from the grasping fingers.

'Do not touch me,' she hissed.

Maggie laughed and moved closer.

'Pretty cloth,' the whore said, testing the wool with her fingertips as if she were thinking to buy. 'Finely woven. Warm, no doubt? And a fine deep hood to hide your face.' She began to pull at it.

'Give it to me,' Kate ordered, understanding at last. She felt light, strong, invincible. The power of the Shadow flowed in her blood and the ghost of Tom Wynter stood at her side. Her thumbs pressed harder against the poppet, her arms bright with its heat.

Isabella cowered.

'You heard her,' Maggie said.

There was a moment's hesitation before Isabella fumbled with the clasp at her neck and the cloak fell away from her shoulders into Maggie's waiting hands. A heartbeat more and Kate was wearing it. Maggie fastened it tight at her throat and lifted the hood, and all the while Kate held the poppet tight, thumbs pressing hard against its breast. Isabella stared, taken aback by this sudden reversal of fortune, the fate she had imagined for herself fading into the dark.

'Go,' Maggie said. She ripped Isabella's purse from her belt, and tucked it into her bodice. 'Call him.'

'No!' The fortune teller found her voice at last, and though she fought against the grip that tightened round her heart, she was no match for the power of the Shadow that surged in Kate's blood. She had been taken by surprise, unprepared for battle. 'No!'

'Gaoler!' Kate was surprised by the calm in her voice and the way she could alter it to mimic her visitor's. 'I am ready.'

She heard his feet tramp down the passage and every step seemed to take an age. Isabella was watching in horror and Maggie held her firmly by the arm, taking no chances.

'Thank you,' Kate said to her friend. 'When you are free again find me at the Cardinal's Cap. I will not forget your kindness.'

The key turned in the lock. Kate kept one thumb hard against the poppet and with the other hand drew the hood lower across her face. The door shuddered open, and as Isabella made one desperate lunge towards it, Kate closed her eyes to see again the shattered reflection of her dream, bending the doll double between her fingers as she did so. Isabella stumbled, reaching a hand to the floor to steady herself. The gaoler appeared in the doorway.

'The poor girl is half-crazed with her terror of the noose,' Kate said. 'I fear my visit has upset her.'

He peered into the cell and, without a moment's pause, walked across the floor to bring the back of his hand so savagely across Isabella's face that she tumbled to the floor, sprawling. Kate exchanged a brief glance with Maggie, then stepped through the door into freedom without another backward glance. She could hear Isabella's cries behind her as the door slammed shut and the key grated harshly in the lock. The poppet was warm in her fingers, still thrumming, and she tightened her grip, thumb still pressed against its breast, thoughts trained towards the shattered image of her dream. She must decide what to do with it, once she was free.

Isabella's screams faded into silence behind her as the gaoler led Kate along the noisome passage, but it was not over yet – first she had to escape the prison. One slip, and the gaoler might notice his mistake. One wrong word, and she could still hang. His broad back filled the corridor in front of her, keys jangling as they swung from his hand, and she strode swiftly behind him, keeping her head bowed and holding the hood close to her face.

The way seemed to go on forever. Darkness threatened at the corners of her vision, the walls threatening to close in around her, like the tunnels in a nightmare. Surely it could not be much further? She clutched the poppet harder as they passed door after door, the reek of pain and hopelessness oozing from the mildewed walls. A woman's shriek made her flinch but she did not slow her steps, still walking close behind the gaoler, eager for the world beyond the prison door.

But the gaoler never looked behind him even once to give her so much as a glance, never thought to examine her. She had paid him well on the inbound journey and he had no reason to doubt her. Inwardly, Kate cursed. She should have thought to take some coins from Isabella's purse – he would expect another payment at the gate and she had nothing at all to give him.

Finally, finally, they came to it. A simple heavy wooden door, bolted and locked, that marked the border between her life and her death. As the gaoler sorted with agonising slowness through his bunch of keys, she waited, forcing herself to be calm when inside her every fibre of her being was screaming for release. Would he realise when she gave him no coin? Would he think to look at her then? Or would he be grateful enough for what she had given him already?

He seemed to take an age to find the great iron key and slip it into the lock, rattling it into place before it would turn. Then, one by one he slid back the three great bolts, took the handle in his fist and opened it. She swept through it without a moment's hesitation, still awaiting his shout, braced for a rough hand to stop her. But there was nothing, and as she strode away at last through the cold of the morning into the bustle of the High Street, her mouth curled slowly into a smile.

Thank you, Tom.

It was my pleasure.

The hood of Isabella's cloak slid back and the bitter bite of winter air had never felt so good against Kate's face.

31

DO AS THE HEAVENS HAVE DONE, FORGET YOUR EVIL; WITH THEM FORGIVE YOURSELF

The winter sun hung low and pale above the rooftops, and the puddles in the street glimmered in its reflection, blinding, so that she had to close her eyes against the brightness of the morning after the dim light of inside the prison walls. Just beyond the doors she halted, letting her eyes adjust as the patter of her heartbeat began to slow. When she opened them again, the first thing they lit upon was Rafe. He was leaning against a wall, arms folded, head tilted in that way she knew so well. And he was watching her, mouth curled in an almost-smile. Her breathing caught and her heartbeat quickened once again. How long had he been standing there? How long had he been watching? She ran an automatic hand across her hair to smooth it as he pushed himself away from the wall and crossed the street towards her. A pair of apprentices crossed between them, and in the instant he was obscured from her sight she felt a flash of panic. But then he was before her again and they stood together for a moment of awkward silence in the cold morning light.

'Kate! How ...?'

She laughed at the bafflement in his eyes as he flicked a glance towards the prison behind her, as if he could see beyond the doors to the cells that lay behind and above them.

'I've learned a thing or two about poppets, these last few days,' she said, and when he held out his arms to her she sank into them and rubbed her face against the leather of his jacket, inhaling his warmth and the smell of him. She had never thought to be in his arms again, never thought to walk beneath the heavens above them.

Taking a step back from him she looked up into his face, and though he was smiling, she could see the lines of weariness etched around his eyes.

'Is my mother safe? Did we save her?'

'She is safe,' he said, 'and she's waiting for you at the Cardinal's Cap.'

Kate let out a long breath of relief.

'Shall we?' He offered her his arm to take, and though she wanted more than anything to take it, desperate to see her mother again and to wash the grime and stench of prison from her skin, she hesitated. First she must dispose of the poppet.

'Come with me to the Cross Bones,' she said. 'There is something I must do.'

For a heartbeat she thought he would refuse. She could see the doubt in his eyes, and the confusion.

'I'll explain on the way,' she said, and then he nodded and offered her his arm again. She took it, grateful for his strength beside her. Now that the first flush of her escape was over, the days of deprivation and hunger were beginning to tell – she could feel the weakness creeping into her limbs, her legs barely able to support her.

It was a short distance from the door of the Marshalsea to Red Cross Street and as they walked together through the bright hard cold of the morning she recounted all that had happened. He listened without a word, grave and pale, and she kept her eyes ahead of her, willing her limbs to obedience. The watery sun hung low above the rooftops, and out of its light the day was bitter.

They stopped at the gate of the Cross Bones and Kate shivered, throwing a glance behind her. The shadow of the prison still seemed to fall at her back, and though Isabella might be caged, she guessed that Nathan would still be free. Would he come after her again? Was he still following her? But she saw only the usual stir of the morning – shop fronts open, housewives and servants with baskets on their arms, a small child with a hoop, and a cluster of older boys kicking a stone in some game with rules of their own. A mangy-looking cat basked in a patch of sunlight close to the fence, watching her.

'Wait for me here.'

Rafe hesitated, reluctant to let her go on without him.

'Keep watch for Nathan.'

He nodded, but she knew he resented the command, wanting instead to stay with her and protect her. And perhaps, too, he wanted to meet Tom Wynter, whose story was so interwoven with his own. Kate shoved open the gate with the weight of her body and stepped inside.

A light frost dappled the grass and weeds, glistening in the sunlight, and by the time she had crossed the graveyard her feet were wet, the cold moisture soaking through the leather of her boots. She stood by Tom's grave with the poppet clutched in her hand, thumb still pressing hard against it, as though she had not yet quite learned to trust in her freedom. She had thought to bury it somewhere here in this unconsecrated ground, an unclean place, as Isabella had buried the poppet that sent Mary to the Shadow. But the earth was frozen hard and she had no tool to dig.

'Good morrow, Tom.'

She expected no answer. In the fair, clear morning, she could barely recall the darkness of the Shadow, and as she lifted her face to meet the sun's caress it seemed like a different world today, full of new promise. But when she lowered her head, Tom was sitting atop his grave, as vivid as his image in her dreams, beautiful and pale. It was hard to remember she was his grandchild, and that he had died long ago.

'Give it to me,' he said, and held out his hand. 'And I'll see it safely home.'

She laid the poppet on his outstretched palm. It seemed to hover against his skin for a moment before it shimmered and faded, disappearing into the air like smoke in a breeze.

'She will trouble you no more.'

'Thank you,' she replied. 'For everything.'

'You are my blood.'

She nodded, and bit back the tears that threatened to come. This was farewell, she knew, and she was sorry for it. She wanted to hold him and wrap herself in the safety of his presence one final time, and as if he understood her need, he held out his hands for her. She stepped between them and he drew her to him, folding her into his cold embrace as she laid her cheek against his chest. There was no heartbeat to hear but she was aware of his love in spite of the chill of him, and she held him tighter, enfolding herself in his protection. After a moment he let his arms slide away and she lifted her head to him – her guardian angel. He was smiling down at her.

'Go now,' he said, 'to your mother, and to Rafe, who loves you.'

She nodded, her heart brimming with the sorrow of his leaving.

'Will I see you again?'

'You have no more need of me,' he replied. 'You have a whole life to live. Use it well.'

Kate wiped at the tears she could no longer stop from falling and when her eyes cleared again, Tom had gone. She stared at the space he had left behind as if she could will him back into being, but she knew this time he had gone for good. So she let the tears rise and fall unchecked and stood crying by the graveside in the bright winter morning until she could weep no more.

By the time they had found their way to the Cardinal's Cap amongst the row of taverns that faced the river on Bankside, the sun had given way to darkening clouds that presaged rain. The tavern had seen better days, Kate thought, as she cast her eyes across the front of it. Rotting window frames and peeling white-wash, the door misshapen with age. The door was locked when she tried it, and no one answered when she knocked, so she hammered with her fist and all that was left of her strength. At the alehouse next door an upstairs window swung open, and a tousled woman's head peered through, squinting into the morning light.

'What do you want?'

'Go back to bed,' Kate returned. ''Tis not your door I want opening.'

'Then stop your hammering.' The head disappeared and at last they heard movement inside. Brisk footsteps sounded on the flag-stones. Then the bolts jarred open, a key turned, and the door was dragged open. In the doorway stood her mother, hair still mussed from sleep, a robe hastily fastened at her waist. Kate had never in her life been so relieved to see her, and as she stepped into the waiting embrace a wash of love and rightness flooded her veins.

'I'm so sorry,' she whispered. 'For everything.'

'Hush,' Mary said, smoothing her daughter's hair with cold quick fingers. ''Tis good to see you, good to have you home. At last.'

Kate stepped back and gestured to Rafe, standing at her shoul-der, made awkward by the women's emotions. 'You've met Rafe?'

Mary nodded and gave him a smile that lit a feeling inside Kate that she could not quite understand. Then her mother, sliding into her old pragmatic self, said, 'Come. You must be hungry.'

With the words Kate's belly twisted, shrunken and beginning to ache with lack of food – she had lost count of the days since she'd eaten anything but mouldy bread. Following her mother into the tavern, she watched as Rosalind laid a meal at the table by the hearth, and though the fare was simple she had almost forgotten such good things existed – fresh white bread, apples, radishes, cheese. It was not food she had dreamt of in the days in prison, but warmth and air and light. The green of trees and the breeze off the river. Rafe's touch. His smile. She turned to him, and took his hand, reassuring herself that he was still there and that he loved her, as Tom had said.

'Eat,' Rosalind said, and they sat at the table. Kate picked at the food and took small sips of wine as her belly groaned in protest at the unaccustomed richness. But the act of eating gave her time to order her thoughts for the questions she knew were coming. Finally, when she could force down no more, she pushed the platter away and lifted her head to meet her mother's gaze. Then, though she had not planned it, she said, 'Tell me about Father's book and how you came to have it. The one Tom Wynter stole.'

She saw her mother exchange a furtive glance with Rosalind, then flick a glance to Rafe, who was sitting close beside Kate, his leg against hers. He gave her a small smile and she wondered again at the weariness in his eyes – she had yet to hear his part in the last few days. But she was grateful for his nearness and protection. For all her witch's power and escape from prison, Nathan's shadow could still wring terror in her guts.

'Isabella came to the gaol to claim it from me,' Kate went on, when her mother said nothing. 'She offered me my freedom in exchange for it. But I took my freedom for myself and Isabella will hang in my place.'

Mary hesitated as she took in her daughter's news, and Kate wondered how much her mother knew, what her role in the story had been. Could it be true that her parents had killed a man? She waited as Mary ran her tongue across her lips, searching for the right words to say. Finally, after a long breath, her mother began to talk, and she seemed to stare into some unknown realm that existed beyond the walls of the tavern.

'The book once belonged to Isabella's father, the sorcerer Alexander, until Tom Wynter took it for his own. In time it came to Toby. And thence to me.'

'That much I already know,' she said. Then, 'Isabella said you murdered her father. You and my father both. Is it true? Tell me – there is nothing can shock me now.'

Mary swallowed. Her eyes flitted across the room, settling on nothing, hands twisting in front of her on the table. She took a sip of wine. Finally, she found the courage she was looking for and brought her gaze to meet her daughter's.

'It's true,' she murmured, and her voice was so low that Kate had to lean forward to catch the words. 'Your father and I. There was a ritual and Alexander had a knife to Toby's throat. I killed him.' Her mother's voice trailed off with the memory and Kate let her eyes drift across the table as her thumb rubbed absently at the edge of it where the wood was worn and smooth. 'I killed him to save your father's life.'

The silence in the room felt thick enough to chew. Kate swallowed, words failing to come to mind though the questions spun wild in her head.

'Isabella wanted revenge,' Mary said. 'And she thought to seduce you into giving her the book. To steal it brings a curse of death. Your grandfather learned that to his cost.'

Kate's gaze slid to rest on the unlit fire in the hearth and cast her mind back. John Lowin had said it was Shakespeare's play that had wrought the curse but perhaps it was all part of the same dark tale – evil forces unleashed on the world, feeding on one another.

In the grate, the ashes were dead and grey, and a single charred piece of wood remained amongst them. Kate remembered it was cold and she shivered, wishing the fire was alight, a sudden need for warmth and brightness. Her hand tightened on Rafe's. She could barely imagine her mother with a part in the story she had told.

Magic, murder, a curse.

A book of power.

Life in a brothel.

No wonder Mary had talked so little of her past. And she, Kate, also a murderess now. She thought of Isabella awaiting her fate and shuddered.

'Is it still at the Bull's Head?'

Rafe nodded. 'Still hidden.'

'We must destroy it,' Mary said, and Kate felt Rafe tense beside her in an echo of her own unwillingness.

Kate stared. 'After all this, why would you destroy it?'

She could feel its call, and the memory of the rite she and Rafe had done together flared in her mind. Despite the terror, she wanted more of it, lusting to have it answer to her as it had answered to her father.

'I promised Tom.' Mary's reply was simple. 'To set him free. So he can rest in peace with Sarah at last.'

Kate was silent. She hadn't known that Tom had come to her mother as he had come to her. A shard of jealousy opened up her insides, sharp and painful, unexpected. She swallowed it down, remembering that Tom had done what he needed to protect them both.

'Can such a book be destroyed?' she asked. Her fingers burned to hold it again, to understand and wield its power, even knowing all she did. She exchanged a glance with Rafe, and knew he was thinking the same.

Mary lifted one shoulder in a shrug. 'Our family's time with it is done. We must throw it in the Thames and let the tide take it where it will. Perhaps it will survive, perhaps not. But it will find its home elsewhere and our family will be free of it.' She began to clear up the remnants of the meal, practical matters to distract herself. 'We'll wait for the tide to turn,' she said, 'to carry it out to sea. Otherwise, it will just wash ashore somewhere nearby and find its way back.'

''Tis a book,' Rosalind said. 'Surely the ink would not survive the water?'

''Tis no ordinary book. Who knows what it can survive?'

'I'll fetch it,' Rafe said, getting to his feet, and Kate felt the cold of his absence already.

'Be quick,' she said. 'Be safe.'

She wanted him near her always, she realised, and the danger of the book hung over them all. Perhaps her mother was right, after all. Perhaps the Winters' time with it was over. She swung her gaze away, suddenly weary, and once more aware of the dirt on her skin and the smell of her clothes.

'I need a bath,' she said. 'And fresh clothes.'

Her mother nodded, got up, and went to the kitchen to see about hot water.

~

Kate sat in the tub that had been brought to Rosalind's chamber and let her mother soap her hair. The hot water was delicious against her skin, the lavender scent of Castile soap sweet in the air. A good fire that roared in the hearth helped chase away the memory of the cold and filth of the prison cell. But every so often she touched her fingers to her throat, as if she could still not quite believe it was free of the threat of the noose. Briefly she thought of Maggie and wondered if she'd find her way to the Cardinal's Cap once she was free. She hoped so.

'You lived here in the brothel,' she said.

Mary's hands stilled briefly at the work of untangling her daughter's hair.

'I did.' She began once more to tease the knots apart, pulling now and then with a tug that made Kate wince. 'And I have known the inside of a prison cell, same as you.'

'For being a …?' she could not bring herself to use the word to her mother.

'I was still a maid when they took me to gaol,' Mary said, 'but by the time I left I was a whore.'

'The scars on your back?'

'Yes.'

'And Father knew?'

'Yes,' her mother replied with a laugh. 'He knew.'

Kate was silent, turning over all she had learned in the last days and hours, the history that Isabella had promised her. 'I always thought you both so proper. So dull.'

Mary yanked hard at a tangle, dragging Kate's head to one side.

'We hoped to leave all of it behind and start afresh. We wanted you to be safe. But the blood of Tom Wynter flows in your veins – I suppose we should have known you'd seek out the truth in the end.'

'I wish I'd known him,' Kate said.

Mary was silent, fingers still busy with the knots. The water was beginning to cool and Kate shivered.

'Rinse it off,' Mary said, and Kate sank obediently into the bath, closing her eyes as the water washed over her face. Then she was up and standing by the fire, skin turning red in its heat as she dried herself. Mary helped her to dress in the fresh robe Rosalind had given her. A soft linen shift. A bodice of rich dark blue with a thick wool skirt to match. Warm woollen stockings. It felt like heaven to be clean again.

BUT THIS ROUGH MAGIC, I HERE ABJURE

Rafe prised the oak panel from the wall in his chamber and reached inside, fingers scrabbling, searching, until they closed at last on the soft cool cloth he had used to wrap the book before he stashed it away. Drawing it out carefully, he brushed off with his fingertips the crumbs of wattle and daub that had stuck to it. Then he teased the panel carefully back into place until he was certain the join was once more invisible.

He let out a long slow breath. The book was heavy in his hands and it seemed to hum, its vibration reaching into his core. Remembering the rite they had done, the presence of the demon he had summoned from another realm, he passed his fingertips across its surface, a loving caress. Long aware of its power, he had yearned to possess it since he first heard of it all those years ago as a student at Oxford. He wanted it. He wanted to keep it for himself. It was a prize to be coveted and here it was, in his hands again, calling to him.

Tearing his gaze away from it he lifted his head towards the window. A pewter sky loured, promising rain, the pale sun of the early morning utterly forgotten. Just along the way at the Cardinal's Cap Kate was waiting for him. She would be clean and fresh and pretty again by the time he returned to her, the taint of prison scrubbed from her skin. He let his thoughts linger on her image – the wide-set eyes that so often challenged him, bright with cleverness, and the rosebud mouth that tasted so sweet to kiss. The lithe boyish lines of her hips, the smoothness of her skin. The touch of her fingers, and her soft warmth when he was inside her.

With the memory of the pleasure they had shared, he gave himself an instinctive smile. In the long cold days of misery in prison, he had revisited every moment they had spent together again and again, and he had fallen a little deeper in love with her each and every time. He had not believed he could ever love again. He had thought he was incapable, that part of him had died along with Ellen and his son. But Kate had reawoken his desire to love and be loved, a life to live together. The thought of her had given him new hope for the future – a wife, children, a family again.

But now he held Tom Wynter's book in his hands, and the darkness called to him with a force that was hard to resist. He could feel its song between his fingers, and the answering throb of his blood, hungry for the knowledge the book contained and the power it could offer him. They could harness it together, he thought – witch and sorcerer, a potent combination. Did they dare? He had seen the reluctance in Kate's eyes to destroy it, her own eagerness to unlock the secrets it contained. She would be willing, he was sure.

He tapped the book with his fingers, tempted. But it was not their book to keep – it belonged to Mary, and she had said that to steal it carried a curse. He recalled Tom Wynter and his untimely death at the end of a rope. Was it his theft of the book that had led him there? The rituals he had performed? No one could ever know the truth of what really happened but there was no doubt that his fate was still tied to it, his peace eluding him until it was gone.

Rafe flicked through the pages once more, longing in his heart. Then, with a sigh of resignation, he tucked the book under his arm, turned away from the hidden panel and began to make his way back to the Cardinal's Cap.

~

Rafe had not long returned when a man's shout rang out from the tavern. Kate was getting settled beside the fire in Rosalind's room to let her mother comb free the last of the tangles from her hair, and all of them looked up in alarm. It was not the usual drunken roar of impatience or laughter, but a more sinister voice, laced with violence. And, Kate realised, a voice she knew.

'Nathan,' she whispered, turning to her mother.

All the colour had drained from Mary's face, and she stared at the door as if transfixed.

'You know him? Isabella's servant?'

Mary nodded, lips compressed. 'He must have come for the book,' she whispered. 'Now that Isabella is gone, he must want it for himself.'

They heard his boots tramp on the stairs that led to the rooms overhead. and Kate's gaze slid to the book where it lay on the bed, awaiting its destruction.

'Take it. Both of you.' Mary raised her head towards Rafe, who had been warming himself at the hearth. 'Quickly. Go through the back.'

Kate hesitated only a moment before she reached for it. Then she fastened Isabella's cloak at her neck as Mary opened the door and peered out.

'Quickly,' she urged again. 'Go. Throw it in the river and let the tide bear it to its fate.'

They slid past her with the book clutched close to Kate's chest, and without looking back they ran along the passage, through the kitchens, and out of the low door into a foul-smelling yard. A gate swung on a broken hinge in a low fence at the back of it and they hurried through to find themselves in the narrow lane that ran between the buildings. Channels of filth had part-frozen in the centre but the rutted mud on either side was hard underfoot. Careful not to slip on the uneven ground, they half walked, half ran, heading west, away from Bankside and the bustling market, seeking the quieter roads beyond.

~

Mary heard the click of the back door that led out into the yard beyond the kitchens, and the outraged squeal of one of the girls overhead as Nathan burst into her room. In a few moments he would be downstairs, and there would be no more time. She scanned the chamber – the bath, the drying sheet, and Kate's prison-soaked clothes: there was nowhere for her to hide any of it in the room that Nathan wouldn't find with just the briefest of searches. She gathered the clothes up in her arms, wrinkling her nose at the smell, then opened the door. Nathan's boots were loud on the boards above and coming this way.

There was no time.

Softly shutting the door again, she carried the bundle to the narrow window that gave on to the wall of the building beside it. Holding the clothes with one hand she turned the latch with the other, but the window stuck in its frame, swollen shut. She rattled it, casting a quick glance to the door. Finally, it gave, and she thrust the gown and shift and stockings through the opening and into the alleyway beyond. They would be gone by the time she returned for them, she guessed, scavenged by a beggar, and briefly she regretted it – beneath the dirt the fabric had been fine. But there was no other way. Pulling the window shut, she smoothed down her skirts and walked smartly to the door, out into the passage and to the tavern itself, where Rosalind was hovering with a cloth in her hand.

Nathan met Mary at the base of the stairs, and she halted, startled by the new and livid wound across his face, and the bright madness of the fever in his eyes. She could smell the purulence from where she stood, and she had to swallow down the thread of vomit that rose in her throat.

'Where is it?' he snarled.

'Where is what?'

'The book,' he snarled. 'The one you cunning bitches of whores took from my mistress.'

'Your mistress is in gaol. What need has she for a book?'

He stared, nonplussed for an instant. Clearly, he had not yet heard the news. But, recovering quickly he lunged towards her, and though she sidestepped smartly to avoid his reaching hand, she was not fast enough; his fingers closed hard around the muscle of her arm. She fought not to gag at the stench, and across the tavern Rosalind cried out as if in pain at her own arm being twisted. 'Where is it?'

'I do not know,' Mary said.

He shoved her roughly backward, and pain sliced into her shoulder.

'And if you did you wouldn't tell me, isn't that right?'

'Perhaps.' She forced a smile, but it was a mistake to provoke him. He let her arm go and brought the back of his hand hard across her face so that she stumbled backward, hitting her hip on a table behind her. She struggled for her balance as he came at her again, grasping her by the shoulders, barrelling her towards the newel post at the bottom of the stairs, pinning her there. His face was an inch from her own as he grabbed a handful of her hair and pulled. She could taste the blood on her lip.

'Tell me,' he breathed, 'or it will be the worse for you.'

'I cannot tell you what I do not know,' she whispered.

His weight against her was crushing her chest, and his fingers twisted cruelly in her hair. Like old times, she thought. Soon he would lift her skirts and help himself to what lay beneath. But she was no longer a whore – those days were long past – and her body wasn't his to take. She spat in his face, a thick gob that hit him just below the eye, and in the instant of shock his grip relaxed just enough for her to bring her knee into his groin. His eyes briefly widened and his breath grew hoarse with pain. For a moment he bent his body forward, winded, but mad with his fever and his rage, he rallied fast. With a final yank at her hair he let her go. Then he turned towards Rosalind who was watching from a distance, and looked her up and down. She shrank away in terror as he strode towards the passage at the back, slamming open the doors that led off it, peering into the store rooms before he came to Rosalind's room. Mary followed at a distance.

He stood in the doorway for what seemed to be a long time, and she tried to see the scene through his eyes. The bathtub, the water growing cold, the unmade bed, the faded cushions and carpets, and a warm fire in the hearth. Would he sense the traces of her daughter, and realise the truth? Would some sixth sense detect her presence, the trail of the book? At last he turned back to face her.

'As you can see, it is not here.'

He gave a smile that made her guts turn. 'I will find it. And I will keep returning to haunt you until the book is in my hands, so you will need to find another place to hide yourself.'

She said nothing, but merely watched him as he brushed past her in the passage, strode across the tavern, and out onto the quayside.

They ran until there was no breath left in Kate's chest and she could run no more. Ahead of her Rafe slowed, then halted, turning at last as she gasped for air. Her head was spinning. The chill of the morning caught at her still-wet hair but she paid it no mind, and when the pain in her chest began finally to lessen she stood upright once more and saw that they had stopped on a grassy expanse of bank where the river's tongue licked at the shore, the tide high and swirling. She was aware of the heaving city not far behind her but it was peaceful here at the water's edge, and easy to forget the danger they had fled. For all that she was grateful for Rafe's presence, Nathan remained a threat, goaded by his desire for the book and the fever that was eating away at his wits. Beside her, Rafe was breathing hard too, his hair damp with sweat, and she thought he had never looked so handsome. Together, they watched a pair of swans glide in to land on the river, elegant and regal, and turned to each other with a smile.

'My father told me once that swans mate for life,' she said. 'But I don't know if they grieve for each other too.'

He took her hand and wound his fingers in hers in answer. Her other hand instinctively tightened on the book before she withdrew it from beneath her cloak. It was still wrapped in cloth and she held it before her, hesitating. Rafe's grip tightened on her fingers, and she was aware of the tightness of his muscles in the way he held himself, and the fierceness of his gaze as it rested on the book. She took a deep breath and raised her head towards him. They exchanged a glance containing volumes – their desire and love for each other with its promise for the future and the debt they owed to Tom Wynter doing battle with their lust for the knowledge contained in the pages in her hand.

In spite of its size the book was heavy, and it seemed to hum against her fingers, calling her. The urge to obey its voice was almost overwhelming, a visceral need in her blood, and it was hard to struggle against it. One more look, the voice in her head urged her, just to see this thing again that had caused men to murder to possess it. But still she hesitated, striving to resist the temptation.

Lifting her head, she looked along the river. On the north bank across from them, a man was chopping wood outside a tumble-down cottage while his dog barked madly at some unknown threat. But on the south side they were alone. She looked along the shore. Just down the bank a way was an old and dilapidated jetty, a structure of rotting planks that reached out over the turbulent tide. All she needed to do was go to the jetty and let the pages slide from her fingers. The Thames would do the rest, bearing the book away to its fate, perhaps to its destruction, or into the hands of another whose life would be blighted by possession of it.

'I don't want to destroy it either,' she said.

'We must,' he replied. But neither one of them moved, caught in the trap of their indecision as the book exerted its will to survive.

The jetty was close, she thought. Just a short walk away. But her legs were reluctant to move. Like in the nightmares of her childhood, when she could not run from the evil that pursued her. She swallowed at the thought of it and turned instinctively to look behind her, seeing only the path that led alongside the river, the trees that overhung it and the last of the cottages, all but hidden behind the bare branches of an apple tree.

Her fingers caressed the wrapping and, without even knowing she had done it, she realised she'd untied the thong that held it so that the piece of cloth fell away. The book seemed to blink in the sudden light as if waking from a sleep. There was no title – the lettering had long since worn away – but she ran her fingertips across the cover, and the leather was still warm from the heat of her skin where she had carried it. Rafe's body seemed to tighten and grow, like an animal with rising hackles, and she was aware of the warmth of the living force inside him – blood beating through his muscles, sinew and bone, the silken stretch of his skin. An answering flame lifted inside her, heartbeat quickening, heat in her belly.

She glanced up again, made afraid by this tide of raw feeling – an animal sense washing over her. The swans were turning on the water, moving in some mysterious dance of their own devising. The woodchopper ceased his work and the day fell silent save for the lapping of the river on the bank, and the waves that slapped against the jetty. Against her will, her fingers opened the cover to the first page. The two names that were written in ink had begun to turn brown with age. Her father and her grandfather.

Tom Wynter.

Toby Chyrche.

She traced the letters with her fingertips. Father and son, their fates tied to the pages in her hand. And Tom, still awaiting the freedom Mary had promised him. She recalled the chill of his embrace at the graveyard and all he had done for her, his love for her. With a sudden sigh of resolution, she shut the book with a snap, wrapped it again inside its cover, and tied the strip of leather tightly around it.

'I'll do it,' she said. But she kept her eyes lowered away from Rafe's, unsure what she would see there, if he would try to stop her. He had long desired the book, she knew, and he had the skills to read it. For half a heartbeat she hesitated, and then she forced her legs into motion and strode for the jetty. Rafe waited on the riverbank, watching.

She was almost to the tip of it, stepping with care across the rotting boards, when a warning crawled over her skin that they were no longer alone.

'Rafe!'

She braced, breath quickening as he swung round, searching wildly. Nathan was already halfway along the jetty and the structure seemed to waver with his movement. The blade of his knife caught in the dull gleam of the morning light as he shifted closer, picking his way across the crumbling timber. How had he slipped past Rafe so easily?

Rafe was thundering towards them, but he drew up sharply when he caught sight of the knife, close enough now to Kate that a single lunge could finish her. A piece of board fell away at the impact and tumbled into the water below. She tightened her grip on the book as it slipped against the sudden sweat on her hands.

'How did you find us?'

'Fate,' he replied, with a shrug. 'Luck, good fortune ... call it what you will.' Then, stepping forward again, treading warily on the treacherous planks. 'You have something of mine, I believe.'

'I don't think so.'

'In your hand.'

'You mean this?' She held it up and his eyes followed it, like a dog will follow a piece of meat in its master's hand. 'This belonged to my father,' she said, 'and now it belongs to me.'

'Then let me show you how to use it,' he coaxed. 'Let me teach you its secrets.'

She said nothing.

'Are you not curious? Think of the possibilities, the power you could wield. For good, if you wish it.'

'My family is done with it,' she answered.

'Then give it to me.'

She held it out above the water.

Nathan's eyes lit up with desperation. 'It cannot be destroyed.' His words were almost swallowed in his gasps for breath. 'It will wash ashore some place we cannot know. Some other man will find it.'

'It matters not. We will be rid of it, and Tom will be free.'

'Fuck Tom,' Nathan hissed, testing his weight on the jetty, stepping closer.

Kate let the book slide from her fingers into the murky water below, and as it fell Nathan lunged towards her. The plank gave way beneath the sudden force and he slipped, but as he flailed to save himself he caught at her skirts with one hand. They fell as one into the rolling tide.

The sudden cold blasted the breath from her body, and in her shock she felt the water flooding into her lungs. Nathan clutched at her gown as she kicked with all her strength to lift herself towards the surface, towards air, trying to heave herself up from the depths with powerful strokes of her arms, obeying the instinctive urge to life. For long heartbeats, she felt the pull of his weight, dragging her down. Then he let her go, swimming away to chase the trail of the book, still resolutely searching in the cold and dark.

But Kate's skirts had filled and spread, dragging her deeper, and though she fought and kicked against the weight of them and the pull of the tide, the brightness of the day above her began to dim, and her strokes grew weaker. Is this it? she wondered. Had the book brought about her death even as she tried to set it free? She struggled harder, but her movements made no headway against the pull of the deep. All around her began to pale and fade, and she could no longer struggle against the downward fall, submitting at last to its watery embrace.

Then, out of nowhere, a strong arm caught her by the waist, and in another moment her head broke the surface.

Rafe.

She gasped and spluttered, her body confused by the sudden inrush of air as he bore her towards the posts of the jetty and from there towards the safety of the shingle and the shore beyond, dragging her from the tide. They lay together on the firm, hard ground, shuddering with the cold as she coughed up the water she had swallowed, her whole body heaving with the effort. She was aware of Rafe's hand on her back, gentle and caressing as she retched and shuddered, and when she trusted that there was no more water left to vomit, she turned towards him, nestling into his arms. His body was hard and reassuring against her and though his jacket was dripping, she rubbed her cheek against it, unable to get close enough; when he moved back a little to place his cloak around her, it felt as though her world had briefly ended. He settled it across her shoulders and she sat up into the circle of his embrace, her body pressed hard against his.

'Thank you,' she whispered, looking up at him.

'You're welcome,' he replied, and gave her a smile that seemed to chase away the chill.

They had done it. The book was gone. Their family was released from the taint of its curse, and Tom Wynter was finally free to go to his rest, wherever he chose to take it. With Sarah, Kate hoped, in Hecate's realm of death.

Only then did she think to look again for Nathan, eyes scanning the river for a sight of him. There was no trace of him at all. Not even a break in the surface of the water, no sign he had ever been there. Peering along the bank, she scanned the northern shore, shielding her eyes with her hand against the brightness, half expecting to see him wading ashore downstream. She waited. Surely a man could not hold his breath for so long? Surely he must surface soon?

'Is he dead?' she wondered out loud.

'I think so,' Rafe replied. 'I've not seen him surface.'

The dog on the far bank resumed its barking and she searched the riverside again with uncertain eyes. But nothing else moved in the winter morning except the tide on the shingle and the waves against the posts of the jetty.

So another life had been claimed by the book, she thought, and though she would not mourn him, she was sorry it had come to this. Had he found it before he breathed his last, dying with it clutched to his chest? Or had he watched it drift away on its journey to a different fate before the water claimed him for its own?

'We should get you home,' Rafe said. 'You're half frozen to the bone.'

'No more than you,' she replied, taking the hand he offered to help her to her feet. Then, arms wrapped around each other, bodies close, they set their feet towards the row of taverns and bawdy houses on Bankside.

Towards home.

33

LET US SIT ON THE GROUND AND TELL
SAD STORIES OF THE DEATH OF KINGS

A few days later, the Thames had frozen hard and the day was so bitter-cold it stung against Mary's face as she stood at the water's edge, gazing out and watching the boys who were playing on the ice, their childish shrieks splitting the air. She smiled at their fun, and hoped the ice would hold their weight. One or two adults were chancing it too and making the crossing on foot – far quicker than taking the bridge, which would be heaving with travellers. The watermen would go hungry tonight.

''Tis an omen.'

Mary turned as a washerwoman came to stand beside her, observing the river. She held a great basket on an ample hip and her cheeks and hands were raw with the cold.

'Of what?'

The woman gave Mary a contemptuous glare at the question. 'Of what will happen when a rightful King is killed. The execution is today. Did you not know?'

'I knew,' Mary answered. But in truth she had barely thought of it. She was bound for another execution, one that touched her far more nearly.

'Will you go? To see him die?'

'Not me.' Mary shook her head.

The woman raised her eyes, shifting her gaze from the icy river to the northern bank, where the tower of St Paul's stood dark against the sky.

'God will take his punishment,' she said, 'and there will be a price to pay.'

There is always a price to pay, Mary thought, but she merely gave the woman a nod and kept her silence.

'I bid you good day,' she said, and, having no trust in the thickness of the ice, she turned from the river and joined the throng of people making their way towards the bridge into the city.

North of the river she walked quickly, growing warm with the movement in spite of the rawness of the day. A cold silver sun hung low in a pale sky and the puddles and ruts were frozen underfoot so she had to tread with care not to slip. But she walked with purpose, and though she was tempted to look about her at a city she had rarely ever visited, she was conscious of the hour and the need to keep her wits about her. On the Strand, a great press of people flowed towards Whitehall. A few joyful faces stood out amongst them but for the most part the expressions were sombre, there not to celebrate the killing of a King but to bear witness to his passing.

It was nearly noon when she finally reached Tyburn, and her blood seemed to shrink inside her at the sight of the great hanging tree at the crossroads, its three great beams bristling with nooses, dangling ready for their victims. Was this where Tom had met his untimely end? she wondered. She had not thought of it before.

Atop the gallows, a young boy crouched in readiness, shivering in the cold, and the crowds around it jostled for position, hawkers moving amongst them, selling ale and apples and cakes, their voices calling high-pitched above the rumble of the crowd. She saw one or two whores touting for trade and had to turn her eyes away. The size of the crowd astonished her. Did no one have to work today? Sliding between the watchers she found a place beside a group of apprentices. The young men shifted to give her room and she thanked them with a smile.

Mary knew when the first hurdle of prisoners had arrived by the change in the noise of the crowd. A quieting, the murmur softening just briefly before the jeers and catcalls started. She heard the rumble of the wheels but she could see nothing over the heads of the mob until the prisoners were shoved one by one from the hurdle that had brought them from the gaol to the cart that would bear them to the noose. As each victim stepped up onto the platform Mary held her breath. Young men, old men, a woman her own age who was sobbing uncontrollably, her wails carrying above the chatter of the throng. The excitement was building in the crowd all around her, a lust for death, and the brutality of it sickened her. She recalled the same roused desire for blood at the beargarden years ago, when she had sometimes plied the crowds in search of customers. But they had been baying then for the blood of an animal as they laid their bets, money changing hands. These frightened creatures before her now were fellow human souls and she had to swallow down the bile that rose in her throat.

High above the throng the boy atop the beam of the hanging tree checked the ropes once more. She waited. Then, finally, Isabella stepped up onto the cart and, though her hands were bound tight before her, she refused all help from the hangman. She stood unbowed as the rope was passed about her neck, her gaze sweeping the crowd with disdain. Briefly, Mary felt a wash of guilt – it was her family's doing that had brought Isabella here. But the feeling did not last long. She had come to witness this woman die as she had seen Alexander die.

With the last noose fastened, the crowd subsided, shouts and jeers dimming down to a murmur that seemed to pulsate. The sobbing woman had fallen silent. A priest began to intone a prayer, and a couple of the condemned called out last words, but Mary paid them no attention. Her gaze was fixed on Isabella.

The woman who had murdered Toby, who had tried to take Kate.

She wanted to be sure of her death. Hadn't trusted that justice would take its course. Even now, she half expected that the fortune teller would still find some way to escape her fate. But her head was raised, eyes searching the crowd until her gaze found Mary at last. The two women locked eyes and Mary felt no pity at all. But as Isabella's mouth curved into a smile, Mary felt the darkness of the Shadow stir.

The hangman gave the signal and the whip fell with a crack that cut the morning. The cart jerked into movement and Isabella's body dropped alongside all the others as they gave their final dance, forms twisting and swinging in the cold morning air. Mary waited till Isabella twitched no more before she turned and shoved her way back through the cheering crowd.

Then she ran, but the chill was still inside her.

THANK YOU!

Thank you for reading Caress of a Witch. If you enjoyed it, I'd be really grateful if you could leave a review on the platform(s) of your choice.

Reviews are like tips for authors, and every one of them helps!

Many thanks,

S.G. Slade

FREE DOWNLOAD

SHORT STORY PREQUEL

Tom's Wynter's life was fated from the start. Read how his story begins in

The Witch's Tale - A Short Story Prequel

Download your short story prequel at
https://www.sgslade.com

ABOUT THE AUTHOR

S.G. Slade originally hails from the historic city of Bristol in
England, and spent many years in London before moving to
Sydney, Australia, where she now lives with her husband and son.
She has worked variously as a bartender, a secretary, a teacher of
English, a shop assistant and a nurse, but a lifelong obsession with
books has never waned.
When she isn't reading or writing (which isn't often), you can find
her either in the garden, going for long walks, or watching old
movies.

She would love you to visit her at https://www.sgslade.com/